Ferryl Shayde

Book 2:

A Student Body

By
Vance Huxley

© 2017 Vance Huxley

Published by Entrada Publishing.

Printed in the United States of America.

Contents

Dedication
To my Noeline and to the Joy of my life

Acknowledgements

Thank you to my editor Sharon Umbaugh,
for turning my words into a book worth reading.

My thanks to Rachel at Entrada
for all her hard work and encouragement.

Mending Fences

The dark red, glistening sack-like creature with thin tendrils groped at the leaf litter on the ground, rearing up as if looking at Abel. It had been inside Henry, controlling him to attack Abel until Abel trapped it. Now Abel felt a strong urge to help it, but the ward tattooed on his arm flashed ice-cold as it stopped the magical compulsion. "Should I use fire or wind glyphs to destroy it?"

The dryad, stood by its tree, pointed a twiggy limb. "We usually drop a branch on anything smelling like that. No fire inside the wood, please." Abel raised both hands, concentrating on imagining wind glyphs in each palm before feeding magic down his arm to activate them. Once again, the sack-creature tried to control Abel, but he launched the two small, tight balls of air. The sack ruptured, splashing the foliage with blood before the creature itself bubbled and disappeared back into pure magic. Abel turned to deal with Henry, laid on the ground nursing a broken arm and staring about in mounting terror.

As he took the first step, the scene vanished.

* * *

Abel Bernard Conroy, only just sixteen and barely a warlock, opened his eyes as the dream ended. He groaned, and not just because the bruises from the fight still hurt. At least he'd finally beaten Henry Copples, so there'd be no more bullying. He'd even managed to cast the glyphs, the magic spells, without Ferryl Shayde to help him.

Abel touched the tattoo of a furry cat-woman on his left bicep, now empty and lifeless. Ferryl, a faded sorceress, had left it to possess a schoolgirl, though Jenny had agreed at the time. She'd been bleeding to death in Abel's arms after he dragged her out of a heap of scaffolding. Jenny made a binding magical bargain: life in return for hosting the sorceress for twenty years.

He touched the strange purplish spikey flower tattoo next to it, his ward against magical attack. Neither were real tattoos. They were magically burned into the bone according to Ferryl, and they'd certainly hurt enough for that. As usual his ward felt calm and reassuring, his own magic welcoming him, but it missed something. Or rather, it missed someone, the real reason for Abel's groans. Kelis.

Kelis, one of his two best friends and his only female friend, had been the first person Abel told about magic. Immediately after explaining, Abel drew a copy of his flower as a ward, magical protection, underneath Kelis' arm. Unfortunately, that created a link, one that might have been why a New Year kiss became six wonderful weeks. Ten days ago, they'd broken the link, then ended their relationship after Ferryl explained that Abel might have magically bound Kelis to him.

The sorceress insisted that even if they didn't want it broken, the link left a dangerous gap in their magical defences. If an attacker gained access to one of them, bound them, the other would have no defence and would be bound as well. Afterwards Kelis and Abel had agreed to stay just good friends for a while. They weren't supposed to kiss or even hug, not until they were totally sure every trace of the link had gone. Now Abel had spent four days refusing to see her, talk to her, or answer emails and texts.

* * *

Abel stopped going around in circles inside his head and sat up. Two ugly scaled creatures, brownies, stopped collecting mud from his boots and scuttled warily out through the too-small crack under the door. A hunting Pictsie hesitated, snatched an earwig in its extravagantly fanged jaws, then somehow slid into the hairline crack between the skirting and the wall. Once again Abel wondered why the ugly magical creatures, mostly blotchy browns, appeared as cute little humanoids in all the stories. Maybe it was a joke by magic users because magical creatures were invisible to all other adults and most children.

Abel winced as muscles stretched, limping to the bathroom for a shower. Eventually he tottered downstairs, to find a note from mum saying she'd gone shopping.

After eating some cereal, Abel took out his phone and turned it on. Four days of texts scrolled down across his screen, a good few from Kelis. There were at least as many from Rob, Abel's other real friend. Abel had ignored him as well, despite Rob calling round to try and see him. Abel turned the phone off and took a deep breath to brace himself. This needed more than a phone call or text. He had to go to see Kelis at home, then

Rob. At least that wouldn't be difficult, there were only three streets and a village green in Brinsford.

On the way Abel noticed rubbish spread around two of the wheelie bins and used a wind glyph to squish a scavenging Thornie. He checked for spectators first, because when a magical creature died it bubbled back into pure magic and became visible to everyone for a few seconds. Abel shouldn't have had to squish the Thornie, not if the goblins had been doing their job. The goblins were allowed to stay in the old church and forage in the village rubbish bins on condition they left no litter and kept creatures like Thornies, Hoplins and rats out of Brinsford. Right now, seeing Kelis worried Abel much more than skiving Goblins.

Abel's steps dragged as he came up the drive to Kelis' door, though at least she hadn't changed the access number on the big iron gates to keep him out. The big, posh two story house showed no sign of the night her dad had finally cracked, and gone from occasional abuse to beating and kicking his wife and daughter. He hesitated, then rang the bell.

"Who is it?" Abel floundered for a moment. He didn't know what Kelis had told her mum or what sort of welcome he'd get.

"It's Abel, Mrs. Ventner. Will Kelis speak to me, please?"

"Come in. Are you feeling better? Kelis said you were injured, something at school and then a fight? Kelis and Rob are in Bonny's Tavern. You know the way." The door lock clicked, so Abel opened it.

"I'm still sore, but better thank you."

"Good. Your mum must be relieved." Abel made his way cautiously through the house to the Tavern, formerly the library. Mrs. Ventner sounded cheerful, so presumably Kelis hadn't told her what actually happened at school. Kelis herself wouldn't be that happy. He approached the door, dithering in front of the flower in a shield sign with 'Bonny's Tavern' above it.

Bonny's Tavern, invented by the three of them, was the mythical setting for a new board game that would hopefully sell well enough to make them all a fortune. Abel knocked, tentatively. Nothing happened for a few moments, then the door opened to reveal a curious Kelis. Her expression smoothed, wiped of all emotion as she looked Abel up and down. He tried to think of what to say, but Kelis got in first. "Guess what the cat's dragged in, Rob?" She looked Abel over again as he tried not to squirm. "At least you aren't covered in Jenny's blood, like the last time I saw you. I suppose we should let you in, though unless you talk fast it might not be for long." She stepped to the side and Abel limped in, eyes downcast so he missed the sudden concern on her face.

Rob sat in an easy chair, scowling as he saw who it was. He stood up, shaking his head. "I'm leaving because Kelis might get violent and I hate the sight of blood. If you survive I want my turn." Abel watched him go, dumbstruck because Rob, his only other real friend, hadn't seemed too bad last night. He'd even smiled when he brought the news about Jenny being alive and well, and learned about Henry finally getting thumped.

Abel turned to Kelis. "I'm sorry. Really, really sorry."

Neither voice nor look seemed impressed. "For what? Letting Ferryl possess Jenny, acting like a complete ass for the last four days, getting into a fight with Henry, binding me, or breaking the binding?" Her voice softened just a little at the last, but not much.

"Guilty on all charges." Abel almost took a step towards her, but he daren't in case a touch reactivated the link. "But very especially the acting like an ass. I shouldn't have turned off my phone and computer."

"I could live with that because of all the crap Henry and Seraph are spreading." Crap was a massive understatement. A chosen clique of the senior students, headed by Seraph, ruled the rest of the pupils at Stourton Comprehensive through a mixture of threats, ridicule and occasional violence. Seraph had added Abel, Rob and later Kelis to her roster of victims from their very first day at the school, causing pain and embarrassment wherever she could. From Kelis' next words the queen of the seraphims had used the current lack of real information about Jenny to demonise Abel. "Some of the idiots from school tried to warn me. Apparently, you are a dangerous nutter at the least, and maybe a murdering rapist. I told the others, the ones who know about magic, that the blood came from Ferryl healing Jenny." Kelis still had her hands on her hips, but her voice wavered a little over the next part. "But you could have spoken to me? You didn't need a phone or computer for that. I'm only two streets away." Abel cringed from the hurt in her voice.

"It was all too much. The calls, and not knowing if the police would turn up or even if Jenny had survived. That's not an excuse. I should have come around. I wanted to but I daren't because, you know, how mad you were about the possessing. I didn't know Ferryl would do that, just that she'd heal Jenny, and then it was too late." Abel whispered the next bit. "And I wasn't sure why I had to see you. I really wanted to come but well, with the link thing…" Abel daren't look up at her eyes. "But I should have tried, stood at the other side of the room or something."

"Fair enough." Kelis threw up her hands. "Well no, not fair, but what about the last one on the list? What on earth were you doing fighting Henry on your own? We are your friends, best friends. That means when there's trouble, we stick together. Idiot! Look at the state you're in."

Abel risked a glance at her and wished he hadn't. Kelis stood over a hundred and eighty centimetres tall, between skinny and very slim with high cheekbones, piercing green-blue eyes, and straight almost-blonde hair falling down well past her shoulders. Stood like this, head up and glaring at him, she looked just like her game character the sorceress K'liss Windcatcher. A little stab of pain in his heart reminded Abel of why he shouldn't dwell on how it made her look drop-dead gorgeous, to him anyway. He kept his voice quiet, wanting to explain without arguing. "It wasn't on purpose. He was inside the wood, where he shouldn't be able to go. The magic boundary should have stopped him."

"Even so, if you hadn't been skulking about on your own instead of us going together as usual we'd have been able to help." Her face showed momentary puzzlement, then cleared again. "No matter how he got there, we'd have squished him." She raised her hand as if to cast a glyph. "You know we both wanted the chance."

Abel mustered a small smile. "It'll be easy now. He's got a broken arm and probably three broken fingers."

Kelis had opened her mouth to continue, but shut it for a moment before answering. Now she definitely looked curious. "Really? Rob said that, but I thought he was winding me up." She looked Abel over more carefully. "He said Henry hit you, more than once from the bruises. Why didn't you zap him first?"

"He'd got magic, some sort of glyph on his chest. He'd also got some gross thing inside him that he puked up. He reckoned when he kissed

Claris it slithered down his throat and it was promising him all sorts of stuff." Abel shivered slightly. "If it wasn't for the dryad he might have got me."

"Henry kissed Claris? Seraph's henchwoman? Maybe he deserved something nasty in his throat. The dryad helping you might be karma, payback because we found it a home." Kelis took a long step forward, then hesitated. "How bad? You I mean."

"Bruises, a lot of them and I've wrenched my knee. Nothing broken this time." Abel hesitated, then pushed on. "The knee is from when I picked up Jenny."

Curiosity banished, Kelis frowned at him. "Yes, Jenny. At least she lived, and I've had time to think about the possession. As a choice it might be better than death. We've got to keep an eye on her, so Ferryl doesn't do anything Jenny wouldn't like." She hesitated. "If we can." This time her face showed just a little concern. "It's a pity Ferryl never taught you that, the healing." Too fast for Abel to react she bent forward and kissed him. Very quickly and gently but only on his cheek, on the livid bruise and scratches where one of Henry's punches had connected.

Abel opened his mouth but couldn't think what to say, because even on his cheek the kiss woke up an echo of that warm, lovely feeling so the link probably wasn't broken. He wished he knew if Kelis still felt it. Eventually he managed "we can't do that, kissing."

That brought a small, wry smile from Kelis. "I didn't think that would matter, just on the cheek." Unfortunately, that still didn't tell Abel if she'd also felt something. "That stupid link is why I can't risk a hug as well, which is your own daft fault for drawing that flower. You are a prize idiot, Abel Conroy, but an idiot who has always looked out for me so I can forgive you most things. Not hiding away and cutting me off; I'm still mad at you for that. Now, why don't you sit down and give me the gory details. Just sit far enough away that I can't hit you when you get to the stupid parts?"

Abel stifled his sigh of relief. Kelis was still mad at him, but she was talking and sort of making jokes. He could settle for that, because he really was an idiot. "Which details? I told you about Jenny when we came home, before, um, well, before."

"Yes, um, before. Before crawling into a hole and locking the trapdoor. You didn't say much anyway, just that Ferryl left the tattoo and possessed Jenny. You said that involved kissing a dying girl and getting drenched in blood, but were more worried about losing all your magic at the time. What actually happened?" Kelis flopped into a chair. "Wait, get a drink first and we'd better have Rob in here as well." She raised her voice. "Rob? Come back in. I've stopped beating on him."

While Abel picked a soft drink from the selection in the small fridge, originally part of Mr. Ventner's concealed bar but restocked for teenagers, Rob poked his head round the door. "Does that mean you aren't throwing him out?" He looked from one to the other. "I was betting evens on you starting up the soggy stuff again, even if it isn't allowed."

"You know why we can't." Abel knew he'd blushed bright red, and Kelis had two spots of red on her cheeks. "I thought you might have taken your chance to move in on Kelis."

"No way." Kelis smirked before aiming a haughty glare at Rob. "A Glyphmistress could easily enchant a Barbarian, but I prefer a challenge." The familiar banter about game characters relaxed all three a little, until Rob and Abel were seated and Kelis tapped the table with a finger end. "Now we both want to know just how big an idiot you've been, and if we can sort it out."

Though even after working it through several times, none of them had any idea what the thing inside Henry had been, nor what Jenny's explanation of her healing would be. The last Abel had seen she had a broken arm, though it had straightened as he watched. She'd stopped coughing up blood before limping away on a foot that had been crushed to pulp when a lorry-load of scaffolding fell on her. Her torn clothes and all the blood would have needed some sort of explanation but it wouldn't be possession.

The vast majority of people wouldn't believe her, because they'd no idea magic even existed. A few knew all about it and if one told the church an archbishop, probably Vicar Creepio Mysterio, would come to investigate. He'd bring God's SAS, the Church Militant, and kill Ferryl. Eventually the three of them settled for trying to corner Jenny or Ferryl, whichever she was, to find out what the possession actually meant. Abel felt sure Jenny had agreed, but she'd been choking to death on her own blood so she hadn't asked for the fine print.

*   *   *

Abel walked home alone, leaving Rob and Kelis to talk about and probably slander him in private. He wasn't happy about Kelis being angry, or Rob, but he couldn't be completely sad. A little bit of him felt happy, because from several things she'd said Kelis had been most upset about him not talking to her. Maybe, when the month was up and he could kiss her again she would still like that, and him, without the magical connection. He really hoped so, especially that the connection really would be gone by then or he'd never get to kiss her again.

The sight of gargoyles in the overgrown churchyard reminded Abel he wanted to see the Goblins. He turned in through the lychgate, looking around for one but none greeted him. Abel frowned, created a very small but hot fire glyph, and tossed it at the stone wall near a gargoyle. "Why did you do that!" The gargoyle became a potbellied green Goblin, the only magical creature legend correctly described, and hopped down off the wall. "You know we catch fire easily." The nearest dozen gargoyles suddenly had Goblin faces, while others only had green eyes. Either way, they all watched him cautiously.

"You were all pretending to be stone so I couldn't talk to you. The glyph was to remind you we have a deal. There's litter around the bins and I just caught a Thornie scavenging." The Goblin looked shifty, definitely hiding something while some of the others reverted to their disguises, grotesque stone gargoyles. "You lot are useless at lying so confess, are the Ratlins back?"

"No, and if they were we'd hunt them and any other small creatures not allowed in the village. We're having trouble with that because there's a gap in your barrier. Someone took up two of the posts, the ones you put hexes on to stop the fae and little creatures." The Goblin glanced at the others. "We couldn't find you to tell you."

"Fair enough, but you could have dealt with the likes of Thornies. Unless you can't be bothered with them now you've got the bins to yourselves?" Abel narrowed his eyes. "That can alter."

"No, don't." A long, thin long tongue came out to lick the Goblin's lips. "The food in there is delicious, but we still eat the creatures you told us we should. Though no pretty birdies or butterflies." Kelis had insisted on that. "It's just that there's bigger ones now, bigger than Thornies so we have to go out in packs. We aren't very tough."

Since a cat could usually keep a pair of goblins off their food, Abel believed that. "What sort of bigger?"

"Skurrits, four of them. They ran away after a dryad strangled one with tree roots but more could come at any time. None of us recognised the other one, the slithery thing. goblins don't live very long you know, and it isn't in our stories." The Goblin looked at Abel's arm. "The sorceress might know?" It sounded cautious. Ferryl frightened all the magical creatures.

"She is busy but I'll let her know and she'll sort it out. Let me or Rob know if anything else turns up that you can't manage." After following directions to the gap, Abel found the hex-inscribed posts thrown aside. He assumed Tyson, Henry's older brother, had done it as payback for Henry's broken arm.

Abel set the posts back in their holes, tapped the tops with a concentrated wind glyph to set them, then drained some magic into the wood to renew the protection. He debated going to Castle House garden to top himself up but like all living things, Abel continuously absorbed a small amount of magic from the air. He'd soon fill up again.

Once he arrived home, Abel's mum wanted to know if he'd apologised. She seemed relieved they were all still friends then wanted more details on the fight with Henry because Abel had gone to bed without explaining much. That explanation took a lot of editing because he couldn't mention magic. After inspecting the worst bruises mum told him to rest, so Abel gratefully headed for his bedroom.

Abel spent most of the day working through his texts and emails, junking the ones accusing him of attempted murder, rape or abduction. Those were a product of Seraph's campaign, based on Abel being covered in Jenny's blood, and would die out with Ferryl/Jenny fit enough to answer them. Seraph, as the self-proclaimed leader of the rich and influential, treated anyone like Abel as a target for harassment. Finding him covered in Jenny's blood had been a perfect opportunity to cause as much trouble as possible. Abel would find out the official version tomorrow, when everyone went back to school after the break.

Most of the rest of the messages were from the betas, local teenagers testing the Bonny's Tavern board game for Kelis, Rob and Abel. Now it was a bit more than a game. After discovering magic, the trio thought it was funny to add a few real magical creatures, and a meditation exercise to levitate a leaf using a glyph. Kelis had also created a sign to hang outside the Tavern as magical protection, using Abel's flower ward in a shield. Because Kelis was magically linked to Abel's mark, she'd accidentally created a true protection hex.

Even so, floating the leaf using pure imagination, without any knowledge of magic, should have been virtually impossible. Unfortunately a few betas drew the Tavern sign, a true magical symbol, on their arms, then found that stroking it while meditating felt really restful. Worse, a few drew the wind glyph on their palms instead of imagining it.

Rob, Kelis and Abel had no idea what the betas were doing, until Petra activated her control of magic and made her leaf flutter. Luckily Abel had added his tattoo as a game character, a cat-sorceress, so Rob put Ferryl Shayde's email address in the game as a way for players to get magical advice. A joke, but the whole thing suddenly seemed a lot less funny after Petra's frantic text to the allegedly fictional cat-sorceress, "one leaf floating. Help."

A short, frantic induction left Petra exhausted but relieved. She immediately insisted that anyone with a funny feeling in their arm while meditating had to be warned, so they didn't panic when the leaf moved. After a short, frantic period those betas activated their magic and became apprentices to Ferryl Shayde's trainees. Unfortunately, the betas were volunteers and not exactly organised, with many still unaware that magic existed. Some had already invited friends and relatives to try the Tavern game, so it had spread to other parts of England and the idea of meditating had spread with them. Now, if it was removed, a lot of non-magical people would ask why.

Abel daren't tell any of them, even those aware of magic and that Ferryl Shayde really lived in his tattoo, about Ferryl possessing Jenny. He wasn't happy about it himself even if Ferryl had told him she usually did this, swapped twenty years of possession for saving a life. Possession sounded awful but Jenny had agreed as an alternative to dying. Now

Abel wished he'd asked for more details about how that worked, but at the time he expected Ferryl to ride in his tattoo for ninety years. Abel answered the magic-aware texts and emails, explaining he'd got bloody holding Jenny while Ferryl healed her. A bland reply to any non-magicals he knew just said he'd tried to help Jenny when he found her.

Unfortunately, none of Abel's social circle knew Jenny personally, or any of her friends. Abel wouldn't find out what Ferryl/Jenny had told either them or her family until the end of the holidays.

*   *   *

Mid-afternoon, despite it being chilly, Abel limped to Castle House on the outskirts of the village. He could use magical heat to keep warm, privately because a powerful repulsion spell kept everyone else except Kelis and Rob out of the gardens. "Blimey, did you have another go at those Copples?" Abel stopped and turned, smiling because Stan would be pleased with the result.

"Only Henry this time." He held out his hands, displaying the skinned knuckles. "No broken fingers this time."

"I told you to come and borrow my shotgun if they gave you more trouble." They both laughed because Stan, allegedly a retired poacher, would never let anyone near his gun. "Did you black his eye again?"

"Yup, and this time he's got the broken fingers."

"Bloody hell. Wish I'd seen that, it's about time. Watch out for Tyson, he'll be annoyed you hurt his little brother." Stan smirked and reached down to stroke Bugsy, his feisty old Jack Russell. "Though that bloody dog of theirs, Cooch, doesn't bother Bugsy since that last run-in with you."

"Mr. Copples promised to tell Tyson to leave me alone, in case I bust his fingers as well." Abel smiled happily. "He told Henry to lay off me in future."

"Blimey, wonders never cease." Stan looked Abel over. "You've filled out a bit lately, put a bit of weight on, but even so I'm definitely impressed. I suppose you'll be going into those gardens again. Have you been in the house?"

"It's all boarded up, and anyway there's some strange stories about that place." There were also some very nasty glyphs protecting the house, but Abel wasn't going to mention them.

"I thought of having a mooch about in the gardens for any stray rabbits, but Bugsy won't go in there. Now you three are tramping all over the gardens scaring everything so there's no point."

Abel knew the real reason was the barrier spell that persuaded Stan to keep out. "Sorry. If I see a rabbit I'll send it your way." Stan laughed and Abel carried on, then paused. Maybe he was just in a good mood, but he decided to give Stan a present. Abel tapped the Land Rover logo on the front of Stan's old vehicle, releasing magic to power it up. "Good motors these." Logos on expensive brands were actually magical protection against Gremlins and other creatures, but the one on Stan's had worn out. Now it would be fully charged and stop a lot of niggling little faults.

Stan frowned, squinting a little, then shook his head as if clearing it. "Was a good motor, and still good enough for me even if it acts up now and then." Abel raised a hand in farewell and left, ignoring the annoyed Gremlin scampering out from under the bonnet. He'd better warn Kelis and Rob that Stan might be one of those rare people who saw hints of magic. Abel's mum saw creatures properly, and had treatment while still a child to stop her hallucinations. Now she knew Abel saw them, and that the wooden plaques with Tavern signs on kept the bad ones away, but didn't know about magic. Abel wasn't going to tell her. According to Ferryl, if someone over twenty-five activated their magic it sent them crazy.

Abel carried on through the gardens to the little cave near the stone slab that had once imprisoned Ferryl, where he finished dealing with the texts. Eventually he just sat there for a while, relaxing and enjoying the peace and the birdsong. Only birds, insects and small animals came in here, because the garden's defences stopped all magical creatures or thinking animals. A few texts came from Kelis and Rob, asking about this and that so they were still chewing over what he'd told them.

The last message brought a big smile. "Tavern meeting at seven. Bring cake." The cake must be his penance, and because his mum baked a really mean fruit cake.

Abel replied, "No marzipan, mum ate it," which was true because it was the last of the Christmas cake. He spent some time catching up on his practice, casting wind, fire, colour-changing and plant growth glyphs. He didn't know many more but hopefully Ferryl would still teach him. Abel daren't experiment, because uncontrolled magic could kill the caster or someone nearby.

*   *   *

When Abel called round for the meeting, Mrs. Ventner wanted to see how badly he had been hurt. "At least those bruises won't hurt you too much." She smiled happily and touched her upper arm. Kelis had drawn a Tavern mark there to stop creatures crawling over her mum in hospital, swearing it was good luck and a meditation symbol to reduce pain. Now Mrs. Ventner thought they all wore them for meditation, especially since it really did make her feel better.

Abel agreed, heading for Bonny's Tavern where two serious faces were waiting. "You've got some explaining to do." Kelis pointed to a chair. "Sit."

"Cake?" Abel put it on the table, hoping it would help as he tried to think what else he'd done wrong.

"That's a start." Kelis kept her face straight but Rob couldn't keep it up, he smirked just a little.

Abel didn't relax because Kelis still seemed serious. "What did I do? Well, what more did I do?"

"Glyphs. You have been learning new ones and never told me." Kelis seemed genuinely annoyed. "How can I be a Glyphmistress if you don't tell me when you learn a new one? My control is as good as yours."

"Better," Rob chipped in, possibly truthfully.

"I've told you them all, everything I know." Puzzled, Abel looked from one to the other. Rob had a little smile and reached for cake.

"So what about the bit where you tangled Henry's feet with brambles? How did you do that?" Kelis pointed at him then wiggled her fingers. "Nothing we've learned up to now would do that, so give."

"It was just the growth one for making the grass and bushes grow. The one I used after the dead tree, the Bound Shade, ripped the gardens up. Just glyphs drawn in the earth. I told you about trying to learn how to burn a glyph to pull magic from a tree root, to activate the growing glyph. I couldn't do it right, burn it under the bark where it wouldn't show." Though now he thought about it, Abel wasn't so sure he'd told them.

"Which is all news to us. You weren't exactly being truthful just then, remember? Hiding your little friend and her special talents?" Kelis glanced at Abel's shoulder. "How does the tattoo feel?"

"Flat and empty. It looks it as well, to me." He showed his cat-woman tattoo and they agreed.

"Right, back to magic brambles. How difficult is the glyph? Does it work on anything? Was the draining one different to the one we use to get magic from a tree?" Kelis really did deserve the Glyphmistress title because she loved them.

"The glyph for drawing magic from a tree is the same for a drawn glyph or a person, though the one to power a glyph doesn't need cutting through the bark. Ferryl puts them under the bark where they can't be seen. The growth glyph is more complicated than the Tavern warding hex, about the same as the colour changing one." Abel shook his head. "I was desperate. If Ferryl hadn't had me crawling around the lawns and through the bushes to fix the greenery I wouldn't have remembered. That took whole afternoons drawing it in lots of different sizes, and must have burned it into my brain."

"Good." Kelis pushed a pen and paper across the table and a smile broke out. "Then you can draw it. Though with a small gap," she paused and they all chorused, "So you don't activate it by mistake." Her eyes narrowed. "Exactly what does it do?"

"Makes things grow? It's the one on the fencepost to help mum's little tree recover. Ah, Ferryl hid that one underground. Crikey, for all I know it will make the carpet grow. Ferryl didn't say." That thought stopped Abel. He'd better test it somehow. "Have you got a plant and pot I could try it on? If the plant grows without the pot getting bigger, we'll know."

"I'll go and find one. Draw the glyph, but don't you dare try it on anything until I get back." Kelis flew out of the room.

Rob swallowed his cake and jabbed Abel in the arm. "I was going to beat on you, verbally at least, but I can't. Kelis is too pleased you pair are talking again, and that you survived Henry. I really, really hope it isn't that magic connection, or I might go all barbarian and cut your arm off to break it."

"I'll volunteer if that's the only way. Don't worry, she tore a proper strip off me first." Abel took the paper and pen. "I suppose I'd better practice with my right hand." At least that got Rob smiling again. Ferryl had used Abel's right hand to draw for homework despite him being a leftie, so now he had to keep it up. By the time Kelis came back with a straggly plant in a medium sized pot, Abel thought he'd got it. "Here. I think it's right."

"I'll try it." Kelis hesitated. "No I won't, or not until I've experimented on some innocent grass in a field. We don't want Jack's beanstalk in here."

Both Rob and Abel inspected the sacrificial plant. "What is that? It shouldn't matter but what should it look like?" The plant had four long twisted stems over a metre long, each having a small bunch of white-veined lopsided half-heart-shaped leaves at the end. Abel poked a couple of leaves. "I don't think it matters, but will the shoots grow up or outwards? I'd better put that in the intent part."

"That is an Angel Wing Begonia, because the leaves look like a wing. It should have been pruned, or re-potted, or maybe fed and watered more. Those leaves should be a lot bigger, all over it, and it has clumps of pink flowers." Her hands gestured, indicating sort of where those should be. Kelis didn't sound happy about the next bit. "Mum loves it but she's been preoccupied just lately since, you know, him."

Kelis meant her dad kicking her mum unconscious and breaking her arm, so Abel moved on. "So we fix it for her." He stood up and concentrated, keeping the glyph really small, imagining it on his palm while pushing magic down his arm and out. The smoky shape hit the stems at the base but nothing happened to start with. "Maybe it should..." Abel stopped as buds pushed out from the first four joints in each stem, the bottom ones opening into small, brand new leaves.

"More." Kelis hovered over the plant, barely touching one of the new leaves. A gleeful smile lit her face. "Do it again."

"Maybe not." Rob pointed at the saucer under the pot, where several small white roots were reaching out. "It needs a bigger pot unless you want it rooting into the table."

"Pot, compost, water, come on!" Kelis chivvied them out of the room and house, down the garden to a greenhouse. Abel thought bringing the plant here would be easier, but wasn't disturbing that happy smile for anything. The three of them came back in past the lounge, where Kelis explained they were potting the Angel Wing on because it had started to sprout. Abel wouldn't want to spoil the happy smile from Mrs. Ventner either.

Though fifteen minutes later he wasn't sure how they'd explain the plant. Rob had been sent back for more, longer canes, because Kelis hadn't been content with Abel's second, slightly stronger attempt or the third. The lush growth now sitting in a much larger pot came after she'd carefully drawn the glyph on her palm, with her finger, and given each stem a definite boost. Abel could see where the Angel Wing name came from. The leaves were bigger than his hands and a delicate red on one side, with white veins and freckles on the dark green front that blushed pink if the light came from behind. Three big clusters of pink blooms cascaded down, just as Kelis had described. "Did your mum see this before you brought it in here?"

"Not recently, I don't think. It lives on the windowsill in the snug. Mum used to go there, you know, for some peace, but she spends most of her time in the lounge now." Kelis tried to lift the plant. "Come on you two, help me. We can't use wind glyphs to move it, not in front of mum."

Fifteen minutes later the suspicious look had gone from Mrs. Ventner's eyes. Abel thought she'd come to the conclusion Kelis had bought her a new plant, but was passing it off as the rejuvenated old one. He decided to ask Kelis for a cutting to grow in the old pot, so he could produce the alleged original at some time. Meanwhile he left the pair of them admiring the flowers while he walked home with Rob.

He half expected more earache about his shortcomings, but Rob concentrated on a bigger problem. "What happens tomorrow? I doubt Henry will be at school, and G… who knows what Jenny-come-Ferryl will say." Rob and Abel avoided saying God, ever since Ferryl pointed out there were several who might be listening. "She'll be sat at the seraphim's table and she's a year ahead of us, so we'll only get the story third hand at best." The two of them chewed it over, deciding to avoid the canteen when they arrived and hope to get some hint from Ferryl-Jenny at break.

Welcome Back

Kelis also wanted to talk about Ferryl/Jenny when she came down her driveway to meet Rob and Abel the following morning. After inspecting Abel she pointed out they could sit in the warm canteen, because answering questions about the bruises and scrapes should divert everyone for a while. The students would be wondering what Henry looked like, because he wouldn't be at school until he could write again.

As usual they sat together on the bus, with Kelis glaring at anyone who scowled at Abel. Some of Seraph's rumours must still be circulating, and the students on the bus had seen Abel coming home covered in blood. A few others glared or muttered when he got off the bus, so Abel chickened out of going to the canteen. It was a bit chilly to walk around the playground, but better than a room full of students and Seraph's remarks when he didn't know the answers. Rob went inside but came back with a glum face. Jenny wasn't there to explain anything.

"What the…!" Kelis brought her hand up and Abel saw a shimmer as the glyph began to form, then it stopped as she looked around. "Around the corner, out of sight. Quick!" Rob and Abel followed, puzzled but not for long. This time Kelis let the wind glyph go and it arrowed across to the box hedge between the path and playing field. The Skurrit, a scruffy, furry magical creature well over a metre from bald tail to pointed nose, hissed and rolled out of cover. As it bared rows of tiny sharp teeth Abel automatically hit it with a fire glyph, tight and very hot. Even alight it began to run but Rob's wind glyph, though not as tight, rolled it over in a tangle of short legs and sharp claws. The fire quickly finished the job.

The three of them stared at the bubbling mess as the dead creature evaporated into raw magic and disappeared, then glanced around but everyone else was inside. "Why is that here on its own?" Abel looked around again, carefully, but there were no others. "Ferryl said they were dangerous but only as pack hunters. One on its own wouldn't dare tackle even an eleven-year-old."

"Why is it here at all? The hexes among the trees along the school fence should deter them. That's why we spent hours of break time putting them there." Even as Rob spoke he tensed and pointed. "What's that?"

The fuzzy ball about fifty centimetres across hurtled over the playing field towards them before bursting apart into a swarm of somethings. Moments later the three of them were surrounded. The creatures were some sort of predatory fae, the magical fliers that preyed on insects and small birds and animals, and should have been repelled by the hexes. This time, as the flower tattoo on Abel's arm turned icy cold, some were getting close enough to sting.

A gust of wind wrapped round them all, flicking the swarm away. "I'll fend them off. Use fire." Kelis cast another wind glyph, curving her hand to swirl it across the swarm as it tried to attack again. Abel tried a burst of flame but only hit a few because they were spread out now and moving too fast. Intent mattered, he remembered—a glyph couldn't miss if the caster watched the target.

"Back up to the wall so they can't get behind us. Small hot glyphs, one at a time Rob. Watch the target." Abel began to throw glyphs with alternate hands, but watching until each one struck slowed him up. Ferryl would have been handy for this. She would have produced a score at a time, every single one on target.

"This will take forever." Though even as he grumbled, Rob roasted fae one after the other. For a few moments it hung in the balance, fae darting around the edge of Kelis' defence while the other two tried to pick them off yet keep killing the rest. Suddenly the survivors turned and headed back across the playing field, towards the trees.

Abel wasn't having that. "I've got it." The fae were leaving, but they'd evaded the hexes so they might be back when non-magical students were out here. His hands moved, shaping the glyph by intent before releasing a disc of fire. Abel's right hand curved, a weak reverse wind glyph to pull the fire back in the middle as it spread out. He watched carefully until halfway across the field the outer edge of the bowl shape overtook the swarm, then he closed his left hand a little. The bowl tightened as the front edge moved past them, all the fae neatly cupped inside. "Now," he breathed, clenching his hand into a fist. The lip of the bowl-shape tightened to seal any escape before the whole thing compressed into in a bright flash of flame. Half a dozen stray fae made it, escaping to disappear between the trees.

"A Skurrit might force its way past, but the hexes should stop fae."

Kelis glared after the escapees, then switched to scowling at the trees. "If the dryads would let us use all that lovely magic in their trees, we could make it much stronger. A few wooden posts with a Tavern hex and a bit of magic obviously isn't enough."

"Why would a dryad care? They've got their tree, and its magic, and don't care about anyone else." Rob kicked moodily at the kerb along the edge of the path. "Several of the Tavern members have spoken to them, but there's only a couple will even bother to reply. Even so you're right, our barrier should stop fae." The school bell interrupted their discussion about if coming through in a tight ball had protected the magical version of hornets.

*   *   *

Getting to class turned into a bit of a rush because they had to put their coats in their lockers and collect folders, but the three of them made it to Graphic Art before Mr. Sanders started on the register. Abel sat at the front, simply so he didn't have to see anyone who'd heard Seraph's rumours frowning or glaring at him. A few whispered, but Mr. Sanders soon shut them up. Halfway through the list of names the classroom door opened bringing a collective gasp from the students. Jenny stood there with a bandage around one arm, a dressing over one ear, and leaning on a walking stick. As she limped in everyone stared at the amount of bandage swathing her leg from someplace under her skirt right down and round her foot.

The seventeen-year-old star of the Acro dancers looked at Abel with a bright smile and headed straight towards him. He hesitated, wondering what he should say or do. Nothing, because Ferryl/Jenny turned and half-sat on Abel's desk, leant down and kissed him! Not a peck either, though it wasn't a Kelis kiss. While the muttering rose behind him, Ferryl's 'voice' in his head explained. "I can't use spooky-phone while I'm possessing a body, but I can contact you if we touch. I told my new dad that you are my secret boyfriend, and that you pulled off the planks and gave me the kiss of life. I've been more or less locked up since. Tell you more at break. Now smile." A low whistle came from someone behind as Ferryl/Jenny broke the lip contact and straightened up.

Abel did his best to smile as instructed, thankful that the rest of the class couldn't see his expression. At least Mr. Sanders didn't notice, too busy frowning at Ferryl/Jenny. "Jennifer Forester, that is not acceptable behaviour on the school grounds!"

Ferryl/Jenny turned with a shy smile, and a little blush on her cheeks. It seemed natural, as if it really was Jenny even if Ferryl had contacted him through her lips. Abel felt his cheeks heat up and concentrated on what Ferryl/Jenny was saying. "Sorry Mr. Sanders. I had an accident on the last day of school, but my boyfriend, Abel, pulled off the planks and gave me the kiss of life." She sounded a little more embarrassed as she continued. "My phone broke and I've been grounded ever since, doctor's orders, so I haven't been in touch. I just had to say thank you." The blush spread slowly over Ferryl/Jenny's cheeks while Abel felt sure his face must be scarlet.

At least the frown had gone as Mr. Sanders looked from one to the other, then back at her injuries. "That's all well and good, but you know the rules." His voice softened a little. "I'm pleased to see you have recovered enough for school. There have been some very graphic stories going about."

"I bled a lot but luckily most of it was skin deep, though I'm off the Acro team until my arm and leg heal up. I really am sorry, sir, I was only going to say thank you, but, well…" Ferryl/Jenny gave Abel a shy smile. He pulled his lips up to smile back, wondering if some of that blushing and voice was Jenny because it seemed totally natural. Except the bit about him being a boyfriend, that wasn't even remotely believable.

"Next time try to catch him before he gets here." A tiny smile touched the teacher's face. "He seems suitably thanked so you'd better get off or you'll be late to your own class."

"Thank you, sir." After another smile aimed at Abel, Ferryl/Jenny limped out and off down the corridor.

Mr. Sanders stopped smiling and banged his desk. "Enough! Quiet please." As the murmuring quietened he looked down at the register. "Sarah Russel?"

"Here sir." Abel could hear the laughter in Sarah's voice, and some of the following ones. He daren't turn around and not just because he was embarrassed, but then he risked a quick glance. Kelis looked as if someone had hit her with a bat, mouth still open in shock. Abel turned away again, realising he'd have to sort out the girlfriend thing within three weeks for the Kelis kiss test. Worse, Ferryl/Jenny would be acting as his girlfriend at the birthday party in a week, the combined one for him and Kelis. Curses, he could hardly pretend it was just a joke if Ferryl/Jenny stood holding his hand right through that.

"Sorry sir." Mr. Sanders had that look that meant he'd spoken to Abel and hadn't got an answer.

"I asked if you were ready to rejoin the rest of us, and perhaps get some work done. Unless you want to nip off down the corridor and interrupt another class, to thank her for the thank you?" Mr. Sanders liked sarcasm, and practiced as often as possible.

"Yes sir. I mean no sir, ready for work." Abel gratefully opened his folder, turned on the computer and tried to lose himself in the lesson. The occasional muttering and giggle from behind and the little paper dart with hearts drawn all over it didn't help.

*   *   *

The lesson seemed to last forever, but finally ended and everyone stampeded for the canteen. "It was a complete surprise." Abel kept his voice down as well as he could.

"Except you never did say why you met up with Jenny outside the school, round the back out of sight. When you saw her accident?" Kelis didn't sound at all happy.

"Pure coincidence, I swear. Later, all right?" Because too many people were interested, or wanted to ask Abel how long he'd been going out with Jenny. A few who were a bit behind the times gave Kelis some odd looks. She'd been Abel's real girlfriend until two weeks ago.

"It had better be good." Kelis straightened and smiled at two students leaning in to try and hear. "That explains why he kept disappearing and coming back with a smile. I wonder what Seraph will make of it?" Deliberate or not, Kelis neatly diverted a good few people as they began to wonder the same thing. With everyone heading to the canteen for morning break, they'd soon find out.

Abel walked in between Kelis and Rob and sat in his usual spot at the geek table, trying to avoid meeting anyone's eyes. Some of the geeks didn't take Graphic Art, but the likes of Sarah were soon filling them in about his visitor. At least the quiet voice behind him stopped anyone asking Abel questions. "Kelis, would you mind moving up one so I can sit next to Abel? I'd sit the opposite side of the table but I can't stretch to hold hands, not until I'm all healed up." Kelis and Abel, and anyone not facing that way, looked round to meet a bright, slightly embarrassed smile.

"Of course Jenny. Are you sure you don't want to drag him off to sit with the seraphims?" A ripple of laughter went around the table, in contrast to the silence spreading across the rest of the canteen.

"I'd prefer it here. I should have come across the last time, when Rob offered, though I'm still not signing up for IT." Kelis stood up but instead of sitting straight away Ferryl/Jenny aimed her smile at Justin, in the next seat. "Would you mind if Kelis sat there, Justin? It's just that she's Abel's best friend so she'll have a million questions. I want us to be friends as well."

"I suppose it was just a matter of time before you lost all sense of shame." It hadn't taken long for Seraph, the self-appointed mistress of her chosen elite, to react. She ruled the older students, and through them most of the rest, and it wasn't a benevolent rule. According to Ferryl, Seraph had enough magic that when she used a certain strident tone it acted as a command. Not true compelling, but enough to make most students feel they should obey her. Only the magically aware students were immune, protected by their wards. Seraph didn't know or she would use real compulsion to help with her bullying and general harassment of anyone she considered inferior.

Seraph didn't wait for Jenny to answer. "Now I'm wondering what you two got up to behind the school that had to be kept secret." There were a few titters, but more of the faces now turned towards Seraph looked disgusted or angry. As a popular member of the school Acro dancers, Jenny had a lot of fans. Some faces showed anticipation. The last time Seraph clashed with the geeks and Jenny had been a laugh.

"I came to sit with my boyfriend, Abel. It's not hard to choose because he already gave me the kiss of life. Sitting at your table again would be more like the kiss of death." Ferryl/Jenny sat down and reached out to take hold of Abel's hand. "I missed you."

Before a startled Abel could answer Seraph spoke again, raising her voice to be heard over the wave of laughter. "You are out of the Acro team as of now, permanently!" The canteen quietened again as they realised what she'd said.

Ferryl/Jenny laughed at her. "Look at me, I'm out anyway. I can't even walk properly let alone perform backflips. In any case you don't decide who's in the team, unless you give Claris and Laurence their instructions?" That set a good few muttering, because Seraph wasn't even in the team but the two captains were both part of her inner circle. Laurence certainly didn't look happy at the idea.

Rob joined in. He had his own score to settle with Seraph. "You could order Jenny to sit with Henry again? That worked out so well last time." Rob made a big show of looking round. "Oh dear, where is he? How will you order people about without your pet, what was it Jenny called him last time, pet bull?"

"Ogre, definitely more ogre than bull." The rest of the geeks had decided to join in, especially since Henry wasn't here.

"Watch out, Seraph's lost an ogre."

"Maybe a minotaur, and he's lost in a labyrinth."

"Henry would get lost on the way to the toilets."

As various people chipped in with increasingly unlikely places Henry could be lost another voice cut through the chatter, silencing them all. "I'd be very interested in an explanation of your last statement, Seraphim Bellamy-Courts." Seraph looked stricken, because she'd made a real mistake. The teacher supervising the canteen this morning was Mr. Beresford, the Sports Master and the teacher in charge of the Acros Dancers. "As Jenny pointed out, Claris and Laurence are the joint captains of the Acro Dancing team. I'm absolutely certain you are in no position to decide who is in the team, or out of it. You can tell me which of us is mistaken in my office at lunchtime."

Seraph sat down looking completely deflated because she absolutely couldn't argue with a teacher. Not only that but Jenny had deserted her clique, publicly, going to the despised geeks and joining them in making fun of the seraphims. Worse still the rest of the students were laughing at Henry while he wasn't here to put the fear of God into them again. To top it all Claris, another of her heavies, had gone missing.

Meanwhile a familiar voice filled Abel's head. "One moment please, while I make skin contact with Kelis." Abel glanced over to see sudden shock on Kelis' face, quickly smoothed out. "I can't manage spooky-phone, Kelis, so it has to be skin to skin. If you wore a shorter skirt we could have touched knees, but the only way is to put my leg across behind yours. Unless we hold hands as well?" This time Abel saw a little smile followed by a quick shake of the head. "I must apologise to both of you, and Rob. The information I learned from Abel's mum as she slept was not complete, and I misunderstood. Chris' thoughts seemed to mean I could be independent at sixteen, but it isn't true freedom. I thought I could save Jenny and keep my oath to Abel Bernard Conroy, but your modern world would not allow it. I did not even think to memorise your telephone numbers. Please allow me time to find a way to complete our bargain."

Abel hid his usual flinch at Ferryl using his mum's first name, Chris, while he wondered how to answer. It was his own fault Ferryl didn't have more information, because he wouldn't let her rummage around in people's heads as they slept. At least Ferryl seemed to be in charge and had access to Jenny's memories. He turned to her. "I missed you during the holidays, Jenny, but I'm really pleased you are feeling better. Can we meet up without the crowd, maybe out of school?" Beyond Ferryl/Jenny, Kelis' eyes narrowed, then she nodded very slightly in understanding. They needed some time to talk about the whole possession away from public scrutiny. Kelis for one would have a lot of searching questions.

Though Ferryl/Jenny had a very good point, one she could make out loud. "I certainly can't sneak off to meet you inside school, not now. With all the bandages, I'm a bit too conspicuous."

"Even if you can't walk very well, perhaps your dad could bring you over to my house. We've got some lovely big comfy chairs in the Tavern so you could put your foot up while we all had a long talk. I'll bet Abel would manage to get rid of me and Rob for a few minutes. Oh, right, you won't know about Bonny's Tavern." Kelis had a little smile now, having a bit of fun. "It's a real home from home."

Rob leant past Abel, determined to have his bit of a laugh even if he couldn't hear Ferryl. "I'm a bit upset you chose Abel, Jenny, but you really are welcome over here. Maybe we could convert you to Bonny's Tavern even if you won't take up Art or IT." The rest of the table laughed. Most of them took Art or IT and over half of them were beta testers for the Tavern game.

"I know about Bonny's Tavern. Diane told me you were really helpful and spent ages helping her. She was so happy I began to wonder if she'd got her own secret boyfriend." Ferryl had decided to have fun as well, because Rob had already been teased about the time he'd spent talking to fourteen-year-old Diane. Ferryl/Jenny turned to Abel. "I want to come and visit as soon as possible, now everybody knows, but dad wants to meet you first. Otherwise I don't think he'll let me out of the house. I had to explain about us and he's gone a bit over the top."

"Ooh, watch out if you visit. You could get a real surprise in Brinsford." Justin, one of the betas who knew about magic, smirked. "He might have another secret girlfriend." Justin meant Ferryl Shayde, living in Abel's tattoo, which was doubly funny under the circumstances.

"Then I'll have to try harder to get there and find out. Though I wasn't sure if dad would even take off the leg-irons to let me come to school." Ferryl/Jenny started explaining, with some exaggeration about handcuffs and security guards, that the doctors had wanted her to rest. Her dad had taken them at their word.

The rest of the students at the table relaxed, because despite being a senior student and a seraphim Jenny had never been the snooty type. Abel assumed Ferryl couldn't talk in his head and through Jenny's mouth at the same time, because she stopped communicating. The whole thing fascinated him because Ferryl/Jenny seemed to be exactly the same as he remembered, totally natural. Except for Jenny holding his hand of course.

The fifteen minutes flew by, but before letting go of his hand Ferryl promised to talk more at dinnertime. Abel went off to English in a sort of daze. He had to meet Mr. Forester? Jenny's dad was some sort of well-off builder, or rather he paid people to build, which summed up everything Abel knew. He really hoped Ferryl/Jenny could hold his hand to give some hints while they talked, then hoped Kelis didn't think it was because of the boyfriend thing. Could he avoid hand holding at the party? Not really because everyone else would expect it. Worse, the ones who had learned about magic would expect Ferryl to talk to them by spooky-phone, from Abel's tattoo.

"I reckon he's really smitten. Did you give Jenny a glyph, or is it some sort of side effect from when you enchanted him?" Rob's voice jerked Abel back to reality.

"I didn't need to give her a glyph, she's got a leotard. Works every time." Kelis had a smile, but Abel thought he heard a bit of a bite in that.

Abel reminded her. "It was all news to me until this morning."

"It's all news to everyone, or it will be by lunchtime. By tomorrow there might be three drunken beggars someplace who won't know, but don't bet on it." Rob nudged Abel. "Wait until I tell them why Henry won't be at school for a while."

"Don't do that, there's no need now. They'll think I'm some sort of martial arts loony." Abel glanced around. "It's bad enough I'm apparently dating a girl a year above me."

"Oh yes, and one of the Acros dancers as well. You'll get some stinky looks from the older boys." Kelis narrowed her eyes. "What about our combined birthday party? I realise Ferryl dumped this on you, but you can't break up with Jenny before then. With her being injured like that, you'd look a real pig. You'll have to invite her."

"I'm more worried about no spooky-phone. The magic-type Taverners will expect to see that at least, even if I hide my tattoo."

A hand slapped Abel on the back. "It must be that country living, all that healthy air and food. Two pretty girls in a week? I'm buying a tent and eating my greens." The boy carried on, laughing as he strode down the corridor to the next turn.

Abel stared after him. "Who was that?" He blushed a little. "It's been two weeks."

"I don't know, he looked like upper-sixth." Something about Kelis' voice made Abel glance at her. She'd started blushing as well, maybe at the pretty bit because Kelis didn't like attention from boys. Abel kept his big mouth shut and headed for English.

*   *   *

At least Abel and Kelis got more information over lunch, because skin-phone worked while Ferryl/Jenny had her mouth full of food. Using the limited information Ferryl had read in Abel's mum's head and her own memories, the sorceress had assumed Jenny could leave home at sixteen. She'd intended healing Jenny then moving in with Abel, but once she could read Jenny's memories that plan crashed. Worse, Jenny's dad had taken her straight to hospital so she'd had to re-injure herself enough to explain the blood and the damage to her clothes. "And believe me that hurt. I couldn't dull the pain because by then I'd used up most of the magic you gave me. I've had no trees to get magic from so I have to manage on the usual amount from the air, which makes finishing the healing much harder."

"So what do you remember from the accident?" Although he spoke quietly, Abel knew others might hear so he daren't ask his real question.

"Everything of course, both from Jenny and you. Oh, you mean Jenny herself? She will remember up to when she let me take over. She has slept since then." Ferryl/Jenny answered aloud. "I remember enough, Abel. You were marvellous."

Abel could see Kelis' frustration growing and tried a way to answer some of the questions about Jenny. "Let's hope you think so in twenty-one years."

"Of course. Even if we break up I'll remember the boy who saved my life." "Twenty-one? You mean when Jenny has her body back? She will remember as much of the years in between as I let her. I will make sure that includes any information from school, and enough of her life so she can recognise people. Keeping the bargain, leaving her as she is today, will be more difficult than usual. In the past the women moved two villages away and nobody knew them or realised they hadn't aged. We will have to talk more." Ferryl had been sealed in a pit for about two hundred years, so the last time she'd switched bodies would be early in Victoria's reign.

"So when do you think your dad will turn you loose?" Abel hoped the answer would be soon, so they could talk properly.

"As soon as possible, so I can get my wits from Castle House gardens. If they include the glyphs for mazzlement, I can confuse and persuade dad to back off. Are all parents like this these days? Maybe he has arranged a marriage and worries you might ruin it. No, you don't do that now. Sorry, I'm still settling in. Will you be able to manage for a few more days?"

Though all she said was "not soon."

"Abel can wait. After all he's already dealt with Henry attempting to beat him to death." The gleam in Kelis' eye and the edge in her voice were familiar, but for once weren't aimed at Abel. Even so, he felt nervous because he didn't want everyone knowing.

Ferryl/Jenny froze, then lifted his hand to look at his knuckles. She turned to lean in and inspected the bruise under Abel's eye, from much too close. "Those are fresh. I thought they were from when you saved me." "Henry did that? Where is he! Wait, he didn't come to school." Amusement coloured Ferryl's mental voice. "Did the Glyphmistress finally get her chance?"

"Those are from when Henry caught Abel. Alone." The edge was aimed at Abel this time, for being so stupid, but a couple of people picked up what Kelis said.

Even as others leaned in to hear better Rob took his chance. He'd been dying to tell someone, anyone. "The scrapes on his knuckles are from when Henry ran into them." He paused for effect. "Hard enough to bust his arm and a few fingers."

Abel lost track of the rest. Ferryl mentally shouted in his head about what she'd do to Henry while apologising for not being there, which combined with Kelis and Rob adding the gory details for everyone else to create some sort of babble. Eventually Ferryl/Jenny calmed down, stroked his hand and face then gently kissed the bruise on his cheek. "I'm a bit late to return the kiss of life." "A girlfriend would do that. It is lucky you broke the link to Kelis when you did. With her as a girlfriend it would have been difficult to explain how often I will be in Brinsford. I must be there to keep our agreement, to teach and protect you."

"Careful with the kissing or the teacher will see you. Mr. Sanders would have a heart attack." Sarah sniggered, glancing towards where a teacher always sat to keep an eye on everyone. "Another one." She tried for the right voice. "That is not acceptable behaviour."

"I forgot. We'll have to be more careful now we are meeting in public." Ferryl/Jenny smiled happily and Abel tried to do the same. He couldn't kiss her because it wasn't Jenny in charge of her lips, and he didn't want Kelis to think he didn't want the kiss test. Complicated didn't even come close even without all the magic mixed in.

"Kissing is a good reason for Jenny to persuade her dad to let her out." Rob switched to Jenny. "How will you get to Brinsford?" He glanced across to where Jenny's younger sister sat answering questions, probably about her sister from the glances. "Diane said you lived in Kielby, six miles away."

"I can ride there once my leg heals up." Ferryl/Jenny beamed at them all. "I've been learning to ride a moped but only on the farm tracks. I'm still a bit wobbly but I'm sure I'll improve." Abel would bet on it because Ferryl would use glyphs to stay upright. "I will persuade Jenny's dad to book me a CBT test. I will pass because Jenny has been studying and Chris's memory held experience in driving. Then I can ride over at any time."

Abel relaxed as the meal progressed, because Ferryl/Jenny would sort something out so she could still train everyone in magic. He still wanted to talk privately about the attack outside the school this morning, the spooky-phone, and about exactly what Ferryl had done to Jenny, but there would be time. Even without Ferryl in his tattoo as a defence Abel wasn't too worried. The three of them had stopped those fae outside, and he'd even beaten Henry without her.

Lunch break ended with some teasing when Ferryl/Jenny held onto Abel's hand and leant on him for support as they left the canteen, smiling sweetly as she passed a baffled Seraph. She hugged him tight before they parted ways to go to class, which set Abel worrying again. Having a row and breaking up looked less and less probable, especially since that would mess up Ferryl/Jenny's reason for visiting Brinsford.

* * *

The next two days were really frustrating because Abel only saw Ferryl/Jenny in public. He couldn't ask any real questions by phone because her dad had the same rules as Abel's mum, occasionally checking her computer contacts. He would definitely read anything from secret boyfriend Abel and he hadn't replaced her phone yet. Even a hastily scribbled note saying "spooky-phone" only led to Ferryl reiterating that she couldn't make one from inside a host.

At least Ferryl got her wits back. Kelis realised that even if Ferryl couldn't get to Brinsford they could take them to school, so Abel dug up the two nubs of bone. They, and an unknown number like them, had been cut from the original Ferryl's bones when the sorcerer imprisoned her. The lumps Ferryl called her wits held her collection of advanced glyphs, magically inscribed as a sort of built-in hard drive as near as Abel could figure it out. Ferryl wanted the rest back but felt sure they were inside Castle House, behind all those deadly magical defences. Until she got them, she wouldn't remember most of her glyphs.

The rest of the table in the canteen wanted to know what was in the secret present, but Ferryl/Jenny wouldn't say. Mentally, through the contact, she sounded ecstatic. The following day Ferryl/Jenny told Abel she'd inserted the wits into Jenny's bones and healed them in place. Abel didn't even want to imagine the pain that must cause. The additional information included the mazzlement glyph, so Ferryl/Jenny could confuse anyone noticing odd behaviour. She'd also found three saplings that were still too small for dryads so she could drain a little magic from each. With the extra magic Ferryl/Jenny could re-damage herself for the doctors, but between appointments she could heal herself.

Meanwhile, everyone else either gently teased Abel about catching an Acro dancer, or Jenny about cradle robbing. Quite a few thought a kiss of life sounded like a good way to catch either a boy or girl. The Tavern members awakened to magic knew from Abel's texts that Ferryl had cured Jenny, so they understood the kiss of life reference. The others assumed he really had revived her, or at least kissed her very thoroughly. At least the magical ones were distracted, because this weekend would be the big party. Abel's birthday, ten days late, and Kelis', all combined with the second meeting of the magically-aware Tavern members.

Their families mixing socially with the Tavern's magical apprentices would have been enough to keep Kelis, Rob and Abel worried, without trying to hide Ferryl/Jenny's possession as well. On top of that two more Tavern beta players discovered magic. Abel had to explain Ferryl couldn't use spooky-phone to reassure them at school, because healing Jenny had taken a lot out of her. One of the other magical trainees, someone living near enough to see the new trainees out of school, explained things. Both were promised more information at the party and given wooden Tavern hexes to stop the small magical creatures they could now see trampling through their dinner and bedrooms. From cautious messages passed in corridors there would also be more people wanting to burn their protection ward down to the bone.

Kelis brought in extra wooden plaques with the Tavern protection hex carved into them, and those were distributed. From the shifty looks Abel suspected the betas were using them to protect other locations, not just their own houses. He couldn't blame them. Watching creatures scuttling about on a friend's or relative's food wasn't easy, not when a little wooden plaque would cure it. Other, rather more teasing remarks were encouraging. From the hints some had made progress in getting finance or actually registering the game, or had development ideas.

*   *   *

Before the weekend Abel had to meet Mr. and Mrs. Forester, Jenny's dad and mum, or his new girlfriend wouldn't be coming to the party. Abel warned his mum he was going home from school in the car with Ferryl/Jenny, which raised eyebrows even if he'd already 'confessed' to having a secret girlfriend. Diane, Ferryl/Jenny's sister, was alight with curiosity because, judging by what she said, Ferryl/Jenny hadn't given many details. She started the inquisition as soon as they were all in the car. At least he could hold hands, so Abel knew what to say. He just hoped he kept it all straight once they arrived.

Abel's main worry failed to materialise. Jenny sat next to him and held on firmly to his hand through the entire conversation, so he could match her story. After a bit of stilted introduction the questioning began to narrow down, and Abel relaxed even more. Her parents weren't worried about him being poor, or from a council house, or being a geek. They were both worried about the secrecy, or the reason for it. At least Ferryl had come up with the right excuse for that—Abel's age. An almost seventeen-year-old star acrobat, one of the Acro team, shouldn't be dating a barely-sixteen-year-old boy. The geek part made the potential for embarrassment even more believable, or would if Jenny had still been herself.

After her accident with the lorry, Ferryl/Jenny had 'confessed' everything to explain the blood on Abel. Both her parents thanked Abel for saving her, which really did make him squirm a bit. Eventually both Abel and Ferryl/Jenny ended up blushing as her dad switched to some mild teasing but that seemed normal and relaxed everyone. The conversation turned to Abel, what he took at school and eventually to the Tavern game. Abel didn't even have to answer most of the Tavern questions, not with Diane leaping in at every opportunity to show what she knew about the characters. Now she wanted her sister to get her some tuition from one of the creators, preferably Rob.

Mr. Forester wasn't completely convinced about nobody else knowing. When he delivered Abel back home, he politely insisted on meeting Abel's mum. Abel and Ferryl/Jenny sat quietly while both parents confirmed, cautiously, that neither had known about the secret relationship. At least Mr. Forester agreed Jenny could come to the party since Abel's, Rob's and Kelis' parent would be there.

When Abel walked Ferryl/Jenny to the car her dad got in first, after pointing out he'd better look away towards the end of the road. Otherwise, he claimed, his daughter would embarrass him by complaining and possibly beating on him. At least Mr. Forester seemed to be more relaxed now. The mischievous smile before Ferryl/Jenny kissed Abel goodbye for definitely too long meant she knew what she'd done. By waiting until they were stood next to the conspicuous shiny new Mercedes, Ferryl had made sure almost everyone in Riverside Close noticed. At least the 'spooky-phone sorted out. At the party,' came as some relief.

*   *   *

On Friday evening, after tea, Rob and Abel collected Kelis for a walk and a very private discussion. Once out of sight in Castle House gardens, Abel took over warming a slow draught of air because he found fire easier to handle, while Kelis orchestrated wind gusts for the rain shield. They ended up sat on the milk crates they'd put in the small cave near where Abel first met Ferryl. "This is going to be a shambles." Kelis flicked a glyph at the dead leaves nearby, scattering them. "My mum has a ward but thinks it's for meditating to soothe pain, and has no idea about magic. Your mum, Abel, can see creatures and knows the hexes carved on doors will stop them, but nothing about wards or that the hexes are magic." She glanced at Rob. "What about your little sister? She's been pestering all the beta players."

He sighed. "Melanie is now a fervent Tavern player, though as yet it's only at home with me so I've steered her away from the meditation part.

Now she'll get to talk to other Taverners. One of them will mention the warding mark, stroking it and the meditation, and imagining making a leaf float so she'll pester me to play properly. Samantha is eighteen so she'll chat up the older boys and probably get too much information, or hints there's more to it than dice. If my mum and dad get on the wrong topic with Abel's mum or yours? Worse, the Taverners will want to talk about magic. How do we stop Melanie from joining in before they realise who she is?" Rob threw a growth glyph at a clump of grass, but only half sprouted which looked really odd.

Kelis sent a little glyph at it. The grass turned brown and drooped. "Curses. I tried to reverse the growth glyph to stunt it again, to get the two sides even, but it doesn't work that way." She sighed. "We need Ferryl back here and as often as possible." Her eyes moved to Abel. "So stop trying to wriggle out of it and be a boyfriend."

"I'm not wriggling." Abel looked from one to the other, baffled.

"She kisses you, so you could at least try kissing her back and put your arm around her when she hugs you. She's not exactly ugly, and you'd have jumped at the chance before... Well, before." Kelis scowled at the dead grass, avoiding Abel's eyes. "You were supposed to try kissing other girls before we tested the binding."

"You don't kiss any boys."

A little smile played over Kelis' lips. "Is that your excuse? Just remember this is my birthday party as well, buster. I'll be sweet sixteen and only kissed by one boy. He's fairly cute, in the right light, but I'll be able to compare just how cute after the party." Her smile grew as she turned towards Abel. "The boy is an idiot, because he's got himself a girlfriend before his party so he won't be able to do the same. Though at least he doesn't have to worry about his girlfriend discovering magic." At least that got them all laughing. Ferryl knew more about magic than everyone else they knew, combined.

"Maybe she can use that mazzlement thing on my family, so they don't notice anything." A calculating look came into Rob's eyes. "I could do with that glyph for when Samantha or Melanie get nosy."

*   *   *

The three of them chewed it all over, and agreed they'd just have to be on their guard. At least they could keep in touch if Ferryl brought spooky-phone. Rob wanted to see where Abel fought Henry so they left through the back gate, into the wood. A harsh creaky voice greeted them. "You should check more often."

"Hello dryad." Abel lifted a hand in greeting to the gnarled twiggy shape standing by its tree. "Check what?"

"For trespassers. There have been attempts to get to the gate. They were not strong enough to even get through this wood, but something is testing." The two light brown eyes switched from one to the other. "Have you checked the other boundaries?"

"We don't know how to. The sorceress will be here tomorrow, so she can do it. I hope." Abel looked around helplessly. "I've no idea if something has been near. I know the protection for this woodland is weaker than the barrier around the main garden, but I've no idea what might get in."

"A small blood-sack tried, much smaller than the one you destroyed. It came in a badger and crossed over the boundary but I could smell it and crushed it under a falling branch." The dryad looked back at the Sycamore tree it lived in. "That is wasteful but my new tree and I are still learning about each other. In time we can strangle something that small with roots."

"What else came, please? I have no honey for answers, but I can bring some tomorrow." Abel glanced at Kelis. "If there's some left?"

"A couple of jars. I've stopped trying to get the dryads in my garden to talk." Kelis nodded towards the dryad and sniggered. "If they find out this one got some, they might change their minds."

"I will trust you. Despite you rescuing me, it is hard to trust magic wielders." The Dryad pointed a stumpy limb and the bunch of twigs on the end to a small clearing nearby. "There is something buried there that is being very secretive. It burrowed in very slowly and stops for long periods, but tree roots are very sensitive." The limb and twigs pointed along the edge of the wood. "Skurrits tried to enter there, and something smaller further along, but the repulsion spell stopped them reaching the trees. The Skurrits must have been compelled or terrified. They tried too hard, until the magic damaged one."

"I'm sorry, we promised this place would be safe for you." Abel looked up and round. "I can't take you inside the main barrier."

The creaking sound that signalled dryad humour, or preparation for an attack, sounded briefly. "I have an adult Sycamore crammed full of the magic it has collected since being a sapling. It is safer than any other tree I know of because your hexes stop all but the strongest, most persistent creatures coming in here, and those are not interested in a mere dryad." The twigs pointed to the clearing again. "Will you need the sorceress to deal with that? It is small, with little magic."

Abel glanced at the other two, and they nodded. "We'll try, just so it doesn't get any further."

"From three directions?" Rob pointed. "If it heads for one of us, the other two get a clear shot from behind."

"Can you see where it is?" Abel scanned the clearing.

"There." Kelis pointed. "The grass and those few nettles are a little bit sickly. I might be wrong?"

"It's worth a try. How do we dig it out?" Rob picked up a piece of old branch and tossed it down. "We need a spade."

"Or not. Remember what happened to the plant roots?" Kelis pointed again and flexed her fingers. "I reckon nettle roots wriggling down around it will startle the whatever at least. I've been practicing."

"So have I, but one thing first." Abel went to a nearby tree and cut the draining glyph deep into the bark. "Sorry tree, but I might need a boost in a hurry." He turned to the others. "I ran out of magic fighting Henry and nearly didn't get to a tree in time. Now I'll only have to slap my hand on the glyph to top up."

"You mentioned it. Good thinking." The other two prepared a tree each. Kelis raised a hand. "Three, two, grow!" Her glyph arrowed into the wilting nettles. There wasn't much reaction at first except the plants straightened and looked a bit greener, but then they began to sprout upwards. Almost immediately they went over as earth flew up and something like a giant grey-brown worm shot out of the ground! Not really a worm, more like half of a fat one sat on the cut segment, but swirly like a tall thin dollop of cream on a bun. The point at the top, nearly shoulder height on Abel, swept in a circle as if looking before the worm tried to head between Kelis and Abel. All three of them hammered it with wind glyphs, but although it fell over twice it wasn't taking damage.

"Abel, use fire. I'm not good enough inside the wood." None of them wanted to use fire in the wood but Rob was right, they had to try. Abel's tight, hot fire glyphs blackened areas of the creature's hide but didn't really penetrate, though the creature felt them. It swerved and either squealed or screamed, a high noise more like a vibration than a sound. All three winced and the glyph-storm faltered as they tried to protect their ears.

"Look out!" The creature turned towards Kelis, away from Abel's fire. It squashed down to half the height, then sprang up and over her, out from between them. All three gaped as it flew up and away like a giant spring, until a branch stretched out from a tree and smashed it back! The creature rolled as it landed back in the clearing but came upright, apparently unhurt, before lunging at Kelis. She abandoned caution to blast it with flame until it swerved away, smashing a sapling to splinters. That gave them all a definite warning about how strong it was.

Rob threw a fireball, setting some weeds on fire, and then a dead branch. That bounced off but gave Abel an idea or rather it sparked his memory. He threw a thick stick in the air before catching it in air glyphs and driving it towards the half-worm. The high vibration rang out as the crude spear finally penetrated its skin. "Physical attack, using magic as power!" A variety of pieces of branch arrowed in or logs bounced off the creature, more penetrated and the vibration intensified. Even so, only the glyphs in the trees gave the trio enough magic to keep fighting.

The creature made one last attempt to escape, falling flat and rolling to crush the sticks now impaling it before trying to burrow. Kelis finally finished the fight. She took a moment to aim, then blew a thick length of wood deep into a hole already made by an earlier branch. The noise stopped, leaving an almost shocking silence before the creature began to bubble and dissolve. For once a magical creature didn't disappear, or not completely. A low mound of dirt and small rocks remained, though when Rob poked it with a stick there were no signs of life.

"What on earth was that?" Kelis and Abel looked at each other, then shook their heads at Rob. There'd never been a hint of anything like this in what Ferryl had told them.

"I do not know." Dryad stood wide-eyed by its Sycamore, one limb firmly connected. "We are ripened with some memory from our forebear, but nothing like that. Though I am a young Dryad, compared to some."

"When I went around asking all the Dryads for help, I looked up some stuff about trees. A Sycamore can live four hundred years. Though dryad's old tree, the one the wind blew over, didn't look really ancient so maybe it isn't that old." Rob looked at the ridge of earth. "Maybe that thing is new, or is supposed to be extinct."

"Ferryl told me the Aryadne's Hound we chased should be extinct, so who knows?" Abel looked up at the tree above the dryad, at the splintered wood along one branch. "Thank you for your help, dryad Sycamore. Does that injury hurt?"

"No, not as you think of it. The tree feels it as a wrongness, but I will direct magic and we will heal it. There is some other damage because trees should not move like that, but we will recover quickly." The dryad's eyes moved to the dirt, and the trampled clearing. "That was very strong even without magic. Can you strengthen the barrier glyphs to stop any other burrowing creature? The effect is weaker underground."

"I'll ask the sorceress. If you are all right, we'll heal the glyphs in these trees and leave you for now." Abel smiled and made a small half-bow. "Though I will bring you honey tomorrow or the day after."

"A rare treat. I thank you, polite magic wielder. Remember to check all the boundaries." Dryad blended back into the tree. The three of them topped up on magic from the trees, healed the cut glyphs, and walked slowly home. Despite going over the whole thing several times they only came up with one solution, one they already knew. They needed a real sorceress, Ferryl Shayde!

* * *

All Saturday morning the tension grew. A text at two pm saying Ferryl/Jenny had left home came as a big relief, to Abel at least. He wanted spooky-phone before the Taverners arrived at the party. According to the text her dad would deliver Ferryl/Jenny to Kelis' house so Abel had better get there sharpish to meet her.

Apart from a quick check to see he'd shone his shoes and tease him about combing his hair for a girl, Abel's mum didn't mind him setting off early. She still found the whole thing funny because after never showing any interest in girls, Abel had found two within weeks. While inspecting his birthday present, a T-shirt with a picture of Bonny's Tavern printed on the front, she commented that his coat seemed a bit tight. Abel daren't tell her Ferryl insisted he spent hours running and lifting small logs, to build up his muscles for magical feedback. He didn't mind practicing running away, because the Bound Shade really had scared him.

At least Kelis' big posh house seemed to reassure Jenny's dad, though when she got out of the car a surprise followed her. "Hello Abel. Can I come to your party? Lots of kids are coming from school, those who play the game. I could get some really good tips." Diane did her best to look innocent, but her giggle didn't help. "You'll want to keep on the right side of your girlfriend's little sister, in case I read her diary." A glance behind her told Abel exactly who thought this was a good idea, Jenny's dad.

Ferryl/Jenny hugged Abel, and kissed him quickly on the cheek. "Wow, is this where Kelis lives? It's huge." "Don't object or dad will wonder why and might stay. We'd never get a chance to talk in private. I'll mazzle Diane if she hears anything about magic."

"Wait until the Taverners arrive, it will soon fill up. Come on then, Diane, I'm sure we can find you cake or a teacher." A real smile broke on Abel's face. "How about Rob?" Rob would go crackers if he had both Diane and his own little sister, Melanie, pestering him about the Tavern. After confirming the party would end at nine, Jenny's dad left and the three of them went in. Sure enough Rob already had Melanie following him around, and Diane made a beeline towards them.

Ferryl/Jenny held firmly onto Abel's hand. "We need a private place for spooky-phone."

"We'll need Kelis as well." Abel wanted her there so she could get her own spooky-phone.

"No we won't. You cannot teach this to anyone. I know how but I have never done it because harnessing the result needs a very unusual vessel." Ferryl/Jenny stood very close, speaking quietly and very seriously instead of using skin contact.

"Kelis will ask." Abel knew he wouldn't refuse if Kelis pushed him.

"You won't know enough to repeat it, and you must tell her I did it all.

Swear, or I will not give you a spooky-phone." Abel gave up and promised, on his true-name. "Good, now kiss me. Several people are watching and this is the first time you have got me alone, away from dad or school. It is expected." Abel complied, careful to keep it friend rather than boyfriend. "That's a start."

"I'm not keen." At least Abel could whisper in her ear now. "Jenny might not like the idea when she wakes up."

"She won't know." When Abel frowned, Ferryl/Jenny tutted in frustration. "We will talk when we have privacy. Now show me the gardens, please."

"Bonny's Tavern would be more private."

"But no good for making a spooky-phone." Ferryl/Jenny tugged his arm, raising her voice. "Come on, show me the gardens, Abel. Please?" As they made for the rear door, Kelis started to follow but Abel shook his head, just enough to let her know. She frowned, but stayed inside. Once in the garden Ferryl/Jenny headed to the far end among the trees and shrubs.

"Remember the security cameras." Abel glanced up to remind her, but Ferryl/Jenny nudged him gently. When he looked at her, her hand moved and glyphs floated gently up towards the nearest cameras.

"They can't see anything now, not with black lenses. I'll reverse it when we've done." Ferryl/Jenny looked around. "This is private enough. Sit here, side by side so the dryads in those trees can't see. They won't understand the magic flows, but might gossip about the result." Ferryl/Jenny sat and patted the grass beside her. "Take off your coat and put it round us both. It'll make a good shield and in any case, we need my tattoo bared." She sighed. "Your tattoo, not mine. I had a lot of fun in there."

Abel wondered why she sounded so sad, but he had something more urgent to worry about right now. Once he draped his coat around them and rolled up his sleeve Ferryl took his left hand, suddenly becoming all business. "No speaking aloud because Dryads can almost hear shadows. Imagine the wind glyph and create a small whirlwind here, this high." She indicated with her other hand. "When I tell you, stop pushing the glyph but keep spilling magic into the actual wind. I'll tell you when to stop." Ferryl/Jenny hesitated for a moment. "This is not a binding. I know

47

you won't accept those. This is servitude in return for life, and at some time you can set it free."

"Nothing dies." Abel had to speak. Any talk of bindings always made him nervous, but the number of times it included death made it worse.

"Nothing dies. Make the whirlwind. Some call them dust devils, but it is not." Ferryl sounded nervous, not something calculated to give Abel peace of mind. He took a deep breath, imagined the wind glyph but only twirling one way, and extended the magic down towards the grass. The result looked really neat. A coil of dust rose from the grass and wobbled there, a miniature twister. Abel concentrated on keeping it stable until suddenly Ferryl reached out, slid her hand under it, and lifted the lot off the ground!

"Steady!" Abel realised his concentration had wavered. He could see Ferryl/Jenny's lips moving but she'd let go of his hand again so he'd no idea what was said, if anything. At least he could tell Kelis the truth, he didn't know what Ferryl had done. The drain on Abel's magic wasn't much, but it continued until he began to wonder if he'd have enough. Eventually Ferryl/Jenny took his hand. "Forget the glyph. Push magic without any form, without intent or shape." Ferryl/Jenny let go again and her lips moved, barely, so she might not be actually talking. Abel did as he was told but it wasn't easy. He remembered someone saying that if you try not to imagine an elephant, all you'd think of was elephant. At least that helped now, taking his mind off the little shape still spinning on Ferryl/Jenny's hand.

She took his left hand again. "Stop now, it is done. I will put her into your tattoo. Her tattoo now. I have explained spooky-phone, English, something of the world and you, and about glyphs and magic. Also how to animate the tattoo, so she can have some fun as well."

"Her?"

"Yes. Your new talking tattoo. I hope she is as happy as I was in there. Hurry up. As soon as she is inside, introduce yourself." Ferryl/Jenny lifted the little swirl of wind, now almost invisible as it had shed the dust, and put it near the cat-woman tattoo. The swirl collapsed, briefly became a small shimmering, and then Abel felt her flow into his arm. Not quite the same feeling as when Ferryl used to, much smaller, or maybe more like

Ferryl when she first arrived. The zing, a small shock that tickled rather than hurt, surprised him but then it was gone. He subvocalized, just as he'd practiced.

"Hello. I am Abel. What is your name?"

"I have a name?" Her voice in his head sounded light and, corny as that seemed, airy.

"You can have, if you like."

"What sort of name?"

"Something that suits you, like Zephyr."

"My name is Zephyr?"

"That's just the first thing I thought of. It's a gentle gust of wind. You can change it?"

"No, I like it. After all, I was a gust of wind before. Now I am a Zephyr. Wind with a name." She sounded a bit overwhelmed, or almost drunk. "Thinking wind."

Abel noticed Ferryl/Jenny watching his face with a little smile on her lips. "Can you connect me to Ferryl Shayde please?"

"Connect?"

"Spooky-phone?"

"Oh, yes." The familiar thin ephemeral line, invisible to anyone who couldn't see magic, stretched to Ferryl/Jenny's sleeve.

"Hi Ferryl."

Ferryl/Jenny took his hand and answered inside Abel's head. "Spooky-phone as requested. Though you will have to answer any questions from others instead of me. The creature will copy my mental voice if you wish."

"Her name is Zephyr."

"A name already? May I speak to her, please?"

"Can't you do that anyway?"

Ferryl's voice had a little laugh in it. "She is your servant so I am being polite. I told her not to talk without your permission."

"That could be awkward, because I have to subvocalize to talk to the tattoo." Talking to Ferryl like that had been a problem sometimes. "If someone asks something and I tell my tattoo the answer, they'll see my lips move."

"Zephyr is a servant, not a rider such as I. She is more closely connected in some ways, less independent. She can take instruction without speech, but only from you, though she can talk to others through the connection."

Abel settled down to find out more. He could talk to Zephyr, and hear her, completely silently. She could talk to others through the spooky-phone but couldn't hear a reply, though if they held hands Abel could hear Ferryl anyway. Abel set into finding out just what Zephyr was. A puff of wind, apparently, given magic and sentience and therefore alive.

According to Ferryl any gust of wind, ripple of water or flicker of flame might pick up enough magic to persist, briefly. If that magic was the decaying remnant of a dead creature it created a Free Spirit, the unthinking and usually short-lived amoeba of the magic world, completely defenceless and the favoured prey of some small fae. Very rarely a Free Spirit absorbed more magic as it drifted here and there and if it survived long enough might grow to become a Feral Spirit. Those felt hunger, seeking out the stray magic leaking from non-magical beings to keep growing. Gradually any who survived long enough, the rarest of Feral Spirits, learned to deliberately take magic from fish eggs or tiny insects. Over many years, possibly centuries, such Feral Spirits could become dangerous enough to kill larger prey for the magic. Even those few were still ephemeral in nature, with few defences, so any magic user or predatory creature might snap them up for their magic.

Zephyr had been taken right through to the last, almost unheard-of stage, self-awareness and truly logical thinking. She understood responsibility and consequences. Abel's magic gave her life and strength while Ferryl had given her purpose, knowledge and then the means to use it. Once the wind became a thinking being, Ferryl knew Abel would not accept binding her. She offered the Spirit the alternatives of freedom to fly away, hoping to survive, or living in the tattoo. The tattoo provided a safe haven and a constant supply of magic while she learned about the world. The price was servitude to Abel, for ninety years or until he chose to let her go.

Abel wasn't keen on the ninety years, but as Ferryl pointed out Zephyr might live for a thousand years after that and every day with Abel increased her chances. After ninety years she would know many glyphs, and understand the dangers much better than she did now. More to the point, from Ferryl's point of view, Abel would be strong enough to not need a watchdog. With Ferryl/Jenny living six miles away, she worried about him being unprotected if another sorceress or Aryadne's Hound turned up.

*   *   *

Abel sat thinking it all through for a little while, getting used to the idea they'd just created a living, thinking being. He waited too long. Just as he opened his mouth to ask about the thing inside Henry, the blood-bag according to the dryad, Abel heard someone calling his name. "Come on, someone has missed us."

As they stood up, Ferryl/Jenny turned and put her arms round him. "At least they're not teachers." Abel barely had time to register the three people looking for him when her lips connected.

"Anyone of a delicate disposition avert your eyes. Now we know why they were missing so long." Abel recognised Shawn, a nineteen-year-old beta drawn into the Tavern by a friend.

Ferryl/Jenny hung onto Abel long enough for everyone to turn and see them, long enough for Abel to use his new spooky-phone. "Why are you insisting on this kissing thing?"

"Because you have to act as if Jenny is your girlfriend. More important, you have to forget what kissing felt like through the magical link to Kelis. Pick another girl for that if you wish, though it would be difficult explaining why I still visit and hold hands." Ferryl/Jenny pulled away from Abel with a blush starting on her cheeks. "Hi Shawn. I just wanted to get Abel somewhere private for a few minutes. We don't get the chance very often." "Now nobody will wonder what else we might have been doing out here."

Abel started blushing even though he knew Ferryl meant magic. As two small glyphs floated up from Ferryl, one to each camera, Shawn winked and lowered his voice. "Sorry but we all wanted to talk to you. If I'd known why you were missing I would have waited a bit longer."

Abel had almost stopped blushing by the time they got indoors, right up until he saw Kelis. She looked from Abel to Ferryl/Jenny and he blushed again, then remembered he could tell her now. Abel concentrated. "Zephyr, spooky-phone to Kelis. Tell her we needed privacy to create you but don't say who you are, not yet." Kelis watched the little wisp grow towards her, spotted the one to Ferryl/Jenny, and started nodding before it connected. Abel rode out various comments about dragging Jenny off into the bushes, while Jenny denied any such thing while giving everyone the impression it was the truth.

*　　*　　*

The next six hours were possibly the most confusing of Abel's life, not least because he had to keep pretending that Zephyr was Ferryl Shayde. If anyone else found out Ferryl had possessed a human, they might be worried enough to talk to a priest or a parent. Abel also stayed on edge until Zephyr had told all the magical Taverners who they shouldn't discuss magic with. Melanie and Diane in particular were quizzing every player about their favourite character and magic symbol.

By the end of the party both the fourteen-year-olds had finally been side-tracked by one of their classmates. Fourteen-year-old Rachel knew how to form glyphs and had her own ward, but didn't enjoy playing the Tavern game with older teenagers. She already knew of two non-magical game players her age, and now recruited Rob's and Jenny's sisters to create their own Tavern. They could play over Skype, with Rachel promising Abel she would try and stop the others activating magic until they were older. That might be difficult. Diane had already scrounged a proper copy of the rules from someone at school so she would be practicing the meditation and trying to float a leaf.

Rob's older sister, Samantha, seemed more interested in the older male players and the costumes some of the girls wore. She wasn't so interested in the game itself, other than asking who some of the more obscure characters were. Petra wore her Ferryl Shayde fur catsuit with leather shorts and Una her Robin D'Ritche mercenary kit with high boots and a plastic sword, but this time they had competition. There were even male and female versions of St. Georgeous the paladin varying from full armour, tinfoil over plywood, to one wearing some metal, silver hot pants and what might be net curtaining over the rest. Rob christened one lass, a Barbarian, Lovingly Sculpted instead of the generic Barbarian name, Roughly Hewn. Abel had to suffer some teasing, because without Ferryl to disguise him with magic he had no costume at all.

As she'd promised Mrs. Ventner took a lot of photos, especially of a selection of the better male costumes posing with Kelis. Kelis wore her robe, and had her hair and makeup fixed again for the occasion so she looked the part. Once her mum went back to the lounge, the sorceress K'liss Windcatcher enchanted several boys to collect her birthday kisses. The extravagant gestures as she allegedly ensnared them might not have been strictly necessary, but kept everyone amused.

Several people wanted to know if Abel had enchanted Jenny, or did a leotard work the same as a glyph? According to Jenny she'd never suspected a thing until pow, she'd suddenly found herself captured. From her comments about collapsing again as often as possible for another kiss of life, Abel wasn't wriggling out of the boyfriend thing any time soon. Luckily the sheer number of Tavern members, twenty-eight this time, kept Abel too busy answering questions for Ferryl/Jenny to push her kissing agenda.

Many of the magic users didn't see each other out of school, or only met over Skype. Now they all wanted to compare their progress or learn new glyphs. Abel really hoped the occasional floating sausage rolls or tiny sparks weren't noticed by the wrong person.

At least the parents stayed in the lounge with the buffet, just circulating now and then to remind everyone they were there. As the evening drew on a small number of teenagers began to hint or downright ask for a proper meeting, somewhere they could talk freely. Some wanted to burn in their protection wards while others had news about protecting the Tavern game, legally. That led to a small meeting in the library, Bonny's Tavern, between Rob, Kelis, Ferryl/Jenny and Abel.

Seven Taverners wanted to burn in a tattoo but there wasn't anyone to check they'd done it properly and hadn't left a weakness. Ferryl's shimmery form had watched over the previous batch, but now she couldn't leave her host's body. If any of the other three watched a Taverner ward themselves, Ferryl warned it could lead to an accidental binding. Worse, when Ferryl tried to explain what to look for, none of the three teenagers could see the magic flows to tell if the warding had worked.

But Zephyr could, though Ferryl advised caution. The puff of animated wind might not understand so soon after her creation. Rob looked at Abel's tattoo. "Can she fly about like Ferryl, or like Ferryl could? If not, she can't watch anyway." Abel concentrated and asked Zephyr.

"May I? Thank you." Ferryl must have taught manners. A moment later a shimmery shape flowed out into the air and hovered, though a spooky-phone stayed connected to Abel. "What should I do now?" Abel had no idea, but Ferryl/Jenny took over. After a few moments she told the rest that Zephyr seemed to be much more aware than expected.

Ferryl/Jenny explained magic flows to Zephyr, then how they should look using the wards on all four of those present as examples. Ferryl/Jenny turned away so the others wouldn't see Zephyr inspect hers, pointing out it had to be hidden by a leotard for Acro dancing. Even after all the explaining, Rob, Kelis and Abel still couldn't see the magic flows.

*   *   *

The placing of wards went well with Rob and Kelis giving each candidate ice and a wad of tissues to bite on. A warded Taverner warned each one about the magical burn, hot pain rather than blistered flesh. Forewarned, each youngster had brought a unique design and decided on a location they could touch through clothes while in public. One after another the candidates imagined their drawing, placed a finger on the spot, and magically burned the tattoo into skin and bone. Zephyr supervised, maintaining spooky-phone contact with Abel to give everyone privacy. As they saw others survive the experience, four more decided to have wards burned in making eleven in total.

While a group of Taverners congratulated the last white-faced teenager on her new tattoo, spooky-phone connected Abel with Ferryl/Jenny, Rob and Kelis. "Time for the meeting, a serious one with the likes of Shannon and Shawn, about the future of the game."

"Not until I tell Melanie and Diane it's private, or they'll try to break in." Rob nodded towards where the two in question were heading his way with curious faces. He smirked at Abel. "That or Diane will be telling her dad how often you snuck off with Jenny." Rob had found a new game, making Abel blush, and it worked again.

Though Abel had an answer, through spooky-phone. "That's another meeting. I've got to sort out the Jenny thing, as opposed to Ferryl."

Kelis nodded understanding, then turned towards the lounge. "I'd better tell the parents we're dealing with Tavern business, or they'll wonder why we keep shutting ourselves away at our own party. I wouldn't want to be accused of enchanting Rob and dragging him off."

Abel already knew who to invite for serious Tavern business. Sarah came as a last-minute addition because she had news about the possible adult warlock in town. "We really must deal with the man in the park near my house. It's the only reason I'm in here for this meeting." Sarah looked a little embarrassed but determined. "I'm getting really worried because he's noticed me, maybe because the creatures leave me alone. I can't avoid the park, not completely, so I walk along the road next to it but he watches me go past. What do I say if he tries to talk to me?"

"Go away or I'll scream?" Shannon shrugged. "It's what mom told me to do if a strange man accosted me."

Prompted by Ferryl's mental voice, Abel got back to the real problem. "Do the creatures still crawl on him? If so he's not a sorcerer, or even a warlock."

"Yes, but he brushes them off so he can definitely see them. The dryad knows I can see it, though it's stopped hiding because I never go near. The man is definitely throwing sweets to it. I saw him taking off wrappers." Sarah smirked. "I've already got a small pot of honey for when we get in contact." She firmed her shoulders. "I'm still only on wind glyphs, so I want someone a bit better at magic to back me up. You said you could organise something."

"Is he there at weekends?" Sarah nodded so Eric turned to Abel.

He shrugged helplessly. "I've no transport."

"I've got a car, sort of? The little blue hatchback I came in." Shannon waved a set of keys. "I finally passed my test so mum lets me borrow her car, but I can only get it at weekends."

"I can take someone on my scooter?" Shawn smiled reassuringly at Sarah. "We want as many as possible." A bit more discussion and there were three with cars who could get away at the right time. A few smiled when Abel asked if Shannon could pick up Jenny on the way, because a woman collecting her would reassure Jenny's dad. The Taverners probably assumed he just wanted to meet his girlfriend away from home, but Abel wanted their only real sorceress on the job.

The next part, setting up a business to market the Tavern game, turned out much simpler than expected. Despite eighteen being the age of full majority, any sixteen-year-old could own shares. As promised Shannon had mugged her parents for several pages of diagrams and flowcharts on how to organise a business, with the legal requirements for setting up a company. Three people had found companies that advertised setting up trademarks or copyrights, and several had downloaded the government information. There were now six Taverners over eighteen, all willing to deal with the contracts and any similar legal problems, but Eric had a better idea. He suggested the three mothers, Abel's, Rob's and Kelis', as the legal owners. The mothers wouldn't even need to know about the magical part.

*   *   *

Now that he could speak freely, Abel told them about being attacked on the first day of school and the creature in the woods behind Castle House. At least he could also talk to Ferryl privately this time, with Ferryl/Jenny replying through his hand. "Why haven't you told me about these attacks?"

"How?" Even while Abel answered, Kelis passed around a sketch of the tough burrower. "Until you made Zephyr I had to talk to you at school, in public. Do you know what that is?"

Warren already knew, sort of. "Blimey, it's either a magical Mr. Whippy ice cream or the Doggy-Doo monster."

Rob laughed because the drawing really looked like one or the other. "It squished down to half that size before boinging up like a spring, so it really did look like dog poop."

"Not ice cream. That thing is tough." Kelis explained how tough.

"Poop-monster then." Warren made a scooping motion with his hand. "We'll need extra-large scoopers and bags."

Meanwhile Abel felt more and more worried as Ferryl explained the reality. "That is a young troll. The earth and rock left behind means a cave troll, which the church claimed they wiped out before I went in the hole. Trolls are protective so a young one like that will have a larger one nearby."

"How big? That thing really was tough."

"As big as a truck, and as they get older the rock and soil bonded into their skin stops even fire. Trolls have little magic of their own outside strengthening rock but are very resistant to magical attacks. Only something that can shatter rock will break through, then the inside can be scoured with magic or blades." Ferryl/Jenny's hand squeezed harder. "You must explain. If anyone sees one, leave it alone."

"What about Castle House gardens? It was trying to burrow in."

"It can't. The main barrier is a globe that includes the rock beneath the house. That is why it takes so many trees to power it. Cut hexes on long thin stakes and drive them deep into the ground around the wood, then fill them with magic. That will stop most intrusions." Ferryl/Jenny leant forward. "So what is it, Abel?"

"A very small cave troll according to Ferryl." He explained, telling them not to even think of fighting a big one. Those present agreed, and would pass sketches and the information to the rest. A Cave Troll would be added to the game so any player seeing a real one would know to run away. Abel moved on to the other attack. "The school attack came through a gap in our barrier. We took a walk along the edge of the field, and one of our stakes had been taken out."

"That's two attacks. How many more?" Abel felt Ferryl/Jenny's hand tighten again. The Acro dancer had a very strong grip.

"None, that's it." He explained silently as Rob told the rest what happened.

"Who would do that? It had to be deliberate to let something in. We need the magic from the trees instead of stakes, then nobody will pull them up." Warren, a fifteen-year-old, scowled, thinking hard. "Is bribing dryads the only way to make the barrier stronger?"

"Yes. Otherwise the dryads will knock over the stakes because stronger hexes will make them uncomfortable." Rob didn't sound happy. He'd spent long hours trying to convince the local dryads to help, without success.

"Some burke, one of the other students, will have seen the stakes and pulled one up for a laugh. Don't worry, we'll find something the dryads want eventually." Petra seemed a lot more confident than Abel felt.

While the rest tried to come up with a way to stop it happening again, Abel took his chance to ask Ferryl about the thing inside Henry. She recognised the description immediately. "A Blood Leech. How big was it?" Abel estimated. It had definitely looked too big to be inside a person but Ferryl explained that. "Much of it is magic so it fits where it wishes, though it could not have been in Henry long enough to grow to that size. There would have been signs."

Abel explained about Henry babbling that he'd kissed Claris before the thing slid into his throat. "I think Claris might be in trouble."

Though Ferryl didn't seem worried. "Not too much trouble, not yet. She was at school before Valentine's so the Leech didn't grow in her either. Very strange. They don't usually move from person to person that quickly, nor do they risk themselves in open attacks." Ferryl hesitated. "It may have left seeds. Those will take a few weeks to show, but then we must check Henry. We will check Claris as well, if she turns up."

"If you two are done staring into each other's eyes, we'd best get back to the party." Several others mirrored Rob's huge grin.

"Not yet. First you all need to know about Blood Leeches, the thing that was inside Henry when I fought him. You all heard the public version, well here's the truth." Abel took a big breath and explained about the magic trap he'd set, and how Henry had vomited up a weird blood-red bag with tentacles. When he explained about Henry getting the thing from Claris, most of those present felt the same as Kelis. Claris probably deserved everything she got, and so did Henry for kissing her.

"Hang on, can I get one of those from kissing anyone?" Una looked more than alarmed, and put a hand on her sword.

"No, not if you've got a ward, a tattoo. Even a Tavern hex on a bit of wood should help." Abel put up his hands at the storm of questions. "No, not a vampire, but sort of close." With Ferryl/Jenny holding his hand and feeding him information, Abel explained properly. Oddly enough, most people thought possession would be worse than the fictional infection depicted in vampire books and films.

"Blood Leeches survive by possessing a human and feeding on the magic in fresh blood. Most find a willing victim, usually demanding forty years of possession in return for curing an otherwise fatal illness. Once vacated the discarded host should be left young and healthy but with no memory of the intervening years. If the Leech has kept the bargain they will then live out their lives normally. Not all Leeches keep the bargain, some leaving the host barely alive or with a seed that will grow into a new Leech. According to Ferryl, Leeches keep a low profile so the church doesn't kill them, so one attacking me was really unusual."

"So will Claris be all right, or have a seed in her?" Petra frowned and then shrugged. "Even for her that sounds a bit rough. If she ever comes back to school, will we be able to tell?"

"Ferryl will. Claris will look hungry, half-starved. We should watch Henry for the same signs then if we see them, we can call in Vicar Creepio to kill it." Abel saw several people, Kelis among them, hesitate before agreeing. At least half of those present had been thumped by Henry at some time.

"Now we really should get back. Mum will notice if both the birthday boy and the girl are missing too long, especially after all those birthday kisses I collected." Kelis glanced back as she headed for the door. "She might tell Jenny's dad you disappeared with her."

"Not quite yet, Kelis." Una looked around the others. "This is a great party, Abel, but we need a proper meeting soon. One without parents and siblings. The new apprentices, the ones who have just found magic, must see the Willow dryads for a description of the sorceress attack. They need a real scare so they understand how important a ward can be." She touched the place her own tattoo hid beneath her clothes. "Sooner or later parents are going to notice all these tattoos, and there'll be hell to pay."

"Tell them to learn fine control of their glyphs, and I can teach them a seeming. They can wrap a cloth around the mark, then the seeming will make the cloth look like skin. The glyph is on one of the wits I've just put in. This is a first step. Casting a seeming on your own skin is very dangerous until you have learned much better control and other, lesser glyphs." Ferryl/Jenny giggled out loud. "I've had to put my ward where it doesn't show while Acro dancing."

After some hilarity over where marks were and if they could be stroked in public, all the experienced Taverners wanted to learn the new seeming glyph. Ferryl/Jenny would only allow Petra, Warren and Una to learn right now, but the rest could learn once their control of air and fire had advanced to a suitable level. Seeing how disappointed the rest were, Abel privately suggested the growth glyph. Ferryl approved, because all those present should have sufficient control for that.

The small Angel Wing cutting Abel had taken soon became a healthy young plant, which led to some searching questions about side effects. Some of those present were keen gardeners, or had parents who were. Learning that not only would the effects last if the plant had proper care, but that vegetables were still edible, brought some very happy smiles. Ferryl, through Abel and Zephyr, promptly warned them all not to grow plants out of season, or too large. After some hilarity about giant veggies winning local competitions, the meeting finally broke up.

Or most of it, because Petra, Warren and Una stayed to have their first lesson on casting a seeming, making a bandage look like skin or anything else they wished. All three were even happier to find out even Abel hadn't seen this one before, and promised competition.

*　　*　　*

One last, small meeting of four had a serious agenda; exactly what the possession entailed. One thing had been settled. From everyone's reaction to Blood Leech possession, Jenny's possession definitely had to stay secret. Abel explained Ferryl saying that Jenny had agreed to the deal, and now her mind slept, then the three of them faced Ferryl/Jenny and waited. "We made an agreement, a very quick one because I can't raise the dead. I am borrowing her body in return for full healing and protection for twenty years, the same bargain I always make. The real Jenny is still in here. Her mind is intact, but really is asleep and slipping deeper. While I control her body I will remember everything, better than she could, so I can give her some memories when I leave."

"In twenty years. How do we know Jenny agreed?" Kelis went straight to the heart of the problem. "Abel says he saw pleading in her eyes but was it for a rescue? From you?"

"No, I swear on all my names." The mention of names tempted Abel, but he didn't want to use Ferryl's true-name to force answers while others were here. She really didn't want more people able to command her, which seemed reasonable.

But the swearing wasn't enough for Kelis. "How do we know you didn't just push your way in? Can't you let her be awake, carry on as usual but with you aboard like you did with Abel?"

"I explained to Abel once before. Forcing possession is difficult and would destroy her mind. The healing meant I had to take over completely so that I understood her body well enough to rebuild it. That's why I never healed Abel, I couldn't spread out through him to understand his body well enough. Possessing someone that completely cannot be undone unless I leave entirely, but I would need another host for that. Meanwhile I have to close down her mind or Jenny will be a very dangerous sorceress when I leave. She will remember every glyph I use but won't have any control." All three flinched at that. They'd spent weeks learning to control wind and fire away from anything breakable or flammable. Even tiny wind glyphs with too much power or intent could splinter wood.

Kelis had one solution. "You could leave her with a bit of control?"

Though Ferryl had an answer. "No, she has to learn that as herself. Even if I could have done that, Jenny would also be able to see all the knowledge on the two wits buried in her bone. I will remove them before she wakes, because some of that knowledge is very dangerous in untrained hands." This time the flinching was worse.

"But how do we know exactly what she agreed to?" Abel bit the bullet. "I'm not kissing back until Jenny tells me it's all right."

"Jenny is slipping deeper, but gradually because that is safest. Right now I can let her have her mind back, enough to see and speak to you. I will make her sit and freeze her limbs, or she may fight. Just reaction and some confusion, I promise. This will take a few minutes." Ferryl/Jenny walked to a chair, sat and stiffened.

The three teenagers sat and watched an immobile girl for a while until she stirred and opened her eyes, suddenly and very wide. "Where am I?" Her voice confirmed both confusion and panic.

Kelis dived straight in. "Kelis' house. Kelis from school. Do you remember the accident and Abel?"

Abel wasn't sure that would go down well, but her reply sounded less worried. "Abel? Where is Abel? I remember. You moved the wood and picked me up. Then a voice in my head." Jenny's eyes moved side to side and she started to panic again. "Why can't I move? Am I paralysed?"

"No, that's Ferryl Shayde. The voice in your head?" Kelis turned to bend and whisper into Abel's ear. "Why didn't Ferryl tell her this?"

"I don't know. Because she had to get on with healing?"

At least the name had registered with Jenny and she calmed down a bit. "Right, Ferryl Shayde. The same as your game. Diane had been rabbiting on about the cat-sorceress in your game. Then she was in my head. Ferryl I mean. I woke up in bed at home, nearly healed. It was like a dream. She said it had only been one day and asked if I remembered wanting to live. That it cost twenty years. I said yes but then I went back to sleep." Jenny's eyes looked alarmed again, darting from side to side. "What day is it?"

"Saturday, ten days after the accident. Ferryl really has healed you, completely. You can remember the bargain?" Abel almost held his breath, because he wasn't sure what to do if she said no.

"Bargain? Oh yes, twenty years or die!" Jenny's voice softened. "I really was dying. Everything had started to fade except the pain and I couldn't breathe. It felt like drowning. My foot and my arm were on fire. Then a voice asked, so I said yes. Of course I said yes, even if I thought it was hallucination. Shit, that magic crap really works?" A nervous chuckle escaped. "It must. So what exactly happens now? Twenty year amnesia?"

"Ferryl Shayde will live in you, but leave you with a seventeen-year-old body in perfect health." Kelis didn't sound keen, even if she tried to lighten it a bit. "I'll be going grey and you'll still be bouncing around Acro dancing."

"But what will she do with me? Crap, what has she done with me? Why am I here, in your house?" The panic started to come back. The following discussion ended up a bit like that, periodic panic mixed with some attempts at dark humour. Eventually Jenny even seemed resigned to the twenty years because, as she put it, the alternative had been worse. Abel explained Ferryl would leave her the memories of who she met and what she learned.

He finally broached his own particular worry. "To explain why I'd got your blood all over me and so she can keep protecting me, Ferryl told everyone I'm your boyfriend." He held up both hands. "Sorry, but it wasn't my idea." He explained about Ferryl teaching and protecting him for ninety years.

"Seriously?" After some explanation and a rerun of the first morning, Jenny accepted that but with definite reservations. "How much of a girlfriend? I can't remember any of it."

"Don't worry." Kelis sounded a lot happier for some reason. "Abel won't even kiss back until you say it's okay. That's why you've been woken up."

"Kiss back? Crap. I thought you said I'd remember? Now even after I get my body back, I'll wonder what she missed out." It wasn't quite panic, but Jenny wasn't happy. "Can't she do that, let me remember it all? Though that might be worse if I can't stop her. If I'm going to be your girlfriend so she can meet you, can we have ground rules? I don't really want to go where a twenty-year relationship usually ends up. Nothing personal, but I'd rather decide for myself who I marry."

"No marriage, or anything remotely like it. After all I don't really know you, and won't with Ferryl in charge." Abel paused, searching for a way to explain.

"He wants to know if it's okay to kiss back, for starters. Without that, being your boyfriend just won't fly." Kelis still looked happier about the kissing than she had other times. "She kisses him with your lips but he won't respond, which is funny for anyone who really looks. So will you allow that, and what sort of a snog?" She'd started having fun. "Not brother and sister, but I know this idiot. I promise it won't stray anyplace you don't want to remember. He'll find a way to get round the girlfriend thing in the end, or he'll never have a real one." Abel blushed while Kelis had started chuckling.

"A bit more than brother might be all right. What is a brother kiss, I haven't got one? How much more? Oh crap, that's impossible to describe." Rob and Kelis spent a few minutes laughing hysterically while Abel started by kissing an immobile Jenny almost too gently to feel. Ferryl must have released some control because she started kissing back. He worked up until Jenny stopped him. "I'd probably give a lad a kiss like that for his birthday or under the mistletoe at Christmas, if he wasn't too gross." At least Jenny had seen the funny side, or Abel's red face amused her. "You aren't really gross so I can live with that, though I'd still rather remember as it happens. How do we tell Ferryl? Where is she?"

"In your head. I'm going to do a bit of magic now to be sure I reach her. She can't use your mouth while you've got it." Zephyr connected while Abel held Jenny's hand to make contact. "Ferryl?"

"I am listening. Jenny can be awake but helpless. I can assure you she will not like that, nor do you want her to learn all my glyphs. Show her some, explain how dangerous such knowledge would be."

It took a little while. Rob managed the invisible hand clap with wind glyphs, he'd been impressed when Petra came up with it. Abel produced heat, then a warm breeze, then a hovering flame. Kelis fluttered strands of hair, picked up coasters, and made the light bulb sway then stop. She topped it off by doubling the size of one shoot on the plant before breaking it off, and that did it. The others could be magician's tricks, but not growing a real plant. After that, learning how much bigger an uncontrolled glyph could get really worried Jenny. She finally accepted that sleeping for twenty years would be safer, but only if Abel, Kelis and Rob promised to watch over her. "All right Ferryl Shayde, if you can hear me. Snow White is ready. Find me a really hot prince for my wakeup kiss."

With that Jenny had gone, though once Ferryl had control again the other three insisted it had to be less than twenty years. Unfortunately none of them could work out how to do that without someone else being possessed. At least when Jenny's dad turned up Ferryl kept the goodbye kiss exactly as agreed, a big relief for Abel. A treacherous little thought pointed out it was actually quite nice, definitely past what he'd expect from a sister. It wasn't long after that before the party gradually wound down as the Taverners left for home. After helping to clear up, Abel headed home with his mum a lot happier about the whole thing. Though now he wondered how mum would feel about helping to run a company.

Fallout

When Abel and his mum came into the lounge and she put the TV on, the few magical creatures began to leave. His mum found a strange sort of satisfaction in finally being proved right, that she'd not been hallucinating for years, and now she even fed the benevolent types in the house. "That's my fault, and yours." Abel's mum took off her Tavern plaque and hung it on the door handle. "Now they'll come back, and closer to me. I've never seen you take yours off." She frowned. "You don't have a necklace, nor do most of those at the party. Jess said hers was drawn on. Does that cat woman tattoo do the same?"

While Abel floundered, not least because of the comment about Kelis' mother, Jess, his phone buzzed. "Just a sec mum."

The text message from Kelis didn't help his peace of mind. 'Mum wants to know if your mum actually sees anything.'

Abel texted an answer. 'Ghosts? My mum knows about drawn wards.'

Another text arrived, from Rob. 'Mum wants to see my tattoo, or I'm to show dad.'

"Let me answer these mum, then I'll turn it off." Abel quickly sent texts explaining he had the same problems, and to do their best. He also texted Jenny to warn her she might get questions about creatures, wards, and the cat-woman on his arm. He half-expected either mum, or Kelis or Rob's parents, to phone Mr. Forester. "Right mum." Abel took a breath. "The tattoo is an attempt to scare the creatures away but I didn't understand so it doesn't work. I had another go." Abel took another deep breath and rolled up his sleeve. "You might recognise the flower."

"You have another tattoo!" Even as Abel braced for the onslaught, his mum's voice quietened. "That looks like the flower in the middle of the shield, your Tavern sign and my plaque, the same sign Jess has drawn on her arm. It was drawn, but she's had it tattooed now. A bit of a wild one in her day, Jess, she's got a few more from then." Abel opened his mouth, then shut it. Quiet, polite Mrs. Ventner a wild child? "That shield carved on top of the doors keeps the nice creatures in and the bad ones away from the house, and my plaque keeps them all away outside. Why did you have a tattoo?"

Abel opened his mouth, closed it, and thought. What had Mrs. Ventner actually said? He went for truth, or some of it. "We aren't allowed jewellery at school so we drew them on our skin but it kept wearing off. Kelis drew the one on her mum in hospital because the creatures were crawling on the beds."

"And it helps her pain. Why doesn't that one help my hip?" Mum pointed at the plaque she'd been wearing. "Would it work if I drew it on me? I can't remember when my hip didn't hurt."

"Maybe? It isn't the drawing, it just focuses the meditation." Abel looked at his mum with mounting apprehension. "How bad is your hip, mum? I didn't think the arthritis bothered you most of the time."

"I don't say much because it's my own fault." She looked at the few creatures still around the saucer of milk. "It isn't arthritis, and now I know it's not my fault. I fell out of a tree when I was seven. A big creature, all teeth and warts, came round the trunk and along my branch. I backed away until the branch broke, and I fractured my hip." She sighed, rubbing her hip for a moment as Abel realised she did it much too often. "It's worse in wet or cold weather, but niggles most of the time. I don't take pain killers because the drugs I had back then made me see the creatures better. I talked about them, and the therapy started." Mum looked lost in memory for a while, not good memories. "Then I find out the hallucinations are real and my son can chase them away. Can you fix my hip as well, Abel?" The last bit came out very quiet and tentative, not at all like his mum.

"The meditation might make it feel a bit better mum, but there's a possible problem. It'll sort of lower your resistance when you relax and you might see the creatures better, much clearer. I don't know why Mrs. Ventner doesn't see them, but it's a blessing." Abel knew all right. Kelis made sure her mum never had a hint about trying to do anything with the nice peaceful feeling, so she didn't activate her magic and go crackers. "It might mess with your head."

"Is this some sort of voodoo, some weird Ouija board type thing!" Mum looked at the creatures, then the plaque hung on the door, then Abel's tattoo, alarm on her face and in her eyes. "What have you got into?"

"No! No, I swear. It's more like hippy stuff, peace and meditation and all that." Abel didn't need to fake the horror in his voice, because he'd just realised that voodoo stuff might be real! "I only started seeing stuff after the fight with Henry when I bust my finger, so maybe the painkillers did it. I saw the creatures keeping clear of some graffiti in town, and drew it on me with biro, but it didn't work." Abel sighed. "The tattoo is a copy of the whole drawing or rather most of it. I'd missed the flower." Crap, now he had to find a wall someplace and get someone to draw a Ferryl Shayde cat on it, with a flower. Abel shut up before he ended up deeper in it.

"Kelis has a flower? And Rob?" Mum's eyes narrowed. "They didn't, or maybe Kelis did but Rob had to more or less strip for his dad after that cat woman tattoo appeared." Abel stared, Rob kept that quiet! Mum sat for a bit, watching the creatures as they fed on the sugar and milk or collected bits of dust and a few of Mrs. Tabitha's cat hairs. She sighed. "Kelis has a tattoo now, her mum told me but not what it was. How much of your game is real, Abel?"

"Not much, mum. We started it long before seeing anything. Then we added a few of the creatures because they looked realistic, and the Tavern sign is just the flower in a shield. We made up the big things like ogres, dragons, animated dinosaur skeletons and slime monsters." Abel smiled slightly, for the first time since getting home. "We made my tattoo into a cat-sorceress, and Kelis makes a great model for a human sorceress."

"That's a relief. I already carry that plaque and see things most other people don't. How much crazier would I get if you drew it on me?" Abel marshalled all sorts of reasons not to, then saw a tear in his mum's eye! "I'll take a chance to sleep properly at nights."

That did it. Ferryl had offered Abel a glyph for his mum's hip after peeking into her head, but never told Abel how bad it was. He thought about those little sighs when his mum sat down in a comfy seat, and how she favoured her hip getting out of the car. "We can draw it with an ordinary felt tip? Then if it doesn't work you can scrub it off. I'll get one." Abel tried for a bright smile. "Any particular colour, to match your hair or something?"

The look meant he hadn't succeeded. "I know you're worried, but now I've got to know." She sighed, heavier this time. "I told Jess about the creatures. When I saw her tattoo I thought she knew so I pointed at one and asked where she fed them. I'll bet Kelis is having a conversation like this. Sort of." Abel stared as his mum giggled, just a bit. "I bet one of those texts was Rob, because his mum saw Jess's tattoo when she explained about the meditation. He'll be stripping off in the bathroom with his dad checking for tattoos, both of them blushing bright red. Sorry."

Abel got out, sharpish, before mum came up with any other things he didn't want to even think about. Halfway up the stairs she called "a light colour, it will be easier to wash off."

Abel concentrated. "Zephyr?"

"Yes?"

"Can you watch, warn me if any magic is leaking from my fingers when I draw it?" Abel really, really didn't want a link to his mum.

"She will not burn it in herself? You told the others it would be better."

"Just a drawing, with no magic from me. The no-magic is very, very important. I'll explain later."

"Good, I have many questions from the party. Life is much more interesting than Ferryl Shayde told me or I expected. But then I never expected life until you gave it to me." The last statement needed a lot of explanation all on its own, but not just now. Abel found his felt tips, and chose a pink one. He argued with himself, without involving Zephyr, all the way back down but that tear did it. He had to risk it now. Though he thought of one problem. "Zephyr, be careful flying about where mum might see you. She might see spooky-phone as well, I'm not sure." He hoped not, because she hadn't mentioned seeing it at the party.

"You will let me fly about? Thank you." At least Zephyr saw that as a plus. Ferryl would have been annoyed by the restriction.

Abel had wondered where the mark would go, but mum had already stood up with her sleeve rolled up. "My left arm. A sort of family tradition." The humour in her glance at his arm came as a relief. "Remember, the flower not the cat. Does it have to be in the shield?"

"It seems to work better, but I don't want to mess about with mine."

"Come on then. It's a good job you finally learned to draw." Abel realised his mum felt as nervous as he did, which helped to keep his hand steady.

Though 'magic leaking' from Zephyr stopped him thinking about mum's nerves so he could concentrate on the actual job. Abel had drawn the Tavern sign as a hex on dozens of windowsills and door frames at school, so it didn't take long. Firm strokes, with intent, worked best according to Ferryl and Abel really did want mum's hip feeling better. He stood back and inspected the result. One of his better efforts. "Leave it a minute, so it doesn't smudge."

"Will that matter?" Mum twisted her arm to look, then used the mirror in the hall. "What now? I didn't feel anything." Abel managed to stifle his sigh of relief at that, because it meant he hadn't connected to her.

"You have to relax. Sit with your hand on it and let your mind go. Think peaceful thoughts. Though you have to believe it will work." Abel wanted to keep away from the mark doing anything other than aid meditation.

He didn't expect the laugh. "Believe in it? Remember, I can see all those disgusting things at work scuttle away from that plaque. A fat ugly thing with boils and lots of arms wandered into Kurbishley's cubicle at work, so I put a plaque by the door to keep it there. Only for a couple of days, but I smiled every time it knocked some of the miserable, nasty sod's papers on the floor." Mum smiled brightly. "I'd like to trap one of those that live in computers in there, the ones that look like little old men. I'm sure they won't do his spreadsheets any good."

Abel managed to shut his mouth when he realised mum was babbling, on edge, waiting for the mark to send her crackers. "Sit down mum. Shut your eyes, put your hand on the flower and stroke it very gently while thinking peaceful thoughts. I'll make you a cuppa." While he put the kettle on Abel listened, but so far so good. He wanted to check, but if his mum saw him peeking it wouldn't help her peace of mind. When he took her the cuppa Abel felt better. Mum had her eyes shut, her hand on the drawing and a little smile on her face. "Cuppa, mum."

"Mmm? Ta. I don't know if it's helped my hip, but this really does feel nice. So far there's no flying unicorns, so here's hoping." She opened her eyes. "Go on, get to your room and text Kelis and Rob. There's probably a dozen waiting from them, or your girlfriend." She closed her eyes so a relieved Abel did as he'd been told.

There were a lot of texts from Rob, but most were relief. After turning down the waistband of his jeans to show his tattoo his mum and dad were satisfied. Both Samantha and Melanie had a million questions, but Melanie had been most excited by the idea of playing the Tavern game with Rachel. Samantha had seen several different tattoos because some of the lads and a couple of girls wanted to show theirs off, and had questions. At least neither of his sisters had broken their rule about sibling indiscretions; they hadn't talked to their parents.

The text from Ferryl/Jenny must be phrased in case her dad saw it. "Dad very interested in what Diane said about the Tavern. He wants to know more. I am telling him what I know but I think he'll want to see the whole file." That would mean the rules and original drawings of characters, and all the notes on how to deal with other game characters and monsters. Abel assumed Mr. Forester wanted to know what Diane might end up seeing, like how much gore was involved.

There were no texts from Kelis, which really worried Abel. He diverted himself by talking to Zephyr, and found it a bit like when Ferryl first moved into his arm. He ended up more or less explaining the whole party to her, minute by minute. His new resident had an insatiable curiosity, and a sheer joy in being alive. Abel came back to her promise to serve him several times, but Zephyr really didn't mind. His magic really had given her life, so Zephyr had absolutely no qualms about serving him for ninety years. She tried a few short flights outside, slipping through an invisible gap around the allegedly draught-proof window trailing the spooky-phone behind her. Abel hoped the torrent of excited commentary would calm down in time.

Just before midnight a short text from Kelis explained her mum understood. Abel's mum had always seen something and now thought she knew what. Abel texted back 'Ghosts?'

'Probably, we decided. Talk tomorrow.'

*　　*　　*

A faint stirring sensation, rather than actual movement, roused Abel and made him smile. He lifted his arm and looked at the tattoo. Both eyes blinked and the whiskers twitched, then the tip of her tail moved just a little. "Good morning. Your mum is awake."

"Good morning. I usually sleep until my alarm goes off. You are moving more." Abel smiled again, remembering conversations with Ferryl about the next bit. "You must keep the tattoo still when others can see you unless I say it's safe." He remembered one difference to talking with Ferryl, no speech necessary. "Once you have control, you can dance in front of Rob or Kelis, or Jenny of course."

"But with clothes." Zephyr's sense of humour sounded familiar.

"Yes. Except with just me. I've got used to Ferryl wandering around my arm in her fur." Abel glanced at the clock but then decided to get up anyway. He wanted to know if mum's ward had worked, if her hip hurt less.

The big smile when he came into the kitchen told at least some of the story. "You're up early. I slept late because that meditation works. I fell asleep on the chair last night, for about an hour, but I wasn't sore when I woke up." Mum rubbed her hip. "I can still feel it, so I'm not sure if I just had a good night or your magic pen worked. If I don't see purple dinosaurs or flying frogs today I want it drawn in permanent marker please."

The magic part in that made Abel twitch. "Just do it yourself, go over that drawing."

"I wondered if it worked better if you did it."

Alarm bells went off in Abel's head. "No. I told you, it's just an aid to meditation." Mum's look still had a bit of suspicion in it. Abel would have to be careful to do nothing at all that might give her any more hints. "Kelis' mum thinks you see ghosts."

"At one time or another I thought I saw ghosts, devils, and aliens. If it's dangerous, maybe I should let her think that's all it is, ghosts." The hug caught Abel by surprise. "But if Jess starts to see things, tell me. I'll explain. I've had a lifetime of it."

"Brilliant. I'll let Kelis know." Mrs. Tabitha came in the cat flap and rubbed around Abel's ankles.

"The guardian! I am supposed to check with her, and the others when I see them." Abel had more or less forgotten about Ferryl Shayde purring to all the local cats, and enhancing their eyes so they could watch out for magical intrusions. Now he realised that with her living six miles away, Ferryl hadn't been getting reports from what she called her guardians.

"Not now, Mum might see." Abel thought quickly. "At night, when you fly about."

"More flying?" Abel hoped Zephyr kept seeing the good side of restrictions. He chatted to mum about the party, some of the costumes, and took a bit of gentle teasing about his new girl. Mum would be a while getting over that. Unfortunately Abel remembered something he hadn't managed to sort out, how to check the wards on Castle House gardens. Maybe Zephyr could see them? After breakfast he went to find out.

*   *   *

While walking around the outside of Brinsford, to come at the gardens from the back, Abel topped up a few of the stakes that created the weak magical boundary. He also used air glyphs to splat several of the larger flying fae because they had nasty stings. Zephyr promptly asked if she could try, but Abel wanted Ferryl/Jenny present for that. Instead he promised plenty of flying once they arrived.

Abel's greeting in the wood reminded him of something else he had forgotten. "Did you bring the honey?"

"My apologies dryad." Abel meant that. Dryads didn't trust magic users so he always tried to keep his word. "Kelis will still be asleep. I will bring it this afternoon."

"Sleeping? Such a waste of time. What lives in your arm? It is not the sorceress." Abel had no idea how dryads knew. The magic-using archbishop Kelis had nicknamed Vicar Creepio Mysterio hadn't been able to detect Ferryl, so there wasn't a magical beacon on his tattoo.

"Fly around, Zephyr. Let the dryad see you. You may speak to it but take care what you say." Abel felt the sprite leave. He preferred to think of her as a sprite rather than an upmarket Feral Spirit.

"This wood feels wonderful. The magic is everywhere, all these trees are full of it. So much magic." Abel knew why. All living things absorbed magic, but everything except plants also leaked some of it. As a result adult trees were the best magic reservoirs in the world, but most had a resident dryad who jealously guarded every drop. This whole protected wood, and Castle House gardens, were the exact opposite. Only one dryad lived in here, in one tree, and had to be given a stone glyph to protect it from the protection spell. All the rest of the magic was freely available for Abel, Kelis and Rob. "When I learn glyphs, this would be a good place to practice. I cannot store much magic of my own." Zephyr soared and swooped, rustling leaves and bending the grass. "This must be what the sorceress called fun."

"You have bound a Wind Spirit, sorcerer?" The dryad didn't sound happy.

A smoky line connected to the dryad. "I am not bound. I am a servant, in return for protection and knowledge." Zephyr swooped low, a shimmer in the air. "I was just a puff of wind until he gave me life."

"How did you do that?" Now the dryad seemed much too interested.

"The sorceress did it, because she can't be here all the time. I'm not sure what she did." Abel racked his brains. "Don't Free Spirits happen all the time?"

"Not like this one." The dryad suddenly sounded much happier, or as happy as a dryad ever sounded. "This Spirit was created to help you strengthen the barriers?"

Abel skirted that part. "We'll be here this afternoon to get started." After explaining how, Abel went into the gardens themselves. Dryads weren't into small talk, or talk at all most of the time. He spent an hour trotting around the overgrown paths, carrying two small logs or creating glyphs on the move. The exercises Ferryl insisted on really had made a difference fighting Henry, allowing Abel to throw heavy logs and branches. Pushing or lifting objects with magic took much less muscle than physically doing so, but Abel wanted to be able to throw or lift as much as possible. Enough to squash the next troll baby under a ton of timber seemed like a good idea.

Zephyr swooped around him the whole time, always connected. She could see the magic feeding the boundary barrier, but had no real idea what the flows did or meant. Abel spent another hour in the cave by the big circular stone slab, practicing glyphs until Zephyr finally calmed down. Before heading home he texted Kelis and Rob, arranging to meet later to deliver honey.

The afternoon went well, back to a sort of normal except for the chatter from Zephyr. The protection hexes carved into long straight-ish branches using penknives weren't the neatest, but did the job once they'd been filled with magic. All three of them used concentrated air glyphs to hammer the branches deep into the ground across the boundary where the troll baby had tunnelled in, much to dryad's relief. Though dryad's happy mood might be from scoffing a whole jar of honey, it had that effect on dryad Chestnut on the village green.

The rest of the barrier would take a little while because Kelis would have to either talk her mum into buying long thin stakes, or the three of them would have to use the tools in her garage to make them.

*　　*　　*

Despite all the potential for disaster the previous weekend, everyone's parents seemed to settle for the explanations - for now at least. During the next week the other students, even Seraph, lost interest in Ferryl/Jenny sitting with the geeks. By Friday Ferryl/Jenny had taken the dressing off her head and the bandage off her foot, but she kept her arm and leg bandaged and still used a stick. Spooky-phone worked overtime, bringing the Taverners up to date and helping to organise the next weekend. Ferryl had to use mazzlement, whatever that did, until her dad agreed to her going out on Saturday afternoon with a group of friends.

At least Abel, and Ferryl, now knew why her dad seemed so concerned. Deep in Jenny's memories, very deep because she hardly remembered it, she had almost died. It had been another accident involving a lorry, which explained why her dad had gone into super-protective mode. On Friday Ferryl/Jenny had a message for Abel. Mr. Forester wanted to talk to all three of the game designers. Would they mind meeting him, either at his house or Kelis'? Since only Mr. Forester had transport they opted for Kelis' house, once her mum agreed.

Early Saturday afternoon Shannon turned up with Jenny to collect Rob and Abel. A bemused Kelis accepted the proffered crash helmet and perched herself on the back of Shawn's scooter. Once she'd said hello a smiling Ferryl/Jenny confirmed she'd passed her CBT, Compulsory Basic Training test for riding a moped. She privately admitted to mazzling the instructor just a little, but now she'd be able to visit Brinsford as often as her dad let her ride over. Ferryl/Jenny sat in the back with Abel, holding hands to 'talk' to him on the way, with Zephyr keeping Rob and Shannon up to date. Abel could see it in his eyes, Rob wanted his own Sprite.

*   *   *

Shawn looked at the twelve teenagers gathered in the car park by Elmwood Park. "We'll scare the poor bloke to death."

"Not frighten, but we want him wary. He's magically aware even if the creatures climb all over him." Abel didn't want anyone getting too confident. "If he found magic in his teens, he could have been using it for twenty or thirty years and might be able to help us with our training. We'll ask him why the creatures climb on him, and if he can't stop them we offer to help. With a group of us backing her up, he'll know Sarah has friends if anything happens to her."

"Yeah, I don't like the idea of that sorceress trying to bind you three. I'm all on my lonesome when I walk home from the school bus." Sarah tried to look relaxed, but her voice squeaked a little.

"He already knows you by sight, so you've got to approach him. Abel has to go with you so you've got Ferryl Shayde as backup, and Jenny because she's welded to his arm." Shawn sounded serious but the rest laughed at the last bit.

"I'm the best with wind, so I should stand nearby." Kelis flexed her fingers. "Just in case."

"With the Barbarian and his club for anything physical." Rob brandished his rounders bat, much smaller than a baseball bat but the carved glyph gave it a tremendous wallop against magical creatures.

"That's five people to meet him, while the rest of us spread out around the park but in sight. Then if he turns on you five, we can move in." Eric didn't sound too confident. "Though if he can fend Ferryl off, we're in trouble."

Abel really hoped it didn't come to that. "We aren't looking for trouble, just to ask questions. Talking, not fighting so nobody throws a glyph unless I start it. He might not be any sort of a threat at all but we have to know one way or another. If the dryad hadn't noticed Sarah coming past every day we could have just ignored both of them. Did you bring the honey for the dryad, Sarah?"

"Yes. You'll be nearby?"

"We all promise." Kelis patted her on the shoulder and wiggled her fingers. "Help is a glyph away." After a quick discussion on who went where, the group split up. The weaker ones teamed up with stronger glyph throwers, because nobody wanted to wait with the cars.

The man didn't take much spotting after Sarah's descriptions, especially since he sat near the only old tree in the park. He had long hair, a straggly beard and well-used clothes, but wasn't as scruffy as Abel expected. The creatures were obvious to those could see them, clustering around him even as he brushed them off. Suddenly most of them drew back a little, and Abel saw the dryad come out of its tree. The shimmer around it meant it had cast a veil so the non-magical wouldn't see the gnarled creature. "Perfect. Go for it, Sarah."

Sarah drew ahead of the others, taking out her pot of honey and unscrewing the lid. Ignoring the man she walked up to the edge of the veil before placing the honey on the grass. "Greetings dryad. I bring honey in return for answers."

The man started to rise, then sat back down and watched intently. The dryad hesitated, torn between caution and honey. Honey won. It moved forward until with a sudden surge the veil reached out round Sarah and the jar full of temptation. "What questions, human? Are you a sorceress?"

"He is using something. I see magic swirling." Zephyr's voice echoed in Abel's head. Her warning explained the vague reddish glow Abel saw.

Ferryl's voice joined it. "The dryad is testing Sarah's magical strength, trying to assess her as a threat. There is no danger."

Sarah wouldn't have noticed because Ferryl had only adapted Abel's, Kelis' and Rob's eyes to be more sensitive to magic, so she answered the dryad. "I am an apprentice. I wanted to know why this man has creatures climbing all over him. He brushes them off, so he can see them but doesn't like them. Is he a sorcerer or warlock, and if so why doesn't he have a ward or a hex?"

"Several questions. Maybe one big one." The dryad eyed the honey. "The payment is enough. You must learn to bargain better, apprentice. The human can see us, but he is not a magic worker. He does not know how to create or activate glyphs. I cannot help. I have no idea how humans work glyphs."

Meanwhile Abel, Ferryl/Jenny, Kelis and Rob walked steadily closer. Sarah stepped back nervously as the dryad extruded a shoot to slurp up the honey. "I thank you dryad. Since he is not a threat we will try to help him with the creatures, if he wishes."

"We?" The dryad stopped slurping and looked around, freezing as it saw the group of four almost at the park bench. "A trap. A clever one. It is an age since I tasted honey." The creature began to ease back towards the tree, calling out to the suddenly wary man. "If they threaten you, run for my tree. I will do my best but three, possibly all four are experienced and strong."

Abel spoke up as the others stopped. "We will not threaten. We simply wanted to make sure he is not a threat to this apprentice because she lives nearby." He turned to address the man. "The dryad says you are not a magic user. We can teach you to use glyphs and send the creatures away, if you wish. That or we can give you a hex that will deter them."

The man looked around the park, half-rising as he spotted the number of people with no creatures near them. "Twelve of you are not a threat? I told you last time, I won't take your job. I can't because I don't know how and I won't pay your price to learn." The sheer bitterness in the last part persuaded Abel he wasn't faking.

"Caution. There is another, hidden, carried by that one." The dryad pointed a twig at Abel and moved closer to the tree, looking longingly at the remaining honey. "My tree is old and strong. Overcoming us will cause noise, and people will notice. Sorcerers don't like that."

Abel took a Tavern hex on a wooden plaque out of his pocket and tossed it towards the park bench. "That will keep the creatures away. Wear it or put it in a pocket. Let the dryad inspect it, to see there is no trap." Abel sketched a slight bow to the dryad. "We will not cheat you out of your honey. Come on Sarah, we'll stand back and let them talk a while." Sarah didn't hesitate, and the five humans walked away out of earshot.

"I can sneak in to hear them, a gentle Zephyr through the grass?"

That might have worked with a non-magical humans, but not that pair. "No sneaking Zephyr, or the dryad will see your magic. Even the human might."

"Not if she dissipates enough. Though it is best not to do that, not yet, not until her sense of self is stronger. Otherwise she will become many tiny, unthinking Free Spirits." Abel passed that on to Zephyr, hoping it would stop her experimenting.

*   *   *

Ten minutes later Abel seriously considered leaving. The man had watched the creatures avoiding the plaque, eventually picking it up along with the honey and taking them to the dryad. The pair of them huddled together under the tree, near the trunk, invisible to most of the world behind the veil. That reminded Abel. "Did you find out how to veil?"

Ferryl sounded despondent. "Not yet, nor how to shield beyond my natural defences. It is not on these wits. The rest must be in the house."

A loud voice interrupted. "Poachers? Who is your master?" Abel and the rest whirled to see a slim man in a suit, possibly about thirty and definitely angry.

"Poaching what? We came to help this man." Abel gestured towards the tree.

"You sold him protection when he refused to buy from us. Stourton is a monopoly my master intends keeping. You will hand over the payment and leave." The man lounged against the lamp post, completely at ease despite the anger on his face. "It is lucky I left something here to keep an eye on him."

"I can see it. Shall I fetch it for you?" Zephyr sounded eager. Abel could almost feel her tugging to be let loose.

"Zephyr wants to collect whatever it is."

So did Ferryl. "Good idea."

Abel barely formed the thought before Zephyr shot out of his arm. The connection flicked out across the park, aimed at a sapling, and something started to rise. Too late. Abel realised she'd caught a bird as Zephyr headed back towards him, leaving a couple of feathers floating gently downwards. The sorcerer, he had to be, raised his hand and a glyph arrowed out. Abel never had time to react, but Ferryl/Jenny did. A puff of steam or smoke rose as her glyph intercepted his. The man whirled, palms out and glyphs stirring, but hesitated at the sight of glyphs forming on Sarah's, Abel's, Ferryl/Jenny's, Kelis' and Rob's palms. Meanwhile Zephyr arrived back, though all Abel could see was the link and a live bird floating inside a shimmer in the air in front of him. Definitely live, because it blinked.

"Interesting." Ferryl/Jenny let go of Abel to reach out towards it, keeping the other hand aimed towards the sorcerer.

"No!" The man closed and twisted one hand, and blood filled the bird's open beak. He'd lost any semblance of relaxation now. "What is that? How did you....?" He stopped and took a breath. "Please understand, if you try to take over Stourton there will be consequences. The business here is not extensive, but my master will not let it go."

"We don't want his business." Abel told Zephyr to let the bird go and hide again. The body bounced on the grass as he felt her flow into the tattoo. "We are not taking over, just dealing with the creatures where nobody else does."

"Protection? The priests will be unhappy if you take the tithes that usually end up in their churches. Those churches cover most of the affluent areas, and the rest won't pay enough to make it worthwhile." At least he sounded nearly as puzzled as he was angry. "So why did you kill my watcher?"

"You killed it. We just stopped it spying on us. We'll collect the next one as well." Abel shouldn't have been stroppy but the bloke had rubbed a raw nerve. Just like the church he didn't care who suffered from creatures if they weren't paying, and killing the bird had been just plain nasty. "We are a charity. The church knows about us, and are interested in how it works out."

Kelis just had to join in. "We had a visit from a Peripatetic Archbishop. He left us a number for God's SAS." Her sunny smile didn't match the glyphs swirling in her palms. "Why don't you try out your crap attitude on him?"

The man's eyes narrowed. "Where are you from? You look like schoolkids, most of you."

"That's us. Most of us are from the comprehensive." Abel figured the bloke would find that out anyway. "We started by protecting the school."

"Some of us are from church schools." Shannon had closed in behind him, close enough to make him jump. A glyph swirled in her palm as well. "I'll bet a Peripatetic Archbishop would take it personally if you hurt us."

Kelis' voice jerked his head back round again. "God's SAS is my name for the church heavies but it fits. We were told they deal with serious problems, the sort that consider levelling villages as collateral." The vicar had suggested it could happen, which meant God's SAS should squish this creep without working up a sweat.

The sorcerer looked startled, then calculating. "An apprentice is not allowed to risk something like that. My master will decide what to do about you. Even if you are a charity, you must claim somewhere as a base. Where?"

"The villages outside Brinsford. Each of us deals with our own and then combine to help those working or living in Stourton." Abel didn't want some sorcerer descending on anyone on their own.

"Where does your sorcerer or sorceress live?" He looked at the swirling glyphs, then closer at Abel, Rob, Kelis and Ferryl/Jenny. "Someone teaches you."

"Our teacher is based in Brinsford, eight miles away." Abel saw the man relax a little so that wasn't going to be a problem. "You'll have to visit if you want to talk."

"My master will want to meet with your," he sneered, "teacher. Probably a witch from the sounds of it." His expression faltered for a moment as he glanced at the bird, then firmed up again. "They will discuss boundaries, and your attitude."

"And yours, we hope?" Kelis kept it light, but she had a low tolerance to threats these days.

"I am a proper apprentice, expected to stand up for my master's rights. Give me your phone number."

Abel waited, not answering, but Ferryl/Jenny smiled sweetly and glanced at him. "His sorcerer doesn't teach manners." Ferryl would find that hilarious after all the reminders about her own manners, when she first lived in the tattoo.

The apprentice glared at her. "Phone number, please. This is not helping."

"I have been taught manners."

"Hush Zephyr, stay hidden."

Abel gave him the mobile number, but not his name. This sorcerer could work for that if he wanted it. "You live in Brinsford?" Abel nodded. "Very well, no more watchers until this is settled." He glowered at the dead bird, turned on his heel and stalked off.

"Just one small heat glyph on that uptight ass?"

Abel glanced at Ferryl/Jenny. "Tempting, but no. Your vocabulary is growing. Uptight ass?"

"I've learned all sorts of things from Jenny. The world really has moved on, especially for women." Ferryl/Jenny turned away as the sorcerer climbed into his car, an almost new BMW.

"What do we do about the man with the dryad? I don't trust the sorcerer not to cause him trouble." Kelis finally lowered her hand, banishing the glyph as the car drove out of sight.

Abel passed on the answer from Ferryl. "The sorcerer will want to speak with our teacher first. Meanwhile the dryad is strong enough to stop low-level harassment. If this man will take a few plaques for his house, that should cover it." He set off back to the tree and the odd couple. "Let's find out."

A lot of the suspicion had gone though not all of it, not from the dryad. "What is the price for this hex?"

"No price dryad, for you or this man. Did you look at it properly?" Abel kept well back with Ferryl/Jenny, Kelis, Rob and Sarah flanking him.

Twigs scraped over the wooden plaque. "A guarding hex I have not seen before, with something else that is not active. Strong enough to deter minor magical beings, but not those such as I."

"There is some soothing and pain relief if it is drawn on skin, where it will also turn minor magical attacks." Abel nodded to the man. "Draw it on yourself if you like, then stroke it and meditate. Otherwise just wear that and the small creatures will leave you alone."

"No price?" The man and dryad glanced at each other.

"We are a sort of charity." Kelis obviously liked that idea. "Just starting. We are trying to help those who can't afford to pay."

"We could teach you how to do it yourself, use a glyph and make your own protection?" Sarah glanced at Abel and shrugged. "I feel sorry for him."

"No!" The man clutched the hex. "That's what they offered. I will not pay that price!"

Abel didn't understand. "What price?" The man looked at the puzzled faces and relaxed.

"You don't know?" Everyone looked at each other, back at him and shook their heads, and that was all it took. Even the dryad relaxed enough to finish polishing the inside of the honey jar as the rest of the Taverners gathered around the man, Frederick. He explained that the sorcerer's apprentice, the one who had just left, had offered to sell him protection. Frederick had no money, not the sort of money needed, so the apprentice made him another offer.

The sorcerer would teach Frederick how to use magic and keep the creatures away. In return Frederick would work for the sorcerer, carrying out magical tasks for twenty years. To ensure obedience, and so Frederick couldn't cheat on the deal, the sorcerer would mark him. It would be a magical leash, which didn't sound too bad until Frederick discussed it with the dryad. The link would be a control, and the sorcerer would leave it in place so Frederick could never be a threat. Frederick would probably have plenty of money, but would spend his life working glyphs to help his master.

After leaving Frederick with seven wooden hexes and Shawn's phone number, a very sober group of Taverners headed back to their transport. Frederick would phone Eric if he wanted tuition, or if anyone magical turned up to harass him. The trainees living in town promised to be there as quickly as possible, and the whole group offered to come to Brinsford when the sorcerer wanted to meet Abel. Most of them thought Ferryl Shayde should just slap the cheeky git down if he started giving ultimatums.

Some of them knew she might not be there, though on the way home in Shannon's car Ferryl had the answer. "Unfortunately, until I recover properly and find my other wits, I can't fight a sorcerer. If I am not there, stand inside Castle House garden. When he tests the barrier, he will find it is too strong and complex for him to unravel. Tell him if he attacks you will run away, and come back after he is dead to try to recapture the response." After a moment's thought she had another idea. "Or dig up the bone glyph we took from the sorceress. That will follow his magical attack back to him, and he'll wake up bound into a brand new tattoo on whoever has the glyph."

Abel vetoed that, though Rob wanted to leave his options open. He voted for having the glyph ready, just in case. When Shannon dropped Ferryl/Jenny off at home, Rob covered his eyes just as he used to for Abel to kiss Kelis goodbye. Abel really wished the kiss felt like a Kelis one, or rather that it was a Kelis one. Though Ferryl might have a point, he wasn't dwelling on that quite as much and Jenny's kiss wasn't exactly awful. Abel, Rob and Shannon spent the journey from Kielby to Brinsford going over this business of magical apprentices and them being leashed.

*   *   *

All weekend Abel expected the sorcerer to ring, but nothing happened. The three of them finished the increased protection around the wood outside the back wall of Castle House garden, with some unexpected help on Sunday afternoon. Warned by a text message the three of them were waiting outside Castle House when Ferryl/Jenny puttered up on her moped, followed by a familiar Mercedes. Ferryl/Jenny smiled as she took off her helmet. "Dad is worried I'll fall off."

"It is your first time out." Mr. Forester looked a little embarrassed. "It will wear off soon, I promise." He looked up at Castle House, then swept his eyes across the gardens. "So this is the mystery wild wood. Is there a way into the house round the back?"

"No, it's all locked or boarded up, every door and window." Abel gestured to include the grounds. "The rest is like this. We like it because nobody bothers us in here."

Ferryl/Jenny hugged her dad, quickly. "I've been dying to explore ever since Abel told me about it. It's all overgrown because nobody has been here for ages. There's even a little cave if it rains." She turned and headed for the gate.

Mr. Forester hesitated. "Typical kids, want someplace private. Who does it belong to?" He eyed the house again. "That would make a really nice place if someone renovated it or turned it into flats." A move towards the gate stopped almost as soon as it started. "I might have a proper look at it sometime."

Abel realised the barrier must be persuading him not to bother right now. "How long is Jenny here for?"

"An hour." Once again, her dad made half a move towards the gate. "Since I'm here I'll wait to make sure Jenny gets home all right." He definitely looked embarrassed this time.

Now he knew why Mr. Forester worried so much, Abel sympathised. He made a suggestion, knowing the barrier would make anything sound good right now. "I'll text mum if you like. She'll stick the kettle on and you can have a cuppa and a natter." Abel held up his phone. "She can probably answer some questions about Bonny's Tavern as well."

It worked. "Are you sure she won't mind?" Abel felt sure his mum would love to grill Mr. Forester about Jenny, and would enjoy showing off the game. She'd taken a drawing of the actual Tavern to work with her, to show everyone what her son and his friends had come up with. Sure enough, a few minutes later Ferryl/Jenny waved her dad goodbye.

"That was mean. You let him off the hook. I wanted to see what sort of daft excuse he'd come up with to leave, yet be here to escort me back." Ferryl/Jenny heaved a big sigh, then put her arms out and twirled. "Free at last! Well not really, but it's nice to stop pretending. No need to limp, or hold hands to talk privately, or talk in code." She looked up as Zephyr flew out of Abel's tattoo and soared up to the treetops, trailing her tether. "Maybe not quite free, not as free as Zephyr." She set off for the cave.

Though Rob wasn't waiting until they were settled. "When can I have a Zephyr, Ferryl? It would make things a lot easier at school. You hold hands with lover-boy here so he can hear you give him private answers, but then he has to pass them on." Rob stopped so fast Abel nearly trampled him. "We should add that to the game. The characters can have an invisible magic companion."

"Yes, I'd like one as well, especially since she saw that watcher bird when nobody else did." Kelis pushed Rob. "Come on, I want to sit down and talk properly."

"I saw it as well, or the magic tether to it when it activated, but couldn't work out what to do. A glyph attack would have been too aggressive just then, and might have started a battle. I forgot how fast Zephyr could move." Ferryl/Jenny shook her head at Rob. "Sorry Rob, no Zephyr for you. You would need a tattoo like Abel's."

"I'll take the grounding when mum finds out. Better still show me the mazzlement glyph, or I can wrap the tattoo in a bandage and practice the seeming glyph." Rob stopped outside the cave. "Curses, there's only three crates."

Kelis grinned at Abel, and then Ferryl/Jenny. "Jenny can sit on her boyfriend's knee."

"Not Jenny so not boyfriend, remember." Abel started to take off his jacket. "I used to sit on this when we started. I can practice fire glyphs if I'm cold."

Rob and Kelis burst out laughing. Ferryl/Jenny and Abel waited patiently until Kelis stopped enough to speak. "Rob reckoned you'd still hold hands and maybe even kiss her while we were on our own, and say it was for practice. I told him you wouldn't."

"Never mind that now. I'm a lot more interested in a Zephyr. Do I have to imagine a tattoo the same as a ward?" Rob paused with his jacket half unzipped. "How much will this hurt?"

"Does it have to be a furry cat-lady? Where would it go?" Kelis inspected Rob but then her eyes opened wide. "Ooh, could Rob have a Lovingly Sculpted on his arm? Though until he saw her, I'd have bet on a Teddy Bear or a Petra cat-girl."

"I'm sorry, you can't have a tattoo like Abel's. I made that tattoo while I had no body, with my true-self blended into his skin, separate yet connected to his magic. I didn't even know if I could do it when I agreed to be a rider without reins, but I was desperate. If Abel had left me in that hole I would have faded completely within a few more years." Ferryl/Jenny's sad face suddenly brightened. "It turned out to be the most fun I've had in centuries. I doubt there is another tattoo like that anywhere, one that allows the inhabitant to leave and fly without any sort of binding. Even Zephyr has to keep contact until Abel releases her from

85

her agreement."

"You could teach us to make one? Oh, we can't get inside ourselves. What about Zephyr? She looks like you did, sort of shimmery." Rob wasn't giving up yet.

"Zephyr couldn't enter you, or anybody, not without being properly bound or possibly blending in a sort of half-possession. She can't make a tattoo like that, and I can't make another without leaving this body. Then I would never get back in, because Jenny is warded now." Ferryl/Jenny glanced up at Zephyr, now hovering and obviously listening. "Zephyr is unique as well." She addressed the shimmer directly. "Nobody will ever work out exactly what you are and you must not let them pry. You are a product of Abel's magic and intent so you absorbed something of him, his character. You also have some of my knowledge, and when I gave you a mind it must have included a part of who I am. The result has exceeded all my expectations, a true thinking being rather than just an obedient servant. A sorcerer might have created something less complex before, or bound a Feral Spirit, but that would not have been given free will."

"But Zephyr isn't completely free." Abel tried wrestling with the idea of Zephyr having his character but left that for now.

"Zephyr chose to serve when she could have flown away. She is a gamble because I broke my promise to you, Abel Bernard Conroy." Jenny's voice sounded totally serious as she looked Abel in the eye. "I needed some way to help you, to protect you in some way when I can't. Zephyr can see magic flows, which even your improved eyesight can't, so she will see magical traps others think are hidden."

"She makes a great retriever as well." Rob sniggered, his hand shooting out and closing as if snatching something from the air. "That wiped the sneer off that apprentice's face."

"Forget him for now. Talking about magic flows has just reminded me that Zephyr needs some tuition. That way, even if you aren't here, we'll know if something has tried to break in." Ferryl promptly insisted on checking the boundaries, immediately, which turned into one long, fascinating lesson. By the end Zephyr understood the magic flows and could spot a problem, even if she couldn't yet fix it. Rob and Kelis learned how to help Abel repair the feeds from the trees, but only if Zephyr found the faults.

*   *   *

Rather than watch Mr. Forester struggle with wanting to come into the gardens while the garden persuaded him not to, the four of them made it back to Abel's house before their hour was up. Once inside they found that sending Jenny's dad here had gone beyond keeping him occupied. He admitted wanting to check out how violent Bonny's Tavern might be but now, after talking with Abel's mum, he made a tentative offer. She'd told him the three mothers would be helping their children to sell the game.

Jenny's dad offered to look into the idea of the game and assess it as a business venture. If it still looked sound, he offered to invest in the potential company and nail down the patent and copyright for Bonny's Tavern, including donating the services of his lawyer and accountant. In return, Mr. Forester asked for a small share of the business, for his daughters. A stunned Abel, Kelis and Rob promised to think about it very seriously.

Once Ferryl/Jenny and her dad left, Abel's mum made a cuppa for everyone. She explained that the offer had very little to do with Abel and Jenny going out together, except that it had brought Bonny's Tavern to Mr. Forester's attention. Diane had been going on about Bonny's Tavern ever since the Abel-Jenny secret came out so he'd tried to buy it for her, and found he couldn't. Jenny had confirmed that the Tavern wanted to legalise the game, which is why he'd wanted a meeting. Explaining that, and answering the tentative questions, kept everyone occupied while they drank their tea.

"Now you three need to sleep on it. Probably for several nights and you'll need at least one Tavern meeting I'm sure. Jenny will probably be in touch, because her dad will be explaining all this once she gets home." Abel's mum ruffled his hair. "You've done it now. That's a serious businessman and he really is interested. Abel mentioned having your mothers as directors, as a possibility, so I hope you two told your mums?" Kelis and Rob nodded, still dumbstruck. "Well you'd best go and tell them it might really happen. I'll talk to Jess and Terri tomorrow and explain everything Mr. Forester said."

Abel saw Rob and Kelis to the door, heading back to the lounge with his head still going in circles. His mum's laugh startled him. "I've never seen you three so serious, not when it's about your blessed game. Cheer up, you don't have to marry the girl." She laughed again at Abel's expression. "We both agreed it'll be a miracle if you pair are still a couple after the summer holidays. Jenny is a year older than you and has entirely different interests, not to mention a very full schedule once she starts Acro training again. The business offer really has nothing to do with how you two feel."

"I wondered if it might be about the accident. You know, a sort of thank you." Which would make Abel feel really guilty. He'd also wondered for a moment if Ferryl had mazzled Jenny's dad, but she hadn't mentioned any of this.

She shook her head. "No, though he really is grateful you saved his daughter. The offer seems to be pure business. I can't help you with finance, Rob's mum and dad aren't exactly flush, and Jess has no idea what she'll end up with after the divorce. This way Mr. Forester picks up the initial costs, and you get to use a proper lawyer and accountant. A few shares for Jenny and Diane are worth nothing now, though you'll have to make sure you three stay in control."

"I've no idea what to think. Worse, I've got school tomorrow so there's homework to finish and my head is scrambled." Even though he finally got it finished, Abel knew he wouldn't get good marks for this homework. The texts from Rob and Kelis told the same story. Neither of them had come to terms with the idea yet, let alone had any serious thoughts.

*   *   *

Ferryl/Jenny's news on Monday morning came as a relief. Her dad wasn't expecting a reply this week, and possibly not the week after. She actually understood the whole thing better than the three designers, because Jenny took Business Studies. That led to Kelis rethinking her options for next year. She had the grades to take Business Studies, but hadn't wanted anything to do with it because of her dad. He'd have used her as cheap labour and the thought of working in the same office terrified her. Now some business knowledge might be a good idea.

The next ten days passed quickly, with Ferryl/Jenny visiting at the weekend and Wednesday nights. Her dad gave up on following the moped after the second visit, though she had to be home well before dusk. During the second week Abel, Rob and Kelis came to a decision. If Jenny's dad really wanted to invest, and the offer wasn't an attempt to rip them off, they'd take it. Even if that didn't happen, Kelis would be taking Business Studies because they'd still push on with Bonny's Tavern.

*   *   *

Meanwhile, Sarah spoke to Frederick whenever she saw him in the park. He sent his thanks for the hexes, telling Sarah the dryad would keep an eye open for watchers and warn him. At the moment Frederick and the dryad were considering the offer of training. They had a strange relationship, where the dryad seemed to really care what happened to the human. Maybe it was lonely because there were no other adult trees or dryads in the park.

Despite occasionally worrying, Abel heard nothing from the sorcerer who allegedly had the monopoly on magic in Stourton. He began to wonder if the man had dismissed him and the rest as irrelevant.

Seraph ignored Ferryl/Jenny, and the geeks, even when Henry came back to school. Henry wasn't much good as a heavy, not with the fingers on one hand strapped up and the other arm in a pot and sling. He had a recorder to help him remember his lessons long enough to make notes, because he had to type them one-fingered. From the slightly haunted look and occasional twitches Henry definitely saw creatures, though despite him looking tired Ferryl declared him leech-free. Henry remained as strong and physically healthy as ever, whereas Leech seed victims were in permanent pain and lost weight quickly as the seed invaded their organs. Claris might be in real trouble, because she still hadn't returned to school.

*   *   *

One surprise, and problem, should have been expected. Rob called for an emergency Tavern meeting on Thursday evening. He arrived waving his phone. "Big problem. Remember all those friends and relatives of our betas setting up their own groups to play the Tavern miles away from here? A lad in Castleton in the Hope Valley has emailed Ferryl Shayde to say he's floated a leaf. Now he wants help, urgently."

That meant he'd activated magic, and obeyed the instructions in the game rules. "I thought the betas weren't going to tell any more recruits about the ward stroking trick? It shouldn't be possible to activate the wind glyph by accident, not if nobody told them to draw a mark on themselves." Kelis looked bewildered. "Or did they?"

"Who knows? He might be one of those people who would have found magic without help, like mum or Frederick. Remember, most of the betas still don't know that magic is possible so they won't see any problem with drawing a Tavern mark on themselves. A good few might never find out, never activate. We can hardly tell every beta to stop now, or they'd wonder why." Abel took a breath to calm down. "It's done now, so we've got to deal with it. First off, we'd best phone round and find out who this guy is. One of the betas must have told him about Bonny's Tavern, hopefully one who has discovered magic. They can talk to him."

"His name is Kieran. I've sent a text from Ferryl telling him to keep quiet and stop meditation until he has advice. I've also told him to draw a Tavern sign on paper to pin up in his room to keep the creatures out." Rob brandished his phone. "He replied straight away, because he thinks the game is coming to life like Jumanji. He's already seeing creatures. I've told him they're real but the game isn't. The game will tell him which little ones to avoid, and the big ones are made up so he needn't worry."

"Ha, yeah, somehow I don't think don't worry will work." Kelis looked from Abel to Rob. "Where is Hope Valley? How near is it?"

Rob's glum look wasn't promising. "The other end of the Peak District National Park, about thirty miles as the crow flies but twice that by road. It's a bit far for Jenny to nip up there on her moped and be back by dark."

"I can't see him upping sticks for a two-day training camp here like Petra did." Kelis hesitated. "He might if he's scared enough, but I'm not sure mum will go for a mystery boy stopping over. At least Petra is a girl, and from the same school."

"First we find out who told him about the game. He'll want a familiar voice." Abel took out his phone. "We'll split the calls between us."

Ten minutes later Kelis raised a fist in triumph. "Got him! He's one of Justin's cousins. Justin is going to ring up and explain it isn't really that scary, and someone will get to him and organise training."

"Any ideas on that?" Rob frowned at his phone. "I've got two offers of transport so far, but only to drop someone off."

"We need someone who can go missing for a weekend, someone advanced enough to give the poor kid confidence." Abel glanced at his arm. "No spooky-phone to help this time, so somebody this Kieran will trust."

"Justin and his sister Rachel can vouch for whoever goes. That should be enough." Kelis started texting.

"We'll need a proper plan for when we get more." Abel looked up and the other two were staring at him. "It will be when, not if. The cat is out of the bag, a great big ugly magical cat."

"Curses." Kelis scowled. "This is when I wish I could swear properly, but I can't risk making it real."

"Crikey flipping bleddering tarnation?"

Kelis' forehead wrinkled in thought for a moment. "What's a bleddering, Rob?"

"I made it up so I don't know and it can't be made real." Rob preened a little. "I could invent a whole string of new curses for sorcerers?" The other two weren't so sure. They'd both started wondering what a bleddering could be and might create some entirely new creature by accident.

An hour later Shawn had agreed to spend the weekend in the Hope Valley. In the game the allegedly magical symbols had to be drawn or carved on wood or rock before activation, but now the fledgling sorcerer would learn the truth. Only one symbol in the game was a true glyph, and all it needed was magic and the intent to activate it. One of the other trainees had a tent and agreed to go as well, to save renting accommodation. Better yet, Kieran would meet another relatively new trainee still practicing with a leaf. The text from Ferryl/Jenny saying "phew" more or less summed it up.

Visitors

Heading home with Rob, Abel carried on discussing ways to deal with new magic users who didn't live near Stourton. When Abel opened his garden gate, Rob stopped talking to point at a stone figurine in the garden.

"A Goblin? Here?" As Rob spoke the dog-like head turned into a round green one though the squat, scaled body and small wings still looked like stone.

"The slippery slithery is still here, sorcerer. We hunted down the Hoplins and other small creatures." It smirked as it spoke. "A pack of us even cornered a Globhoblin. It was delicious."

"Sorry, we've been very busy." Abel turned to Rob and explained the missing barrier posts and what the goblins had told him.

"So where is the, what did you call it, a slippery slithery? Where is it hiding?"

The Stonelin turned to Rob. "It lives in the old Ratlin tunnels, under the churchyard. It stung two of us and ate them, drained their magic. We sealed up all the holes inside the walls but it has other exits so we can only look for food in packs. Where is the sorceress?" Its eyes moved to Abel's sleeve. "The new creature in your arm does not seem as strong."

"Can we get to see it, get an idea of what we're dealing with?" Abel needed a better description before he phoned Ferryl/Jenny, so she could tell him if they'd got a real problem.

"It is across the road, under the lilac bush. It follows you, apprentice." As Rob and Abel turned to look the Goblin continued. "It knows when you leave the house. It follows and finds a place to watch, though it cannot get into the Dead Wood or the Sorcerer's Keep."

"Does it talk to anyone, or have a magical tether?" Abel thought of the watcher in the park.

"We have not seen it speak, nor any magical connections though a sorcerer might hide one."

"I can snatch it?" Zephyr had also thought of the watcher.

"No Zephyr, not until we see how big it is." Abel tried to see under the bush, but either the creature had blurred the view or it blended into the shoots and leaves. "Rob, smack the bush with a wind glyph please. I'll be ready if it breaks cover." The smoky shape shot across the road, dead leaves flew up into the air, and something long and low shot out of the shadows. Abel and Rob got an impression of a long scaled shape, pointed head, a crest on its back and two stumpy chicken-legs almost blurring as it ran off. It disappeared, leaving Abel with a half-formed flame glyph on his hand.

"It never did that before, ran." The Goblin had turned completely into a fat green munchkin to come to the gate and look, but now it looked guilty and turned back into stone. The mouth and eyes turned green again. "Sorry. We didn't think it could balance on those two little legs. I wonder if the wings work as well?"

"That bit on the back is wings?" Rob looked in the direction the creature had gone. "That's towards the churchyard so it probably went to ground. We'll need Ferryl to burn it out of those tunnels like we did the Ratlins. That's if fire bothers those scales."

"I'm more worried about it spying on me." Abel turned to the Stonelin. "What does it do if I'm not here?"

"It follows him or the other one." It looked at Rob. "Or watches your houses and families."

That settled it. Rob wasn't having some creature creeping round after his little sister, especially after he found out it killed a rat. If it could hurt real animals as well as magical it had to go as soon as possible. While he stomped off home to collect his enchanted rounders bat, Abel texted Kelis. On the way to collect her, he asked the Goblin how to find the thing, but Zephyr already had the answer. "I can find it now. There are many magical signs in the village, many creatures moving about and each sort has a magical taste. I did not realise that one should not be here." Zephyr must be seeing or tasting Batlins, fae, faeries, Piskies and the other small creatures either encouraged or tolerated by Abel and his friends. "I can go down the tunnels and search?"

The Goblin stopped that idea, because Zephyr wouldn't be strong enough and might be caught in the narrow tunnels. Unfortunately, the creature would run away from anyone strong enough to hurt it. When Abel explained everything to Kelis, she only had one question. "It follows you? So if you went for a walk it would follow Abel?" The Goblin agreed and Kelis pointed along the road. "So walk up there, Abel, towards Castle House."

Abel didn't fancy it, especially when Kelis insisted that Zephyr couldn't contact anyone else. The creature might see the spooky-phone, and realise it was a trap. According to the Goblin, Abel was stronger than the slithery so with Kelis he should be able to clobber it. Just in case it got away Rob volunteered to guard the middle of its three escape tunnels. He could always run to the others if the intruder went that way.

The three of them hesitated but none of them liked the idea of this thing creeping around their families, families unaware of magic and so unprepared for any attack. Zephyr flew up high, reporting that the creature now lurked at the entrance to the nearest tunnel to Abel. It really seemed interested in him, which meant he had to try.

*　　*　　*

Abel felt twitchy as he walked up the road alone in the dark. Zephyr flew high above, but only connected to him because if she talked to the others the slithery might see the magical phone lines. He paused at the gate, but still nothing happened so he went into Castle House gardens. Once he'd crossed the lawn Abel hid behind a tree and watched the road.

This time he saw the long, chicken-headed shape clearly as it slithered across the grass to hide in the depression where the Bound Shade, a dead tree, had once stood. A warning from Zephyr meant Abel already had a glyph forming when Kelis' flew from behind a garden wall near the slithery. He started running, a second fire glyph growing in the other hand.

Because Kelis had sneaked past to strike from behind, the wind glyph bowled the slithery out of the hollow towards the road. For a moment the slithery had an open escape route away from Brinsford, but it ran towards the safety of the tunnels giving Abel a clear shot. Both fire glyphs hit, one on a leg and the other on that scaled tail. The leg buckled for a moment and a loud hissing filled the night, but the scales deflected the other attack.

"Tell Kelis and Rob, fire is no good on the scales." Though as Zephyr's spooky-phone snaked out to connect to them and pass the message Abel could see that Kelis had stuck to her favourite, wind. A tight glyph struck the beaked head, knocking it sideways and the creature staggered, slowing long enough for Abel to hit his target leg twice more. That slowed it up, but instead of limping onward what looked like a crest on its back blurred, and the creature flew upwards!

Even as the long shape swooped back towards Kelis, beak agape to show rows of tiny teeth, Zephyr broadcast a reminder. "Watch the tail sting!" Kelis had already launched one glyph at the beak, but her second swatted the tail aside. Neither was as powerful as the first ones, because Kelis had no time to concentrate now. Abel had the same problem, especially while running. His two quick wind glyphs barely knocked the creature aside far enough to miss Kelis.

Rubbish rained down out of the sky, all around it! Small rocks, bits of pizza and a chicken carcase mixed with tin cans and other less identifiable objects bounced off its wings and head. The creature looked up, hissing angrily and zooming higher where small dark shapes scattered. "Batlins!" That impressed Abel because batlins were small, secretive and fragile and definitely shouldn't have been confronting something as strong as the slithery. Zephyr dropped out of the sky and skimmed the ground as she suddenly found herself the target.

"Towards me!" Abel had been given a moment to concentrate, and now the target followed Zephyr as she turned his way. He created two tight fire glyphs, very hot, and launched both at that blurring. The ruff around slithery's neck looked like feathers, so with a bit of luck... A flash of flame, a startled squawk, and the beak, ruff and then the full scaled length smacked into the road, skidding along the tarmac for several metres. Before Abel or Kelis could follow up it doubled back along its own length and staggered into the village again, all thought of fighting forgotten. A streamer of smoke and the stink of burned feathers probably meant it wouldn't be flying again very soon.

Though despite two more wind glyphs from Kelis it made the relative safety of Brinsford Main Street, half-running, half slithering along the tarmac. Abel and Kelis tried to keep up, firing off wind glyphs, but they had to be careful. Not only might fire glyphs frighten the villagers, but any deflected glyphs could damage windows or cars. As it was, anyone looking outside would have wondered why the pair of them were racing down the street in the gloom, waving their arms about. The creature staggered a few times but didn't go down, eventually disappearing into the gardens around the old churchyard.

"Wrong tunnel. Rob came this way, it went that." Not exactly coherent, but Abel and Kelis got the message. They followed the spooky-phone attachments as Zephyr swerved off across the gardens in pursuit. Without the improved night vision gifted by Ferryl they'd have hurt themselves in the chase that followed.

*   *   *

Abel staggered as he dropped over yet another fence, pausing to catch his breath. The slithery must be tiring because he could see it, but he could also see its escape tunnel. Abel created two very tight, very hot fire glyphs, as Kelis came over the fence beside him. "Curses." He heard her trying to steady her breathing to concentrate as he lifted both hands.

The goblins nearly made a very big mistake. Abel stifled a yelp of pain as he snuffed the glyphs and burned his hands rather than burn them as a horde poured over the churchyard wall. The goblins pelting the beaked head with everything from a piece of a gravestone to a handful of weeds, stopping it in its tracks.

Slippery slithery hesitated for a moment, then lowered its head to charge. The goblins kept yelling and throwing, but from the way they flinched from the beak and raised tail none of them wanted to actually fight. Even as Abel strengthened wind glyphs he saw Kelis raise her hands, but he doubted hitting it from behind would stop the thing moving towards safety. Kelis hesitated as a blur shot down from up high, levelling out to hit the creature in the head with a loud smack. With a screech of pain the beak snapped at its assailant, but Zephyr had already bulleted away towards Abel.

The creature hesitated, it really wanted payback and no wonder. One eye looked as if someone had hit it with a hammer! Abel and Kelis let their glyphs go, but as expected they did no more than make it stumble as it turned back towards escape. The goblins scattered, the last two leaping over the wall as the slithery tottered towards its tunnel, then its head jerked round. Rob charged into sight, swinging his rounders bat underhand. With a shout of triumph he connected with the underside of the beak.

A crack echoed as the carved ward on the bat met magical resistance, followed by a flash of light as the creature's head came up and over. The whole front end followed as its legs crumpled, it overbalanced, and the lot fell over in a thrashing mess of scaled tail, beak and claws. Its tail came up, poised, but Rob had his bat ready. The crack wasn't as loud this time but the end of its tail drooped, swinging loosely. Abel called out "use fire" and let the flame build in his palms as he ran forward. With no goblins in the line of fire and a clear shot at the creature's head, Abel didn't hold back. He added a bit of wind, flinching at the brief flamethrower effect before it shut off!

"Oh yeah, barbecue." Rob belted the charred head while Kelis stepped closer, aimed carefully and arrowed two hot glyphs into the least damaged eye.

Abel didn't get fancy again. He stuck to pure fire as he and Kelis, with Rob smacking the legs when the creature tried to stand, concentrated on the parts without scales. Moments later the three of them watched the two metre length bubble and melt away into nothing.

A woman's voice jerked all their heads round as light from an open door lit up the lawn. "Oi, what are you three doing in my garden?"

Both Kelis and Rob moved across a bit to block Mrs. Turner's view of the largest bubbling bits. "Sorry Mrs. Turner. We saw a fox and chased it so it didn't get Stan's chickens. It went down that hole." Abel pointed at the Ratlin hole the creature had aimed for and hoped Mrs. Turner didn't see the last scraps bubbling away or the scattered feathers. "We'll get a spade and fill it in."

Mrs. Turner sniffed in distain. Not everyone approved of Stan. "You should let it try for the chickens, then at least Stan can shoot something legal." She looked closer. "Feathers? It really got one?"

"A chicken or maybe a grouse, or hen pheasant?" With luck she couldn't tell in the gathering dark. "Don't worry, we'll sort it out."

"Try not to make so much noise." Mrs. Turner squinted, then gave up on the feathers. "You scared the living daylights out of me." All three heaved a sigh of relief as she shut her door.

"We'll get a spade? Gee, thanks, I love digging." Rob bent over the feathers. "Why didn't these turn to gunk?" He picked one up. "It looks like a rooster feather, coloured. Yeuk! It's got things moving on it." While Rob wiped his hand three fire glyphs incinerated the feathers.

"Is it dead?" A green head popped up over the wall in time to see the last bits bubble away. "Good."

"Can you fill in the holes, please, to stop anything else moving in?" Abel remembered the rain of rubbish. "And pick up the stuff the batlins dropped?"

More goblins looked over the wall. "The batlins should pick that up." Abel thought that unlikely. By now the batlins would be off hunting insects, faerie and fae.

"Some of it is food. Pizza and chicken?" goblins wouldn't mind the dirt.

"All right." A long thin tongue dropped from this one's mouth to give a long, slow, typically Goblin slurp. "But just the food." Considering what goblins would eat that meant anything remotely organic, so Abel thanked it and left.

As Rob and Abel walked Kelis home, Zephyr swooped back into her tattoo. "What did you hit that thing with, Zephyr? I thought you couldn't use glyphs or pick anything up?"

"Not yet. That was me, squished down into a small hard ball. I made me dizzy for a moment." Abel could feel her tattoo moving, just a little, and hear the excitement in her voice.

"Just be careful Zephyr." Rob cowered away. "And don't punch me like that, ever."

Kelis looked more thoughtful. "Though a Flying Fist of Doom would have come in handy before we learned magic, for dealing with the likes of Henry."

"I am here to help protect Abel Bernard Conroy. Ferryl Shayde told me that is why he gave me life."

"Not really, even if I appreciate the help. You mustn't risk yourself. I don't want you to die." Now Abel wondered just what Ferryl had said to the Sprite. By the time he'd dropped off Kelis, and arrived back home, Abel thought he and Rob had explained. Zephyr could help, but not risk capture or dying.

* * *

Friday and the weekend were an anti-climax after that, except maybe for what the creature was. From the description Ferryl/Jenny recognised a Kalkatrie, a supposedly extinct creature. Centuries ago they would be sent out by Greek Gods to either spy or to lead hunters to their prey. Kalkatrie had large eyes that could detect the slightest trail in the faintest light, and see both magic and heat. Their sting would only make the victim sleep so that others could capture it, but the Kalkatrie could easily kill the sleeping victim with its beak.

A second extinct creature from ancient Greece, a dedicated hunter and spy, meant whoever sent the Aryadne's Hound must still be out there and testing. Though if the Kalkatrie didn't leave the village and Zephyr saw no magical tether, whoever sent it didn't get a report this time. All they could do was watch for the next spy and hope it gave them a clue of some sort.

While Abel, Kelis and Rob chased the Kalkatrie, Ferryl/Jenny had been at home thinking about the Blood Leeches in Henry and the badger. If two came to Brinsford, it might mean a nest of them in Stourton. Back when Ferryl went into the hole the Leeches had been a minor problem that both Church and sorceresses destroyed on sight. A persistent problem, unfortunately, because they were difficult to spot once the seed had grown large enough to take full control.

Something had changed, because back then an adult would definitely not have risked attracting attention by attacking Abel directly. Ferryl didn't like them, and since one had attacked Abel the others were prepared to glyph first and ask questions later. Despite a lot of discussion, none of them were sure if the Leeches and Kalkatrie were connected, though neither were welcome.

* * *

Over the weekend Mr. Forester visited twice, to ask questions and make suggestions about the game. At home Ferryl/Jenny kept as close an eye on him as possible, and he really seemed genuine though she warned he would try to get more than a few shares. That wasn't a total surprise; all three mothers expected that at least. On Sunday he seemed intrigued by mention of charitable work and promised to look into that as well. Even if Bonny's Tavern itself didn't become a charity, supporting one would be a good way to reduce tax if they ever paid any.

Ferryl/Jenny spent a little longer in Brinsford this weekend, and checked progress on casting a seeming onto a cloth. The glyph seemed similar in style to the colouring one, but more complicated. In addition it had to be adapted and shaped to copy specific nearby colours, shapes and textures even in changing light. Rob, Ferryl and Kelis began to realise just what an advantage all the extra magic from trees gave them. It meant they could practice much longer than those relying on the magic they absorbed each day. Though despite Rob pushing, none of them would be learning mazzlement until they became much more proficient. One tiny mistake could leave the victim missing large parts of their memory, even forgetting how to walk or speak.

Ferryl/Jenny only visiting occasionally led to a change in their training. "I intended bringing this in gradually, building up from a ripple in a natural progression as we did with wind and fire. Now you will have to practice the glyph and decide when to progress without me. First you learned air, then flame which is slightly less ephemeral. You are all adept, as was shown when you fought the Troll baby and then the Kalkatrie, so now you progress to a more solid glyph. Water." She sloshed the bottle taken from the box on the back of her moped, and spread out four saucers. "You will be making ripples to start with, without using wind." Ferryl/Jenny leant forward to draw a glyph on the ground. "This is water and can be very useful. In a fight some of the water in a living being's own body can be drawn into its lungs to drown it, or the water in a river can pluck the unwary off the bank. With heat it is steam, or heat reversed on shaped water makes ice darts. Those can be directed using air. The three glyphs together can be potent."

"Providing there's a convenient puddle." Rob wasn't actually complaining but Ferryl/Jenny smirked at him.

"But there is always water, even in deserts, another advantage of controlling this glyph." Her hand raised, casting a glyph that hovered. A tiny blur appeared in the air, slowly expanding into a small mist cloud which then became droplets of water. "An instant drink of pure water. I am working the glyph slowly so you can see me taking the moisture from the air. Water can also come from grass, a tree or the ground. Be careful with your intent when drawing water from a living being. I have seen a whole room full of people fall to the ground, shrivelled husks, because the sorceress had no time to be specific." The droplets coalesced into a clear wobbly globe before descending to splash gently into a saucer.

"Control, but not aimed towards anything living." Abel hitched forward. "So how do we persuade water to ripple?"

A large yellow star appeared over Abel. "Good student. Persuade, don't force. Water is slippery, but tough. It cannot be pushed and pulled unless frozen with a reverse heat glyph." During the lesson Abel could feel Zephyr's interest. He'd got used to it, but now he worried she might try out a glyph and wreck something. Once Ferryl/Jenny finished, he let Zephyr out to hover and her connections shot out to everyone.

"Zephyr wants to work glyphs. She says she has little magic, but wants to help." Abel glanced at the eager shimmer. "But I won't let her try in case it isn't safe."

Ferryl/Jenny thought about it for some time. "Zephyr can work glyphs, certainly wind glyphs. Her problem will be forming them with pure imagination and then keeping control. Luckily, as you said, she has little magic." Everyone smiled at the next bit. "Ask her to float a leaf." Abel asked and a glyph smoked out of the shimmer to pluck a leaf from the ground. Moments later it hovered, almost rock steady. Ferryl/Jenny's eyes narrowed. "Gravel?" The little cloud of dust rose to become a small, neat heap in mid-air. "That is not a first attempt."

The dust fell in an untidy cloud. "I am sorry." The shimmer couldn't squirm but it tried. "But I tried a glyph while flying about visiting the guardians and it is a lot of fun. I only tried air, because I am wind so I thought it couldn't hurt. You said I should have fun?" Zephyr bobbed up and down. "Can I keep practicing? Please? Then I can bop fae hard enough to stun? You don't like fae."

"First off, whatever we decide you stick to, right?" Abel kept his face straight but Rob had a little smile and Kelis' lip twitched. Bop Fae?

"Sorry. I will obey. I agreed that, but you didn't say not about blowing air?"

Zephyr didn't sound all that sorry. Unfortunately Abel knew just how exciting learning that first glyph could be, so he had trouble sounding stern. "No glyphs without agreement. That doesn't mean not ever."

"Yeah!" The shimmer shot up, trailing the spooky-phone connections, looped the loop and dropped back to hover attentively. The excitement through the connection never wavered as Ferryl/Jenny laid down the law about not using any other glyph yet, and not putting too much intent into the practice. As the four of them walked the boundaries, checking, a shimmer above them snatched individual dead leaves from the ground and tried to turn them into aerial acrobats.

*   *   *

Sunday evening a long message from Shawn told them Kieran, the new magic user in the Hope Valley, would like another visit. He'd got past the first shock, and finding that the hexes really did frighten off creatures reassured him. Kieran would be practicing with a leaf during every waking moment, until he could float instead of flutter. Shawn couldn't go, he had commitments next weekend, so it would have to be someone else or at a later date. Meanwhile Justin and his sister Rachel would keep in touch with their cousin Kieran, even if Rachel spent much of her spare time playing Bonny's Tavern with Diane, Melanie and the other fourteen-year-olds.

Zephyr continued learning and developing, and not just her wind glyph. Now she could turn her tattoo's head, change her expression, raise a hand and wave her tail properly. Some of her broader education came from the internet while Abel slept. After burning out a TV remote control with magic the sprite learned to tap buttons with just her wind, and could use the keyboard or a mouse. Mornings became a silent conversation lasting up to breakfast as Abel put right her impressions of the world, or admired her increasing control of the tattoo. As a side effect he learned reams of probably useless facts Zephyr found on the internet.

Most of the betas were preoccupied with exams right now, or rather the run-in to them. Almost all the originals were in the same year as Abel, fifteen or just sixteen years old, and would take their GCSEs in June. The majority expected to stay at school through the sixth form, years twelve and thirteen, and they wanted good results so they could take their preferred A-Level subjects. Only a few wanted to take apprenticeships or the vocational courses that were the alternatives for sixteen to eighteen-year-olds.

Even Ferryl/Jenny in year twelve needed good grades because they counted towards A-levels next year. Claris would struggle to catch up, or pass her A-levels, because she still hadn't returned to school. The police came around interviewing her friends but then rumours spread that she had been found. Nobody could be certain why but Claris had definitely left school, and might have left home as well. Abel, Kelis, Rob and Ferryl/Jenny feared the worst, a Leech seed, but couldn't be certain without finding her.

April progressed with most of the older students struggling with mounting school homework. Mr. Forester only contacted Abel once, to say he thought the charity work and business of selling the game should be separate. Meanwhile, despite their schoolwork, various betas found time to suggest extra characters. Some were traditional such as a thief and a hunter but Rob wanted a sprite catcher, a character who caught and trained wild magical Sprites to use as watchdogs or hunters. He still hoped to get his own Zephyr somehow.

* * *

Abel had almost forgotten the sorcerer's apprentice, so a phone call one Friday evening asking for a meeting caught him out. The stilted voice introduced himself as Elrond, senior apprentice to Pendragon, and seemed totally serious about the fantasy names. Abel bit back jokes about pointy ears or if any of them had found a precious or a sword in a stone, agreeing to meet up on the road outside the village Saturday afternoon. He thought he heard a little bit of interest when he said outside Castle House would be best, but Elrond didn't make any comment.

At least Abel had time to contact Ferryl/Jenny so their sorceress would be present. So would Kelis and Rob, though none of them had a real plan. Tempting though it was, asking more Tavern members to come might look like a threat or that they were frightened. Abel tried to concentrate on homework because no matter what happened, that came first right now.

By Saturday lunchtime Abel felt decidedly nervous, so Ferryl/Jenny's moped zooming up to the house came as a big relief. While Ferryl/Jenny said a quick hello to his mum Abel texted Kelis and Rob, and they were both raring to go as well. Fifteen minutes later the four of them were trudging along the edge of the village to come into the gardens through what the dryad called the Dead Wood. Abel had learned his lesson. He called out to the dryad before entering but this time there were no nasty surprises waiting.

A comment about two birds trying to come inside made them all smile. The sorcerer or his apprentice had been testing, because ordinary birds would have had no problem. With that in mind Abel turned Zephyr loose to search but she reported the area clear of watchers. She flew ahead to check the gardens and even as the four of them reached the little cave, reported a visitor arriving. "A car has just stopped outside the village boundary stakes. Two watcher birds have been released, but they have not crossed over."

"They might not be able to." Ferryl/Jenny looked decidedly smug. "They definitely won't get into the wood or gardens."

"I could catch one? Or both?" Zephyr definitely liked hunting. Once Abel had agreed he didn't like the flying predatory fae near pets or children, she caught any getting too close.

"No, because he's being polite. Sort of polite though he's nearly an hour early so he's planning something." Abel concentrated, though the mental contact came easier now. "Keep out of sight, including magical sight, but try to see if the apprentice is there as well."

Within minutes Zephyr found him, or probably did. "There is another car waiting further back. There are no little watchers there." Abel called her back to watch the first car, and the occupant and watchers. "A man is getting out. He has magic swirling all round him. He is inspecting a boundary stake. A watcher-bird is trying to approach the stake but does not want to. Oh. It kept coming nearer until it dropped. I can see the life fading. He has released another bird but it is staying clear."

"We should show ourselves before the nasty git kills any more birds." Kelis glanced up at the sky. "Better yet, if we get him inside the village boundary he can't release any more."

"Is he the one who's been testing us, Ferryl?" Rob didn't seem happy either, gripping his bat.

"No, or I think not. He is using living animals controlled by magic, not magical creatures. Though it would be a good idea to stop him carrying out more tests." She turned to Abel. "Keep Zephyr hidden, and do not use spooky-phone. He will not guess exactly what she is, but why give him any hints?" A reluctant Zephyr came back to hide in the tattoo.

*   *   *

By the time the four of them came out of the trees the tall, slim man with neat black hair, blue eyes and a short pointed beard had crossed the village boundary. He stood by the first fencepost he came to, a hand up to test the barrier around Castle House. Abel called out to get his attention before he learned anything useful. "You are early. That is, I'm assuming you are Pendragon? I expected someone with a sword. Or a stone with a sword in it?" Abel heard Rob snigger, but he really hadn't been able to resist an Arthur joke.

The piercing ice-blue eyes weren't amused. "The names are chosen by our master when we are apprenticed. Your master or mistress should have done that for you, though my apprentice claims you are only witches and warlocks." He tapped the air a good metre away from the fence, as if testing it. "This is a bit more advanced than a witch could manage, and has been worked on recently. I wish to speak to all of you including the sorcerer or sorceress, please."

Ferryl/Jenny's hand gripped Abel's. "Careful because he is shielded, so probably expecting trouble. He wants to be sure we are all here. I would bet his apprentice is going to test the rest of the boundary and maybe the barrier. Elrond is human and a sorcerer, so he may be able to enter the wood. It would hurt and possibly injure him, but this man wouldn't care about that."

That would explain the other car stopping well back. "I'm afraid you'll have to deal with me. Your apprentice will have to deal with something much more unpleasant if he insists on trying to come through the boundary anywhere but here." Abel tried for a faint, enigmatic smile. "We have watchers as well."

"And hunters. He tells me you have one perched on your shoulder, a very fast one. Could I see it?"

Abel deliberately misunderstood. "I doubt it, or not soon enough to make any difference. I thought we were here for a friendly discussion?"

"Hopefully, now I have seen this barrier." He tapped the air again, then gestured towards the two watchers perched on the trees near his car. One flew off. "Elrond will be here shortly. I'm used to the Arthurian references but please don't make elf jokes, especially about his ears. He is already upset about you killing his pet. It is the first creature I have allowed him to control, and now he has to earn another."

The git wasn't pushing the blame for that on Abel, or Zephyr. "The hunter caught it alive. Your elf killed it."

"Really?" The tone barely changed but Abel felt a little shiver as Pendragon continued. "I must chastise him. I insist on honesty, from apprentices at least." He concentrated briefly. "He will be hurrying now."

"I saw it! There is a link. He just used it. Stronger than the flicker when he sent the bird."

"Thank you Zephyr. If I move so your tattoo touches Ferryl's shoulder, can you use spooky-phone without him knowing? If so, tell her about the link."

"I will try."

A moment later Ferryl/Jenny squeezed Abel's hand. "Clever. I will put my other hand behind me and hope Rob or Kelis takes the hint."

Pendragon didn't seem to notice. "After your little scene in Elmwood Park, I investigated. Much to my surprise, the church really does know about you though I couldn't find out how or why. Now I am not totally sure if the Archbishop part is true or not."

Kelis reached past Abel, holding up a business card. "He's real. Call this number, but God's SAS might turn up." The sorcerer's eyes flickered and Abel could have sworn they turned brown for a moment.

Ferryl's snigger echoed in his head. "He lost control of the seeming, just for a moment when he altered his eyes to try and see the small print."

"Seeming?"

"He is smaller and fatter." Abel bit back a snigger of his own. The bloke had put on a sorcerer disguise to impress them.

Though now he knew Abel just couldn't resist tweaking Pendragon. That appearance with that name was just so over the top. "Zephyr, or Ferryl, is he still shielded?" Two affirmatives echoed in his head. "I'm Abel and this is Jenny, while these two are Rob and Kelis. Now we all know each other you may as well relax, drop the seeming and the shield. It's a waste of magic unless you've got something better than an Archbishop and his bodyguard?"

The startled glance at the house probably meant no. "He brought a bodyguard? What have you got in there?" His eyes narrowed. "I looked into this place, and the information is very sparse. Lots of dire warnings about something unpleasant, and the names of several powerful entities that tried to enter and were never heard of again. It was all long ago and sometimes it's best to let sleeping houses lay, especially when annoying them might ruin a profitable contract or two. Then last summer my apprentices reported a surge of magic. I was abroad at the time so I missed it, though I wondered if the owner had called by." He glanced back as Elrond came in view, the same man as had been at Elmwood Park but limping with his face screwed up in pain. "At last. You obviously needed the encouragement."

Elrond straightened with obvious relief. "I came as quickly as possible, master."

"That is where the link goes! The sorcerer just stopped whatever he did." Abel would bet the nasty git had given the apprentice his limp, then told him to hurry. From the little hand squeeze, Ferryl had seen the same or heard Zephyr.

"Sir will do. We are being informal, apparently. We will talk later about how you actually lost your pet." Pendragon turned back to Abel, to Elrond's obvious relief. "If the pleasantries are over, we had better sort out our little differences. Would you like to sit in my car? It would be more comfortable." It certainly would, he'd come in a dark green Bentley with personalised number plates. PEN 1 had to be from right back when numbers started.

"Would you like to come into the garden? It's really pretty, and there are daffodils further inside." Kelis didn't hide her distaste. "Though you would probably want your apprentice to come in first." Abel assumed she'd either worked out what the sorcerer had done, or maybe just didn't like his manner.

"That is one reason for having apprentices, to go into suspicious places first. My main concern is my monopoly in Stourton. Elrond told me you are a charity." The magnificent sneer and glance at Elrond meant he didn't believe it.

"It's a new approach, since none of you sorcerers seemed interested in helping Brinsford." Abel tried for nonchalance. "So far, so good, though as yet we've concentrated on the villages."

Pendragon waved a negligent hand. "There's no money out here. The witches were supposed to deal with it." He glanced at the house. "Though a sorcerer claimed this village and the nearby area. Nobody has heard of him in over a hundred years, but that doesn't really prove anything. You being in his garden does. You can have all the villages if you give me access to the house and gardens."

"No!"

Abel didn't need Ferryl to tell him that was a bad idea. "No. You don't want the villages anyway, and the garden alone will kill you." He skipped around the house part. "We want to carry out charity work in Stourton in any area that isn't protected, especially where our trainees live. Since we won't charge, it isn't affecting your income."

"That will not be acceptable. Once word spreads, my customers will flock to get free protection and will then want you to carry out other work. I paid a substantial sum to get the Stourton monopoly because of the business park, and will not let that go." Pendragon braced himself. "I will take all of you as apprentices? Judging by your performance to date," he cast a withering glance at Elrond, "senior apprentices. That is a very good offer for anyone your age. You will be provided with a good income for not too much work and will progress to be a sorcerer or sorceress." His eyes swept the group. "The competition would sharpen up my current apprentices."

"You missed a bit. The magical tether." Ferryl/Jenny pointed, no doubt straight at where it came from. "We've just seen how that works."

Pendragon's eyes narrowed, then he gave a short laugh. "Very good.

You really can see through the seeming, can't you?" Elrond looked startled when his boss shimmered and became a shorter, stouter man with brown eyes, wearing jeans and a casual jacket. "You are right of course, this is more comfortable. Now I really am interested in having you as apprentices, enough to make your income very tempting. I'd like to know how you did that without using a glyph, and I'd love to meet that hunter."

"He would not! I could black his eye now his shield has gone."

"No, Zephyr. We are safe in here and don't want to make an enemy." Abel answered Pendragon with a shake of the head. "No thanks, because you'll still want a tether."

"Are none of your trainees tethered?" Abel shook his head. "So they could join me?"

"Providing you explain the tether first, you can approach any of the Taverners. You must tell them exactly what it does." Abel looked at Elrond to make his point. He would be ringing around to warn the entire Tavern as soon as this bloke left.

"Don't try to snatch any or trick them. There are a lot of us, and not just around here." From his voice, Abel could picture how Rob had gripped his bat. "It would be expensive if we nipped down to the industrial estate to make a few free offers, like hexes for instance. You'd never have enough watchers to stop us all."

"Though if you leave us be, we promise not to poach." Abel thought he'd better take some of the threat out of that.

"You really do need training. I can't snatch the trainees, as you put it, without their agreement. Well I can, but forcing a tether past a ward might kill them or drive them insane. I tested that new hex of yours very carefully, the one some of them wear as a ward, and it is surprisingly efficient. How you did that is another question I'd like answered. It's not as good as the true wards the others have, but it would be troublesome." Pendragon seemed genuinely puzzled. "How did you learn to see the tether and about seemings, and tame that hunter, without knowing the basics? I really would like to meet your teacher."

"You might have. He or she might be here, now." She was, stood right next to Abel.

Pendragon looked from one to the other. "No, you are all too young and it isn't a seeming. My apprentices watched you at school, and a seeming would have shown with all the physical contact. Not only that, but a sorcerer or sorceress isn't going to spend all day attending lessons. Very well, until I know more you may carry out your charity work providing you do not impact my business. I will be making enquiries. One day we may have a very different conversation, one where you had better hope your mentor is present." With that he turned on his heel and headed back to the car!

Elrond glared at Abel then followed, quickly overtaking his master. Once they reached the boundary Abel found out why, Pendragon swerved and reached out a hand to grab a boundary post. "Hey!" Even as Abel called out a Ferryl glyph flew from Jenny's hand, growing and becoming more solid as it sped across the gap. Elrond must have been waiting for it, immediately sending a glyph to intercept.

Even as Abel raised his hand, Ferryl/Jenny's glyph split into four pieces and swerved around Elrond's. His glyph hit one piece, producing smoke or steam, but the other three recombined and knocked a startled Pendragon's hand aside. Meanwhile Kelis reached past Abel and released her glyph, though she missed Elrond. Elrond raised a hand, then sneered as he saw the glyph flying wide, assuming that Kelis must be barely trained. It passed him at knee height, then his eyes widened and he staggered as his leg buckled. Kelis had reversed the wind, yanking it back behind his knee. "Gotcha, sucker." At least Kelis only murmured that though Elrond raised his hand again, face twisted in anger and embarrassment.

Pendragon inspected the hand Ferryl had hit, raising the other to stop Elrond. The growing glyph disappeared. The sorcerer raised both hands, backs towards Abel to demonstrate he wasn't threatening, though as he did Zephyr murmured, "His shield is back."

"My apologies. I only wanted to tempt you into showing your hunter. Instead I learned that you are both capable and very restrained." Pendragon looked from one to another. "You've just confirmed my initial assessment. You all have too much knowledge and skill for your age. Worse, none of you are under control. I really will investigate and might even take it to the Council, though I would rather recruit you all?"

"No thanks, but after that attempt we have to expect more. We will take away one business in Stourton for every boundary post you or yours remove." Abel suddenly wondered if the sorcerer pulled up the others, at school. "From anywhere."

"I would not be so petty." He bent to put a card on the ground. "My business card, if you change your minds. Once you report to your teacher, he or she might agree to see me." Once again the sorcerer turned and walked away, but this time he got into his Bentley and his two watchers followed. Elrond trotted off down the road towards his BMW.

"I may take it to the Council." Kelis hadn't got the tone quite right, but near enough. "What Council? The County Council? They haven't even fixed the road properly since the Shade ripped it up last year." She turned to Ferryl/Jenny. "Any ideas?"

"Maybe. There is a Magical Council, though without a leader it hasn't really had any authority for hundreds of years. Not unless a very strong sorcerer seized power while I was imprisoned." Ferryl/Jenny sounded quite cheerful. "Pendragon will be really annoyed at not getting to see Zephyr. Could you ask her to make sure the cars and watchers have left, please?"

A thought sent the sprite winging upwards, but only far enough to hide in the treetops. "They are driving away. There are no watchers, or any others trying to break the boundary." Zephyr swooped, then flew back up to snatch a fae. As usual it bubbled and disappeared when she closed around it.

"She is feeding well, and growing faster than expected. It must be all the flying and hunting."

"Maybe she can split in two or have babies if she gets too big, then I could raise one?" Rob laughed at everyone's expressions. "Hey, I can dream. I also dream of a proper seeming now. I'd really like to do that, stay in my jeans instead of bothering with school uniform." The rest started teasing him about wanting a pointy beard, before settling down to discuss the sorcerer. He might not be the one testing the defences, because Pendragon seemed to think he could come to a business agreement with whoever was in charge.

"Another car is coming. It has different magic, like that around Shannon's and Mark's crosses."

"Hide in your tattoo when it gets near, Zephyr. If this is Vicar Creepio, he is very dangerous." A car bearing church magic made Abel wary. "Why would he visit now?" Nobody had any idea, but nobody thought it would be good.

Though when the car drew up and the Vicar, as he preferred being called, strolled over, he seemed to be in a good mood. "So Pendragon didn't recruit you? Quelle surprise. Though I half expected a cloud of smoke or something unpleasant rampaging across the countryside. Sorcerers do not take rejection very well."

Kelis laughed, possibly in relief because the other man, the magical bodyguard, stayed in the car this time. "He's even agreed we can carry out charity work in Stourton."

"Really? Impressive. Did your shy friend persuade him?" The Vicar meant Ferryl, who he'd never seen though he really wanted to.

"No." Abel smiled happily. "He did a trick, we did one, and he left."

"Did you take my name in vain again?" Mysterio didn't seem quite as happy now. "I dislike sorcerers poking their noses into my business. As I understand it someone used me as a threat."

"No, we just said an Archbishop knew about the charity work."

Rob interrupted Abel. "Shannon said you would be unhappy if he attacked a member of the church, one who went to a church school."

"I would be, and that is another worry. You are tempting possible clergy away from mother church. Though I am both intrigued and reassured that your new hex does not seem to find the church a threat. I spoke to a young man who wore both a cross and a wooden plaque." The Vicar frowned, looking at Abel's arm and then briefly inspecting the rest of them. "He is very confused about how magic and faith can exist together."

"I'll bet he's called Mark. When we first found out about magic, some of the new users were churchgoers so we found out a cross and a hex on wood do the same job. Since we aren't anti-church, the church-goers kept playing the game though Mark is really worried. I'm pleased someone from the church finally listened to him. He's been trying to get his local priest to discuss magic but keeps being told to pray creatures out of existence." Kelis leant forward. "Did you reassure him? He still believes in your God and wants to know if he's sinning."

"The priests usually report someone who keeps complaining of strange visions, and that works its way up to clergy with more knowledge. Then a Bishop will arrange to meet the young man." Creepio smiled a little wryly. "Or woman now, in some cases, since we have relaxed the criteria a little. They are offered counselling and eventually a position in the church, in a branch that handles magic. Someone suitable will speak to Mark now I have alerted them. I do not recruit, I investigate problems."

"Are we a problem?" Abel knew Castle House interested the church, but the sorcerer seemed more worried about trainees running around without control.

"Oddly enough, no. Or not yet. When Pendragon came to see you I half expected to be forced to step in, then you would have owed me a favour. Now I find myself in the strange position of having to ask for your help without any leverage." Vicar Mysterio actually looked a little embarrassed.

"From us?" All four voices answered in unison, which made him smile.

"Yes, I know, it is a change of pace from threatening God's SAS. I looked into this game, Bonny's Tavern, because Mark really seemed taken by it. When I first met you, I mentioned how the old compact betwixt believer and unbeliever, magic and faith, had been forgotten?" He looked enquiringly at Abel and Kelis.

"God wars and all that, and gaps in the magical protection of the countryside. We've noticed gaps in town as well." Abel didn't hide his distaste. "Where they can't afford you or a sorcerer."

"I wish it were otherwise, but God wars are expensive. Your game may help but your storyline is a little loose. Players just choose a character and head off on a quest for no real reason."

Now all four of them really were lost. "That's how most games are. There's some sort of vague background as an excuse, or an overall campaign to save humanity or become the king, but the quests or missions are the gameplay." Abel shrugged. "The quests build up skills and expertise, with special weapons or prizes at the end which are why the characters choose them. Why else would a bunch of misfits and rivals meeting in a tavern join together to risk their lives?"

"Because the ancient pact betwixt magic and faith has broken down? The poor peasants are being preyed upon while the sorcerers and churchmen sit in their castles, fat and happy." Creepio chuckled. "That really is true about the sorcerers, and too many churchmen for my peace of mind. A storyline like that could be used to embarrass a few into trying harder."

"Seriously? You want us to take the… Er, make fun of the church?" Rob floundered for a moment. "Won't God's SAS be upset?"

"Not really. They have a sense of humour, allegedly. I'm reliably informed some of them find your nickname for them amusing. The real reason I am asking is that just having the truth out there, even disguised as a story, may help. Education these days, as far as that bit of history is concerned, really is falling down very badly. I don't mean in schools because it isn't their job. Priests and witches used to deal with anyone magically inclined, helping and training them." Creepio looked from one to the other, his expression totally serious. "Now, as you can see, there is a real problem. Witches are dying out, and we are taking away all the magically inclined members of the clergy for God wars. The lay preachers or priests have no idea what is happening when dealing with magical awakening." His usual attitude had disappeared; right now the Archbishop seemed to be just a man with a problem.

Abel looked at the other three. Ferryl/Jenny didn't look keen, but Ferryl hated the church anyway. "It wouldn't be a problem, and won't even alter the gameplay much. We could have more quests to rescue villagers from something or other, including grasping sorcerers and Bishops? Others would appeal to rogues and thieves, like robbing cathedrals instead of just castles."

"We could even put in the charitable bit, maybe quests setting up or supporting some type of food and shelter for the victims of wars, plagues or high taxes. Saint Georgeous would go for that." Abel saw the Vicar's lip twitch when Kelis mentioned the beautiful but androgynous paladin. "Most players would still go for the grab, bash and battle options, but others might fancy a truly noble quest."

The vicar switched to Ferryl/Jenny, curious about her obvious reluctance. "You don't seem keen. Are you a new recruit?" Mysterio seemed to be back on balance, with a slightly mocking glance at where she held Abel's hand.

"A recent one. Abel used magic to help me after an accident and suddenly I could see a very different world." Ferryl/Jenny smiled sweetly, "And a whole new Abel."

"Though we've got players discovering magic in other places as well, without being told or shown. Some are a bit too far away for us to help them easily." Abel hesitated about mentioning Kieran by name, then decided against it for now.

"If they are church members, let your local Bishop know. He will make sure someone goes to help them. You may lose a recruit?" Now Mysterio had gone back to being cautious.

"But they won't think they've gone crazy. We'll call if necessary." Kelis seemed happy with the idea, as was Abel. "We aren't deliberately recruiting, and have never asked anyone to choose us over the church. Nor do we use tethers."

A smile broke over the Vicar's face. "Your skill and knowledge grows, but you all still have morals. This gets more and more interesting. I hope you and your refreshingly new outlook survive contact with real life." He looked up and down the road, then up at the house with a small frown. "Speaking of surviving contact, the house still seems to be firmly locked down. I half expected you to be tempted into trying to get inside. Have you made any progress?" If Abel hadn't been paying close attention, he'd have missed the slight edge to the last question.

"Not without a key. We are definitely not breaking in."

"Very wise." Creepio's manner became more brisk, business-like. "If you could adjust that game, I really would be grateful. Even if only a couple of hundred young people ever see it, that would help the four or five who might need guidance."

"Grateful enough to give us a chance to sort out a problem, rather than bring in the big guns? We don't want Brinsford included in the collateral if something gets out of the house." It had to be worth trying, because in the past the vicar hadn't seemed too worried about dead unbelievers.

He'd more or less promised total war if something nasty escaped from Castle House.

Vicar Mysterio really thought about it before answering. "I cannot make promises, but if you can help the church by spreading knowledge of the old compact I will try. I will stress that it would be in the best interests of Mother Church to carefully consider any possible damage to innocents in this area, especially before unleashing our less controllable and more violent assets. That is the best I can promise."

The careful wording persuaded Abel, the Vicar meant it. "We will seriously consider adding to the back story behind Bonny's Tavern. We will not send the result for church approval, nor will we be kind to the church. From where we see it, the church is just as greedy as the sorcerers."

"I could argue about the ways we spend the income, but accept the point." Mysterio suddenly brightened. "I am suddenly looking forward to seeing the reaction in some places, and wishing your little project every success." He turned towards his car, then turned back. "Pendragon left a watcher at the turnoff from the main road, to see who visits Brinsford. I will remove it on the way back. Call it a gesture of good faith."

"You'll kill the bird?" Kelis scowled at him.

"Oh no, I'll break the magical compulsion and release it. That will be much more annoying." Vicar Mysterio turned and headed for his car, whistling happily in a very not-Creepio way.

"I don't trust him."

"You don't trust the church, full stop." Abel smiled happily, because his mum would have been part of any collateral. "I reckon he meant it."

"We could have a Mysterio Creepio in the game, a church investigator with henchmen." Rob sniggered. "See if he laughs at that."

"According to the betas we need at least another six characters, so why not?" Kelis flexed her fingers. "I'd better get started on some drawings. It's a good job I hammered my homework last night." By the time they'd discussed characters and how they'd look, then the new back story and the sorcerer's visit, Ferryl/Jenny had to head for home. She'd finally conceded that the church wasn't getting any real favours, while using the historic compact as a storyline might help accidental magic users. Any help presupposed people reading about Bonny's Tavern, which led to Rob suggesting the church should advertise it on their notice boards.

*   *   *

During the following week word about the sorcerer's offer spread among the magically-aware Tavern betas. Some liked the idea of a well-paid job, but not if it meant a tether that could make them limp with just a thought. Three reported they'd had flashes of cold from their wards, usually a sign that it had protected them from magic. There'd been no obvious attack, so those might have been the sorcerer checking. There wouldn't be much 'charity work' to worry him anyway, not for a couple of months. The teachers had ramped up the homework again, and set the first mock exams. Those would continue right through next week, up to Easter.

Despite being busy, Sarah and several more of the Stourton Tavern took time to check on Frederick. They were worried about Pendragon harassing an old, lonely and magically defenceless man. It might have been the defenceless part that led to Frederick telling the older lads that the Taverners could use his front room for meetings. The Taverners were cautious until he explained he had a big house and lived alone, so they could practice magic in peace.

Mr. Forester passed a couple of messages, one at the weekend when he'd seen the new game scenario about the broken magical agreement. He thought it would sell the game better than the previous vague background, but needed more polishing. With Ferryl/Jenny obviously buried in school work, her dad didn't press hard.

*   *   *

Another week went by, sheer bedlam this time because a good part of the school were taking mock exams. Everyone involved staggered home on Thursday with a huge sigh of relief. They had ten whole days to rest, the Easter Holidays, even if the teachers had given them a stack of revision to complete.

For the rest of Easter Abel and his two friends needed the peace and quiet of Castle House Gardens, and glyph practice, to cheer them up now and then. Ferryl/Jenny came to Brinsford for a few hours almost every day, except Easter Sunday when her extended family gathered.

Abel begged off because Jenny wasn't a genuine friend, not really. He still intended finding another host for Ferryl, one who needed medical aid long-term and could be his friend, not girlfriend. He spent Easter with his mum, as usual. Kelis' aunty visited for two days, bringing her eggs and a card. A few cards arrived for Kelis from other relatives but they'd given up on her mum years ago, driven off by Mr. Ventner.

Kelis saved some chocolate egg for the Goblins, carefully sharing out the tiny pieces, and gave a larger piece to dryad Chestnut. When she told him, Abel donated some of his egg to the dryad in Dead Wood, as a reward for keeping watch. Rob had eaten most of his chocolate before he found out, but then he finally forgave the Willow dryads for tricking him and gave all three a few pieces.

*   *   *

Abel didn't have time to practice glyphs very often once school started again. The teachers were in hyper-drive, hammering information into reluctant brains so it would be fresh in June. Tavern meetings during the week were abandoned by all the students, as was any development of characters. The only progress with Bonny's Tavern came when Mr. Forester called a meeting during the Mayday weekend. Forewarned that it would be serious business, all three mothers attended.

Mr. Forester didn't beat about the bush. "Someone is making enquiries about the legal status of your game. You need to copyright and trademark Bonny's Tavern as soon as possible."

"It isn't ready." Abel darted a glance at Ferryl/Jenny. She hadn't said a word.

Mr. Forester noticed. "I didn't tell Jenny. She needs to concentrate on exams. That's why I want to sort it all out now, then she can go to school on Tuesday without thinking about any distractions."

"You want us to sign up now?" Jess, Kelis' mum, sounded rightly suspicious.

"Not right this moment. We can thrash out the details, amend these papers, and I'll leave them and this." He put a bundle of twenty-pound notes on the table. "Part of the loan in these documents. Pay me back if you don't sign, or get a receipt if you do and it goes through the accounts.

That money will pay for you to see a lawyer, any lawyer not involved with me, to have the papers looked over. If your lawyer gives them a clean bill of health, we'll all sign. Then I'll make a phone call and anyone trying to claim copyright, or trademark the name, will be out of luck."

"What if they already started?" Abel's mum, Chris, glanced at Abel. "The betas have been messing about with it for over a year so it's been sort of public."

"We'll sue, and win, and then claim costs and damages. I'm betting one of these three," he nodded at Abel, Kelis and Rob, "have some old computer files from when they started. They'll be dated. According to my lawyer that's all we'll need. We won't be fighting over the use of an established name like Ford or Heinz." Mr. Forester leant back. "How far back do your files go?"

He'd looked at Abel, but both Abel and Kelis looked at Rob. Rob shrugged, a little bit embarrassed. "I've probably got the original sketches, and scans of them, and the first concept notes. Eighteen months back, or a bit more?" He nodded towards Kelis and Abel. "They always tease me, but the old stuff might come in handy."

"Those files are pure gold if anyone is trying to hijack Bonny's Tavern." Opening a file, Mr. Forester pushed it towards Terri, Rob's mum, and then another towards the other two women. "I'm already on first terms with Chris and Jess." He held out a hand to Rob's mum. "My name is Jake. Let's hope we are still speaking when I leave."

Abel felt fairly sure some of the next bit went past everybody at the table except Mr. Forester. They'd definitely need a lawyer, though the bones of the agreement were very clear. Mr. Forester would put in ten thousand pounds, as a loan to a new company called Bonny's Taverners. He'd already registered it, but a hundred of the pounds on the table bought the company and name from him. Ninety-six of the pounds in the end, because the first big tussle came over the amount his daughters would get.

The teenagers, all four, kept out of it. Mr. Forester wanted to buy five percent for each of his two kids, and offered to settle for four when the mums weren't happy with that. He hadn't reckoned on three mothers fighting for their children. Jess, Chris and Terri made no bones about it;

their kids had sweated blood for a year and a half over Bonny's Tavern and they weren't giving it all away. In the end Jenny's dad settled for four percent, split between Diane and Jenny. Abel would never be sure if he meant the last bit, that it wasn't that important. If the game took off then four percent of millions would make both girls wealthy, but if it didn't then even ten percent of hundreds or possibly thousands wouldn't help them much. Abel exchanged glances with his mum. Ten percent of hundreds looked like a lot to them.

Mr. Forester won one concession; he got to be on the board with a two percent stake. To be honest, Abel felt relieved. With the businessman trying to make money for himself and his daughters, there wouldn't be much wrong with the actual business plan. The negotiations continued with the three mums doing their best for their kids, down to insisting directors weren't paid until there were serious profits. Eventually Kelis opened the little bar built into the bookshelves and everyone drank a toast to success, in soft drinks.

Mr. Forester didn't get it quite right. All four teenagers kept worrying until Thursday. A lawyer in Stourton took until then making sure the mothers knew exactly what they'd be agreeing to. Pens and paper met the same afternoon, and Bonny's Taverners changed hands. Mr. Forester told them he'd get the copyright and trademark sorted out, then leave it all until the holidays. They should forget about it until then. The students did their best to comply, ably assisted by increasingly frantic teachers and heaps of work.

Abel had one more minor interruption, a mystery phone call asking if he wanted the key to Castle House. When he asked how much she wanted for it, the woman's voice said he'd find out nearer the school holidays and rang off. Despite him being intrigued the first of Abel's GCSEs, Graphic Art, drove the phone call out of his head. From then until the last of the GCSEs he never gave it a thought.

*　　*　　*

The last exam left Abel drained and sort of numb, relieved and privately very proud. Pass or fail he'd done it all honestly. Abel had been very sorely tempted in some exams, because Zephyr could have been the ultimate cheat sheet. She'd watched all his lessons and revision through his eyes, and listened to the teachers. Abel had even recited swathes of his notes to her. It started as a way to help Zephyr learn to read, but then he'd found he remembered the notes better afterwards. If he'd been truly desperate Abel could have left her with his textbooks and notes, hidden in his locker, to give him the answers down the spooky-link.

Rob grumbled he would have done that, used Zephyr. He only believed Abel hadn't because Abel was an idiot, too stupid to realise that if he had a cheat sheet in his head that was the same as knowing. Kelis seemed to breeze through the lot, calm and unruffled and pointing out that after glyphs, maths was a doddle. Abel couldn't see how, and Rob didn't look so sure.

Though the following day Abel felt in a terrific mood, relieved, and so did the others. They wanted a way to let off steam, perhaps with some extravagant glyph-throwing in the Dead Wood? Spooky-phone shot out to connect all three. "Can I join in to try out my glyph as well?"

The trio agreed that watching Zephyr playing with wind might be even better. The sprite soon showed she'd been practicing control of her one allowed glyph. Her leaf performed gentle gymnastics, barely fluttering, while her handful of gravel lifted, fell, spread out to a thin layer then came together into a ball, all in mid-air. Even with what Ferryl said, that with wind as her element Zephyr would find the glyph easy, the three examiners were impressed. After all, Zephyr couldn't draw on her hand so the glyphs were formed and controlled with pure imagination.

"Good enough?" Abel looked around and Kelis and Rob nodded. "Fire?" Both looked apprehensive, but nodded. Zephyr could be exuberant sometimes. Adopting Kelis' casually suggested 'Flying Fist of Doom' as a nickname sort of personified that. Abel turned to the hovering ripple. "Fire, but very, very small and aim at the ground. Better yet, as practice, scour a small area clear with wind first." A small whirlwind, reminiscent of Zephyr's first appearance, polished a patch of earth. "Do you know the glyph?"

"Yes. I remember every glyph I have seen you throw. But please draw it so I am really sure." Abel drew the glyph in the dust, with a tiny break so it didn't activate.

Abel, Kelis and Rob found themselves repeating all the warnings and precautions Ferryl had drilled into them. Eventually Abel pointed.

"Right there, in the middle of the bare bit." They all saw the glyph, a tiny one, but it didn't seem to have any effect. Abel hesitated. The glyph might have been wrong or maybe Zephyr simply didn't put enough into it. Unfortunately none of them knew if a wrong glyph would be visible. "A bit stronger Zephyr. Whoa!"

"That was a little bit?" Kelis leant forward to inspect the black, glazed patch in the dirt, still smoking.

"Maybe I had too much intent?" Kelis and Rob rolled about laughing at that. The one part Zephyr needn't worry about was intent. "The difference between very little and a bit more is hard to judge, harder than wind. Maybe I can't work any other glyph?"

Rob chuckled and held out his hands as if warming them on the scorch mark. "I reckon anything on the other end of that would agree you can work the glyph. Now you just need to dial it down from charred to medium rare."

A disheartened Zephyr didn't recognise Rob's joke. "I am sorry. I thought I might inherit fire control from Abel, because it is his favourite glyph."

"I can show you? You can sort of judge from the magic flows?" Abel wasn't sure if her magic vision worked like that, but he cheered up Zephyr. The three teenagers spent a happy hour varying the amount of heat they threw into the earth or a selection of bits of leaf and twig. After each attempt, an excited puff of wind tried to copy them.

After that the three humans practiced water, watched by a very interested Zephyr though she promised to make no attempt at it whatsoever. Water glyphs led to magnificent Glyphmistress smug because Kelis had taken to this one really well. She claimed it felt even easier than wind, and Kelis hadn't chosen Windcatcher as a game name by coincidence. Rob grumbled that they were all a pain, air or fire or water, though he could now get the currents to swirl where he wanted to in his saucer. Abel managed to make his mist produce a few drops of rain, and could create a whirlpool in his saucer. Neither came close to Kelis' waterspout, using almost all the water in her saucer. She even directed it out and across the grass until it 'tripped' over a clump of grass and splashed them. Once again Zephyr watched intently. Being allowed to play with fire seemed to have really fired her up, as it were.

Before leaving, Zephyr practiced her fire again. Ferryl/Jenny had two more exams before she could visit, by which time the three of them were going to get the sprite trained.

Three days later, the celebration after the end of Jenny's exams and the big reveal of Zephyr's fire skills led to a pop and crisp party, and some very silly Glyphmistress dancing. Anyone walking past Castle House must have heard, though the barrier spell might make it sound like witches and monsters having a rave-up.

A Bloody Bargain

Abel's good mood lasted all the next day, Friday, until late evening when his phone rang. The "People are Strange" ringtone meant an unknown number, and Abel certainly didn't recognise the woman's voice.

"Outside Castle House. Be quick because we did not feed the youngling today. She has a message, but will need fresh blood to survive long enough to show you. Hurry." The caller rang off.

Abel wasn't falling for that. He called Rob and Kelis first, because Ferryl/Jenny wouldn't be allowed to come to Brinsford this late. When they met Rob suggested sending a couple of Goblins, maybe Batlins, to take a look. While Rob negotiated with the munchkins, Abel escorted Kelis home for some leftovers as a bribe. Abel hadn't spoken to Chestnut for weeks, so the greeting on the way back past the village green came as a surprise.

"I hope you have not brought more trouble into our lives."

"What sort of trouble, dryad Chestnut? That is a question you want to answer, so there will be no payment." Though Abel wasn't sure he'd get away with that. Chestnut liked its honey.

"That is unkind, but just. You allowed the scaled watcher inside the village, and then hunted it openly for all to see. You should have trapped it quietly, or not let it in."

"It didn't want to be trapped. It's your fault it got in, or dryads in general. None of you will help with protection, so we have to use stakes which can be pulled out. Nobody would pull trees up." Abel smiled happily. He hoped that idea would eventually persuade the dryads to contribute tree magic for the boundary.

"Not yet, young but usually polite apprentice. I still do not trust you even if the wind whispers of a dryad who has been given a new tree." Abel knew it wasn't the wind. The dryad meant snatches of impressions gathered from birds and fae, or larger animals. "You could have trapped the creature in its tunnels, then asked the church trees to strangle it."

"The dryads in the church trees won't talk to us. We've stopped even trying." Rob had spent months trying to recruit them.

"Next time you get something like that, ask. Some creatures just need killing. Has the other apprentice got honey?"

"No, Kelis brought scraps for Goblins." Abel glanced at Kelis, who had stopped and turned back. "We want them to look at what might be a problem." Abel explained.

"Braeth Huntian has left your arm. What you have now is much smaller and weaker, but intriguing. Did the sorceress desert you?" As usual dryad Chestnut wasn't mincing words, though the dryad's alternative name for Ferryl Shayde confused Abel for a moment.

"No, she has a real host now but still trains us. This passenger is young and inexperienced, which is why we want goblins to help her scout the area. No charge for the answers." Abel hoped the creaking after his joke meant humour.

Kelis opened the plastic bag full of bribe. "Hello dryad Chestnut." She peered inside. "There's some icing in here, because mum dropped a slice of cake. It's sweet so would you like to try it?"

"What is icing? Anything sweet would be welcome. There has been a sad lack lately." Kelis didn't answer, just fishing out the treat and throwing it to the dryad who tested it carefully. "This might be worth trading for answers another time, occasionally generous apprentice." Abel and Kelis left it with the treat, to find that Rob had volunteers. Three goblins shared the scraps, then headed for Castle House with Zephyr flying high above them. Kelis, Rob and Abel followed but cautiously, with only Abel connected so anyone waiting would think he came alone.

Zephyr reported back long before they were in sight of the garden. "It is a person, laid in the hollow where the Kalkatrie hid. A woman and she is alive but not moving. The goblins are getting closer. May I connect to a Goblin?"

"No Zephyr. Ferryl warned against letting anyone know who you are, and the contact might tell them too much. Please search the area, for other people as well as anything magical." Abel passed the message to the other two.

"There is faint magic inside her, not hers but not like Ferryl Shayde. I will search."

When Abel repeated that Kelis stopped dead. "You said something about blood and feeding. Can you remember what the phone call said, exactly?" Abel did his best. "Whoever that is has a Blood Leech in them. Or a seed, maybe that's what a youngling means." She started walking again. "You dealt with a grown one, Abel, so we three can tackle a youngster." She sniggered and pointed upwards. "Especially with the flying fist of doom helping out."

The flying fist of doom reported the area clear of anything that might threaten three humans. As the teenagers came out of the village, the three ornamental stone figures in the grass reported in. The woman had hardly moved, possibly injured because the goblins could smell blood but not see any. She had something inside her that stank. Abel remembered the dryad saying the Blood Leech smelled bad.

Everything made sense once they saw the woman. "Claris!" Kelis started forward then stopped, looking around.

"Pale, scrawny, weak, those are all the signs according to Ferryl." Rob edged closer, his bat raised. "I'm not into whomping women, but if she goes for anyone?" He peered at her. "Flipping flopping curses, she looks starved!"

The voices roused Claris, or something inside her. "Are you the sorcerer, Abel Conroy?" Before he could answer, Claris' voice continued. "Yes, this host recognises you. I have a message for you, and a place to take you. If you want the key to Castle House you must feed this one. She must be stronger to make the trip." A wave of feeling swept over Abel, a wish to help, but it wasn't strong and his ward barely chilled as it banished the attempt.

Kelis pushed forward and glared down at Claris. "Don't try that again. Any of us can crush you, let alone all three. Is Claris alive?"

"Yes, a host must stay alive. But not for long if we do not get blood." The hissing cackle sounded nothing like Claris, "If you kill me, your school-friend dies."

"Friend? Hah!" Rob hesitated, because even if he disliked Claris intensely he wouldn't actually kill her. "The nearest you get to blood is a beef sandwich."

"Blood, it must be blood. I cannot use any other food until I grow.

Fresh blood with the magic still in it. If all three of you open a vein, I could get a little from each?" A fainter version of the compulsion started but then stopped.

"A rare steak?" Abel looked from Kelis to Rob, trying to get his head round it. The Leech might be conning them, but everything it said sort of gelled with Ferryl's description. "Blood sausage? Black pudding?"

"Fresh, it must be to have the magic still in it. This is where we need a local blood bank, open for withdrawals." Kelis rubbed her wrist. "I'm not letting it suck on me. Next thing I'll have a seed as well. Vampires! The cursed thing really is a vampire."

"Near enough for the legends." Abel racked his brains. "We have to find blood to keep her going until Ferryl gets here, which will be tomorrow. Though I've no idea how to do that."

"Does the blood have to be human? We could see if Stan has nobbled a rabbit? Or use a chicken?" Rob shuddered. "I don't fancy that either."

"It must be human blood." Claris struggled half-upright. "Soon. We have not fed today."

"How do we know it really is we, that Claris isn't dead?" Kelis' eyes narrowed. "Prove it, wake her up. Let her speak."

"She is already awake. If I let her speak, we will get blood?"

"Yes." Kelis stared at Abel so he gave the tiniest of shrugs. "Zephyr, tell Kelis and Rob I don't mind lying to this thing." When the spooky-phone connected Kelis gave a tiny nod.

"Of course we will, but only if Claris is free to speak." Kelis stopped speaking as Claris' eyes opened wider, her face showing pure terror.

"Help me! Oh God, please help me. I can't stop it. It hurts and hurts, and then it makes me drink..... Oh god, stop it. Please!" Her face smoothed out and her voice calmed. "Now give me my blood."

"That's all wrong! Ferryl said the host shouldn't remember." Rob hesitated, then turned to Kelis. "Maybe we shouldn't have woken her up like that."

Abel wasn't getting side-tracked, though Claris' reaction had shocked him as well. "We'll find out when Ferryl gets here. Right now we need a chicken." He wondered just how ill Claris was. "Can you walk?" He didn't fancy feeding her here, or carrying her through the village.

"Yes if I get blood, for strength. But it must be human. You promised."

"No it doesn't. Any animal blood will do." Kelis sneered at the thing looking out of Claris' eyes. "One of you, a blood-sack, came into the wood in a badger." Her lip lifted in a snarl. "The dryad killed it. One of you living in a badger means you can drink chicken blood, or rat blood if necessary. Make up your mind, chicken blood or die."

Rob looked from Claris to Kelis to Abel and opened his mouth but Abel had already contacted Zephyr. "Tell Rob to keep quiet. Kelis is calling its bluff because she's right about the badger." Zephyr must have passed it on because Rob subsided.

"A chicken then. But it must be fresh, with the magic in it. If you get the chicken, I will kill it?" The thing seemed much too keen on that, but none of them fancied doing it themselves.

"How do we get a chicken from someone?" Rob glanced towards the houses. "Stan is nearest." He shrugged. "We'll have to come up with a reason for whoever we go to, something better than fancying a late-night chicken curry."

"We'll tell him we want to put a chicken in the garden, in our meeting place." Kelis hesitated then grinned. "Because we've got ants? So they'll be eaten up by morning?" That lightened the mood, but after a quick discussion it was the best they could come up with.

"What about money? How much is a chicken?" Abel patted his pockets. "I'm skint."

"The Tavern fund will pay." Kelis turned towards home. "One of you had better come with me. Mum will go crackers if I walk through the village on my own at this time of night. She's not as worried about dad these days, but it's best not to wind her up again."

"I'll go and talk to Stan first. We get on all right, and I reckon he'll trust me for the money until tomorrow." Abel really didn't fancy it, but braced himself. "We've got to get Claris away from here before someone coming past stops their car to see what we're up to." He turned to Claris, who watched him intently. "If someone comes, you act completely human. No mention of blood. You've sprained an ankle and we are here to help you home."

"Then I get blood?" Abel didn't answer. He headed across the road at an angle towards Stan's, the first house in Brinsford, but hesitated at the front gate. When Bugsy started barking, Abel braced himself, opened the gate and went round to the back door. He knocked, hoping Stan could hear him over the row.

"Abel? What are you doing here at this time of night?" Stan glanced down. "Bugsy, hush." The Jack Russel stopped immediately. "Friend." Stan looked up again. "Come in lad. I presume this is private." He grinned. "Want some advice about your love life?"

Abel laughed because he had to. "No Stan, but thanks." He came into the small kitchen, closing the door behind him. "I've got a really odd request. You know we go into those gardens? Well, we have a little cave where we can keep out of the rain." Abel went into a little spiel about how they must have attracted ants by dropping crisps and crumbs, and wanted a chicken. Stan didn't mind selling one, though he had a definitely curious look about him, but then it all started to go wrong. First Stan told him to call back in the morning and Abel had to explain it had to be tonight. He got the impression the old poacher thought he knew Abel was lying, especially when Stan asked if Kelis and Rob were still waiting across the road. "Yes." Stan looked at him for a long time, then shook his head sadly.

The next words floored Abel completely. "They're not devils or gods, y'know. You can't ask them for stuff, or communicate. I thought they might be ghosts, but if they are then some folk are bloody nasty even after they die." Stan held Abel's eyes. "Is this some sort of bloody stupid black magic crap? A blood sacrifice, or for you to write some daft shite on a wall?"

"Bloo… No Stan! I swear!" Abel's mind went round in circles. Black magic?

"So why are you three over there in the grass with something bloody weird moving around near you. Bugsy warned me earlier so I had a look out the window. They look like garden ornaments half the time then well, if Bugsy couldn't see them I'd wonder about booking a room in the loony-bin." Abel's mind skittered around searching for an answer, but goblins were clearly visible to anyone. "I know you're like your mum, see stuff. I keep quiet, though I should have told her when she had all that trouble as a nipper. I didn't want the same treatment."

"So you…?" Now Abel wondered how many people could actually see something, a bit of the magic.

"I see stuff, out the corner of my eye, especially when me and Bugsy are wandering about at night." A wry smile accepted Stan wasn't just wandering about. "I even tried shooting a few, back when I were younger and dafter. It don't work on most, and makes some of the big ones look even worse." His face and voice sobered. "Some of them are nasty and will attack small animals. I've lost chicks and even young pullets now and then. I had to train Bugsy to let them be after he got stung a couple of times. Now young fella, why do you want a live chicken right now, tonight?"

Abel sat and thought for a few minutes but Stan didn't interrupt, sitting quietly and stroking Bugsy. Eventually Abel couldn't come up with anything more believable than the truth. "A school friend has got one of the bad ones inside her. Tomorrow we can get someone to come and get it out but it's hungry, and hurting her. We have to feed it fresh blood to keep her going tonight. She got as far as the hollow over there, but unless we feed it she'll not make it through the village."

Stan didn't react at first, just stroking his dog and thinking. He took a deep breath. "I'd be a lot more worried if I hadn't seen you three at Halloween. You really were chasing things out of Brinsford, though back then I couldn't be sure it was deliberate. Then I saw a couple of other odd things round you three, and a sort of spark when you tapped my Land Rover." He darted a quick glance at Abel. "It runs better now." Abel kept quiet. "Now the little critturs that usually run about in here have gone and hid. You frighten them lad, and that's good enough for me."

He stood and went to a cupboard, reaching inside. Abel heard a clink and a clatter and Stan took out his shotgun, pulling a chain out of the trigger guard. He broke the weapon and slid in two cartridges. "Just in case. I'm not happy about those statue things."

"Kelis and Rob will have chased them off by now." Abel made sure they did. "Zephyr, please contact Kelis. Ask her to get the goblins to hide, because Stan is coming with a shotgun. Explain what he said, and what I told him." Bugsy's eyes followed Zephyr as she flew out through the crack around the door, but Stan didn't notice that or the spooky-phone.

"I'm coming over there to weigh the job up first. If it all looks like you said I'll give you blood for the lass. Though I'll want to see her tomorrow, once you've got it sorted out." With a smirk he opened the fridge. "I like to make me own black pudding." Abel stared at the big carton. "Yes lad, blood from the butcher, though I add some rabbit if I catch one."

"Brilliant, Stan. The idea of killing something makes my stomach turn." Though Abel's mind raced because he wasn't sure the thing would take it. Dead blood might not have magic in it. "Don't mention where it's from in front of Claris. The thing seems to get off on the fresh part."

"It'll know anyway. That's cold, unless you want it warmed up." He paused. "Does your mum know? About what you see?"

"She knows I see stuff, and that I can keep the creatures out of the house."

A big smile broke over Stan's face. "In that case that's what the blood will cost you. I knew you'd turn out to be useful one day. That's if you can fix my place up to keep them out, and the chicken pen?"

"Deal." Abel followed Stan and Bugsy out the door, his head spinning. "How many other people in Brinsford can see the creatures, Stan?"

"Just me and your mum, as far as I know. It's why I live here, near Castle House where there aren't so many weird things wandering about. That place seems to scare them away. Are there any in the gardens?"

"Not many. Maybe that's what started all the stories about the place." As they talked about why there were fewer creatures, Abel realised Stan didn't push for answers. The old poacher always liked to know everything, but not this time. Despite his caution Stan didn't close and cock the shotgun as they crossed the road, watching Bugsy rather the group ahead.

Stan relaxed when he came nearer Kelis and Rob. "Those two scare the things away as well. Good to know."

Claris had sat up, with Kelis holding her. The Leech must have had instructions, because Claris looked and sounded like a scared schoolgirl with something painful inside. After asking her name, and a few more questions, Stan asked straight out if she really needed blood. Abel had to give the Leech credit, it managed to copy some of the fear and revulsion Claris showed earlier. Meanwhile Bugsy wouldn't go too near her, and growled a little.

"All right, I'm convinced and Bugsy reckons there's something wrong with her. I don't want to know any more, Claris, except I want to see you tomorrow after you've been cured." Stan looked around the rest of them. "I've come too near to going crazy too many times to ask more questions. Some things are best left alone. If you get in real trouble, me and Bugsy are always here." Stan patted his shotgun. "This works on some of them, and they ain't people so I'll shoot. Stay here and I'll bring the blood, in a jug. I'm not trying to drain a chicken at the side of the road."

As he headed away Claris opened her mouth to object but Abel bent to stop her. "Fresh blood in a mug or he'll be suspicious and maybe call a priest." Her mouth clamped shut. "Zephyr, tell Kelis and Rob the blood is from the fridge, cold with no magic. Be ready if the Leech acts up."

Both frowned for a moment, then Kelis stepped back out of Claris' line of sight. She raised both hands, slightly cupped as if casting a glyph. "I'll hold the glass or mug for Claris. We wouldn't want her to spill any and waste the magic." At "magic" she waggled her fingers and Abel had to stifle the smile.

"Be quick, to make sure it's still warm."

"Oh yes." Kelis smirked, then sneered at the back of Claris' head.

Five minutes later Stan came back across the road, without his shotgun but carrying a jug and a glass. "Anyone squeamish had better look away. I know you modern kids have weak stomachs." He held out the jug and glass. "Now drink it while it's still warm." He'd obviously thought that bit out himself. Kelis stood in front of Stan, her back to the Leech as Stan filled the glass, then turned and held it for Claris to drink. The jug filled the glass three times, and Claris drank the lot. "I wasn't absolutely certain you'd drink it. Kids can be sneaky." Stan prodded Abel. "Whatever that is in yon lass, kill it." Behind him Claris jerked and opened her mouth, but kept quiet when Rob prodded her with his bat.

"We'll get it sorted, I promise. It might take a couple of days, but I'm not totally sure without the expert." Abel thought he'd best go for it now. "If we need a bit more blood, for a day or so?"

"All right, just for a couple of days but no more. Is your expert that vicar?" Stan smirked at the look of surprise. "I live right there, where I can see everyone coming and going."

"Not the vicar though he could do it. This one is shy but much better for this job, gentler. I really do owe you, Stan." More than Stan would ever know, hopefully.

"You know how to pay." The old poacher turned to Claris, concern on his face. "It's all right love. They're an odd lot, these three, but they'll look after you." With that he picked up the glass, called Bugsy to heel and left.

"Can you walk now?" Claris stood up without answering. "Good, now let's get you...." Abel tailed off into silence as he realised he'd no idea where Claris could sleep.

"It's not getting near mum." Kelis had moved away from Claris now Stan had gone.

"Nor my family." Rob tapped his bat into his palm. "I really don't trust it to stay put inside Claris. You said the one in Henry came out."

"It did, he heaved it up like being sick. It's definitely not sleeping on my couch." The three of them tried to work out just where Claris, and her passenger, could be kept safe. Even with her tied up, that Leech might get out and wriggle away. Worse, it might compel someone healthier to let it inside them, or maybe offer their neck.

"Do you have more sweet sticky fruity stuff?" All three stopped talking to stare at the Goblins. They'd crept up, imitating stone while listening, but one had turned its head green to talk.

"Sorry, I've already emptied the kitchen bin. Thank you for helping but you may as well go home now." Kelis stayed polite, even though the Goblin obsession with food could be annoying.

"But more sticky nice stuff and we will watch the stinky." The Goblin's glance at Claris wasn't strictly necessary. "If you tie it up, we can stop little stinky crawling away. A little stinky might even be tasty."

That put a whole new gremlin in among the pigeons. "What sticky stuff exactly? What was in the bin, Kelis?" Abel eyed up the Goblins.

Three of them could probably deal with even the large Leech Abel had seen, and they ate rats and Globhoblins so a Leech really might be on the menu.

"Maybe it means cake? You gave the dryad the icing." Rob's face fell. "Sticky, sweet and fruity, it's your mum's fruit cake Abel."

Abel's face fell as well, he really had been enjoying the extra fruitcake his mum made from the ingredients left over after the birthday party. Though if the goblins would guard Claris and the Leech? "We could put her in the church, if the rest of the goblins don't mind? It'll be a bit chilly but I'll bring a coat."

"I can take a quilt from one of the spare bedrooms?" Kelis turned to the Goblins. "You have to watch all night, no snoozing or nipping off for a snack." She turned back to Abel and Rob. "We'll need rope."

"Gaffer tape would be better. There's a roll in the shed." Abel glanced at the Goblins. "I'll give up half the cake we've got left, though I'd best take off the marzipan for mum."

"That'll do for tonight, then I can use what's left of the wedge your mum gave us if it takes another night." Kelis relaxed with a big sigh. "Now let's get Claris and it tucked up before mum sends out a search party." She brandished her phone. "I've already had to reassure her I've not been kidnapped by aliens." Kelis cautiously prodded Claris. "Come on you, we've got you a room for the night."

Claris seemed much stronger, walking through Brinsford to the church without any help. On the way the Leech gloated about how much richer and stronger chicken blood was than expected, probably because the carton had said ox blood. Despite its promises, Abel didn't expect it to survive long enough to take him to meet the Firstseed. That must be the woman on the phone and Abel would love to meet her, if only to stop her opening Castle House. Ferryl wanted the key because after inspecting the door to Castle House, the sorceress couldn't see any other way to turn off the cluster of protective glyphs. While Rob and Kelis took Claris into the churchyard, Abel ran home to fetch the Gaffer tape.

On the way back dryad Chestnut called out. "Careful, that one has a blood bag. Just a small one, but it will grow." The creaking had to be humour this time when it continued. "If you let it walk under my tree I can deal with it?"

"No thank you. We want to get the Leech out but save Claris. We hope Ferryl knows how." Abel turned to go, then a thought struck him. If he'd been able to cast a veil like the dryad used, that would have kept the goblins hidden from Stan. "I wonder how much honey a dryad might ask for, to teach me the glyph for a veil?" Abel didn't look at the dryad, taking care not to ask a question that would require payment.

"If anyone wanted to know that, they would ask the sorceress who trained them. If she still trained them." Dryad wanted answers as well, without paying.

"Perhaps a sorceress would tell students they should be able to find out themselves, that it would be good practice." The truth, that Ferryl hadn't found the bone wit containing the right glyph, would embarrass her.

"It might be worth it, to a dryad, just to spoil her fun. There would be a whole pot of honey as well, the larger size, in case Braeth Huntian didn't like the joke." That almost diverted Abel, because he wanted to know why Dryad Chestnut kept calling Ferryl that.

"A student would find that a good deal." Abel laughed and headed for the churchyard, hearing the creak of dryad laughter behind him.

"Another glyph? Will I be able to cast this one?"

Abel answered silently in case the dryad could still hear. "I've no idea Zephyr. We'll have to work on your control first, to see if you can draw and activate rather than imagine the glyph. Don't mention me buying the glyph to anyone but Ferryl Shayde, Kelis and Rob."

Gaffer tape did a really good job, trussing Claris up at her ankles, wrists and knees with a couple of turns round her body. As Rob remarked, they'd have felt guilty taping up most people but they all owed Claris a bit of payback. Even so Abel felt a tug of sympathy for her, lying helpless on the floor in a ragged, stained dress with her painfully thin limbs in plain view. From the look of her clothing she'd been going to a party or on a night out. Rob and Abel laid her on the quilt behind the altar and wrapped it around her. The three goblins perched on top, looking down at Claris. "I'll bring cake in the morning." Abel turned to Claris. "Leech, remember what they said." He looked round at a small crowd of goblins who had come to have a look. "A small Leech might be tasty."

"The Firstseed told me to stay. You will feed me every day to strengthen the host, so that we can go to collect the key." Abel didn't argue - not tonight. He walked back home fervently hoping Ferryl could force the thing out.

*   *   *

Ferryl/Jenny finally arrived just before midday on Saturday, curious about the "Claris, leech seed, safe, waiting" text. After greeting Abel's mum she went straight to the church to have a look at the captive. Unfortunately Ferryl couldn't physically rip the Leech out, not without seriously damaging Claris.

All four went to Kelis' house so the Leech didn't hear them plotting. If the creature could make Claris walk and talk, it already had tendrils into and through major organs including her brain. Even immediate intensive care wouldn't save Claris if the Leech was destroyed, because Leeches always connected themselves to large blood vessels. Ferryl admitted she had seen both the church and sorcerers remove them forcibly, but even if the seed was very small the hosts died.

Ferryl might kill the Leech and save Claris by leaving Jenny and possessing the older girl, but she couldn't do that immediately. Jenny had now spent months in a deep sleep, one expected to last for twenty years. Before leaving, Ferryl had to wake Jenny gradually so she could assimilate memories of what happened since the accident. That would be slow, delicate work, altering each memory to remove magical knowledge. Normally Ferryl didn't give back detailed memories because the host's old life, friends and family lay far behind them. In the early eighteen hundreds most people died before reaching forty, and two villages away was a whole new world.

All the work had to be done at night because Jenny must stay functional for school and her family. The whole process would take about two weeks, and even then Jenny might still be a little confused as her memories settled in around the gaps. She would also be aware, magically, so Ferryl would leave enough knowledge to flutter a leaf. From there Jenny had to learn glyphs and magic the same as anyone else.

That left the Leech still growing in Claris for the next two weeks.

Worse, they'd have to find enough blood until then, though they all found it funny the Leech liked the refrigerated stuff. That still left one big problem, where to buy and store the stuff. "It can't go in our fridge. Mum would go crazy." Kelis shook her head. "Not even the little fridge in here. She'd think I'd flipped." The rest agreed. Cartons of blood would lead to pointed questions for any of them.

"We could put a second-hand fridge in the church? In that little office bit at the side, the vestry or whatever. If the electricity still works we'd be set and the church will pay the bill." Rob glanced towards the cash box. "Can we spend Tavern money on a fridge? We could put a camp bed in there for Claris, and pay the goblins to be guards. Cursing bogglewigs, we'd need a shedload of cake."

"Or two shedloads of pizza." Serious discussion led to the conclusion that saving a life had to be a good use for the donations. Some searching on the internet led to two local butchers who sold blood for sausages or pudding, and a slaughterhouse ten miles the wrong side of Stourton. Ferryl/Jenny on her moped or maybe a Taverner with transport could go there in an emergency.

The big flaw kept coming up again and again. No matter how much they disliked Claris none of them liked the idea of a Blood Leech growing inside her, twisting itself throughout her body, inflicting more pain and terror. Maybe this Leech could be persuaded or forced to slow down, and repair what damage it had done. Ferryl asked about that several times, how terrified Claris had been, and couldn't understand it. The Leeches supposedly kept their victims unaware, then released them at the end of forty years.

"At the least it could let Claris sleep. She can obviously remember everything it does, and the pain." Kelis shuddered, her face screwed up in disgust. "Who knows how it got the blood, but even feeling it growing inside and drinking fresh blood from a glass?" She shuddered again.

"It wanted to kill the chicken, really wanted to." Abel shook his head. "We've got to work out how keep it as small as possible, stop it hurting Claris, and keep it restrained. If we can't, Jenny will just have to be badly confused and lose a few memories."

"We can do a deal, promise not to kill it if it's nice to Claris and comes

137

out peacefully at the end?" Rob made a half-gesture with his bat. "Though I don't fancy turning it loose."

"Can you think of any way to persuade it to leave instead of pulling it out, Ferryl?" Kelis sounded desperate now. "Has it ever happened?"

"Never, not unless the Leech chose another host. Even then, Claris will have those memories forever and she'll end up babbling to the wrong person. Then the church will be looking for the Leech nest and kill them all. It just doesn't make sense for Leeches to risk that." Ferryl/Jenny thought for a long time before coming to some decision. "There is one chance. The Leech seed will have been given memories, implanted by the Firstseed. If it has the right memories, I might stop it hurting Claris." She stood up. "I can frighten it, and maybe persuade it to come out voluntarily, but only if I really will let it live. Our communication will not allow me to lie."

"Would it agree to help us get the key to Castle House once it's out? That would be a reason for us to let it live." At the look from Ferryl/Jenny, Abel realised he'd missed out that part. "Claris is here to arrange a meeting, for me to get the key. The Leech inside her has a phone number and an address."

"That would be a very good reason for me to show mercy. If there is a key out there, I'd rather have it than some creature or sorcerer turn up with it and let out whatever is locked inside Castle House. Let's go and find out if that sounds like a good enough reason." Ferryl/Jenny paused. "Though we will still have to restrain it for two weeks, because after we have spoken it will want to escape."

"It's a pity we don't know a punk or a Hell's Angel. They'd have plenty of chains." Rob sniggered and nudged Abel, "Maybe handcuffs. Do you reckon your girlfriend's dad would mind her buying some?"

At least wrangling and teasing each other over who might buy handcuffs for who kept them occupied all the way to the church.

*   *   *

Goblins were a lot stronger than they looked, and gentle when Abel insisted. Two of them soon had Claris laid in the little side room off the church that held an old desk and a couple of chairs. "I want everyone to leave except Abel Bernard Conroy, please." Ferryl/Jenny's look wasn't accepting any argument. "I must show my true-self. I may need him to remind me of who I am now."

"What about Zephyr?" Kelis glanced at Abel's arm.

"She knows what I am, but will never speak of it. We have our own bargain." Ferryl/Jenny stood, waiting, until a puzzled and slightly miffed Kelis and Rob followed the goblins out.

"True-self?"

Ferryl/Jenny took Abel's hand. "The Leech must not hear this. You met me when I had faded down almost to nothing. In that state I would have done anything to survive. What did I ask you to do, to give me strength?"

Abel thought, and she had to mean... He asked Zephyr to connect him. "Give you blood, or hold Henry down on the slab so you could drain him. You were angry Cooch didn't bleed more."

"The Leech must see that side of me, know who I am, that it is prey not the hunter. I need you here in case the hunger becomes too strong. I really am a hunter, Abel, usually of magical creatures but I sometimes drained blood for the magic. Hunter is what the dryad's name for me, Huntian, means. Our agreement means I have forsaken that life for ninety years." Ferryl/Jenny looked uneasy. "But I still feel the need, sometimes."

"But you can control it."

"Maybe not if I show the Leech my true nature. Be ready to stop me." Ferryl/Jenny hesitated. "It must be a command but you must not use my true-name, Pungh Hmmshtfun. If you say that name I will kill Claris to keep it secret. Do not let Zephyr stay in contact or I may turn on even her in frustration, and she is perhaps the only creature I would grieve for."

"What about me? Am I safe?"

The little smile looked totally natural, even if it wasn't Jenny's. "I cannot hurt you, Abel, and not just because of your ward or our bargain. Some part of me still lives in that tattoo." Ferryl/Jenny turned to Claris, letting go of Abel's hand and kneeling next to the trussed-up girl. "Leech, look at me. I will touch you, and show my true-self. If you survive, it will be because this human wishes it. Remember that when we talk afterwards."

The Leech wasn't impressed. Claris' face sneered. "If you kill me, the host dies."

"In a moment you will know just how little that matters to me." Ferryl knelt astride Claris, clamped Jenny's hands either side of Claris' head and looked down into her eyes. "Behold the hunter."

Abel knew the exact moment Ferryl connected her true-self, because Claris' eyes bugged out and her body arched. Her bound heels drummed on the floor as she tried to tear herself away but Ferryl/Jenny stayed right there, pinning her. "No! No! No. No…" The last one became more of a whimper. "Braeth Huntian. The hunter in the shadows. You were gone. I did not know. Spare me?" Claris dragged her eyes to a shocked Abel, her voice a bare whisper. "Help me, please?"

"Maybe." Abel tried not to be swayed by the sheer terror looking at him, or the sudden surge of hope at the maybe. The Leech totally and absolutely believed in Ferryl, or whatever she was. "Remember this."

"Too late." Abel didn't need more than the tone to tell him what he needed to do, he could hear the hunger in Jenny's voice.

"Ferryl Shayde! Stop! Now!" For long moments Abel didn't think she'd heard, watching the flash of hope fading in Claris' eyes as the Leech waited to die. "Ferryl! No! We need it alive! Stop!" The Leech wasn't even trying to get away now.

Ferryl/Jenny shuddered, and the tension slowly left her arms and body. She took several deep breaths, then released Claris' head and stood up with her back still turned to Abel. She turned slowly, apprehension and guilt stamped all over her face. "I am sorry."

"You warned me, and you stopped." Abel glanced down at Claris but her eyes were screwed tight shut and she'd curled up as best she could with her arms behind her. "Are you under control again?"

"Yes. I truly am sorry. I thought I could control it but I had to show the hunger, and the Leech tried to escape. When the prey flees from the hunter?" She stopped, hesitating over what to say next.

Abel thought he'd got most of the shock off his face, though his voice wasn't quite firm. "It's a natural thing in hunters. All the wildlife programmes show the same thing. Mrs. Tabitha can't resist chasing moving things, even a dot of light." He took a deep breath. "I'm convinced, and from Claris' eyes so is that thing."

Ferryl/Jenny reached out, tentatively, so Abel took her hand and asked Zephyr to connect him. "Will you tell Kelis and Rob?"

Ferryl wasn't forbidding him. Abel struggled with it for a few moments, but if Kelis pushed he'd end up confessing. Telling her part of it straight away might stop her prying. "They'll have heard me shout. I'll just say that you are very, very scary to Leeches, but I couldn't see exactly what you did." A sudden thought hit him. "Are they safe, Kelis and Rob?"

"I once told you, and them. I will never harm anyone Abel Bernard Conroy cares for." Ferryl/Jenny straightened properly. "Leech! Turn this way and open your eyes."

Claris' body turned, reluctantly, and her eyes went from Ferryl/Jenny to Abel. "You will not let it kill me?"

"I might not be able to stop her if you run, though I can persuade her to let you live if you give me what I want." Abel waited for a tiny, reluctant nod. "You will not tell anyone exactly who the hunter is, or I will not stand in her way. You understand?" After another tiny nod Abel relaxed a bit. "Zephyr, ask Kelis and Rob to come in, please."

Claris looked startled when a shimmer flew out to hover threateningly over her. "A tethered Hunter? I was told none of you are real sorcerers. The Firstseed knew nothing of hunters, of any sort." Now the Leech seemed nervous of Abel as well, a welcome change because most people and things sneered. Though actually it seemed frightened of Zephyr, which sort of restored Abel's sense of right.

Which did bring one question to mind. "It seems to think you and Zephyr are the same."

"Warning the seeds about me prepares them for other, lesser hunters. It recognises the urge to chase. You know Zephyr does that, but she has some of you in her. She will never be like me." Ferryl's mental voice didn't seem upset about that.

A wary Claris watched Zephyr leave, then return with Kelis and Rob.

141

"I told you. They hold hands in private as well." Rob looked triumphant, but Kelis seemed worried.

"Not private." Abel looked pointedly at Claris. "The Leech has got the message. It will negotiate, if we let it live." Rob took that in and opened his mouth. "Shut up Rob. We don't have to say what sort of life." Not a good one, Abel thought, not going by the look Kelis gave Claris.

"From the way Claris is eying Jenny and Zephyr, I vote we leave it to think scary thoughts for a bit. In any case I'm hungry and we don't know how long this will take. We can bring back some drinks as well." Kelis turned to Claris. "Do you need proper food, or water to drink?"

"Blood." Kelis waited. "The host needs water as well. Bring that and blood."

"The first thing you'd better learn is manners because from the look of you when I came in you'll be asking, not demanding. No blood yet, it will encourage you." Kelis turned on her heel, calling out to the Goblins. "A small piece of cake and a packet of fish fingers if you keep the Leech in here today." The only bit the goblins wanted to negotiate was if they could eat the stinky if it tried to escape.

*   *   *

On the way to Kelis' house she wanted to know why the Leech looked frightened. "Ferryl used to be a hunter of sorts, before she went in the hole. The Leech boss, the Firstseed, passed on a memory of Ferryl."

"You must have been mucho scary, to be remembered for two hundred years." Kelis eyed Ferryl/Jenny. "We heard you shout, tell her we needed it alive."

"It knew I would kill it, but had to learn that Abel can save it. Leeches pass from host to host so some live a long time, longer than I stayed in that hole. They pass some memory to their seeds, a way of warning their young of the dangers out there. When I hunted Leeches, I would move on before the church heard too many rumours. A hundred years could pass before I returned to an area, so some prey learned not to forget me." Ferryl/Jenny seemed to relish that last part.

"You are the Leech-kiddy bogey-man, or woman?" Rob hunched and raised his arms with his fingers clawed, trying to produce a Disney witch's cackling voice. "Beware, children. Drink up your chicken or the dreaded Ferryl will get you." Though even if Rob found it funny, Abel could see that Kelis still had questions. He'd best be ready when Ferryl/Jenny went home.

Kelis insisted on eating her sandwiches at home in case the Leech in Claris said or did something gross, so they went through what they wanted. No more pain or bad memories for Claris, no more growing, and it had to leave her as healthy as possible when came out. Ferryl also wanted the key to Castle House, if only to stop anyone else getting in. Then came the practicalities, because Abel for one now felt sure the Leech would run at the first chance.

An internet search for handcuffs had them all scandalised, then laughing. There were plenty for sale, or chains and manacles, but a good percentage were covered in velvet or had bits of fur, leather or bows on them. They'd have to talk to an older Taverner such as Eric, one who wouldn't be embarrassed buying restraints. After flicking through the prices, their fund looked smaller and smaller.

*   *   *

From the first negotiations with the Leech it became clear the Tavern fund might not be enough. The Leech agreed to grow very slowly, and to keep out of most major organs, but it needed a daily supply of blood. It couldn't repair all the intrusions and release Claris' heart, but could allow her to eat enough normal food to keep her stomach functioning. Toilet facilities went onto the list, along with clothes and a sleeping bag.

One big demand turned out to be impossible. The Leech couldn't keep Claris asleep like Ferryl did with Jenny. It couldn't operate a human body, so the Leech needed the host awake to control her through compulsion. In the end the Leech allowed Claris to speak, so she could understand what was happening. With Ferryl/Jenny poised and Zephyr hovering, it promised to keep very, very still so it caused no pain while they talked.

The Leech kept its word. After her first yelling for release Claris calmed down and listened. She'd seen and heard everything but in a sort of nightmare, so didn't really understand though she seemed wary of Ferryl/Jenny. Claris just wanted it out of her, any way necessary, as soon as possible. Gradually she accepted the thing had to stay in her for now, but it wouldn't hurt her as much and would leave her in a few weeks.

Abel hesitated before explaining the rest. In the interim Claris still had to drink glasses of blood to stay alive, but she'd get some real food as well. Whatever had happened before must have been awful. Claris readily agreed to drinking blood from a glass as long as she could live in this room and didn't have to kill anything else. Promising she could be in charge for a while every day to talk to Kelis, Rob, Abel or Jenny, seemed to help. Claris might not have fully understood everything because she kept flipping back into sheer terror.

Unfortunately, the Leech hadn't agreed to all that before freeing Claris to speak. Once back in control it used the demands to negotiate hard for more than just keeping its life. It wanted a new host, a young, healthy one, once it left. Otherwise it swore it might as well stay in Claris, in a host they cared for. If the hunter tried to force it out every last tendril would hang on, physical and magical, damaging the host's brain as well as body. It insisted it must grow a little, get stronger, and refused to spend the time laid on the floor bound like this. Lastly the information about the key would only be revealed once it had the new body, because the Firstseed insisted the Leech must lead Abel to the meeting. Abel agreed but privately gave up on the key; he wasn't letting this thing lead him anywhere.

More potential problems came up. Claris had been phoning her mother every few days to stop her mounting a search. After getting back in touch with her mother a Leech-controlled Claris had promised to go for counselling, and treatment for her alleged drug problem. She hadn't. Ferryl/Jenny took Abel's hand. "If her mother comes the Leech might influence her, to go to the police. You will not be able to stop the police if they insist on seeing her alone."

Zephyr hovered over Abel's shoulder when he turned to Claris. "If Claris' mother insists on seeing you, don't use that as a way to ask for the police. I will turn both hunters loose. One will already be in the room, invisible to the woman or any police, and neither will care about laws." The flash of fear before it agreed showed the Leech understood. Now all Claris had to do was keep her mother from getting too worried.

Even when that had all been sort of settled, Stan had to agree. Kelis and Rob went to get him and today's blood, while Ferryl/Jenny explained the rules to the Leech. "A man will come, the one from last night. He knows very little of magic, so don't mention it. You are a schoolgirl who has something small and nasty living inside. You understand it will be removed, but it takes time and you must drink blood until then."

Abel took over. "You are frightened but grateful. The thing might take over and try to run off, so you have agreed to be chained so you are safe. The man has no ward but you will not use compulsion, except to persuade him to accept the situation." Abel didn't want even that but he didn't think Stan would stand for it otherwise. He directed a thought at Zephyr so she flew over to hover above Claris. "The man will not see her. At the first sign you are trying to escape or get inside him, the hunter will attack."

"Tell it. I will force it from Claris' mind first so it cannot control her, then the damage will be less when I kill it." Abel passed that on.

Ferryl/Jenny smiled. "The huntress learns. With Claris' mind free, I need not be gentle. Do you understand?" Claris nodded nervously.

Abel felt nervous as well; he hadn't realised Zephyr was that strong. "Can you do that?"

"Not yet but I think I can drive the Leech from her mind and hold out until Ferryl Shayde arrives. I am not strong enough to kill it, not while it is in a body."

There was a big problem in that. "Warn it if it starts to stray. Dive close as a reminder, because Ferryl won't be in Brinsford all the time. Even if she is, she might harm Jenny by leaving suddenly."

"I will keep it frightened." Abel accepted that. He also felt reassured after Ferryl/Jenny added her sixpennorth. She made it clear that if Stan didn't accept the situation, she could see no point in letting the Leech live any longer. Claris' infestation seemed very keen after that.

Abel didn't think Stan would have gone along with them, even with Claris' superb act, without the compulsion. The old poacher might have second thoughts later, but for now seemed convinced. He even offered a length of chain and two padlocks so she could move about. A confused but agreeable Stan finally left with the two Tavern hexes Kelis gave him to put near his food for now.

Rob nipped off for the chain while Abel escorted Kelis home for her to get some clean clothes for Claris. They wouldn't fit, but neither would they be torn or spattered with old blood and mud. After padding Claris' leg, they padlocked the chain around it while the other end went around the desk where it couldn't slide free. The tape stayed on her wrists for now, and a Goblin sat in the room. Finally, the Leech gave up control while Claris talked to her mum. Claris kept her word not to say where she was or mention the Leech, but sobbed her socks off during the call. That might be why her mother started pushing for a meeting, probably not reassured by Claris telling her she needed a couple of weeks to get herself right. At least the brief freedom from control allowed Claris to confirm the Leech wasn't hurting as much. The day dragged on like that, ups and downs, but by mid-afternoon Claris slept peacefully and the four teenagers could leave her.

Abel kissed Ferryl/Jenny goodbye and waved her off, then turned to meet two glum faces. "What happened to all the fun? New glyphs, dancing leaves, and making hexes. Chasing Hoplins and tweaking dryads?" Kelis hooked an arm though Abel's, careful to do so very loosely. Abel thought he felt a little something, but since Kelis didn't it wasn't a magical link. "I'm too young to grow old, and a wizard's beard just won't suit you."

Rob hooked his arm through Kelis' free one. "I can actually use the last glyph properly, the growth one. It seems easier than the basic ones." Rob smirked as he spoke. "I've been making every third tomato plant grow faster than the rest. Samantha is supposed to feed them so mum's giving her grief about not doing it properly. It's driving her crackers."

"I've been boosting mum's flower border and the fruit bushes, just a bit. The gooseberries will have a bumper crop this year." A little smile lit Abel's face. "How about hiding one of Samantha's tomato plants, then revealing it the next day? If Kelis gets her last jar of honey, we'll ask dryad Chestnut to sell us the veil glyph." Anyone looking out of their window in Brinsford would have been puzzled by the sight of three teenagers, laughing and more or less dancing down the street, calling to each other before howling with laughter again. Even if someone heard "Melanie's Teddy Bears," "mum's handbag," "the phone while it's ringing," or "every third tomato" they wouldn't understand.

*   *   *

Nobody in Brinsford saw the glyph lesson because Dryad Chestnut set a veil once Abel checked that nobody was looking straight at them. When it drew the shape in the dust the glyph seemed easy, a circle of dashes with a dot in the middle. "That's it?"

"For me, yes. Mine is cast through my tree, so naturally reaches as far as the branches or roots and remains as long as necessary." They all looked up at the leaves overhead in sudden comprehension. "Remember it must rotate, spin. I am sure such good students will soon learn how to control the size? Maybe the speed of spin will make a difference, or the direction?" Creaky dryad laughter sounded at the apprehensive looks on three student faces.

"How do we shut it off? Does it move with us?" Rob frowned at the glyph in the dirt.

"If it moves with us we can't break it by walking through the edge, the usual way." Abel stopped fretting and smiled at the dryad. "Our thanks, dryad Chestnut. It looks as if it will still be hard work, but we expect that. Ferryl Shayde will be startled."

"I will stay alert in case she doesn't laugh afterwards." That really tickled dryad going by the creaking, or maybe the honey had made him a bit squiffy again. "Farewell, polite and sometimes generous apprentices. Ask again if your lessons are too hard."

On the way home they all agreed they would practice control until they found out all the answers, then surprise Ferryl. She knew Abel had negotiated, but not when he would get the glyph. The idea of getting a magical one-up on the sorceress cheered them all, for now at least.

*   *   *

Claris' jailers were very keen, and very hungry. At first most of the Goblin bribe consisted of packets of out-of-date food, then anything from home that none of them liked. Once those were gone Jenny shopped on the way to Brinsford, buying the cheapest offers in the supermarkets. Goblins loved junk food like cheap pizzas, sausages and burgers.

When Rob, Kelis and Abel had a proper look around inside the church the prison facilities improved. They discovered a toilet with a sink on the other side of the building, kept reasonably clean by the pixies and brownies. Kelis would escort Claris with two goblins as backup, or

Ferryl/Claris could oversee toilet visits if she was visiting. Stan produced two big staples and Rob found a second chain in the garage at home, heavily rusted but still sound. The tape came off Claris' hands for the last time, replaced by a well-padded chain round her neck to supplement the one on her ankle. Meanwhile the Leech used compulsion every time Stan visited to keep him from changing his mind.

The old poacher definitely seemed happy about Abel, Rob and Kelis spending one Saturday morning creature-proofing his house, garage, the chicken hut and their mesh run. Bugsy followed Abel around, watching, though Stan stayed well clear. He really didn't want to look too closely at what anyone did, though he'd see the actual plaques and drawings. Towards the end of the hex-drawing, Zephyr flew very slowly out of Abel's tattoo and hovered in front of Bugsy.

Abel opened his mouth to ask why, then shut up as a spooky-phone extended very, very slowly. Bugsy growled, a few hairs on his back went up, and Abel tensed ready to leg it. The old Jack Russel could be a bit sharp even on a good day. The ephemeral line touched, and Bugsy froze. After a few moments he relaxed a little and his hairs flattened. Abel tried to whisper in his head. "Zephyr, what are you doing?"

"Greeting another hunter. Hunter and guard, just as I am. He knows you are different, because of me, and worries about what you are doing. I am explaining."

"You speak dog?" Abel remembered Ferryl purring to cats, but Zephyr never made a noise.

"No. We understand enough, but not like words. He knows I am your hunter and guard, and we mean no harm. I am letting him know that what we do will protect the Stan." As the spooky-phone retracted, Bugsy actually twitched his tail and gave a tiny whine. "I will ask Ferryl if she can gift him something to help."

"Maybe better sight? She does that for cats so they can be guardians and see creatures better." She'd also enrolled them to help watch the village. "Will she make Bugsy a guardian?"

"She cannot. He has his own god, the Stan." Abel went back to work. That needed way too much explanation, or very little but he might not like the answers. Remembering Ferryl Shayde had denied being a goddess came as a big relief.

* * *

Abel didn't mind losing his cake when, on the sixth day of being allowed to talk, Claris actually smiled. She still started off looking terrified, but couldn't help it. Claris could feel the Leech controlling her all the time and knew she couldn't do anything about it, so she spent most of the time wondering what it would make her do next. Claris reported that the pains inside had died back, so the Leech had stopped growing into her organs. Better yet, the Leech had stopped doing gross things when it came here. Claris wouldn't define gross. Since she didn't seem too upset about drinking blood or having a Goblin in the room all the time, nobody pushed for details.

Even though it would have made her feel better, they daren't tell Claris her daily blood came from a shop in case the Leech objected. Whoever handed Claris the glass warmed it and added the magic out of sight, so the Leech wouldn't find out. For now Ferryl/Jenny bought more every three days and put it in a cool box in the church. Abel, Rob and Kelis took turns to re-freeze the cool box packs at home.

Nine magically aware Taverner players made the trip to Brinsford to meet Claris, to speak to her when the Leech didn't have total control. They came in ones and twos, reporting back to the rest. To Abel's great relief nobody asked for their donations back, though some made it clear that once the Leech left her Claris had to earn her own keep. Several sent out-of-date food for the Goblins, or old clothes for Claris. Most of the clothes hung on her, because she still wasn't putting on much weight.

Between dealing with Claris, exercising, practicing glyphs and patrolling Brinsford to top up the boundary, Abel had plenty on his plate. He still had to cram them in around school, though at least the homework had stopped after the exams. The evening boundary patrol wasn't too bad, a time to just walk and let himself relax a little.

"Food for Claris! May I, please?"

"Yes, go on Zephyr. As long as it isn't a mouse again." Zephyr left on "yes." She'd been crestfallen to find that the mouse she caught two days ago wasn't suitable. The Leech might have eaten it, but Claris didn't need that memory.

"Yes!" Triumph rang through the connection. "Please come, Abel. I cannot lift it."

That definitely intrigued Abel. He followed the spooky-line into the tall grass and nettles until he saw a plump rabbit laid on its side with Zephyr shimmering right above it. "You killed that?"

"The flying fist of doom strikes! Not killed. I thought the blood is better alive?"

Abel smiled, Zephyr loved Kelis' nickname for her. Then he didn't feel anything like as happy because now he had to kill the rabbit. "Will it stay unconscious until I can get it to Stan, so he can kill it? I don't fancy it." Abel could kill a Blood Leech or something attacking him, but not an unconscious bunny.

"I took care to hit hard enough so it would not escape, but without killing." The shimmering tightened around the rabbit's head. It barely quivered, its chest heaved a couple of times, and then it stilled. Zephyr took off again. "Is that better?"

"Perfect, thank you. Um, check with me another time please, in case I want something kept alive?" That had been quick, efficient, and without any hesitation. Ferryl claimed Zephyr took her character from him, so was he a killer at heart? Abel gingerly picked the floppy body up by the back feet, feeling definitely un-murderish. "I hope it hasn't got fleas."

"Shall I kill them?"

That came as a relief, both Zephyr asking and that she'd get rid of the fleas. "Yes please." Zephyr flowed over the rabbit's fur then soared into the sky.

"All gone. I was not sure I could knock a rabbit down without getting dizzy. You told me not to do that. I have been practicing being tight and hard. A flying fist of doom." Zephyr swooped and soared. "The next time there is trouble, I can help more. Do we want another?" She came down to hover in front of him. Abel felt sure if Zephyr had a tail it would be wagging.

"Not just now, thank you. We'd best take this to Stan." Abel giggled. "Or we could ask Kelis if she wants rabbit stew." Though he took this one to Stan. Zephyr caught the next one at the weekend so Ferryl/Jenny quickly and expertly drained, skinned and gutted it. The goblins scoffed all the gunky stuff including the fur, but Kelis still didn't want the meat. She felt sure her mum would run a mile from the bloody lumps. Instead, Abel surprised his mum with the joints, claiming Stan had caught too many. When rabbit stew turned out to be better than expected Abel hoped Zephyr caught more, though he still didn't fancy learning to skin them.

* * *

The two weeks after the exams weren't a holiday because school hadn't officially finished. Instead everyone attended but year eleven did little work while year thirteen were leaving school anyway. The attitude of some of the seraphims had eased after Jenny took to sitting with the geeks. Now, with the relaxation after the exams, a few of the seraphims became really interested in the Tavern game. That might have been due to Jenny adopting it, or just an excuse to mix with geeks and talk to her. After all, many were her friends or co-members of the Acro dancers.

If the weather let them the students now spent breaks out on the school field instead of in the canteen. One or two at a time, seraphims or teenagers who normally had nothing to do with geeks joined a growing group to discuss characters. The idea of making up people complete with their appearance and character appealed to a wide variety of teenagers. One seventeen-year-old in particular, Laurence Sperrick, seemed to find more and more reasons to ask Kelis questions.

Laurence even came up with a character. He suggested a rakish wastrel, the disgraced, disowned fourth son of a noble who hung around chatting up Bonny the Barmaid and tried to act like a bold, dangerous adventurer. Laurence spent some time with Kelis trying to design the character, called Spenz F'Lorinze. The result, tall and gangling with a hooked nose, bore a definite resemblance to Laurence. The original even promised to try to get a big hat with a feather, striped tights, a frilled shirt and a rapier if he could get an invite to a Taverner party.

When Kelis perfected the drawing Laurence strutted up and down in front of the Taverners, waving his imaginary rapier and spouting flowery compliments to demonstrate how Spenz should act. As he bent over Kelis' hand, pretending to kiss it, a familiar voice cut through the laughter. This voice didn't usually come out here on the school field at break time.

Seraph preferred to stay in the canteen rather than wallow about in the mud while she ate, as she put it. "Laurence Horatio Sperrick, you will stop that ridiculous behaviour now. Come away from that disgusting peasant, and never go anywhere near her again."

Laurence let go of Kelis' hand and stood, turning to face Seraph, and for a moment Abel thought he'd do as he was told. Instead another familiar voice rang out. "Laurence Horatio Sperrick, ignore her." Heads turned to see Ferryl/Jenny glaring but at Seraph, not Laurence. "Seraph Angelique Bellamy-Courts, you will be quiet! I do not wish to hear that tone of voice from you ever again. Do you understand?" It wasn't aimed at him, but the sheer compulsion in Ferryl/Jenny's voice pulled at Abel and probably everyone else there. At least his ward didn't chill, so nobody except Seraph was in danger of being actually commanded.

Seraph, however, never had a chance. Unlike her own semi-magical instructions, this was full magical compulsion. Her face blanked before she whispered "yes."

Ferryl/Jenny wasn't done. "You keep ordering people about, or insulting and bullying them, and that must stop right now. No more of it, ever again. Do you understand?"

"Yes."

Now people were starting to look puzzled, or even a bit alarmed. Abel tugged at Ferryl/Jenny's hand, speaking through Zephyr. "Ferryl, stop it. Everyone is looking. Enough."

Ferryl/Jenny took a deep breath, let it go and Abel sighed in relief. Too soon. "I think we need a little more. She could be dangerous to you if she keeps her influence with these young people when she leaves school. I will not allow that." A bright smile spread over Ferryl/Jenny's face. "Now look, you've made me sound just like you. Tell me Seraph, why do you do that, insult people and order them about?" Abel heard the little bit of command in the last bit.

Ferryl already had Seraph under control so she answered without hesitation. "I am jealous." Muttering and a few giggles broke out but Ferryl wasn't done.

"Why? Who are you jealous of?"

"Laurence. He is poor but has blue blood. Even though my father has more money Laurence will always get preference over me, always be invited to the best places. I hate the Acro dancers. Just because they are fit and show off in those leotards everyone likes them. That skinny wretch Kelis and her scruffy friends are actually popular because of a stupid game, which is totally unfair. I despise those musclebound idiots in the rugby team, especially Henry, but I have to tolerate the lout so I can use him to beat others into line."

"Enough. I think we all understand. Goodbye, Seraph."

Seraph staggered slightly, then looked puzzled. Comprehension, or maybe memory, spread over her face followed by a magnificent blush before she turned away. The erstwhile leader of the seraphims ran from the playing field followed by enough laughter to burn her soul for ever, from the very people she despised. At least the laughter, and the immediate discussions about what Seraph said, stopped most of them thinking about why she'd said it.

Laurence looked totally confused. "I don't understand. I never tell anyone about father's title and all that."

"Are you a really a disgraced fourth son?" Kelis nudged him. "That would explain your way with women. You've even managed to charm a sorceress." Abel looked away as Laurence turned towards her with a sweeping bow, and occupied himself by watching everyone else. Rob and a small group of geeks and betas, including Diane, were rolling about laughing. A triumphant Diane gave her big sister a double thumbs-up when Ferryl/Jenny looked that way.

"You got away with the magic, I think. What will your instructions do to Seraph?"

"I've no real idea. Telling her not to order people about might mean she can't order a drink in a café, but I doubt it will work that well." Intense satisfaction filled Ferryl's mental voice. "She certainly won't be repeating the sort of thing she tried with Jenny."

Surprised, Abel forgot to use Zephyr. Instead he turned to whisper. "With Jenny? After she refused to sit with Henry?"

"Seraph kept pushing after that, harassment that got worse. Jenny's body must have been barely aware of magic, because Seraph's voice didn't work. Even so the commands pulled at her, made her confused. Seraph would tell her she wasn't good enough for the Acro team so Jenny would wonder, then fail at routines she'd performed flawlessly at other times. I have been waking Jenny at night, and now I have her last memories. I finally found out why she hid round the back of the school." Ferryl/Jenny's hand tightened as she leaned closer to whisper in Abel's ear. "I never read the last memories or they might have roused her, but they were fresh in Jenny's mind when she woke up."

"What did she do? Seraph I mean?"

"Gave Jenny an ultimatum to think about over the holiday. Jenny could come back to sit at Seraph's table, apologise and sit next to Henry as instructed, or she could stop Acro dancing. The team captains would drop her, permanently. It seems Seraph really did give Claris and Laurence their orders.

Abel actually put his arm round Ferryl/Jenny, without thought, because he could hear how that had hurt Jenny even second-hand through Ferryl. "She had her head in her hands when I saw her, but then she ran away." He paused. "Round the corner and under the lorry."

"I'll show Jenny what happened here, but not how I did it." Ferryl/Jenny hugged him hard for a moment. "You'll have to stop this soon."

Abel realised what they were doing, hugging each other and whispering, and noticed the amused faces nearby. He glanced towards Kelis and froze. She had her arm around Laurence, looking right at Ferryl/Jenny with a little smile. Laurence put his arm round her, said something, and she laughed and turned away. With a pang Abel realised they were the same height, made for each other. Ferryl/Jenny's voice whispered in his ear. "Be happy, the link is broken." When he turned to her their faces nearly touched and she kissed him on the nose. "Now smile." Abel did, just about.

*　　*　　*

Several of the Taverners descended on Abel and Ferryl/Jenny, mostly to congratulate her on trimming Seraph down to size. The talk turned to the Tavern game, with some wanting to know when the next real meeting could be held. Others wanted to know the progress on the new characters. Some were interested in both; they wanted to see if Kelis could persuade Laurence to wear tights. Apparently most other people had already assumed if the pair weren't a couple now, it wouldn't be long. Except Abel, who had missed it entirely.

He'd caught up by the time break ended because Laurence still had an arm round Kelis as they went back in, only breaking away to go to his class. Abel, preoccupied, found his way blocked by Henry. "Not now Henry. I'm really not in the mood." He felt Zephyr move slightly in the tattoo, poised to act.

Ferryl/Jenny squeezed his hand. "Behave, everyone is watching."

True, when Abel glanced round, but Henry wasn't looking for trouble. "Do I have to join your game? To make the things go away. They don't bother you." His eyes moved to Ferryl/Jenny. "Or you, any of those playing that game. I can't sleep, they crawl on me, and in my food." Henry looked tired, sounded desperate, and had a definite twitch.

For long moments Abel considered telling him to go to hell, but he'd already had all the revenge he needed. Seraph had just totally humiliated Henry in front of the whole school, and instead of going crackers he'd come begging to the wimp who broke his arm. "I'll get you something. It'll keep them away. Catch me at the lockers before we go home." Abel brushed past. He didn't want any more to do with Henry than he had to.

Ferryl/Jenny leaned close. "You will give him a hex, a real one?" Abel could feel Zephyr's interest.

"Yes, enough of them so he can eat and sleep free of creatures. I can't even hate him anymore. He won't bother us again, and even Kelis has stopped complaining she never got to beat on him." Abel turned to Ferryl/Jenny, changing the subject. "Another week or so to the big breakup."

"Small, quiet breakup. I have been studying these things and talking to Jenny. We will all remain friends, because Jenny will need tuition. Not only that, she is a shareholder." A quick hug and she left for her classes.

"I thought you'd pounce on Kelis once Jenny woke up." Rob spoke quietly, teasing Abel but gently. "She must have got tired of waiting."

"Maybe she just found someone the right height."

"It'll save her carrying a stepladder about for when someone wants to kiss her." For some reason Rob found that funny, giggling all the way to class.

Abel didn't have to say much to Henry. No sooner had he handed over a few Tavern hexes, with instructions about using them, when several students pounced. They really wanted a meeting of some sort, someplace, for everyone who could cast a glyph. A couple of them suggested Frederick's house would be ideal. Frederick had already given the Taverners a big room to use, and there really was a private garden with plenty of room to throw magic.

They'd been a bit wary at first but Frederick seemed to be just what he'd looked like, a lonely old man in a big empty house. A couple of visits showed that the magical creatures nobody else could see really did upset him, because he stuck to the few rooms he had hexes for. At first the Taverners always arranged to meet up there in groups, but now they trickled in and out more or less at will at the weekends. Frederick always seemed pleased to see them. That might be because his visitors helped him with magic, or because they'd started putting hexes in the rest of his house.

Abel added that to his list of things to sort out, but right now getting the Leech out of Claris filled the top ten places.

*   *   *

According to Rob, each time he turned Claris' phone on for her to call her mum it showed missed calls from a withheld number. Whoever had the key must be impatient. Not as impatient as Claris' mum, though she had been mollified by promises to meet up in a couple weeks.

As the end of term came nearer, Abel, Kelis and Rob realised they'd ignored one big problem. They had to convince the Blood Leech it would go into another person, yet stop it doing so. The problem soon became urgent, because the Leech knew the time must be getting close and asked to see its new body.

"If we go to the hospital we can find someone with a terminal illness. That is how adult Leeches find victims." Ferryl couldn't see a problem. "From what I see in Jenny's memory, people find out about cancer while they are still healthy. The Leech would have very little to fix."

"I'd even consider that, except now we know the poor sucker will be awake all the time." Abel shivered. "Can you imagine the state someone will be in after forty years of being compelled to kill and then drink the blood. Claris knows it'll be out of her soon but it's still driving her crackers." Claris still started her conscious periods in a blind panic, and hated having to go back under control. She hadn't hesitated for a moment about Ferryl possessing her after the Leech left, because Jenny looked both happy and healthy.

"Maybe not, because I'm sure Leeches usually leave the hosts happy and healthy, with no memory of bloodshed. Perhaps this only happens when a new seed grows." Ferryl/Claris looked a little guilty. "I never cared much. I just killed any Leeches I found and drank their magic, providing I could do so without alerting the church. Now I wish I'd asked a few questions."

"We could keep the new host here, make a deal so they weren't hurt like we did with Claris?" Kelis slumped. "No we can't, not even if the Leech can scramble Stan's head enough to accept another prisoner. We can't afford the food and Goblin bribery, and if we could someone will notice the squatter in the church sooner or later. There'll be a funeral here or something and a vicar will come and discover everything."

"Then the church rips the Leech out, and the host dies." Abel turned to Kelis, suddenly curious. "That smile when I said we'd offer the Leech a life, but it didn't have to be a good one. What did you think of?"

That same smile flitted across Kelis' face, perhaps more malicious, before she answered. "I thought of a rat, unless we could find a big enough toad? Kept in a cage, with enough sedatives in the blood we fed it so the host never felt a thing. It would be so spaced the Leech wouldn't be able to hurt it to get its kicks."

"That amount of sleeping pills or whatever would kill a rat or toad." Rob looked at Abel for confirmation but he shrugged.

Kelis chipped in. "No it wouldn't. The Leech would have to work non-stop to keep the host alive, or die as well."

"It might not fit in a rat." Abel frowned. He'd seen the size of what Henry upchucked.

"You've seen that wooden block in our kitchen, the one with all the knives in it?" Puzzled, Abel and Rob nodded so Kelis continued. "I'll bring the cleaver to make sure it fits. After all, if it can heal Claris then healing itself should be easy. Perhaps some pain might convince it to go easy on future hosts."

"Ouch." Rob mock-winced, or maybe really did. "Remind me to never, ever get you properly mad at me."

"You need reminding? This is K'liss Windcatcher, and I believe she is becoming a real Glyphmistress at last." Ferryl/Jenny didn't see Kelis' shocked look.

"We'd never get the Leech to go into a rat anyway. It will tear Claris' mind to shreds first. Not unless we can disguise a rat's mouth as a healthy human one." Rob shrugged at the sceptical looks. "Maybe we can persuade it to come outside Claris, towards another host, then grab it."

"Unlikely." Ferryl/Jenny shook her head. "It would want mouth to mouth contact so there wouldn't be much to grab. Worse, a Blood Leech is slippery. Not just with blood, but because much of it is magic. Hands would slither through or off it." They all sat thinking hard.

For once, Zephyr interrupted a serious discussion. "Can it slither away from the flying fist of doom?" Smiles broke out and they began to really think about ways and means.

* * *

The last day of school, Kelis looked really thoughtful when the three of them got off the bus. The other two were happy to be finished for six weeks, and making vague plans for a Tavern meeting, but she never said a word. Rob stopped talking and watched her for a few moments. "She's got the dreaded lurgy."

"The what?" Abel actually looked to see if there were spots before he noticed Rob's little smile. "What are the symptoms?"

"Mostly withdrawal. Though if she puts a big hat with a feather on a broom handle to carry around with her that should make her feel better."

"I am not moping about Laurence!" Kelis glowered, but it didn't have the usual force and soon faltered. "But he is funny, and I've sort of got used to seeing him. He's not as stuck-up as I thought, not really."

"Ooh, the Glyphmistress has struck again. Is he properly entranced?" Rob opened his eyes wide in shock. "Or did it bounce, and you are now putty in his hands?"

Abel finally got his chance, after all the digs from Kelis. "No, it's the leotard. Remember, Kelis always said it had a strange effect, but we thought she meant on the boys."

"Stop it! It's not glyphs, not magic like, you know. Me and Abel." Kelis had a faint smile as she turned to Abel. "It's not the leotard you idiot. He's nice to me, without being pushy, all right? And he takes the mickey out of himself instead of me."

"Maybe he'll phone, or drive over here to see you in the holidays?" Abel tried to say the next bit with a straight face. "He might even join the Tavern."

"He has." Kelis shut up but too late.

"Phoned you?"

"He's coming here or he's joining the Tavern?" Abel really wanted to laugh now, but Kelis looked really flustered. Rob laughed anyway.

"Both. All three maybe. Yes he's phoned, several times. He's already started going to Tavern games in town, any of them who'll fit him in. I thought they'd said something?" She relaxed a bit as both Rob and Abel shook their heads. "I thought someone might have said things. About him and me. Because of the Tavern drawing."

"When is he coming here?" Abel almost choked swallowing a snigger. "Have you mentioned him to your mum? From experience suddenly producing a secret boyfriend or girlfriend can cause severe earache."

"No! He can't come here." Kelis hesitated. "Or not until the Claris thing is sorted out. One glimpse and he'll recognise her. She's the joint captain of the Acros, or was at least." She kicked moodily at the gravel still filling the smaller holes where the Bound Shade had damaged the road. "By the time that's done Laurence will have lost interest anyway so it's not worth telling mum. It's not like we're going out or anything."

"What you need is cheering up. Then you won't care about some disowned fourth son." Rob gestured to Castle House as they passed. "We can have plenty of glyph practice now there's no school."

A shy little smile flitted over Kelis' face. "He's not a disowned fourth son. He's the second son of an Earl, though I had to prise that out of him." She glanced at the gardens. "I enjoy practice, but I've not had much chance while we've been dealing with Claris. I should keep my hand in, just in case Laurence flutters a leaf."

"You should learn to hide in case you change your mind about him." Abel had just thought of something to cheer Kelis up. "I've been practicing the invisibility now and then and I've sort of got it, but we've never really compared notes. How about a final rehearsal before we spring it on Ferryl?"

As expected two big smiles greeted the idea, though he didn't expect another reaction. "Can I practice as well? To show her how much I've improved my fire and the colour glyph?" Abel had let Zephyr practice colour changes because that one couldn't hurt anything.

"Good idea Zephyr." Abel barely finished before a flying fist of doom shot skywards, connecting to all three and doing her best to sing 'Ring of Fire.' That finally broke Kelis' mood, and she agreed to meet up straight after tea and Claris-feeding.

* * *

When she arrived in Castle House garden Kelis pointed out they couldn't be sure how well the veil worked, because from inside it was invisible. That stopped them all. Veils were clear from inside, and as magic users they could all see through one from outside. The most they'd see was a shimmer like the one when a dryad cast it. Zephyr had a sort of solution. She could see the magic flows, and Abel's veil looked different to dryad's although the effect on the humans inside it was almost the same. If all three cast a veil Zephyr could tell if it was a human-dryad difference or a fault in casting. Because she could see the effect of the magic on whatever lay inside the veil, and they knew a dryad veil worked, Zephyr could also tell if it made people invisible. When they tried, all three humans produced slightly different flows with the ones cast by dryads very much the odd one out. None of them affected the human inside in quite the same way as the dryad's veil did, so they might still be visible. After some serious experimentation all three humans cast veils with smooth magic flows that were virtually identical, and according to Zephyr they hid the person inside.

As a bonus, the sprite claimed she now knew how to cast one herself. Although invisible to ordinary eyes anyway, Zephyr thought that might be useful to hide objects if Abel wanted her to. She wouldn't try yet, not until Abel and Ferryl gave her permission. Now all three could reach Zephyr's high standards, Kelis in particular wanted to experiment. That led to answers but more questions.

The faster they imagined the glyph spinning anti-clockwise, the more the veil hid. The first, slower spin hid living beings and any item held by or attached to the caster. A faster spin hid plants as well as manmade solids such as glass and metal but not rocks, while even faster hid dead organics such as wood or leather. Eventually, at the fastest they could manage, everything including Zephyr disappeared from even magical sight. No shimmer, no flicker, just a bare patch of earth, but none of them could get that fast for more than a second or two.

The fastest spin used huge amounts of magic, too much to be practical unless the caster drew magic directly from a tree. According to Zephyr she could still see the magic flows, but nothing inside except earth or rock. Increasing the spin using an identical but clockwise glyph extended the veil outward in a globe.

Cast at the ground the glyph produced a static veil, one that could be broken by walking out of it. None of them wanted to cast it at a person, so they settled for a stick. Carrying the stick moved the veil, so a solid object could be hidden and left. Eventually all three took a break to absorb it all and rest. Even if the veil had no weight or substance, casting still tired them. The last experiment would be trying to alter the size while hiding, two glyphs moving opposite directions at different speeds, but not until they'd rested.

Zephyr gleefully threw herself into fire-practice. Abel had let her use fire glyphs to singe fae while walking the boundaries, but felt sure she'd been sneaking extra practice at night when she contacted the village cats. After running through her repertoire Zephyr switched to colour, soon turning a nearby bush into a kaleidoscope of brightly coloured leaves. After more coaching on shades, because Zephyr tended to bright and garish, the three judges insisted she made the leaves natural green again. Once the sprite managed that, they all agreed she could showcase her own skills during the big veil reveal. Tomorrow they decided, if Jenny could get over to Brinsford. It would give them all a bit of a boost before trying to de-Leech Claris. That could still go very wrong.

Nobody even thought about Leeches the following day when all four apprentices flaunted their glyphs for Ferryl/Jenny. Although pleased to get the glyph, being the least adept really annoyed the sorceress until she saw the funny side. She was the real sorceress, actually teaching glyphs, and now she had to play catch-up. The following celebration included more very silly Glyphmistress dancing including a sprite variation. The pop and crisp party, with snatches of songs about magic, fire and any lyric vaguely concerning invisibility, should have amused anyone hearing them. Instead, if enough sound had escaped the magical barrier, it would have scared passersby senseless as the magic used it to dissuade anyone from investigating.

*   *   *

The next four days before Jenny's awakening were tense. If she ran off to her dad or the church, screaming about possession, all hell would break loose. Ferryl couldn't be certain, because Jenny could be pretending agreement just to get her out. Two days before J-Day, or C-Day, a special meeting of Bonny's Tavern took place in the church. This time Ferryl let go completely, withdrew deep inside to give Jenny complete control.

Jenny looked around her, stood up and walked up and down the church, swinging her arms. "We usually do this at night. I've been dying to be really free when I'm not in bed, to walk about all by myself." She held Kelis', Rob's and Abel's eye in turn. "But I'm not free yet, and that still freaks me out a bit. I'm not even sure if Ferryl Shayde isn't the only reason I'm not shrieking and beating on the walls."

Abel held her gaze. "You are in complete control right now. Ferryl promised."

"She might be lying."

"Ferryl doesn't lie to me."

"She can't lie to Abel."

"Not to him."

Jenny concentrated on Abel. "Why not? Do you control her like you do the thing in your arm?"

"Ferryl is free. I did her a big favour once so she will never hurt me even with a lie. Zephyr is also free if she asks to be. She wants to stay, to

162

be safe and to learn." Abel threw his hands up in frustration. "Now you'll say I might be lying?"

"I was going to say that, but I remember Rob teasing you about being honest. That thing, sorry, Zephyr, could have given you every single answer in the exams, but didn't." Jenny walked up the church and back, thinking hard. "Anyone might be lying but I've got to believe someone, and every memory says you are probably the best bet." The little laugh had some bitterness in it. "Though I know my memories aren't totally true. I'm not to be trusted with some things. Is it true, what you said about how hard magic is to control and how dangerous it is? Because what you actually showed wasn't scary when I had a chance to think about it, you just said it could be."

"You have to learn to control glyphs slowly but then you can do really serious damage." Kelis smiled slightly. "I remember the first time I saw Abel practicing, just floating a leaf." She searched in her pockets and brought out a permanent marker. "Now I can do this, but it took many, many hours." The pen hovered over Kelis' hand then flew up, twirling in the air before suddenly driving down to embed itself deep into the wooden floor. Jenny's chair rose, twirled and set back down. "That is the simplest glyph, air." Another glyph produced a small cloud of mist that rained for a few moments. "That is harder."

"Then there's this." Abel cast reverse fire to freeze the cloud, leaving ice dust drifting slowly downwards. He cast a tight, hot fire glyph across the church to leave a circular black mark, still smoking a little, on the stone wall. "I can freeze more, a person, or the flame can be much, much bigger, and hot enough to light the church ablaze. Kelis could do her trick with a tree branch, I've seen it. How big do we have to go to persuade you?" Jenny looked at Rob with the question in her eyes.

"Instead of a few leaves on a house plant I can take you outside and make a clump of grass grow two or three metres in seconds? You saw growth, but a mistake and the plant turns brown and dead just as quick. So do people if you get it wrong with that cloud glyph." Rob tapped his rounders bat, in his belt as usual. "This thing has a glyph that makes it an iron hammer to magical creatures, but I'd need a creature to demonstrate. We can disappear so only the magically aware can see us. Just think of how dangerous that can be, to the user as well if you step into the road and the driver can't see you. All it takes is practice."

Jenny sat back down. "So anyone can do it, because you three are like chalk and cheese. You're very different to each other but you all learned. That's what Ferryl Shayde said." She took a deep breath. "Right." She pointed at the black mark on the wall, the melting ice and the pen, still embedded in the floor. "Those alone are truly dangerous so I'll accept the rest are, and that me chucking them about without practice could kill someone." Her rueful smile accepted she had to believe some of it. "After all, I'm alive and that had to be very strong magic. Is the memory about Seraph being humiliated true? She really never came back to school?" They all nodded and she smiled happily. "Then I owe you all for that one."

"So you'll keep quiet about all this? The magic? Though you'll have to burn a ward, a tattoo, unless that one Ferryl did works." Kelis looked sceptical. "It's supposed to be burned using your own will."

Jenny glanced down at her clothes. "She tells me she used my will to survive when she woke me briefly, just after the accident, so the tattoo is mine. My memory of that is confused, genuinely not Ferryl's doing." Two spots of red grew on her cheeks. "Have you seen it?"

Jenny looked straight at Abel, so he answered. "Nobody has." He wasn't sure if his own cheeks were pink. "We weren't really boyfriend and girlfriend you know."

"No I didn't, not for certain, not until now." Jenny looked down with a little smile. "It's really pretty, but I hope it stays a secret for a long while yet."

"Well if you've got a ward you are protected, so you can ignore the whole magic thing if you like. That tattoo will protect against quite serious magic, compulsion like Seraph's, or any attempt to magically leash or possess you. Even Ferryl can't get back inside you once she's left so there's no need to learn any glyphs." Kelis glanced at Abel. "He didn't have much choice, and I certainly wasn't going to let him do that stuff without learning how, but not every beta knows about magic."

"I know. Ferryl has been explaining it all. I just needed to be sure it was true." Jenny chuckled, her face finally relaxing. "Not learn any glyphs? Hah! Diane will be throwing glyphs around all over the place by the time she's my age. You really think I want my little sister pulling magical pranks when I can't fight back?" She took a deep breath before looking around the empty church. "So how do we manage it? Does Ferryl just float out? She said it's to save Claris but I'd have to do some of it at the last minute. To be honest my memories of Claris are more about her being a bitch than this problem, but I'll do it to get my life back."

"We need you to get well clear once Ferryl moves over, though you'll feel weak at first. Just before then you will sleep for a few hours, in Castle House gardens. You'll be safe, but you don't want to remember the painful bit, right?" Kelis glanced at the males. "I'll be right there with you, but not these two."

"We'll be nearby but out of sight, standing guard." Rob gestured at Abel. "Though nobody else should be able to get in that garden anyway. After that there'll be some messy stuff, a really nasty looking thing that we have to cram into a new home. Don't try to interfere, even if it looks as if Claris or Rob is in real trouble. Just remember, Ferryl fixed you so she can fix them."

The serious faces made their own point. Jenny nodded but then glanced at one of the internal doors. "Can I see Claris? While I'm like this I mean. So I know. Can you make the Leech let me talk to her without Ferryl there?" She looked unsure. "Ferryl hasn't let me remember much about what's in Claris, while my earlier memories tell me she might deserve all she gets."

"She doesn't deserve this. Nobody does. You'll need someone in there to keep the Leech in order, but not one of us three. Try to ignore the hovering fist of doom. Zephyr won't tell me what you say to each other, but she scares the crap out of the Leech." Abel grinned. "You've seen Zephyr with Ferryl's eyes, now here's what we see." He hardly needed to switch mental gears these days. "Zephyr, just a bit of gentle flying please."

The shimmer barely moved at first, trailing her connection very slowly out about a metre before performing a couple of slow loops. Jenny watched entranced. "Like heat haze on a line of smoke. She's another secret. Ferryl won't let me remember how Zephyr got into your arm."

"We don't know either. As far as I can gather, you and Abel had a magical love-child. Oh, er..." Rob looked frantically from one to the other. "Bl.. Curses, er, not really, honest. It's just they made her, Ferryl and Abel. Out in the garden behind the bushes. Out of sight. Well no, not like that. Ferryl just blanked the cameras."

"Shut up Rob." Kelis had trouble speaking through her giggles. Abel knew his face was on fire and he'd turned away from the horrified look on Jenny's face. "He means they used Abel's magic and Ferryl's knowledge and skill to bring a puff of wind to life. Zephyr, get it? Nothing else, except they probably held hands."

"Only so the dryads didn't hear." Abel still daren't look up. "Would you like to see Claris now?" He hoped so, if only until Kelis stopped giggling and he stopped blushing.

"It might be a good idea." Jenny's voice sounded strange. "Providing our love-child will keep watch." As Abel glanced up she burst out laughing. "Your face is a picture. I'll miss seeing you blush at the slightest excuse." Her face sobered. "Ah, right. After we split up I'd rather we didn't see much of each other, not for a while. I don't dislike you but it feels a bit weird, you know? After the holding hands and kissing. We'll meet, but I'd rather someone else taught me magic, another Taverner?"

"Okay, no problem. Anything less than you being totally creeped out is a plus." Abel stood up. "I'll just nip through there and terrify a Leech."

"Not likely. The flying fist of doom will do that." Kelis suddenly looked thoughtful. "I could design you a FFOD logo to put on a shirt."

"Come on fuffod, your tattoo carrier needs you."

"This is not much fun. I am not allowed to hurt the Leech, because it would hurt Claris."

"Just hover menacingly, and if it argues pretend I'm holding you back."

"You are." Abel wondered if answering back and the developing sense of humour were his, Ferryl's, or all Zephyr.

However it worked, the Leech didn't argue about Claris getting extra free time. It had met the new host and approved, so the sooner it transferred and could leave the church the better. Jenny spent some time in there, but Abel didn't ask Zephyr what was said. They soon knew the gist. A sober-faced Jenny pointed out that after talking to Claris, a few months or even twenty years with Ferryl in charge wasn't that bad a deal. She'd told Claris how it felt, to make her feel better. Rob took Jenny outside and made a few weeds and a clump of grass explode in growth to take her mind off it a bit. As a bonus, Jenny met goblins for real and wanted one for her front garden.

When Jenny came back in she sat and told them she needed to sleep on it. Ferryl must have been waiting. The schoolgirl barely swayed but the three teenagers could see a difference in the way she held herself, or maybe in her expression. They fed Claris and took her to the washroom before Ferryl/Jenny went home and the others split up. Abel and Zephyr went to practice, Kelis to carve a complicated glyph into a piece of wood, and Rob to worry about his part.

* * ** * ** * ** * ** * ** * *~

Too Many Possessions

Mr. Forester asked about a meeting, and the Taverners all wanted to have a proper get-together now they were on holiday, but Claris came first. The magical Taverners understood, even if they weren't aware of the Ferryl possession part. They still thought Ferryl lived in Abel's arm, especially now that Zephyr had real control of the tattoo. While not yet as versatile as Ferryl, the sprite had her own definite ideas.

Zephyr had created her own special version of the tattoo for the transfer, though Claris' Leech wouldn't see it. Abel's bicep sported a large red boxing glove with a cloud of smoke behind and FFOD across it in big letters. At least that lightened the mood a little when Abel showed her to Jenny, Kelis and Rob, a welcome distraction after the preparations for removing Claris' Leech. Eventually everything possible had been done, so Rob, Abel and Kelis went to collect her. When her three captors arrived, Claris stood up with a big smile. "Now?" Claris looked curious when the chains came off completely. "Where is Huntian?"

Rob ignored the odd name for Ferryl. The Leech seemed frightened by it, which was good enough. "We're doing this somewhere else, so let's get going." His nerves hadn't been helped by spending over an hour sat in Castle House gardens, in earshot but out of sight of Jenny and Kelis. Ferryl had screamed while removing her bone glyphs, then spent a long time healing both Jenny's bone and the holes out through her flesh. Once she'd given Abel her wits Ferryl removed Jenny's memories of pain and any knowledge of the magic she'd used. Jenny woke up fully for the final time, ready to control her own body during the changeover. Right now Jenny and Ferryl were going over exactly what that meant.

"You'll walk down the street with us, happy and smiling. Hold this." Abel gave Claris a pebble engraved with the glyph that allowed her to pass through the Castle House barrier. "Remember, the hunter will be right above you as we walk." As Zephyr flew out of Abel's arm and hovered as promised, Claris nodded.

"Can I walk with him. The host?" Claris smiled hungrily at Rob. "You are a fool to give yourself to save this host, because she never liked you." The Leech held out Claris' hand. "Most of our nest is female. Our

Firstseed prefers them but I might enjoy being different."

Rob looked at the hand in disgust. "I think not. I really don't want to touch you until I have to. I don't want to touch you at all, but I can't leave you in a pretty girl like Claris. Not even a girl I don't like. Now shut up. If I change my mind you've got no-place to go."

"Yes, and try not to damage him. Remember, when we go to this meeting I'll be buying Rob back. I want him fit to walk out once you leave." Abel got between them. "Let's go. You don't want Huntian to come looking."

"You don't want your boss to refuse to sell Rob either, or Huntian will be leading us all on a Leech-hunt. Remember to tell her that." Kelis moved to the other side of Claris as they came through the lychgate and headed towards Castle House. Even walking under her own steam the Leech-infested teenager still looked anorexic thin and very pale.

Despite that she made good time to Castle House. Rob stopped her at the gate. "If you drop that pebble, you'll die. Don't try to run off in there." Claris nodded and walked through the gate without any hesitation, following Rob to the cave.

Ferryl/Jenny, already waiting, didn't waste any time. She pointed to the pair of pillows on the ground. "Rob, lie there with your mouth open. You must agree completely or your ward will bar entry, then the Leech will not leave Claris willingly. You understand?"

Rob gave her the macho answer they'd come up with to explain why he'd volunteered. "Yes. We went through all this and I told you, and the Leech. I'm only agreeing because Claris is a girl. I'm a lad so I'm tougher and can stand it until Abel buys me back." He glared at Claris, or rather the Leech. "If he can't buy me, kill this thing even if it kills me. I don't want forty years of what Claris had."

"Deal." Abel pushed Claris towards one of the pillows on the ground. "You lie here so Ferryl can get into Claris straight away. Remember, if Ferryl can't save her we'll rip you out of Rob. You won't be able to damage him badly enough fast enough to stop Ferryl saving him."

"I understand. You already told me." Claris' face eagerly watched Rob lie down to put his head on the other pillow. "You will let me leave this place afterwards? If not I will never take you for the key, and this one will suffer."

"We can't stop Rob leaving. The barrier recognises him so he can just walk through." Abel reached down and took the bat from Rob's belt. "Though we'll hang onto this. Now lie down and get on with it." He glanced at Jenny. "Ready?"

Jenny nodded nervously, really Jenny because Ferryl had disengaged ready to leave. "I kneel here, to the side of Claris. As soon as the Leech leaves I put my mouth on Claris', even if her mouth is bloody, so Ferryl can cross over." Her little laugh sounded shaky. "Which is mean because I distinctly remember asking for a hot prince to kiss me. I'd have settled for doing the kissing, but Claris isn't a prince or even a lad."

"But you get time off for good behaviour. Kelis will be right behind you to help because you will feel faint afterwards." Abel stood a metre below Rob's and Claris' feet looking at Claris. "I'll just make sure there's no cheating. No choking Claris on the way out or anything like that."

"But the hunter stays inside you?" Claris looked nervously at Abel's shoulder. "And you stay back there, too far away to interfere."

"Yes, now do it."

Claris turned to Rob and put her hands either side of his face, opened her mouth and went to make contact. Rob recoiled. "Not a chance! That's disgusting." He looked up at Abel with a helpless shrug. "I know it's going into me, but her mouth and breath stink of rotten blood. Can't it sort of jump over?"

"Can you?" Abel almost held his breath, because everything depended on the Leech's reaction. Hopefully it wouldn't think too hard or too long with a fresh healthy body waiting.

"No, I cannot move around easily outside a host." Claris looked sulky. "You promised. It makes no difference what I smell like, I'll be inside."

"If you kneel above his mouth, can you sort of drop in?" Abel switched to Rob. "You could hold your breath?"

Rob considered it, then nodded slowly. "All right, but I still need a bit of room." He shuddered. "You haven't smelled it, Abel."

"Not too far." Now Claris looked suspicious, but at least the Leech had accepted some sort of gap.

"This?" Rob held his hands apart and Claris' head shook. Rob sighed and moved them closer in stages, stopping at about thirty centimetres apart. "That's it, I'm not getting closer than that."

For a few moments Claris looked from Abel to Rob, and his hands. "That will do if he takes the hunter further away. I will get a grip on you before I leave this host, so I will know your ward is not defending you. Before I release her throat I will be far enough into yours that the hunter cannot stop me. Are you still willing?" Real anger showed. "If this is all a trick I will tear this host to shreds!"

Abel took a long step back. He wasn't actually watching Claris, so he caught the slight nod from Jenny and heard a quiet affirmative in his head. "I'll stay here, but I'll crouch down to watch. Now can we get on with it?"

"Yes, because I really am bricking it here." Rob looked it, pale and nervous as the moment came closer. Claris got to her knees and knelt over Rob, leaning down until he put up a hand to stop her getting closer. "That's what we agreed, coffin-breath. Be quick, while I hold my breath." Rob snatched a quick breath, opened his mouth, and Claris' throat bulged. At the second heave tendrils reached out of her mouth to snag Rob's lips, and pulled. A wet bag slid out of Claris' mouth until the front end touched Rob's lips.

"Go!" Abel really hoped they'd got it right, that the thing would have released Claris' brain by now ready to slide across into Rob's throat. The flicker wasn't even a blur as Claris' head jerked to the side, away from Abel. Blood spattered from Rob's mouth, then flooded from Claris' as Zephyr tore the rest of the Leech free. Even as it rolled away, fighting furiously with a shimmering ball of fury, Jenny pulled Claris over and bent to kiss her. Abel summoned fire and watched the fight, while Kelis stood beside Jenny, a glyph boiling in her hand. Neither of them dare cast in case they hit Zephyr. "Zephyr, release!"

"Trying." That sounded strained. The tangle kept rolling back and forth, tendrils thrashing and blood splattering. Rob turned onto his hands and knees, one hand to his bloody mouth, and staggered to his feet. For a moment Kelis, Rob and Abel all stood poised, then Jenny collapsed. She rolled away from Claris who now laid coughing blood and shuddering, her limbs twitching and thrashing. The Leech must have done terrible damage inside her throat.

Kelis remembered her part. "Here, Jenny." She banished her wind glyph and bent, picking up the pebble Claris had dropped and putting it into Jenny's right hand. "Hold that tight." She more or less heaved Jenny to her feet, helping her towards a tree before pushing Jenny's left hand onto a mark cut into the bark. "Come on Jenny, push magic. Through your palm like Ferryl showed you. Connect with the glyph." As Jenny froze, then started to straighten up, a loud bang echoed.

Zephyr and the Leech flew apart. A slightly smoking blur shot back into Abel's arm, where he could feel her trembling. "Sorry. Couldn't get away. Then wanted more. Sorry."

Abel tried to radiate reassurance because Zephyr seemed frightened. She shouldn't be, because the Leech had definitely come off second best. Several tendrils hung askew, others had been burned off and a large black, charred patch across the main body bubbled both blood and magic. That slowly sealed as Abel watched. "No, Rob."

Rob glanced over, anger on his face. He lowered the hand from his dripping mouth to show the deep cuts on his lips. "Payback" he slurred, gesturing with the fire glyph. "It can't hurt anyone now."

"Firstly Ferryl promised, though she wouldn't care if we broke it. Second, and more important, we might still get the key to the house. You wouldn't want to waste Kelis' work." Abel glanced at the Leech. "It's hurting now, because the garden will be trying to terrify it enough to leave and it can't. We agreed capture not kill."

"That depends on Claris living." They both looked at her. Claris lay on her back, a fine spray of blood coming with every exhale, but the choking and most of the thrashing about had stopped. The spray stopped after a few more breaths, her limbs finally stilled, and Claris' eyes opened. Calm eyes, which meant Ferryl had her. Meanwhile Jenny had gone from collapse to hugging the tree, giggling madly with her hand still firmly over the glyph. Kelis left her, coming back to Claris. "I'll sit Claris up. She'll want to see that thing get its new home."

Rob glared at the Leech, still thrashing about in the grass. "I hope you can understand. If we just leave you, the garden will kill you with fear. I'm going to give you an option." He stopped to wipe more blood from his lips but they kept dripping. "I hope you refuse. You'll die screaming in terror, as bad as anything you put Claris through." The glyph disappeared from his palm as he turned to reach into the bushes. Rob's smile looked awful, still dripping red as he held the cage up. "A young, healthy body as promised. A toad body, but you can't have everything. Now either you figure out how to get in there, or Kelis can start carving lumps off until you fit." Any reticence Rob had about that had long gone.

Abel took the cage. "Zephyr, if I let my glyph die, are you ready if it tries anything?" He wanted Rob free to staunch his mouth rather than looking for a chance, any chance, to burn the blood-bag.

"I am, but I will not try to hold it, just hit it. When it fought, I held tighter and then began to slide inside. I nearly went all the way in, it was suddenly easy." Abel felt a shudder through the tattoo. "I don't know how to control that, or if I'd get out. I don't want to be in that thing so I cast fire, from partly inside it. Don't ask me to hold it again, please?"

"A Fiery Flying Fist of Doom, that's all we'll need." A faint mental giggle answered, though a nervous one. "Okay Rob, we've got it. You'd better sort your mouth out." Abel turned to the Leech, putting the cage down as Rob started pulling his shirt off. "The hunter is watching so be good. Kelis carved a glyph on the wooden bottom of this cage. If you crawl in here you'll be protected from the garden, so the terror will stop. Though if you don't possess the toad, you'll die of starvation anyway." The toad had backed into a corner, awake because none of them knew how to safely knock it out. The consensus was it might not understand what happened, whereas a rat or any other similar sized mammal probably would. It wasn't a question Jenny could ask the pet shop assistant.

The Leech froze, so it understood some of what was said. A wave of compulsion bounced off Abel's ward, and probably Rob's and Kelis' from their expressions. Jenny looked startled and glanced down, probably at the sudden chill from her ward. Ferryl/Claris gave the Leech a bloody smile, a hungry, eager one. Her voice sounded rough, but understandable. "That only works on prey. Like a toad or a Leech." That did it. The Leech crawled towards the cage where the toad waddled forward and obediently opened its mouth. As the Leech wriggled inside magic boiled away and blood spurted, shrinking its body until it would fit.

Jenny, now sat leaning against the tree, gave a little giggle. "That is gross, but I'm too drunk to care. Maybe drunk. I've never been drunk, just a bit squiffy one Christmas. No wonder you all like magic." She patted the tree. "My new booze cupboard."

"You'll have to move now, I'm afraid." Abel helped Kelis to get Ferryl/Claris to her feet. "Claris needs a little drinky as well." Jenny shuffled aside as Abel lifted Ferryl/Claris' hand and placed it on the mark in the bark. "Drink up, Ferryl."

There wasn't much outward sign except Ferryl/Claris' breathing steadied, and when she spoke her voice sounded stronger though still rough. "This will take time. The Leech tore her throat, but also holes in her heart and several big blood vessels. It probably meant to keep me busy so I couldn't interfere." Ferryl/Claris turned to glare at the toad. "It worried about the wrong hunter."

"I worried about Zephyr being fast enough. I didn't really see her, just a flicker and bap!" From the replies nobody saw much more.

"Hey Ferryl, can you spare a bit of healing for my lips?" Rob pulled his wadded shirt away from his mouth, letting blood gush from some of the cuts. He quickly put the shirt back to try and staunch them.

"Not heal, but I can do some very crude repairs to stop the bleeding. I can make them scab, so they heal naturally. You will heal a little faster than you used to anyway, because your magic helps now you are aware of it." Ferryl/Claris raised her hand, then looked embarrassed. "No I can't. No connection."

"Zephyr? Connect to Ferryl." The spooky-phone shot out. "Ferryl, can you use this connection?"

"No, or rather yes but it would be too dangerous. I could show Zephyr so she could help but that would mean touching Rob with her wind form. Unfortunately she would have to go partway into his skin, and might find it impossible get back out. She might not want to."

"I can do it. I stopped myself going any further into the Leech." Zephyr's mental voice dropped to a bare whisper. "I don't like it. I don't want to do that. It feels all wrong."

As Ferryl/Claris stared at Abel a slow smile grew, which looked awful on her bruised and bloody face. "Truly your child, not mine. Explain to

174

Rob."

Abel tried, without the child comments. After listening to Zephyr's comments on spooky-phone, Rob went for it. Either that or he'd have to get to a hospital for stitches, urgently because five gashes still gushed blood whenever he moved his shirt away. The actual scabbing took a while, because Zephyr would only do a little at a time. She kept returning to her tattoo to break any connections except to Abel, then flowing out to do more. The sprite told Abel, privately, that she needed to return to remind herself where she belonged and who she was.

While Zephyr worked Ferryl/Claris explained why she couldn't do it herself. Ferryl could heal any body she possessed, because she understood it intimately. She also understood how all human bodies worked, from being in several, but not precisely enough for fast or perfect repairs because they were all different. Magic users could only heal one person properly - themselves.

After that statement even Jenny wanted to know how, as soon as possible. Ferryl suggested they start with grazes, then if the experiments marred the skin the injury could be repaired later. All anyone magical had to do was understand their own bodies precisely enough to grow new tissue, using a variant of the plant growth glyph. Precise, after more explanation, seemed to mean down to cell structure. Kelis and a stunned Jenny suggested medical books as a first step although Jenny agreed she had to learn control, a lot of control, before experimenting. Now Abel understood why Ferryl never healed him. She'd never possessed his body so she never fully understood it.

Rob asked about eyes because Ferryl had given all three of them night sight. Modifying healthy lenses and receptors came under adapting healthy tissue, adjusting rather than growing. That was much easier with parts that weren't quite as alive, such as lenses, teeth and finger nails. Receptors in eyes could be slightly adapted, but Ferryl couldn't repair physically damaged eyes. Jenny promptly wanted night vision, but once Ferryl explained the process she backed off rather than let an amateur play in her eyeballs. Zephyr would have some tuition before practicing on rabbits or mice, and then on something larger before tackling a human.

The talk and slow healing of Rob's lips gave them all a chance to wind down, and Ferryl a chance to carry out more repairs to Claris. Deeper inside the Leech had left even more extensive wounds as it pulled free, though they weren't immediately life-threatening. Staying next to a tree, a ready supply of magic, meant Ferryl could get everything functioning. Finishing the healing properly would take time, but not quite as much magic.

Zephyr ended up with one more task. After further instructions, she cleaned the blood from everyone's clothes, including Rob's sodden shirt, just as Ferryl had when she first met Abel. Afterwards Zephyr looked darker, more visible, and complained it made her feel heavy. She turned into a little whirlwind for a few seconds, leaving a neat pile of black dust once she stopped. Ferryl confessed she'd used Abel's and Cooch's blood-dust to help form the ragged shape she'd taken coming out of the hole.

"Are we all ready?" Abel helped Ferryl/Claris up from where she sat with Jenny against the tree. "We'd better let Stan see Claris and tell him she won't need any more blood. He'll be relieved."

"What about that?" Rob gestured towards the toad. "It'll need some blood, if we really need it alive."

"Zephyr can kill mice or something similar, and the toad can eat them while they're fresh. The Leech is smaller now so it won't need much blood or magic." Abel gestured. "Come on, I want to sit down and have a drink. Will your mum mind Claris visiting, Kelis?"

"No, she's used to your women popping in and out." Kelis giggled, followed by Jenny. "Your face is a picture. Mum won't mind if we say Claris is getting Tavern help for her illness." She turned and knelt in front of the cage, now placed in the small cave. "Remember, blood-sack. If you escape from the cage, you will die screaming and rolling about in terror. If you are good, and help us get the key, I will bring you a little bit of blood and the occasional worm. You will want to be kind to toad, because it might be your host for a long, long time." A glyph sprang up in her raised palm. "Or no time at all, if you annoy me enough."

The toad backed slowly away into a corner. "Come on Kelis, it got the message." Rob reached down to help Jenny to her feet. "Watch out Abel, we're outnumbered now."

"Good, then you won't get any ideas." Jenny took Rob's head very gently in her hands and kissed his swollen and scabbed lips. "There, the hero's reward. You risked that foul thing getting inside you to save Claris, even if you don't like her." With a little shudder Jenny glanced at Ferryl/ Claris. "You won't want that mouth to kiss you, not until it's been well scrubbed." Turning to look at Abel her familiar bright smile came back. "Better yet, if Abel needs taking down a peg you can remind him you got a kiss without me being possessed first."

Between teasing a flustered Rob and mocking a protesting Abel the three women definitely cheered up. They all sobered when Ferryl/Claris tried to walk. Despite stopping the bleeding and gaining control of her limbs she needed Rob and Abel to help. Her magic couldn't keep Claris' damaged organs working as well as overcome the wasting of her muscles. While topping up from a tree again, just before leaving the garden, Ferryl/ Claris pointed out she could eat a Goblin let alone real food. She badly needed solid nourishment to turn into muscle.

Bugsy sniffed them all suspiciously when they arrived at Stan's, but didn't growl at anyone which reassured Stan. Either the dog didn't detect Ferryl inside Claris, or considered her a friend. Maybe she smelled like Zephyr. Once he knew the thing had gone Stan fussed round Ferryl/ Claris, offering her a chair and a cuppa. When Rob came in and Stan got a good look at the scabs, he glanced at the gun cupboard and wanted to know what the hell happened. Rob explained the thing had fought back, but lost. At least Stan didn't push for details, just knowing the whatever had been dealt with seemed enough.

When the five teenagers arrived at Kelis' house, her mum took one look at Rob's mouth and phoned to let his mum know her son was on the way home. His swollen lips and seven huge scabs weren't acceptable, meditation tattoo or not. At least Rob had been practicing his excuse. He claimed to have been showing off to the girls on the little cliff in Castle House gardens, but slipped and kissed the rocks on the way down. Shortly after leaving, Rob texted to say dad was taking him to hospital to get the gashes cleaned and treated. A later text pointed out he wasn't impressed with the tetanus shot.

Kelis' mum reacted much the same as Stan when she saw Ferryl/ Claris, offering her a seat and fussing round her. She didn't question the vague story about recovering from an illness, anyone ill who wanted Tavern help could call any time. Mrs. Ventner spent some time reassuring

Ferryl/Claris that the drawing she'd get on her arm really would help, then stuffed her with sandwiches, soup, ice cream and cake to help get some weight back on.

*   *   *

While they waited for Rob to come back from hospital, the others had a quiet celebration in Bonny's Tavern. Even remembering that Ferryl/Claris still had to sleep in the church didn't break the happy mood. In theory Claris could go home, but Ferryl wasn't leaving Brinsford again. Unfortunately, none of them thought producing an anorexic teenager who'd run away from home and wanted lodgings would work on parents.

Jenny stayed on a bit of a high after all the tree magic, wanting to know if it always felt like that. She'd drawn the glyph on her palm under Ferryl's instruction, but hadn't realised how tired she'd be when Ferryl drained her. Tree magic had come as an absolutely mind-blowing revelation. Abel remembered his first taste, and from the little glance so did Kelis. Jenny teased him about no more hand holding and kisses, then teased Kelis about Laurence. Her mood came as a huge relief to Abel at least.

When Rob came back and joined in Kelis finally admitted to coaching Laurence in pushing magic, or rather meditating with a Tavern mark. He still hadn't floated a leaf, and Kelis had been careful not to say he could, but with Laurence attending every Tavern game possible he wouldn't take long. The local players all practiced the 'meditation' before a game, and many knew the real reason so they'd recognise the signs.

The pair had been texting, and talking on the phone but now Laurence wanted to come to a Bonny's Tavern meeting. When Jenny had finally left, promising to keep in touch but only by phone for now, Rob, Ferryl/Claris and Abel sat looking at Kelis. The two boys had little smiles but nobody said anything until Kelis gave a big sigh. "Yes, Laurence really wants to see me, properly not just at school. He's nice to me and I like him. Get over it."

Abel held up his hands in surrender while Rob managed a magnificent cringe, then spoiled it by laughing. "I didn't say anything."

Kelis' glare turned into a wry smile. "No, but it was the looks. It's just that Abel keeps collecting girlfriends, and sooner or later some poor innocent will fall for your helpless buffoon act. I've got to get over my thing about boys. Laurence seemed about the right height, and he's funny." She sniggered, then blushed a little. "Do you think I can really persuade him to wear stripy tights?"

Abel sat in shock while Rob answered, pointing out she could probably charm the sucker into anything including a tutu. Finally Abel collected his scattered wits enough to get the words out. "Collecting girlfriends?"

Kelis glanced at Ferryl/Claris. "Ferryl is your teacher and protector so she will stay close to you. More than that you will have to hold her hand to get answers so Zephyr can pretend to be Ferryl Shayde. Well, skin to skin contact but hand holding is probably the most socially acceptable option." She smiled sweetly as Ferryl/Claris took Abel's hand.

"She's right, though I never thought of it. Perhaps we should tell everyone I have possessed Claris to save her? Then you won't have to pretend."

"No, you can't!" Abel explained and the other two agreed. Going by the reaction to Leech possession, even when everyone thought it was relatively benevolent, nobody would be happy about Claris being possessed. At least Claris had actually agreed, clearly and upfront, to sleep for a while until Ferryl could find another host so that wasn't a problem this time. The ex-Leech host hadn't even asked them to hurry because she wanted time to let the horror fade. Despite that Abel wasn't going for the boyfriend part this time.

At least during the holidays there could be a gap between breaking up with Jenny and a situation where he needed to hold hands with Ferryl/Claris to speak privately. Abel bid Kelis goodnight, then Ferryl/Claris at the church, then suffered Rob's teasing about girlfriends and Jenny's kiss until he arrived home. Zephyr crowing about bashing the Leech and healing Rob came as a relief.

* * *

Within days Abel's mum called him downstairs to point at her phone. "You broke up with Jenny?"

"Not quite, it was sort of mutual."

"Why?" Abel recognised that tone, the mum-ready-to-defend-her-boy one. He really, really didn't want to talk about girlfriends to his mum, but he'd best calm her down before she went on the warpath.

Abel took the easiest route, at least some of it true. "Mr. Forester and you got it right, we haven't got that much in common. Sneaking a bit of time to be together seemed exciting but then everyone knew. Then we found that outside of the Tavern game and complaining about Seraph we hadn't got much to talk about. That and, well, to be honest Jenny is kinda serious, grown up at times." Abel sighed. "We only got talking because we were both looking for a quiet spot after Seraph picked on us. Maybe that's all it would have been without the accident." Abel hoped he wasn't overdoing it, that his mum didn't think he was upset and hiding it. She'd say something to Jenny or Mr. Forester.

"Are you going to be all right? You've not been sat up there moping like you did about Kelis, have you?" Yup, his mum thought the hussy might have dumped him and he was hiding it.

Abel sighed again, swallowing the little smile at that thought and trying to sound a bit sad. "Kelis was my first girlfriend." He squirmed a bit because he really hadn't got past Kelis, not yet. "Can we not talk about that? Or Jenny? She's staying clear for a bit but we agreed to still be friends." Abel forced a chuckle. "Just as well since we're in business together. Now can we talk about the weather or something?"

"I'd hope you are still friends. After all, according to her your kiss saved her life. All right, I'll drop it." His mum's voice seemed more amused than worried now, so Abel relaxed a bit. "Though you might have mentioned it." She brandished the phone again. "Instead of Jake assuming I knew? I felt a complete fool."

"Mr. Forester?" Abel stared at the phone. "Oh."

"Yes, oh. He wanted to know if there'd be a problem with Jenny attending meetings. She's a shareholder remember, and Jake wants her involved but he doesn't fancy you two looking daggers at each other."

Abel laughed, genuinely this time. "Not likely. I mean it, neither of us is mad at the other. Her dad will want Jenny in the meetings to help her with business studies." Now he'd stopped fending off questions about Jenny, Abel wondered why her dad wanted a meeting. "Does Mr. Forester want a proper meeting? Has he got it all sorted out, the game?"

"No, not even close. He wants to talk about where we go from here and even the highlights are giving me grey hairs. Apparently you need a proper graphic designer for the board and cards, editors for the rule books, all that sort of thing so they can be printed professionally. Then marketing, sales outlets, and probably a zillion other things. Ten thousand quid is more cash than I've ever seen in my life, but now I'm wondering if it's going to be enough." Now his mum looked worried, so Abel gave her a quick hug.

"You've seen the drawings, and the computer-drawn versions of some. Kelis has top-range graphics software on her laptop and Rob and me, well, we borrowed it so a printing firm should be able to use everything we've got. We've even designed a game-board with the lands around the Tavern and a few details here and there. The rest has to be discovered and some can alter with a dice throw. Here be monsters stuff. There's enough to get started, I think." Though now Abel began to wonder. "We all take Graphic Art so it's decent quality. We can even put it on a DVD to sell, then people can print their own. Maybe it can be sold like that on eBay for starters? I'm not sure how we get anyone to actually buy it though."

"I have a strong suspicion Jake is thinking of a little bit more than that. We'll have to be ready to jump in if he gets too carried away." The glare about the next bit didn't have too much heat in it, probably because of the bigger problem. "We'd better get all your computers legal for starters." At least talking about practicalities took the conversation away from not keeping mum up to date on Abel's social life. Though now he had to crowbar Ferryl/Claris in there, somehow. She'd be coming to Tavern meetings, and Kelis' mum would mention her even if Abel didn't.

Abel thought he'd better get it over with. "There's a girl came over a couple of times, Claris from school. She's recovering from an illness." Abel sighed and went into the prepared story. "Actually she missed all the exams. Everyone wondered why. We, Kelis Rob and me, found out, or rather Claris came and told us. She got into drugs and stuff and ended up in a house with some people. Bad ones, she won't say much. She had a moment of sanity or something and got out, and we're helping her get straight. She's scared to death of whoever it was she ended up with and daren't go home yet." Abel paused, but he may as well get it all out in the open. "She's even worried about meeting her mum. She wants me, Kelis and Rob to be there, sort of moral support."

"Are you taking this charitable bit seriously? Where are they meeting?" Mum thought a moment. "Where is she living? There won't be any of her drug friends about, will there?"

"No, just us and her mum in the coffee shop inside the big shopping centre. Nice and public." Abel skipped Claris' current home.

"In that case I'll take you three." The look meant his mum wasn't taking no as an answer. Abel's mind spun. How would they get Claris there? Would one of the other Taverners come and get her if they weren't picking up Abel or his friends? A good few were decidedly lukewarm about Claris because she'd been Seraph's henchwoman. "When are you meeting?"

"Er, when Claris sorts it out, sometime convenient for her mum? Now it'll be when it's convenient for you as well." Because if Abel even looked like he'd tried to wriggle out of it, mum would just dig deeper.

The small break while his mum checked her diary gave Abel time to think, but there wasn't a way out of it. "Unless I'm called in suddenly, these are the days and times I'm free for the next two weeks. I'm at work most days because of staff holidays." Abel took the scribbled list, hoping Claris' mum would be free as well. The next bit threw him again. "If you've got that to sort out in the daytime, we'd better have the meeting with Jake in the evening. Does it matter what date?"

"Er, no." Abel had relaxed too soon. He held up the list. "I'll have a word with Rob and Kelis, and Claris."

"You could just call Claris now." Mum was definitely pushing a bit.

"She keeps her phone turned off, so those people don't keep pestering her. I'll catch her this evening just before she calls her mum." Abel hoped he kept the fibs straight in his head. He'd always tried to be honest, mainly because with his lousy memory and tendency to blush he got caught too easily. Ferryl Shayde had changed the honesty bit right from the start but kept track of the porkies for him, but not now.

Explaining that to Zephyr, and why it might be okay to lie to his mum sometimes but not others, distracted Abel a little but not for long. He really hoped Zephyr's offer to keep track of the porkies wasn't just to make him feel better.

*   *   *

When Abel collected Rob and called round to explain to Kelis, she sat very quietly for a few minutes. "I could get transport for Claris?"

"Your mum? Can she drive?" None of them had ever seen Mrs. Ventner on the lawn mower, let alone driving a car. "Or were you going to try to rope in your aunty again?" Abel stopped guessing as he saw the little smile on Rob's face and the two spots of colour in Kelis' cheeks.

"Mum can't drive but, um, well. Laurence can. Drive I mean. He's even got a car, but his dad won't let him take it to school. He has to pay for petrol out of his allowance. But that's not a problem. Not if, well, not for coming here. To meet me. For the Tavern." Abel started to smile as the normally calm, collected Kelis floundered. "I just thought. Well, you know. He's been asking about coming to pick me up. If I went to Stourton with him, he might pick up Claris as well?" She finally looked up at the two big smiles. "If he will."

"Oh, from the sounds of that I think he's sufficiently well glyphed. You could even leave Claris in town so he could drive you back by the scenic route. She could catch a bus." Rob looked on the edge of laughter.

"No! I couldn't. Well, you know, she hasn't got money. Anyway...." Kelis stopped, taking a breath before glaring at the two of them. "I'm just trying to help!"

"Actually that would work. You could sit and hold his hand, Abel could hold Claris' hand." Rob looked around with a little smile. "Maybe Claris' mum will want her hand held."

"Stop it. There'll be no hand holding." Kelis opened her mouth to argue so Abel took the easiest option. "Well maybe for some people. At least Laurence won't ask awkward questions in front of adults."

"Oh G... curses. Mum!" Kelis looked horrified. "She'll go crackers if Laurence turns up to drag me off in his car. She's never even met him and she's still half-expecting me to be kidnapped by Dad. Even if Laurence doesn't come here, your mum will mention him." She slumped.

Seeing how despondent Kelis looked settled one thing. Abel finally abandoned the kiss test, because Kelis really had moved on. "What if

Claris is in his car when he arrives?" Though he could still tweak her. "You could ask your mum to come as well, as a chaperone?"

Kelis didn't bite. From the sound of it she'd even considered the possibility because Laurence would meet her mum sooner rather than later. He'd already started pushing, gently, to meet up. In the end they decided on a Tavern meeting in Kelis' house, a non-magical one where Kelis' mum could get the third degree out of the way. Kelis warmed to that, because then Laurence could pick Claris up outside Castle House so nobody realised she lived in the church.

Claris' mother, Mrs. Ellsworth, promptly accepted the first opportunity for a meeting. Unfortunately she immediately launched into an attempt to get Claris to come home. She'd try even harder at the meeting, because although Ferryl/Claris could now walk without help she still looked thin and sickly. Building her body back up so she remained healthy without magical help would take time and food. At least the junk food for the goblins came in handy, because Ferryl/Claris stuffed it down and converted it into healthy girl.

*   *   *

As expected, by Rob and Abel at least, Laurence could come to a Tavern meeting with Kelis any time. He stuttered a bit over picking up Claris but Kelis just insisted he had to keep it quiet until there'd been time to explain. When Laurence and Ferryl/Claris drove up Kelis' drive he looked unhappy but resigned, though Kelis' mum greeting Ferryl/Claris reassured him. Most of the visit Laurence spent sat in the lounge talking to Mrs. Ventner, a prolonged, gentle interrogation. Her mum still felt very protective after all the trouble.

The meeting afterwards in Bonny's Tavern didn't take long. Laurence sat with Kelis and she walked him out to his car afterwards though Ferryl/Claris stayed behind, allegedly to catch a bus. She reported intense cross-questioning when Laurence picked her up, about both her condition and what happened. He seemed to buy the drug story, telling Claris she was a fool and should have phoned him for help.

Three days later Kelis waved her mum goodbye as a smiling Laurence held open the door of his second-hand but nippy hot hatch, a red Corsa. It wasn't nippy on the way into town, because Abel's mum led the way.

Once the short, stout woman had more or less flown across the coffee shop to crush her wayward daughter in a bear hug, everyone met Mrs. Ellsworth. She wanted privacy, but conceded defeat after tearful pleas from Ferryl/Claris. Ferryl/Claris swore she'd had a terrible time, she'd been in an awful place, and she insisted on sitting with Abel, Kelis and Rob. That brought the first curious looks from Abel's mum.

The garbled tale about getting away and wanting a place nobody would look for her poured out. Claris had chosen Brinsford because there'd be no druggies, and nobody would expect her to run to these three. She hadn't been sure they'd help, because they hadn't been friends, but she'd hoped the charity bit in their game was real. Now Claris daren't tell anyone where she lived or go home in case the bad people found her.

More tears and clinging to Abel got her through not going to the police in case the criminals wanted revenge. Abel had no idea where Ferryl got some of that, probably some film she'd watched while he slept. He felt sure it only worked due to copious tears, and Ferryl/Claris clinging to him every time going home was mentioned.

Now he could see how badly Mrs. Ellsworth wanted her daughter home, Abel felt guilty because he knew Ferryl/Claris could go right now. Ferryl only refused so she could stay in Brinsford and protect him. Finally Ferryl/Claris suggested the two mothers should talk so her mum could ask embarrassing questions about Abel, Kelis and Rob. A flustered Mrs. Ellsworth hesitated but then agreed, no doubt hoping she could find out why Claris had gone to Brinsford, or where she was living now.

*　　*　　*

The five teenagers went for a wander around the shopping centre, where a definite trend developed. Laurence kept asking what sort of place Rob, Abel or Ferryl/Claris liked to go on days out. They soon realised he wanted someone, anyone, to make up a three or foursome so he could take Kelis out. Laurence worked through a variety of places including amusement parks, concerts and a Shire Horse centre until Abel thought he'd probably settle for a funeral if that's all there was.

Abel didn't volunteer because he couldn't work out if either of them wanted company or not. Kelis had always shied clear of boys, so maybe she'd got cold feet about being alone with Laurence. Eventually Rob looked from one to the other and shook his head, smiling. "Ask, you daft burkes. Do you want me, Claris or Abel? We'll all come if it makes you feel better, and even wander off and leave you alone now and then?" He watched with delight while both Kelis and Laurence floundered over the last bit.

"I can't come along without Abel. I wouldn't want to be on my own." Ferryl/Claris glanced at Rob with a little smile. Abel opened his mouth to point out organising that might be impossible so Rob could chaperone.

Too late, Rob struck first. "Perfect. Abel and Claris because two couples will look better and you won't want to take someone on their own, a gooseberry. If I come I'll have to bring Melanie so I have someone to talk to."

Abel didn't have to look to know Laurence would move heaven and earth to avoid having Rob's kid sister along. He still meant to object until he saw the happy little smile on Kelis' face. Either she found the idea of dragging Abel and Ferryl/Claris around as a couple funny, or just felt happy for any solution, but either way Abel gave in. Laurence promptly launched into a list of places they could go.

Meanwhile Ferryl/Claris had been nudging Abel closer to the shop windows as they passed until she suddenly stopped. Since she still had an arm round him and hung onto his hand, so did Abel and the rest turned, curious. "That is beautiful. The Sprite, nymph. The silver one." Ferryl's mental voice spoke to Abe. "Can we buy it?"

"Crikey, Claris, that's twenty quid." At least Abel could use Zephyr to answer now. "Why do you want it?"

"To pay my way." Ferryl/Claris looked wistful. "My room is so bare. I would like just one beautiful thing in there, just to remind me of home." She sighed. "Something not expensive enough to be tempted to sell it."

"Are you broke? Your mum would give you money." Laurence looked puzzled, because from the meeting Mrs. Ellsworth would mortgage the house if Claris needed it. "Blimey, I'll loan you a few quid if you need it."

"I emptied my bank account, or rather the people I was with did. I gave them the card and PIN number to get my fixes. Now I don't want to ask mum for more because without cash I can't buy the shit, so I can't be hooked again. Worse, those nasty bastards might hear about it. I'd end up back in that house, and, well, it would be worse this time." Ferryl/ Claris shuddered. "Once I've really recovered I can stay clean but right now I'd be tempted." She glanced down, ashamed. "I'm still not really clear." Once again Abel wondered if she'd got all this from a film.

"I'll buy you the fairy." Laurence looked at the array of ornaments and jewellery in the window. "What about that one sat on a toadstool? It's a bit bigger, and her wings are stretched out. She'll look better all on her own."

Despite Abel's mental objections, Ferryl/Claris let Laurence buy her a lovely silver fairy for sixty-three quid. Allegedly it was the least he could do to apologise for not realising she'd got in trouble. By the time they arrived back in the coffee shop Abel thought he knew at least part of the reason Laurence insisted. Kelis now wore a necklace holding another silver fairy, one with tiny diamond chips sparkling on her wings. According to Laurence he "couldn't buy something for one lovely lady without treating the other."

Abel tried hard, but Ferryl wouldn't tell him what she'd got in mind. He had to banish Zephyr because his mum might see spooky-phone, so Abel gave up until he got home. There'd been some real discussion between the mothers, some of it about Ferryl/Claris' second-hand clothes. A big bag of Claris' clothes and her makeup and God only knew what else would be ready tomorrow. Laurence promptly volunteered to collect it all, though Ferryl/Claris insisted it went to Brinsford rather than give up her address.

The goodbye turned into a tearjerker of course. Abel insisted on letting go to step back, allowing Mrs. Ellsworth to hug her daughter and have a few totally private words. Though before Mrs. Ellsworth left Abel also got a big hug and a tearful thank you, as did a startled Kelis and Rob.

Once again Ferryl/Claris insisted she'd get home from Brinsford by herself, but Kelis diverted any questions by walking Laurence to his car to say goodnight. Abel missed it because his mum took him straight home to answer some questions. Despite the third degree Abel felt sure she wasn't satisfied but he couldn't work out why. Was it because Ferryl/ Claris came to him rather than friends or because she wouldn't go home? He steadfastly refused to admit he knew where Ferryl/Claris lived, or give her phone number.

When he finally got to Bonny's Tavern Abel collapsed with a soft drink. "We've got to find someplace for Ferryl to live, somewhere she can take Claris' mum." He took a swig. "Just to stop the third degree. My throat is raw. I'll get more when mum remembers Claris hanging onto my hand."

"It would be better if I could get lodgings in Brinsford. Then I could walk about openly and we could meet up easier. Someone will notice me eventually." Ferryl/Claris smiled at Kelis, with just a bit of wicked in it. "At least we will be out of Brinsford some of the time, with Laurence. I can get to see a bit of the modern world."

"Why is Laurence so keen, Kelis?" Abel laughed at her look. "I meant to cram in so many days out, not to see you."

"He's only got a few weeks to enjoy the holidays, then just before we go back to school he's off to Europe for a fortnight. It's a big family thing. They've got relatives in France and Germany who all meet up at a chalet in the mountains. After that holiday Laurence has to start work so he's making the most of these last few weeks of freedom."

"Blimey, how the other half live." Rob raised his drink in a salute. "Cash in Kelis."

She looked down at the fairy necklace. "It's not like that. I don't want his money. I just wanted to enjoy myself a bit now I'm finally rid of dad, and Laurence is nice. I didn't expect the trips or gifts." Her eyes narrowed. "I wouldn't have got jewellery if someone hadn't been casting greedy eyes over something else."

"Tomorrow. I have some careful glyphs to cast, and can't be sure how well it will work. This might be a way to support myself in this modern world." Ferryl/Claris looked decidedly smug. "If it works, Laurence will get his money back and you will all be working very hard on glyphs."

*　*　*

The following morning, as soon as Abel, Rob and Kelis had all eaten breakfast, they headed for the church. Kelis stopped Rob and Abel before they went indoors. "I know it's short notice, Abel, but Laurence will be over just after ten to bring Claris her clothes." Kelis looked from Abel to the church, where Ferryl/Claris would be eating or sleeping, the best ways to let Ferryl heal her.

"No problem. He doesn't even have to meet Claris, just drop them off. That might be best because he looked a bit curious about why she didn't go back to Stourton with him." Rob shook his head. "We've got to sort that out sooner or later."

"Ah. Well. It's just that Laurence called last night. He wondered if I, we, wanted to go someplace today. I sort of panicked and said how about a zoo. Apparently there's one not too far by car. Near Chapel-en-le Frith? The Chestnut Centre? There's owls and things? Well?" Kelis stopped babbling and waited warily.

"You pulled that out of your head?" Abel couldn't name a nearby zoo and very few anyplace. "Why a zoo?"

"Because it's public and a zoo is the first thing I thought of? I'm a bit wary. He's nearly eighteen and well, my only other boyfriend lived next door and never took me out of the village?" She giggled nervously. "He sounded a bit panicky. I think he looked up zoos while we were talking." Kelis poked Abel with a finger. "Don't you dare wander off."

"Really? You want a gooseberry?"

"This time at least, so no smart comments. Just remember, I can see you when you use a veil." Kelis smirked. "Gooseberries, because Claris will be going as well."

"What! How come? She's supposed to be in Stourton." Abel turned to look at the church. "Ferryl wanted to work on something today."

"Last night so it'll be done. It's just that, well, Rob threatened to bring Melanie." Rob tried to look penitent but the smile kept spoiling it. "Then I thought Laurence might think it's weird, bringing my ex along. If you've got Claris hung on your arm it'll look better." Kelis looked determined.

"And you aren't sure how I'd react if you hinted I got lost for a few minutes." Abel grinned at her wary expression. "Relax, I got the message. Kiss test cancelled, link broken, move on. Though we'll still have to talk fast to cover Claris being here."

* * *

Though once the three of them crammed into Ferryl/Claris' little room it wasn't excuses for Laurence anyone wanted to talk about. Rob got over the initial shock first, reaching out cautiously. "Is that a seeming, or the colour glyph?" He picked up the fairy figurine and hefted it. "It's heavier than I thought."

"Gold is heavy." Ferryl/Claris smirked. "Much heavier than silver, and worth about fifty times as much going by my rough calculations."

"Real gold?" Kelis took the fairy from Rob, inspecting it. "Crikey, why haven't you been making gold bars? Was the glyph for this on your wits?" She passed the ornament to Abel.

"No, Ferryl could always make gold." Abel remembered now, he'd thought the same when Ferryl made a diamond out of rock. "Remember you had to give that big shiny stone back to me for a while, so it didn't turn to dust overnight?"

"You weren't just being silly, it's a real magical gem? I know it's not diamond, because I can see a blurry bit in the middle." Kelis grinned, pretending to swing something from one hand. "I really did consider putting it on a chain, either as bling or to brain Henry with, but it's too big to be anything but glass or plastic."

Abel grinned back. "Wrong, it's a real diamond, but only as long as there's enough magic in that blur to keep it that way. Ferryl can make gold bricks from ordinary ones, but they've got a glyph right inside and if they are melted down, hammered into another shape or run out of magic, ping. Back to a clay brick. I asked, because it seemed a terrific way to make money, but goldsmiths will have a magic detector."

"No they don't, though most of them used to have one when I went in the hole." Ferryl/Claris took the ornament. "The shop this came from hasn't got any magical anything, nor had most of the other shops. If gold sovereigns were still used as money I could make dozens of them. They take longer because of the shaping and stamping, but are worth a lot of money now." She handed the ornament to Kelis. "Sell that as gold. The money will pay for my food and Jenny's petrol money to get it. Better yet, I can rent a proper room in Brinsford."

"If someone will rent you one." Rob looked round the room. "Anything has to be better than this."

"Not really, this is pure luxury for a rich man if you go back far enough back." Ferryl/Claris gestured at the fairy. "Well? We can buy more silver, in ornaments so nobody will melt or reshape them, then sell them as gold at fifty times the price. I can make the ornaments from clay but it takes much longer."

"But what about when the glyph runs down?" Rob took the alleged gold and inspected it. "Someone is going to be really, really pissed off." He turned to Kelis, sniggering. "So your diamond will turn to dust? It's a good job you dumped the cheapskate."

"The diamond will last several normal lifetimes, or forever if you keep putting magic into it now and then. At the time I thought Abel might be trying to attract you, or buy your favours, so I put plenty of his magic in there." Ferryl/Claris continued, oblivious to Kelis' silently mouthed 'buy my favours' or Abel's scarlet face. "I have put a similar amount in here. The purchaser and their heirs will be long dead before it crumbles."

"Good enough for me." Rob seemed convinced. "Make it their great-great grandkids, because you can get plenty of magic from the trees in the garden. Then nobody is being swindled, not really." He shrugged. "They'll still have the silver, and just think it was never real."

"Unless it gets stolen. Then the thief melts it down and gets a lump of silver. I can live with that." Kelis touched her necklace. "Though I'll keep this one as silver. It would be mean to change a gift." She looked at the rest in turn. "It can't really be that easy?"

"We only make gold to get Claris sorted out, to get lodgings and maybe a few quid towards the game development. Then once we get an income, any income, we stop. I know it's one or two hundred years in the future but we're still cheating someone eventually." Abel knew it felt wrong, but the hundred quid or so profit would be the price of a packet of crisps by then. Though it still niggled. "How much will it fetch?"

"Over three thousand pounds, just by weight. I told you, I looked in those windows and worked it out." Ferryl/Claris looked triumphant. "You never asked for riches, Abel Conroy, but now you can have them as well."

"Three..." That stumped Abel.

"So how do you do it? Is it the same as the colour glyph? I could get dad a gold watch for his birthday." Rob looked around the room. "How big a thing can you change? How about a gold desk?"

"The size depends on the supply of magic and concentration, and control of course. It isn't so much a glyph, more a rearranging of the inside of the metal." The three teenagers sat on chairs or the bed as Ferryl/Claris went into teacher mode. Though once they began to realise just what transformation involved, none of them expected to learn it soon. According to Ferryl they had to let magic penetrate the metal just a little, and read the way the parts were arranged. Once they had that memorised, then the students must look into a rock and re-arrange the structure to match that of gold. Shedding parts or taking some from earth or air might be necessary depending on the transformation. A locking glyph kept the result in place.

Kelis got it first. Molecular reconstruction. Ferryl didn't understand that, and none of them were good enough at science to be sure, but it had to be similar. Though Ferryl couldn't make just anything, she'd only memorised the arrangements for gems and valuable metals. Gold for value of course, but also because the weight made it a good store for magic. She had to mean density because lead came a close second though she'd never memorised that. Gems were excellent magic stores, but useless for selling because of the glyph in the centre. According to Ferryl, the staffs that wizards were always shown with had gems and gold just for the magic storage.

Despite the lovely golden fairy now placed on the table between them, the three teenagers were a lot more interested in magical storage. They'd all had to top up halfway through fighting the Troll baby. Now Abel at least wanted a store of magic to carry about, and asked why Ferryl hadn't mentioned it. He finally found out how the wits worked. The knowledge really did work like memory, there if needed, rather than a file Ferryl could browse. She'd started changing silver to gold, and remembered another reason for doing so.

The trees in Castle House garden gave them an almost endless supply of magic, because they had no dryads. Anywhere else dryads guarded their trees so anyone running low on magic had to wait until they absorbed more the usual way, slowly from the air around them. If the three of them could carry free magic around with them, they could get around that restriction.

Discussing storing magic came back to another skill none of them had yet, because sorceresses already had a way to carry extra magic. "So we can't carry spare magic until we can heal ourselves, because the diamonds or gold have to be set into our bones?" Rob looked down at himself and touched his lips. "I can't even heal a scratch. No wonder sorcerers are miserable if they have to keep burning tattoos and embedding stuff inside them."

"Does it have to be inside, Ferryl?" Abel might be the keenest on having a spare magical battery, because Henry had nearly got him.

"In the flesh at least, because you might dislodge anything else in a fight. The pain is no more than burning a ward, and the bone part isn't usually a problem. By the time a sorceress learns to make gems or gold to store magic she has mastered healing herself. Learning to make a gem can take several hundred years of trial and error, because nobody ever teaches anyone else. Healing is more important because that's the only way to live long enough, and also why only sorceresses can do it. Witches never become adept. They are people who activate their magic but can't progress beyond simple glyphs, so the best any can manage is to slow their aging a little. Some of your Taverners will die before ever becoming sorcerers and sorceresses."

"Die? Of old age? But sorceresses don't? So how long does learning the healing take?" Kelis frowned. "Is that why sorcerers look old?"

"They look old if they want to, though many die before learning that." Ferryl/Claris turned to Abel, suddenly serious. "Your bargain was better than you realised at the time. I never thought it through because the cost was not significant, not to gain my freedom and a sanctuary. Sorceresses usually have apprentices, but might only teach them simple glyphs for twenty years. Maybe not even as complicated as the growth glyph. The apprentices will pay for the training by setting or topping up protection hexes, or any other similar minor tasks."

"Is that what Pendragon does, uses Elrond and the rest to power protection hexes for businesses and lawnmowers?" Kelis looked puzzled. "It doesn't seem much of a service."

"Not to you. Remember, they will not have access to tree magic so work like that can be a serious drain on them. Then a sorceress may demand another twenty years servitude for the first hints on healing, or a veil, perhaps a seeming. Age, accident or meeting the wrong opponent can kill the apprentice long before they learn properly."

Her eyes went to Kelis and Rob. "Because you are his friends, and Abel insists, you are also benefitting. Many apprentices never learn how to heal properly before leaving their mistress, and definitely never make gold or gems, or bone wits, until they are free. You have already absorbed ten or fifteen years of lessons, though as yet you have not polished those skills. Though with limitless magic you are getting years of practice in just weeks. What you will learn in ninety years is truly priceless." Ferryl/Claris' face broke into a big smile. "Or a small price to pay for my life."

When Kelis' phone struck up with "I don't want to be Royal" she gave everyone an embarrassed look and ran outside to answer it. The others followed, slowly, but she'd already gone through the lychgate to flag down Laurence's car. Abel looked at his watch. "That old thing about time flying and having fun works. Ten on the dot."

"This should be fun. We were supposed to find a reason for Claris to be here." Rob raised a hand to answer Laurence's wave when he saw the three of them. "Better get there sharpish before Kelis gets inventive. She doesn't fire on all cylinders round Laurence and she's got a strange sense of humour when it comes to you, Abel."

Both seemed to be true when the three of them came out of the churchyard. Kelis turned away from Laurence's car with a bright smile. "I've just had to explain why Claris is already here. I'm sorry Abel, Claris, your secret is out. Though at least you can relax and act natural while we're out together instead of pretending to be just friends." Her smile had a real struggle not to turn into a giggle at least as she started walking towards Abel. Abel turned to Rob and Ferryl/Claris but Rob had turned away. The way his shoulders were shaking he must be strangling hysterical laughter.

Laurence looked past Kelis, definitely not convinced. "Claris? What's going on?" A relieved Abel reached for Claris' hand to tell her to scotch the idea as Kelis' little joke, hesitated because that looked bad, and then Ferryl/Claris had brushed past him and Kelis to the car. She bent down to talk to Laurence, too quietly for Abel to hear.

Kelis took another step to come near enough to whisper. "Sorry, it was the first thing I came up with." She finally giggled, but quietly. "Your

194

face is priceless. Don't worry, Ferryl will put him right then I'll laugh and we'll all tease you a bit."

"Then I'll tell him it's really Rob she's seeing and see how he likes that." Abel glared at Rob, who promptly turned away again and started shaking. "He'll not find that anything like as funny." Even as Kelis giggled again, Ferryl/Claris stood upright, turned and came back towards them with a big smile.

Abel caught the mischief in Ferryl/Claris' smile much too late. "I'm sorry Abel, I've had to tell Laurence it's true." She hugged Abel gently and turned to face a startled Kelis and gobsmacked Rob, slipping an arm round Abel's waist. "It's a relief in a way. Now it won't matter if I forget and put my arm round you while we're out with him and Kelis." Her other hand came over to catch hold of Abel's, making skin contact.

"This works out perfectly. I have to stay close to you, and now it won't seem strange. I can get lodgings in Brinsford for as long as necessary and see you every day. If there are more attacks, I will be here."

Zephyr connected Abel to Claris. "No you can't! I'm nearly two years younger than you and you've left school." Abel took a mental breath. "Laugh, tell him it's a joke. He's never going to believe I've somehow bamboozled Kelis, Jenny and you into going out with me within six months. Look at me I'm a bloo....ming wimp, a geek!" Abel fought not to look horrified about Ferryl/Claris' little surprise, or laugh at Kelis' face now her joke had bitten back. "Is that a good idea, us going out together properly?"

"You've filled out a bit with all that exercise, so not quite a wimp." The mental laughter with that didn't help. "Laurence and all the rest of the boys will be impressed and the girls will be curious." Ferryl/Claris leant on his shoulder, pretending to whisper too quietly to be heard. "Some of the young blades would have a score of women in a year. They were much admired." Out loud she said, "Don't you want to?" Her voice sounded really upset.

Abel stifled a groan as he pretended to smile at whatever she'd supposedly said. "It's just that you are a bit confused right now." He'd thought Ferryl got over her early Elizabethan ideas of morals. "Two hundred years out of date, Ferryl. The blokes will think I'm a slimeball who took advantage while you were drugged and the girls won't go near me, ever. Anyway, you know I won't play that game without the girl agreeing. We sorted that out with Jenny but not with Claris. Now she's fast asleep and doesn't want waking." This mental communication worked a lot faster than speaking. Even so Abel turned to pretend to whisper in her ear to avoid an awkward silence and maybe someone asking questions. Both Kelis and Laurence were poised, waiting.

Ferryl/Claris moved her lips again as if whispering, then kissed his ear. "I made the Leech release Claris' mind several times so I could explain what happened after it left. I mentioned wanting to keep close to you because we had a bargain, and that doing so might involve kissing. She said she'd kiss you, Rob, Kelis and the rest of the school to get that thing out of her."

Abel kept the fixed smile on his face as Kelis' face went from startled to suspicious to worried. Rob had moved from gobsmacked to definitely intrigued, and he'd started to smile. Laurence looked definitely suspicious, so he wasn't convinced at all and Abel wasn't surprised. He probably thought Claris still took something to help her come off the drugs, and Abel had taken advantage. "One kiss isn't permission for you to suddenly make us a couple, especially now the Leech is out. Claris has got enough in her head when she wakes up. She doesn't need me as well. Not only that but Laurence doesn't believe you." He really wished pretending to whisper wasn't confirming what everyone must be thinking.

"I told Claris she might only have to kiss you, but several times. She said she'd snog your brains out as often as necessary to get her life back. Apparently you'll taste a lot better than anything the Leech made her drink." Ferryl/Claris hugged gently and her mental tone took on a hint of mischief. "Maybe I should do that to persuade Laurence, snog your brains out? I think I know what she meant." Her voice sounded determined, and a little bit worried when she spoke loud enough for everyone to hear. "I'm not confused about this, Abel. I thought you liked me now."

"Maybe I'll persuade him." Abel gently removed Claris' arm and headed past Kelis, winking at her. "I think Laurence and I need a few words, just so nobody gets the wrong idea." He bent down to talk to a definitely unhappy Laurence, keeping his voice low. "Because you don't believe a word of that rubbish Kelis and Claris came out with about me and her, do you?"

"No, or not all of it. What really happened with Jenny? Or Kelis because she was the first." Laurence really kept his voice low, so he definitely didn't want Kelis hearing. Luckily she'd gone to have a low, intense conversation of her own with Ferryl/Claris.

"I kissed Kelis at New Year, when the chimes started up. Stone cold sober but we'd been dancing and it was her first kiss, and mine, so very special. By February we both realised it wasn't eternal love. Come on Laurence, look at her, Kelis could be a model in a year or two. I look like a flipping dwarf next to her." Abel grinned, a totally genuine one. "I'd need neck surgery after a month or two."

A little smile touched Laurence's lips. "She really is tall for a girl, as tall as me. I never noticed until after Christmas but suddenly she was there, more or less spitting in Seraph's eye, without a sign of the shy skinny little thing she used to be." The smile died. "So what about Jenny and now Claris?"

Abel ran through his now practiced explanation about Jenny and paused, and Laurence nodded gently. "A few people wondered about the gratitude thing, but it was a bit more. Jenny obviously liked you." A bright smile suddenly lit his face. "Jenny really ripped into Seraph just before school broke up. Personally I give you credit for that, for giving her confidence to do it." His eyes narrowed. "Now what about Claris?"

This time Abel played on what Ferryl/Claris had told her mum. "Now I'm worried if I just refuse to have anything to do with her, she'll crack. She's off all the drugs, but bloody terrified of whoever it was had her. She's latched onto me as some sort of anchor, but thinks it's more." Abel shrugged, trying to radiate innocence or maybe just stupidity. "So I'll put an arm round her, hold her hand, talk to her and act like a couple. Maybe a kiss or two but that's all. Then when she gets her head together she can go back to real life with no harm done."

"So you don't like her? You shouldn't, not the way she used to talk about you."

"I don't hold grudges. Ask Henry. Jenny finished any influence Seraph had, and now she's left so I don't think Claris will be the same. Especially after all this drugs stuff." Abel shrugged again and smiled, a completely natural shy one because the next bit was true. "To be honest I think she's kinda pretty now she's not snarling at me. It won't exactly harm my street cred if she hangs on my arm for a month or so. I might even end up with a real girlfriend, one who doesn't have to nearly die first."

Laurence almost choked over that, trying to stifle the laugh. "Looks aren't everything. Claris isn't really that nice, or wasn't because she seems different now. How bad was it?"

"I don't know, but from the bits she told us I don't want to know the rest." Abel took a breath. "So if we wander about arm in arm, hold hands, maybe kiss now and then, you'll go along with it?"

"Oh yes. If she reverts to bitch mode afterwards, I'll have a lot of fun reminding her about you." Laurence might know Claris well enough to have wanted to help her, but from the gleam in his eye he wasn't above payback sometime. "As long as, you know, you don't lead her on."

"Cross my heart. Now laugh and relax before Kelis thinks I'm competing for you." The other three wouldn't know what the completely natural laughter was about but all three faces relaxed a bit as Abel turned. As he walked past Kelis spooky-phone connected and Zephyr filled them all in.

Kelis turned back to Laurence. "I sort of sprung today on them. Can Claris get changed at my place while Abel tells his mum he's going out for the day with his new girl?" Her big smile from the look on Abel's face after that comment lasted while she helped Rob, Laurence and Claris lug two suitcases and a backpack into Kelis' house. Abel hadn't any sort of smile as he called mum and absolutely and definitely skipped around Claris coming. At least with mum being at work she couldn't give him a real grilling by text. Abel almost chickened out when Ferryl/Claris came back from Kelis' bedroom, made up and wearing her own clothes. She might still be thin enough that her clothes didn't really fit properly, but she looked much too old and pretty to be with him.

Despite a lot of hints from Laurence, Ferryl/Claris insisted on leaving her clothes at Brinsford rather than dropping them off where she lived. Rob quietly promised to get them to the church, then swear blind he'd conned his sister into delivering them to Stourton. Despite Abel's misgivings, when Laurence finally drove out of Brinsford he didn't start any third degree. Instead he started talking about zoos, or rather animal ecosystems and preservation. Laurence had been studying towards a job in estate management because his extended family owned huge tracts of moors and woodland, especially in Scotland, France and Germany.

Chestnut Centre turned out to be Chestnut Centre Otter, Owl and Wildlife Park. It wasn't very exotic as otters and owls, some of them foreign, covered most of the creatures there. Laurence seemed to be in his element, explaining how both species had been threatened by the modern world but were recovering. Abel heard all Laurence's explanations because Kelis made no move to get any privacy, while Ferryl/Claris hung on every word. Zoo meant menagerie back in her day, a private, personal status symbol for the rich not a public display. Capturing otters and birds of prey rather than killing them astounded her.

Abel ended up enjoying his day out even if he missed Rob's jokes. Kelis certainly looked happy while Ferryl/Claris behaved, just hand-holding with arms around each other now and then. Despite protesting, Kelis, Abel and Ferryl/Claris accepted Laurence's offer of lunch when he threatened to make them sit and watch him eat it. Laurence hadn't given anyone an option over tickets. He'd paid over his phone while Ferryl/Claris and Kelis went to get changed and told them afterwards.

Abel agreed to going out again in three days, Ferryl/Claris agreed she could make it, and Laurence finally roared off away from Brinsford with a big smile. A smile mirrored by Kelis, though hers had some relief. Rob teased them, then took them to see Ferryl/Claris' refurbished home. That included what Ferryl/Claris' memory said had been her favourite quilt cover and several pictures from her bedroom. Unfortunately her TV and DVD player wouldn't work without electricity. The heap of toiletries and makeup looked incongruous in the little toilet and washroom.

*   *   *

Someone in Stourton, probably Mrs. Turner, had seen the foursome either set off or arrive back and mentioned Abel's new girl. After another third degree his mum accepted that Abel now had yet another girlfriend, a skinny redhead even older than Jenny. Jenny helped, especially when Claris' name came up at the meetings with her Dad, and even came over on her own to make sure the stories tied up. After all, as she put it privately, she'd been in a similar position even if she'd taken a less traumatic route.

There wasn't a lot of chance for Jenny to say much at the meetings, because her dad had moved into full businessman mode. He'd talked to friends in various branches of business, and thought Bonny's Tavern had enough unique aspects to stand out among the plethora of other offerings. Mr. Forester really pushed the charitable part of the scenario as a way to get free advertising, as well as add a unique perspective to the gameplay. He really fancied the idea of making it true, involving the Tavern in real charity work somehow. Abel promised to get the beta players on working out ways and means.

Meeting with Magic

Involving all the betas meant two meetings. First the magically active Taverners had to gather somewhere they could talk freely, then the whole Tavern could meet in Brinsford. Organising the first one didn't take long because everyone who knew about it wanted to talk about the Leech as soon as possible. When his usual visitors mentioned finding a suitable place, Frederick offered his house and gardens. All the Taverners who had been there agreed the place would be perfect, providing they brought their own food and pop. Frederick couldn't afford to cater for them beyond a few cups of tea.

When Eric, Jenny, Abel, Rob and Ferryl/Claris arrived outside a big, rambling, rundown house in Jenny's dad's pickup, there wasn't any doubt they'd found the right place. Petra, resplendent in her fur catsuit and shorts, wasn't exactly inconspicuous. She looked up the road behind them with real curiosity. "Where's Kelis and Laurence?" She smiled wickedly. "Has he got lost or run out of petrol?"

"No, Kelis has made the ultimate sacrifice. Laurence is going to have a problem when he finds out. She finally agreed to him dragging her home to meet his family, and on her own in the car without a chaperone so he's really chuffed. He doesn't know about this meeting, but can't be too miffy with Kelis. He'd have insisted on coming if he'd known, a bit awkward with everyone else doing magic tricks." Abel chuckled. "Or not actually tricks, which is the problem."

"Not for long. You do know he's playing the Tavern game every night if he can find a meeting or crash a Skype game? I reckon some of them have coached him a bit because he's drawn a Tavern mark on his arm, and Shannon swears his leaf trembled last time." Petra turned to sweep an arm across the house and garden behind her. "How do you like the Stourton Tavern? Frederick nearly bust a gut to volunteer, and as a bonus he'll get the whole house plastered with hexes. Those who are good at them are running classes for the amateurs."

"Hah! We're all amateurs, according to Ferryl." Rob glanced at Abel so he took off his jacket and the cat-woman tattoo version of Zephyr took a bow. "Though other magical apprentices apparently take twenty years to learn some of what we've got, and other glyphs take a hundred years." Rob glanced round. "Worse, some of us won't ever be able to cast advanced glyphs. Anyone really struggling with the plant growth glyph or lesser ones might never get any further, which makes them potential Witches and Warlocks."

"Crap, that won't go down well. We'd better have a meeting with those who are definitely past that stage and work out how to deal with it. Meanwhile, come on in and let Frederick give you the tour." Petra pointed to a big gate in the wall at the side of the house. "There's a big garden through there, with an overgrown orchard. There's dryads but Frederick didn't know. You know what they're like, the miserable gits." As they went through the gate she started pointing at various people wandering about dressed in anything from ordinary clothes up to full Bonny's Tavern character costume. "About half the Taverners have some sort of costume this time. Some of us even wear them to play, if we can get together instead of using Skype. Una's got her sword at last, with a soft steel blade that won't sharpen properly because it's a prop for re-enactments."

Petra chattered on while Abel got his head round the crowd of young people casually levitating with wind, producing flames, creating little bursts of fresh growth on bushes or discussing glyphs. The size of the house came as a shock all on its own. "Hello Frederick. Thanks for letting us use your place. I didn't realise you'd got a mansion."

"Not quite. Big old houses are actually cheap, especially in the wrong part of town, but I didn't realise the running costs when I bought it. My neighbours are mostly nursing homes or they've been converted into cheap bedsits." His frown must be a trip down memory lane. "When my wife finally couldn't stand me jumping at shadows she didn't want the house, just everything else. After that the creatures seemed to get worse and I had a bit of a breakdown. Now I can only get minimum wage jobs so I've been padding out the income by flogging this and that on eBay. You know, buy the right thing from a boot sale, sell it on?"

"You don't seem to be too bad now?" Ferryl had said people like Frederick could go crackers, but Frederick seemed to have managed to get right again.

Frederick looked round with a big smile. "I did mention a bit of a breakdown? In the end it was Dryad Elm who probably saved my sanity, the hallucination who talked back. When he asked for sweets, and ate the one I threw, I finally knew the creatures were real but not all bad. Though my sanity has still been a slippery thing now and then. I'm a lot better after meeting your Taverners." He gestured at the young people all around them, chattering happily. Someone upstairs had started using a vacuum cleaner. "This lot have opened rooms I've not been in for years because of the creatures. Now they're even getting rid of the worst of the dust. I went to the park to escape my house, because most of the things left me alone when I talked to Dryad Elm."

Frederick stopped, his face suddenly sad. "He's not in an Elm because all the Elm trees died of disease. He's still sad about that but seems to be a bit better since I first met him. Maybe he's getting over it." The bearded and still nothing like neat and tidy man turned to the stairs. "Come on. I'm really enjoying this, showing everyone around. I've even got Pictsies and Pixies helping now."

After an extensive tour of the three-storeyed house and the cellar and a look at the gardens Abel found himself in the lounge, a huge front-to-back room which had been cleared of furniture to get everyone in. Following a chant of "Ferryl, Ferryl" he turned for his shoulder to take a bow, then say hi to everyone through spooky-phone. Abel held Ferryl/Claris' hand when the questions started, so he could answer magical questions, but that led to the expected reaction.

"I heard, but seeing is actually believing." Both sixteen-year-old Justin and his younger sister Rachel were scowling at Ferryl/Claris. "I'm surprised you had the nerve to ask Abel for help."

"I didn't. The Leech made me go to Brinsford and make him an offer. Instead of saying yes or no, him, Kelis, Rob and Jenny fooled the damn thing and got it out. I really am sorry about being a bitch in the past." Ferryl/Claris gave them a sad smile. "I got it back in spades, believe me. Then I found out how nice the awful geeks are really, and then how reassuring one in particular is." She put her arm round Abel and kissed him on the cheek. "On the cheek, so don't give me a lecture."

The murmuring from those nearby stopped as Jenny squeezed through to the front, with a good few bracing themselves for fireworks. Instead Jenny came up to the other side of Abel, turned to face the rest and hooked her arm through his. "I can vouch for that. Believe me, I'm the last person to give Claris any sympathy but she really has been in a very bad place. So was I in a different way, and Abel helped me as well so I can see her point."

Abel had to smile, which seemed to amuse Justin. "Proper little white knight, our Abel."

"White wizard." Rachel hadn't been able to keep her mouth shut. "We should call him Gandalf."

"I'm too short for Gandalf. More like a hobbit?" Abel grinned and hugged with both arms. "I've managed to find two preciouses?"

"Ooh, smooth. Actually, Kelis could be an elven princess. She's got that tall, haughty all-knowing look dead right." Warren turned to Rob. "Gimli? You'll need to build some muscle, and shrink, or maybe Abel can go on a body-building course. Though you've got the axe, the magical rounders bat." The room descended into suggestions about which Lord of the Rings characters others could be.

Rachel came back to the start of it. "I still reckon Abel is Gandalf. He keeps rescuing maidens and wanting us to carry out charity work, but he kicks magical ass when necessary. Especially bullies, which is something the whole Tavern should get behind. All he needs is to grow a beard like Frederick's."

"He can't, not yet. Abel is a poor innocent adolescent adrift in a world of magic and wicked women." Una pushed through and looked Ferryl/Claris up and down with a scowl totally at odds with her opening joke. "We've run into a sorcerer, Pendragon, so perhaps he's stumbled over Morgana Le Fay. If so she'd better be careful. Some of the women here have swords, and might be a bit pissed off if she hurts Abel." She tapped the hilt of hers.

"Some don't need swords, just magic. Have you learned yet, Claris?" The rubber ball bouncing up and down above Petra's hand wasn't actually touching her, just being blown and sucked in mid-air. Several others casually levitated this or that or produced flames from their hands.

"Yes, barely. I've learned to float a leaf, sort of." Ferryl/Claris looked suitably chastised. "I wouldn't hurt Abel. I really have changed."

Abel let Zephyr reach out with spooky-phones again, pretending to be Ferryl. "Claris was possessed by the Blood Leech, controlled but able to see, hear and feel everything. That included feeling its tendrils growing into her heart, liver, lungs and brain. It made her drink blood from living human victims. That's enough to change most people." Her tone lightened. "Now if you have all done with Abel's love life we have news about the game, and new glyphs."

Nobody had been able to talk properly about Claris over a phone, just in case a parent caught something. Only a few older Taverners like Eric and Warren had actually been to see her, so the bald facts hit hard. Now Abel, Rob and Jenny answered a series of questions about Claris' appearance and how they'd got the Leech out. The truth worked for once, without mentioning actual possession or keeping the Leech alive. "From the sounds of that, Claris should be holding your hand, not Abel's." Warren watched, delighted, as a flustered Rob tried to find an answer.

"Maybe he's not as forgiving as Abel, or as much as a sucker for Acro dancers." Petra gave Jenny and then Claris pointed looks, before wagging her hips to make her tail wave. "Though if Claris had been wearing fur?"

"He might not want the traditional reward anyway, not while his lips are like that." Several young women and a few lads made a big thing of inspecting Rob's lips and deciding he wouldn't mind the pain if the right girl kissed him.

Rob certainly distracted everyone from Abel and Claris, more so when Jenny sauntered over and put an arm round him. "Too late girls. Now it might have been his bravery, or it might have been magic, but Claris wasn't up to it and I thought someone should say thank you." She puckered her lips at Rob, who really couldn't handle being on the wrong end of this sort of teasing. Despite protesting, he couldn't escape as half a dozen laughing young women took turns to administer a gentle kiss to his swollen lips and ask how it compared.

Abel smiled happily, not just because of the teasing Kelis would give Rob once she knew. Rob really did deserve some recognition. He always insisted he came along as the joker or the brute barbarian, all club and no brains, but he'd always done his part. Before offering himself as Leech bait, Rob's club had driven back the sorceress's wolf shade to let Ferryl deal with it, and stopped the Kalkatrie escaping down its tunnel. Now, once the laughter died down, several newer trainees seemed to have adopted him as their mascot or role model.

*   *   *

Eric and Frederick wanting to know about the Tavern game as a business, and others asking about new glyphs, finally got Rob off the hook.

The first part, the Tavern game actually being involved in real charity work, seemed to be a done deal. After Kelis' comments about charity, back when they first met Frederick and Elrond the apprentice, the idea had spread. Now a good few Taverners were interested in how it would work. Some, like Rachel, had already embraced the whole idea and wanted to get started. She pointed out that as a white wizard had shown them magic, and was their leader, the Tavern had to be a force for good.

Despite Abel's scarlet face, most of those present seemed to accept they needed some sort of real mission beyond learning magic. They were all having fun, but the world wasn't a nice place and magic could be used to improve it a bit. Actually getting involved in charity seemed ridiculously simple. Frederick had already offered his house as a hostel of sorts for those suffering from creatures or anyone needing to get away from a sorcerer. There were seven rooms upstairs that were big enough for bedsits, and other rooms that could be connected to make another six at least. They'd be really popular because the occupants could use the main kitchen and this huge lounge instead of having to live in their room.

Before having his marriage-and-creature-induced breakdown, Frederick had even put en-suites in some bedrooms. Now he agreed to take in a battered wife or two, or someone like that, making the place a charitable refuge. He had one proviso; Frederick needed a few magic users on call in case of trouble. If Pendragon decided to act up, Frederick's very rudimentary magic skills wouldn't hold out for more than a few seconds.

Within minutes Frederick had two magical lodgers, Taverners with jobs who would provide protection, lessons and help with fixing the place in return for a cheap room each. At least one other considered it, as a way to leave home and be free to practice magic while she mastered her glyphs. While the rest moved on to adapting the game and creating new characters, she negotiated with Frederick to rent a room once the place had been cleaned up. Frederick could do with the rent, especially if he had to get the place up to scratch as a refuge. A few quick searches on the internet showed that this charity business might not be as easy as expected, because of all the legalities. Just how hard it would be depended on some serious research on the internet, and what Mr. Forester's lawyer came up with.

*   *   *

The whole charity business was abandoned for now when Justin introduced his cousin Kieran from Hope Valley. The flustered teenager confessed to being overwhelmed and sick with worry, but not now. Seeing most of the thirty-seven local magic users in one spot had changed his entire outlook. They ranged from fourteen to mid-twenties, fifties if they included Frederick, and from fluttering leaves to colour changes and juggling sparks. Learning that the experts had taken a nasty creature from inside a victim got rid of the last of his worries. Now he wanted to know how he could learn more, and what he could do in return.

After serious discussion with several Taverners, Kieran agreed to be the liaison in the Hope Valley, to visit anyone local to him who emailed Ferryl Shayde. He could get to the nearest big towns by bus or train in an emergency, to deliver hexes and calm someone down until the Tavern could organise a real visit. According to Kieran at least one of his own friends might be emailing very soon. She seemed determined to float her leaf even if that wasn't meant to be possible.

The other Taverner from out of town had come from further afield. Luckily she had floated her leaf in the holidays so she'd been able to come and visit relatives for training. Since those relatives had been the ones who told her about the Tavern game, that only seemed fair. Now she demonstrated how her leaf leapt and fluttered, listened to the experts, and watched the adepts make various objects dance or burn on command.

At least the first rush of new magic users had eased off, now that nobody passed on hints about drawing a Tavern mark on skin and stroking it while meditating. There would still be occasional breakthroughs because some seemed almost there before they started, the sort who saw shadows move. Shawn had brought another new member, one who had never played Bonny's Tavern or fluttered a leaf. "I'd like to introduce Effy. Epiphany for her sins but if you call her that, duck." The slim, studious-looking young woman raised a hand in greeting. "I noticed her at work, flinching from creatures so I knew she could see them. I introduced her to the Tavern hexes so she could clear her workspace. Effy's got news about how the sorcerers make their money."

Everyone's interest sharpened. They'd been told the sorcerers and sorceresses were all in big cities where they could earn more money with their talents. Despite that Pendragon claimed to have valuable contracts in Stourton, which was only a small market town. The Taverners had been keeping an eye open but couldn't see many signs of magical protection or apprentices, except around churches which wouldn't be paying Pendragon. The few very expensive blocks of flats or houses that were avoided by creatures, and protecting the units on the industrial park, couldn't be much of an income. Vicar Creepio Mysterio and Pendragon weren't particularly chatty so any extra news would help.

"Hi everyone. I'm still a bit nervous about all the magic, but once I'd got this," Effy touched the Tavern hex on a leather string around her neck, "it answered lots of questions. I've always seen creatures but mostly hints and shadows. I thought they were ghosts, spirits of the dead, so it seemed odd when I found a place at work without any. It's where the lawnmowers are finished prior to being shipped out."

"Lawnmowers?" Shannon looked puzzled, as did others.

"The place we work at puts various bits of gardening gear together, a production line. The thing is, that logo goes on at the very end." Shawn indicated Effy.

"I only noticed because I like to eat my sandwiches by the doors to the warehouse, the clear place?" Everyone nodded, some magical creatures were attracted to food. "There's a man comes to fit the logos, just that, which seemed odd. The thing is, the creatures leave him alone. Not only that but when I showed Shawn he says they have magic in them, the logos. He says I'll be able to tell when I can float a leaf. There'll be a very faint red glow?"

Or a bright red glow if Abel, Rob or Kelis looked, but they'd had their eyes adapted by Ferryl. "True, and you'll be able to see the creatures better as well." Abel turned to Shawn. "Do you know who the man is?"

"No but he's not the one from Elmwood Park, Elrond. I'm on the production line but I asked a few of the office types, casually, about strangers working on the stock. He also comes in to fit the logos on a few other items we put together, top of the range stuff. Other parts arrive with the logo fitted, but those don't have magic in them." Abel nodded, he'd already worked out only expensive brands paid to have their products protected from gremlins. "He has to be a warlock or possibly a sorcerer and comes from Sheffield twice a month." Shawn hesitated. "I'd approach him, but I want backup first. That sorceress who attacked you three worries me."

"Would something like that provide a decent income?" Shannon looked puzzled. "It seems really inefficient as well, someone travelling around like that."

"Maybe it's tradition, from when they came by horseback to visit village craftsmen." The young man with a big grin suddenly sobered. "Actually that might be true. Pendragon does sound like a traditional sort of person."

"Sheffield is thirty miles away from Stourton, a hell of a trip to stick a label on. It must pay enough to be worthwhile. Maybe he visits several places, makes a day of it?" Abel asked Ferryl her opinion via spooky-phone.

She answered aloud. "He has to be a sorcerer, or maybe an apprentice." Ferryl/Claris noticed the curious looks, realising as a newcomer she shouldn't be so sure. "I'm going by what I've been told. Abel has explained some of this while I've been recuperating." She preened just a little. "He gave me some tuition which is why I've managed to flutter a leaf so quickly." A big smile lit her face. "I'm a real believer now, and want to be able to fry the next slimy little blood-bag." The suspicion turned to enthusiastic agreement on that part.

"Don't tell Kieran that. He'll be after some private lessons from Robin D'Ritche or Petra the cat-sorceress now he's met them." Eric, the nineteen-year-old introduced to the game and magic by his younger brother, didn't let teasing side-track him for long. "I agree that Shawn shouldn't brace him alone, or maybe not at all."

"I suggest we watch him, when someone has time, and maybe follow him to see if Pendragon has an office in town. It would be handy if we want to talk to a sorcerer in a hurry sometime. He's not that nice, but in an emergency he's the only one we know." Shannon looked around the room. "Better yet, if he gives us trouble, we can find him to return the favour. There's enough of us in the holidays to switch the watchers around so he doesn't notice, though we'll have to be careful."

When asked, Ferryl couldn't provide any sort of magical tracker glyph, which left hiding as the best idea. "Just remember, he'll be able to see creatures avoiding you. Stay behind other people if possible."

"Back to the lawnmowers. Why do some items have magic added?" Shannon looked over at Abel. "You know why, don't you? You nodded when Shawn said some were delivered without." Abel realised it just hadn't come up before. He explained about logos on expensive items having magic, so they deterred gremlins and ran better, but this time there were questions. Experimentation in Frederick's house soon showed that although a few cheaper logos accepted magic, others simply wouldn't so they'd never been designed as hexes. All the Taverners decided to test every logo they came across and make a list of the ones they could just active. The rest would still need drawn Tavern hexes to protect them.

"But that's just testing old hexes. Today we've brought news of a new glyph." Kelis beamed back at all the excited smiles. "None of us have enough control to use it, but we can start learning what we'll need when we get to that stage."

*   *   *

The announcement that the new glyph would help them heal themselves took everyone's mind off other sorcerers and really set the place buzzing. They weren't told it could prolong life but Abel had been adamant when discussing it with Ferryl. If healing took a long time to learn, everyone should start as soon as possible. Kelis, Rob, and Abel explained that trainees would only be taught the glyph once they could create a seeming, a bandage that looked like skin to hide tattoos. By then each of them would have made mistakes and wrecked the cloth, a graphic warning of what might happen to flesh. For now all three stressed that every trainee should study medical books while getting to that level, to help them later. The news that being alive to magic helped everyone to heal anyway took away some of the disappointment at the delay.

Everyone who thought they were good enough at casting glyphs came forward to be tested. Several of those who hadn't bothered too much with the disguise glyph, because showing their tattoo didn't matter, complained a little. Not too much, if they were adept enough then some serious practice would rectify that and the prize provided plenty of incentive. Only eight could cast a seeming on a bandage so it looked enough like their unblemished skin to satisfy Ferryl. Those were taken outside where nobody could overhear. Though before anyone learned, Zephyr connected and passed on Ferryl's lecture about starting with grazes because she couldn't heal them if they made a mistake.

After the healing lesson Abel looked around the small group. "Learning that will take lots of practice, years of it so it's not much use right now. You'll learn a second new glyph today, to practice when healing is boring you silly. This one is the next stage after air and fire and only you eight get to know yet."

"Earth?" Petra looked down at the ground and smirked. "You're going to make the earth move?"

"Water. It shouldn't take long to perfect and then yes, you'll get the other element." Abel grinned because he'd had a real argument with Ferryl about the next bit. "You'll also be learning the beginnings of the fourth while you practice water, but you don't get the glyph to make it work. To earn that you have to control your own personal waterspout and also make a small cloud and produce rain, both without heat or wind." Abel pointed at his shoulder. "Ferryl will decide when you are ready. Water is boring practice in a way, similar to wind, so we thought you'd want an incentive."

Rob shook his head sadly. "I've scraped a pass, just. Kelis has aced it of course which means it's a pity she's not here. Abel will demonstrate to spare my blushes." Several Taverners smiled as he added his usual rider. "Though I reckon Abel hasn't actually learned any glyphs. Ferryl does it all for him."

Zephyr connected to them all. "Not likely. I've no intention of riding about in an amateur, though I sometimes wonder if Kelis might have been a better choice. Now, if Rob has the water, Abel will demonstrate."

Rob drew the basic water glyph and variations in the dust, and each student carefully copied them into little notebooks but with tiny breaks. When Abel actually used the glyphs on a dish of water to produce a waterspout, then created a tiny raincloud, everyone looked a lot more interested. Several made the leap to using steam or ice and wind in combinations without any prompting. A couple thought it could be handy in really hot, dry weather, a cloud of their own cool, moist air, or to make a sudden shower avoid them. After everyone had tried to make a dish of water react, eyes turned back to Abel.

"Right, I can practice that at home until my fingers go wrinkly from the wet." Una's eyes narrowed. "Now what did you mean by starting on an earth glyph, something to control the earth?"

"Just a little bit of it." Abel glanced at Rob. This would be training towards making gold from bricks, a first baby step, but he wouldn't tell anyone that part for a long time. "I'll make a little bit of soft earth move, as Petra put it, but as a piece of rock."

"Transformation? Is that possible?" Even as Warren asked, several people suddenly got a gleam in their eye.

"No, not transformation. Sorry to get your hopes up. You'll see in a moment. Right, we want someone good with wind, and someone who prefers fire. The rest of you use glyphs to remove earth from there among the trees and make three small heaps on this flagstone." Abel waited as the Taverners discussed who might be best at what. Soon the three heaps sat on the stone, waiting.

"I'm the wind witch, or I am since Kelis isn't here." Petra looked at the nearest heap. "What shall I do with that?"

"Pick it up and crush it as hard as you can with wind, just wind, into a tight ball." Abel pointed to the second. "Warren, you pick that up with wind but then burn it, try to bake it into a really small hard ball."

"Warning, a watcher has arrived. It flew past a boundary post, so it has better protection." Zephyr connected to Ferryl/Claris without being asked and her eyes sharpened.

"Wait a moment, we need a better place." "Where is it?" Abel asked both Zephyr and Ferryl, but only Zephyr answered.

"The hawthorn by the garden wall, beyond Una's left shoulder. It will be ready for me this time, so I need to be closer. Unless you want a kill?"

"I can't see, not without turning which might warn it." Ferryl sounded frustrated at the next part. "Even then, I can only use glyphs."

Abel pointed at the three heaps first and then halfway along the path, speaking aloud. "Petra, Una, Warren, please move the earth over here where we can't be seen from the house. We don't want the beginners trying this." "Zephyr, when you are sure, capture it alive. Get close enough to be sure it doesn't die. I want Pendragon to understand how vulnerable those birds are."

As the small group moved several chattered about what Abel might be going to demonstrate, while Abel made no attempt to hurry them. He didn't even glance at the bush, nor did Rob who had now been warned. Abel felt Zephyr's interest sharpen, and then she went! The rest stopped, exclaiming as Zephyr came back a little slower but carrying something. Not for the first time Abel reflected that Zephyr on the link acted like a big frog's tongue. Zoom, splat, and back came the target.

"Aw, why did you do that Ferryl? It's only a bird." Petra looked closer at the sparrow. "It's still alive!" Several others asked Ferryl to let it go, worried the bird might die of fright.

"Not just a bird I reckon." Shawn scowled around in general. "That's a spy, isn't it, like the one in the park? Where's the sorcerer or that snotty apprentice?"

"A long way away from a crowd like us." Eric sneered. "He wouldn't want to get himself snared the same way."

"What do we do with it? It looks so helpless." Ferryl/Claris put out a hand to touch the sparrow for a moment. It blinked.

"I'm not sure." Abel wanted the sorcerer to stop spying but wasn't sure how to persuade him. He couldn't break a link like Creepio did. "I'd rather not kill it."

"Saw it! A link like the last one. I can only see it when the sorcerer or the bird use it." Zephyr sounded triumphant.

Ferryl's 'voice' sounded thoughtful. "Yes, and this time I can inspect it properly because he won't see me as a threat. I'm a newcomer so a complete amateur. Talk to the sorcerer through the bird, Abel, but don't try to get near or touch. It will have passed information about being captured, and he will want to listen to whatever you say."

Abel looked straight into the sparrow's eye as Zephyr held it suspended in a ball of rippling air. "Pendragon I assume, unless you gave Elrond another pet. We talked about this, about being left alone. You stay clear of us, we don't poach." The bird blinked again, curiously unafraid or rigidly controlled by the link.

"Yes! Again!" Zephyr beat Ferryl to it, just.

"Talk again, Abel. I want to understand the link, so we can either follow or break it." Aloud Ferryl/Claris spoke to the sparrow, putting a finger through the rippling air to gently stroke the bird again. "It's all right little birdy. Nobody wants to hurt you."

"She's right, Pendragon. We don't want to hurt your watchers so I'm going to send this one back alive. Strengthening them against the barrier won't work again, because I will set alarms. The next one will be caught and set free." Abel paused for effect. "Or did you think the one by Brinsford just wandered off?" He hoped Creepio really had freed it.

"Keep going."

"It didn't die. It's flying around the countryside being a bird again. Though it is a real pain breaking the links without killing them, and uses up magic, so I'll be annoyed if another one turns up." Abel gestured behind him to the house. "You've seen how many of us there are. I'll send those people out across Stourton and the countryside nearby, and they'll wipe out all your watchers. Then they'll do it again, and again." Abel paused again.

"Got it. It will take time to work out how to manipulate the link, but I understand the flows now. Release or kill the bird."

"I have been reading the flows as well. I can help. Shall I kill it?"

Abel shook his head, he couldn't kill a slave though Zephyr would without a thought. "Remember Pendragon, every time you make another one to send you will have wasted time and magic. Let it go, hunter. If it comes near again, kill it." The bird, suddenly released, flapped madly and then darted away over the wall. Abel raised his hand against the avalanche of questions. Eventually everyone understood, he didn't want to kill the bird so he'd bluffed. The sorcerer had no idea a sorceress lived in Abel's tattoo, only that she was a hunter and could detect his spies. "Well spotted Zephyr. It's a good job you saw it."

"I am guard as well as hunter. I always watch over you. The wind never sleeps." That sounded a bit creepy, but very reassuring.

"Now we haven't got a watcher, will Petra and Warren do their thing with that earth please?" All the speculation stopped as two heaps of earth levitated. One became a ball, uneven but then smoother and smaller before Petra lowered it gently. The other glowed with heat before contracting.

"Best I can do."

"And me." Warren's blackened ball still smoked as it settled.

"First off, I'm sorry about this but it's a part of the lesson. Rob, stomp on them please." Rob stamped twice and both balls were crushed. "Those were hard enough to hurt if they hit you, but a long way from a rock. Here's the trick. Rock is earth with the spaces removed." A wind glyph collected the last heap and held it above Abel's hand. The earth shifted, rippling a little in the air as Abel tried to do what Ferryl told him, move the pieces about until there were no softer materials. He also had to remove the gaps in the remainder until the whole lot packed together as a solid.

The little bits seemed to wriggle in his magical grip as he tried to read them, control them, and tease out the not-dirt bits. He separated some bits and closed the gaps, maybe, then everything slid out of place again. "I see it! I know how! You use magic differently to me. Can I help, please?" Abel wasn't getting near enough success for the original scheme to work so Zephyr's voice came as a big relief. Performing in public had ruined his concentration.

"Go on. Should I let go?"

"No, keep trying. It is right, but not controlled enough because you are not reading the differences properly. If you let me I can do that and alter your flows, just a little. Your glyphs and magic are stronger than mine, surer. You understand it better, what the dirt should be, but I can see what it is now." As Zephyr spoke Abel could feel her, a sort of tickling in his palm where the magic flowed. A twisting followed and a tweaking that he could almost follow, then he lost track. Abel stuck to doing what he knew, leaving the rest to Zephyr, and the earth began to contract faster.

Suddenly, with a last tiny puff of dust, a rough stone hovered over Abel's hand! He quickly formed the locking glyph and fed it magic.

Ferryl/Claris squeezed his hand. "How did you do that?" Abel understood the surprise. He'd planned on making a solid shape, the best he could though still as fragile as those crushed under Rob's heel. When he gave it to Ferryl/Claris to pass round she'd finish the job, unseen in her hand.

While Zephyr explained Abel passed Ferryl/Claris the stone, definitely a stone. She held it between thumb and forefinger in clear sight and passed it to Una. "I think Abel wants it stomped, but it feels like a rock to me so be careful."

Una stamped, gently then a little harder. Several others tried, their smiles growing as even when the stone split in half the material didn't crumble. Eric's had a definite edge of excitement. "All the space between? Do you mean down to the atoms?" His eyes narrowed. "How long did it take you to learn that?"

"I haven't." Abel laughed. "I got started then Ferryl finished it." The tattoo on his arm took a bow as the audience applauded. Several people had a closer look at the small stone. "This is the first stage in learning to manipulate solids." Abel explained about recognising the individual components and removing the air or softer materials, but without mentioning altering anything. Everyone seemed really excited about working down to atomic level, maybe atomic because Abel couldn't confirm that. As he pointed out, he wasn't actually sure and Ferryl didn't know what atoms were. He finished with a final warning. "Remember, not a word to beginners. You don't want them turning something or even someone to dust because it went the wrong way."

"The crumble-wall glyph. Handy if a door won't open." Eric grinned, he'd been the one asked about getting restraints. "Or handcuffs."

"Dryad! Just the eyes." Ferryl/Claris opened her mouth to say more but just pointed at a nearby tree. "It opened its eyes to see. I was about to order it to come out, but that might raise a few eyebrows."

"Zephyr, be ready." Abel pointed at the tree. "Dryad, you are in Frederick's garden, so it would be polite to talk." He waited patiently for a while. "There are enough magic-users here to insist." Something creaked.

"An attack would be hot and fatal for your tree."

"We were here before the human." Only two eyes and a rent appeared, though Abel wasn't sure if it spoke through the rent or used it for effect.

"But not before humans, not in an orchard. He has not disturbed your trees."

"He dare not." Abel never spoke though he saw glyphs forming in several hands. "You are right, too many magic-users now. But why must we leave?"

"Who said that? But if you stay, you should take care of him. Another owner of the house might prefer a lawn here." Abel looked around the old, gnarled fruit trees. "As it happens, he likes dryads. He didn't know about you but he talks to the one in Elmwood Park."

"The place of dead trees? The last dryad still endures?"

"Yes and has honey sometimes." Abel heard Rob snigger because of how dryads usually reacted to honey. Sure enough…

"You have honey for answers?"

"Maybe honey for a little vigilance. You saw the watcher, the bird?" Abel gestured to where it had been, in the bush.

"They come and go."

"Not any more. That or I find more guards and they get the sweet rewards."

The dryad wasn't buying it. "No. We will tell the human if there are more, but we will not join wars between magic users. Dryads always die, or their trees do." Several nearby trees rustled agreement, so other dryads were listening.

Unfortunately Abel felt sure the dryad told the truth. Sorcerers like Pendragon would burn an inconvenient tree if the dryad became a nuisance, and not lose a minute's sleep. "Accepted. There may be occasional treats if you speak to him, or deal with magical creatures that intrude. I will find another way to deal with watchers."

Ferryl/Claris had one. "Burn one tree. The rest will obey." Though aloud she looked overwhelmed. "A real dryad, right here in Frederick's back garden. Now will you take me to see the willow ones?" Abel ignored the smirks because all those present had met those three.

"I will when we get back, and you can help me organise some guards." By then the group were back at the house and surrounded by Taverners wanting to know what had happened, what had Ferryl been teaching? Though before he finally left Abel had a long talk to Frederick about the local area, and if he wanted more lodgers.

*　　*　　*

Abel and Rob weren't going to mention the meeting to Kelis when she arrived back with Laurence, because he shouldn't know. It turned out Laurence already knew and seemed definitely annoyed, but also a little worried. "You could have told me about a Tavern meeting. Kelis could have come home another day." He looked at her and smiled. "Though I really am pleased to get her to meet my parents. They've been fraying my ears because Kelis' mother isn't in their usual circle of friends." His smile grew just a little bit, but seemed more nervous. "Has the reason anything to do with what Kelis told me when, er, on the way back?"

Before Rob could say a word, Kelis dived in. "We stopped for some meditation, to practice leaf floating, because I was a bag of nerves after the visit." She glowered at Rob's snigger. "Laurence mentioned he'd got this funny sensation down his arm, and asked if that should happen. I fluttered my leaf. After all, the others were told before they actually did that, so they weren't scared witless." She looked defiant now because there'd been a discussion before each revelation.

The expression on Laurence's face caught Abel's eye. He looked decidedly warier now. "What did Kelis say, Laurence?"

"That the funny feeling meant I'd nearly fluttered the leaf so I had to talk to you. That you'd explain about Ferryl Shayde. I thought." He looked at Kelis, hesitating. "Well, it's just, Kelis gets nervous when we're alone."

"I'm getting better with practice?" Kelis realised what she'd said and tried frantically to find a way out.

Laurence ploughed on, rescuing her from Rob and her own big mouth. "I thought Kelis blew on the leaf as an excuse to head home, because we'd been sat there meditating for a while. Now she just said she'd fluttered her leaf and you two never batted an eyelid. On the way back Kelis said if

I'd done that a couple of days ago I could have come to the meeting, and explained which one. It's real, isn't it?" He looked at Rob's smiling face. "Unless it's a really complicated setup?"

"No setup Laurence. In a day or week your leaf will flutter up off your palm and you'll blame a draught or a sigh. Then it will do it again and you'll email Ferryl Shayde, still thinking she's a joke, a game character. After that but before you see too many magical creatures, you'll meet her, or her voice anyway." Rob laughed, because he could show Laurence a magical creature right now. "Kelis, do you want to take Laurence to collect Claris from outside the church? He could admire the gargoyles."

Abel watched the shock, then understanding, then the humour as Kelis took that in before asking, "Will that speed it up?"

"I think so. Then you won't have to find excuses for getting him to park up in quiet places. Unless you like the practice." Rob burst out laughing at the spluttered denials, soon joined by Abel and eventually Kelis and Laurence. Once Kelis and Laurence left, with Laurence asking how come Claris would be outside the church, Abel sent Zephyr to pass a warning. Ferry/Claris would be waiting, and would know exactly what had been said. It would be a big relief in a way for Laurence to know about magic, even if he didn't need to know everything just yet.

Laurence didn't leave until after dark, though he still didn't really know what happened at the big Taverner meeting. He'd not even pushed, being completely floored by seeing the Goblins. According to him, and Kelis, his home had plenty of gargoyles and stone statues, but Kelis didn't think any were alive. Unfortunately even her enhanced eyes didn't have proper magical sight like Zephyr, and she couldn't go round tapping them all with a warm glyph to be sure. Now Laurence wanted a way to find out, and asked if he could adopt some from the church if necessary. He left with a fistful of hexes and a warning he'd want a way to put them near food once his sight cleared.

Once he'd left Ferryl/Claris showed them another missed message on her phone, from a withheld number. She promised to start digging into Claris' memories of the Leech, even if she wasn't keen, to see if Claris had seen anything about this key. If not they may as well finish off the Leech, because it probably wouldn't tell them now even if it could communicate.

Kelis wanted to know what really happened at the Taverner meeting, keeping strictly to that when Rob asked about leaf practice and how long the journey home had taken. Though after hearing all she needed to, Kelis did talk about where Laurence lived. Not a stately home, the sort with safari parks and guided tours, but possibly hoping to grow into one. It had the big lawns and tree-lined driveway and paths, and the big steps and ornate stonework round doors and windows, but only eight of the fifteen bedrooms were fit to sleep in. Laurence's words apparently, which had them all laughing.

On the way home Rob wanted Abel to help him smuggle a Goblin into the boot of Laurence's car. They decided the Goblin would start asking for food much too soon, probably before Laurence got out of Brinsford.

*   *   *

Within days, on the way to a theme park, Laurence told them he'd moved his leaf. He'd even done so twice to be sure. After a test to confirm it the day became a bit of a celebration, with Kelis definitely unwinding. With a smirk to Abel and Ferryl/Claris she told them they wouldn't want to be in the same car on any tunnel rides, not now she knew Laurence would be magically protected. Maybe, but Abel whispered to Ferryl/Claris that he definitely looked to have been glyphed after the first one. Since they were left to their own devices a bit more Abel found out Ferryl liked bareknuckle rides, the faster and scarier the better. Abel wasn't a fan, but at least he figured he could soften any impact with wind glyphs.

Laurence didn't want to be rid of the other couple when he stopped on the way home. He'd started to see creatures and would like lots of tuition, as soon as possible please. Considering the size of his home, Laurence wanted to start banishing them or preferably for Abel and Rob to visit. The bottom line turned out to be Laurence bricking it about what might be lurking in the old, empty rooms on the upper floors and attic. "If we can clear them the Tavern can raid the storage for anything that will make a costume. Some of it has been in the attic for donkey's years so mother and father won't object."

"A real Spenz F'Lorinze?" Kelis giggled, then glanced at Abel. "Sorry, Laurence didn't mention this and then the thought of him in tights?" She giggled again.

"Not quite." Laurence smiled at her. "Though if it helps to persuade you I can get a real rapier, a big feather and the frilly shirt, and the rest must be for hire?" His smile suddenly grew. "There's about twenty little rooms in the attic that were for servants in the bad old days. When we were younger we used to drag out bits of curtain for cloaks and old helmets and clothes. Dad barred us from up there for a year when he caught my big brother chasing me with a real sword."

"So if you were disowned you'd have a sword and helmet at least." Abel had a little smile but wasn't convinced yet. Kelis seemed torn, worried about how long it would take the three of them even if she knew Ferryl/Claris would make it four. Eventually Abel agreed to coming over with Rob and Claris just to look. "Though won't your parents think it strange if you don't invite your usual friends?"

"Seraph? I sometimes wonder why I used to invite her so often, because she's worse than Claris. Sorry Claris, than you were." Laurence looked a bit puzzled. "Mother calls her the blue-bloodsucker, throwing money about and trying to latch onto connections to nobility. I used to think of inviting others, but somehow I always ended up with Seraph and her friends." A smile flickered over his face. "I think Kelis came as a real relief for my parents."

"Yes, she would. I was a real bitch then but I promise to be nicer this time." Ferryl/Claris looked suitably remorseful.

"Will they mind us wandering about poking in corners?" Abel glanced at Ferryl/Claris. They'd not want parental supervision for drawing or fixing hexes.

"We'll wander about the grounds first and look at statues, then it'll just be me showing the place off." Laurence shrugged uncomfortably. "I don't usually, but they'll be interested in me making new friends. Mother nags sometimes."

Kelis wiggled her fingers. "I hope nobody comes over all posh and uppity." Abel heard the bite in that, and Laurence must have. He promised his parents weren't like that, and the staff weren't at all posh.

*   *   *

While Laurence worked on magical protection for his home, Frederick sent more information about the area around his house. With two resident magic users, a score of magical visitors and one enthusiastic beginner, Effy, to help him, Frederick checked for any magical protection or large magical creatures nearby. The dryads had spoken to him, and had no problem dealing with purely magical trespassers. Nothing like a Hoplin or even a Skurrit would be venturing into Frederick's garden, not after he scattered the first bag of boiled sweets among the trees. Better yet, many of the big old houses on the street had old trees in their huge back gardens, so they also had dryads who might be bribed into being watchers.

Armed with the information Abel, Kelis, Ferryl/Claris and Rob visited the churchyard to talk to the Goblins. As usual the gargoyles had moved about and changed shape, though the ones in plain view from the street always looked the same. Abel chose a dragonish one perched on a sarcophagus. "We'd like to talk to a few of you at the same time, a serious talk."

"More bribery? More cake and pizza?" A long green tongue dropped from the stone mouth to slurp noisily. "Another little stinky?"

"Are you always hungry because you are a Goblin, or because there isn't enough food in Brinsford?" Kelis turned to the other three. "It just occurred to me it could be real hunger."

Even Ferryl/Claris looked curious, so she didn't know. "We are not as hungry, not since you drove out the competition." The green eyes looked up at the church, and the small crowd of mainly stone spectators.

Rob eyed them as well. "What Kelis means is are there too many of you for the food supply in Brinsford?"

"Possibly, but what can we do? Even though we are strong enough to pass through your boundary to hunt outside, lone goblins would soon be caught by Skurrit packs or larger hunters. A big pack would be safe, but cannot hide out there. Gargoyles do not belong in fields."

"What about moving into a big town? There would be bins to raid." Abel held the Goblin's eye. "With care of course, without leaving litter."

Instead of looking keen, the Goblin looked uncertain. "That would split the meld, those who have grown together. We never do that in the stories, our history. Each meld just keeps growing." The stone spectators now had green Goblin heads or had turned completely into Goblins, none of them looking keen.

"But how did that work? Why didn't you end up overrunning the area?"

"They did. I told you about fires when goblins slept near hearths, and them being hunted down." Ferryl/Claris looked thoughtful. "There were always more, like rats. Actually they kept the rats down. Some sorcerers believe a huge Goblin infestation spreading from northern England stopped the Black Death by eating all the rats. When such infestations grew too big, a Lord or sorcerer would organise a Goblin hunt."

"Our stories say many died because the church declared us demons and the sorcerers burned us as entertainment." This Goblin, a little larger than most, crawled down a drainpipe to join the discussion. "This meld fled such a hunt, by a sorcerer. Our Old added that to the stories. We were few, but hid on a farm near here. When the church barrier around the village fell, we moved in. So much food! The meld grew, to where we had trouble finding enough to eat. Then you came and drove out the Ratlins and other scavengers, so we had enough again." This Goblin looked as if its skin had been glazed badly, covered in tiny cracks.

"Are you an old one?" Kelis inspected several others. "Why is your skin like that?"

"I am an Old, beginning my crumbling. All goblins crumble, but Stonelins faster than others. The constant changing, looking like stone, weakens our skin so it fails sooner, then the gas and magic inside escape and mix. If the rest of the meld are lucky, we are alone so none perish with us." The Goblin looked at the four humans. "Soon, some Old must search for a flame, so the younger meld can eat. We always increase so the Old must make way."

"You commit suicide?" All four looked around as Rob spoke, realisation dawning. "Haven't you got birth control, or, well, er, restraint?"

"We have no birth as you know it but the meld increases, always. Some of our magic returns to the air, so we live on but not in the same form." The old Goblin didn't seem comforted by that.

"So you wouldn't rather move, just some of you to start a new pack, meld?" Rob looked around baffled by the lack of understanding.

The goblins simply didn't see how or didn't want to. "Even if a meld tries to move to find food, other melds will not allow it. They would drive us away. It is in the stories."

"What if there isn't another meld there?"

The goblins looked at Rob, baffled, then from one to the other in total disbelief. A smooth one, so probably younger, jumped off a gravestone. "That is not possible. Even if the church and sorcerers drive us out, they always miss some. The meld only needs one to grow again." It shuddered. "We do not want to be used as entertainment."

"Sorcerers don't do that anymore, heat you up so you pop and burn. We have fireworks. You saw them." Rob threw his hands up in exasperation. "We explained."

"But we thought you meant here, since Sorcerer's Keep fell empty." Now the goblins looked completely baffled.

"Listen properly this time, please." The four humans sat down surrounded by goblins in various stages of gargoyle and, now the humans were looking, varying degrees of smoothness. The goblins weren't actually accusing anyone of lying, certainly not magic users with fire glyphs, but they weren't convinced either. Instead of coming away with an agreement for volunteers, the best the humans could get was a promise to talk about it. At least the goblins could pester Ferryl/Claris for answers because she lived there.

*   *   *

When the four of them discussed the Goblins' reluctance, Ferryl/Claris confirmed there had always been Goblins, everywhere. Despite her memories, the investigations around Frederick's house hadn't found a single sign of them. Ferryl/Claris wanted to find out why, but selling the gold ornament had a higher priority so she could get lodgings. Not to get a better bed, though that would be nice, but to get her clothes clean. Without a launderette nearby, the lack of a washing machine had become a real problem.

Tonight Kelis took some of Ferryl/Claris' clothes home, to mix in with her own for washing. Now Claris spent so much time in public, grubby wrinkled clothing wasn't acceptable. Meanwhile Abel hoped he could get the quilt cover and sheets through the washer at home and back here without his mum noticing. The clothing couldn't even be dried here; a washing line in the churchyard would have attracted notice.

In between visiting here and there with Laurence, practicing their new glyphs and persuading the goblins to consider a move, Abel, Kelis and Rob attended several meetings with Mr. Forester. He really had pushed ahead, finding contractors and negotiating the printing of real game boards and packs of cards. The booklets first had been produced containing the monsters and rules for the players or the Barmaid, their version of a Dungeon Master-type referee. The first example of the proposed box and the board came as a stunning shock to all three teenagers. Suddenly Bonny's Tavern looked like the real thing!

Mr. Forester brought Jenny every time, because he wanted her to actually organise the whole launch of the game. With his supervision of course, but Jenny's dad really liked the idea of her getting practical experience to back up her studies. There were several suggestions for improving the board, and another rewriting of the background scenario because Mr. Forester really did like the charity aspect. He had already started the paperwork to establish Frederick's house as a charity. Jenny thought that even if that wasn't completed the game itself might be ready to launch by Christmas.

After each meeting, while the adults chatted, Jenny went for a walk with the others to see Ferryl/Claris. She also met the three young willow dryads as herself rather than Ferryl, claiming that the meeting came a close second to her first dose of tree magic. Jenny had tried hard to find her own supply but as with most Taverners every mature tree Jenny tried had a dryad guardian.

After a couple of visits, as a special treat, Jenny held an inscribed stone for protection while she topped up from a tree in Castle House gardens. Any memory of the magic in the trees, apart from the one she used straight after Ferryl left, had been removed from Jenny's mind so finding out how much magic lay unused blew her away all over again. She immediately negotiated for a regular visit and joined the discussion on ways to store magic that weren't in bone. All the Taverners would progress faster if they could store extra for when they had time and space to practice.

Even Laurence brought up that problem, reinforced by the visit to his home. His mum and dad really were charming, and left the six teenagers to their own devices. Six because once she knew about the visit, Jenny volunteered herself as Rob's companion because she'd never seen the place. The group needed as much help as possible to place hexes because even the boating lake had magical creatures swimming in it. Laurence and Jenny had their first practical lesson in drawing glyphs to protect the rowing boats.

Zephyr investigated the woodland as the humans walked past. As Laurence told them, all the trees were claimed, but the visit answered some questions about forests. Zephyr's sight disclosed that each dryad in the woods claimed several trees, at least one adult and one a sapling, magically linking them together.

The house turned out both easier and harder to protect than expected. Ferryl and Zephyr noticed that a small deer's head with intricately twisted horns, part of the Sperrick coat of arms, formed a hex. All the big rooms with fancy carvings had a coat of arms somewhere, so Laurence could protect them just by pouring magic into the deer heads. Though as he pointed out, that could take months without a tree to supply extra magic.

The attic turned out to be an entirely different proposition. The first half had the usual collection of small creatures but those petered out as the group moved up the corridor. Ferryl/Claris suddenly stopped them. "Caution. Something large and powerful is in the rooms ahead."

"I see magic, seeping through the floor and around the doors. I could check?" Zephyr had loved flying about outside but became bored with hexing the rooms.

"No!" Ferryl/Claris spent some time with her palm towards the suspect area, concentrating hard. According to Zephyr she would be trying to read the magic ahead, to identify what it was. Eventually Ferryl relaxed, but gestured for the rest to fall back. "That is a Fursomnium, a creature that feeds on dreams. It is infesting the walls in that half of the attic. It sleeps, probably still sated after feeding on all the servants that once lived there."

"We've got to get rid of it!" Laurence clenched his fists. "Does it reach the bedrooms below? There's nobody directly under it, because my parents sleep at this end of the house."

Ferryl checked the next two floors, hexing the bedrooms in regular use to stop the creature spreading into the walls. Laurence still wanted it removed, but Ferryl worried that if roused Fursomnium might be too big to kill. Then it would tear at any unprotected minds nearby or move to prey on someone else. She proposed a full meeting of the magical members of the Tavern, here in the house, to trap and destroy it.

Laurence agreed to work on persuading his parents to host a Tavern meeting. He had already played the game, so it would be a natural progression at some time. The serious discussion about him needing more magic for such a big place led to the usual one about ways to store some. When he stretched the gold links on his expanding watch bracelet, pointing out that it should hold some, Ferryl looked thoughtful and promised to look into it. Just before the group left, Laurence produced what he'd wanted to find up in the attic, a gold-painted plastic headband with paste gems for Kelis' Windcatcher outfit.

Once back in Brinsford Kelis took him to a dryad-free oak in the Dead Wood, as a thank you but also to help him ward more of his home. She didn't tell Laurence there were more trees, but a dose of oak magic encouraged Laurence to plant a small copse at home. It would take a few years to mature, but then he'd have a personal supply.

*   *   *

Oblivious to any human plans, the goblins finally wanted to talk about their population problem just as Abel, Kelis and Ferryl/Claris were leaving for a day out. "Sorceresses, sorcerer, the meld have considered."

Abel looked carefully, and he thought this one must be the old Goblin from last time. The cracking on its skin looked worse, once it banished the stone seeming of a gargoyle. "Are you all right? You look worse."

"I am nearer the flame, but will not need to look for it if you agree. Some of the young have only ever known hunger and wish to take a chance. Keeping the seeming strong enough to stay disguised takes much food." It glanced back where green faces peered round the corner of the church and some gravestones. "If you take me and another Old, we will look. We will return to tell the young if there truly is food with no other meld to challenge for it. If the price is not too high some young will go, with two Old to offer advice and teach our stories until crumbling."

"The price will be to watch over one house and gardens, to make sure others do not intrude or spy. A sorcerer sends birds as bound watchers." Abel stopped, because the Goblin had bared its rows of tiny, sharp teeth.

"Will there be a place for Batlins? We will try hard, but birds are swift and we do not fly." It cocked its head to one side, suddenly curious. "Why do you not ward the garden as you do Sorcerer's Keep and Dead Wood?"

"There are dryads. They have been there a long time, and a strong barrier would drive them out. The house itself will be protected." Abel glanced at his watch. "We'll be leaving in a minute, but will be back this evening. How soon will you be ready?"

"We were ready, but now the Batlin meld must consider moving as well. By stopping them from catching what she calls the pretties, this sorceress has reduced their prey and your hunter takes some of the magical ones." It glanced at Abel's shoulder. "She is also hungry, and the batlins dare not challenge her. They have listened to us talk, so they will decide quickly." The Goblin looked back at the other eager green faces. "I will tell them two more days, if you agree?"

"Agreed." Abel texted Rob, asking if he could polish a gargoyle. "Explain to Rob please. He'll be here as soon as he can get away." Rob would be busy helping Melanie with her costume because even if she only played over Skype, his little sister wanted to look the part. She wanted to be Cackle the Crone, even if that wasn't a playable character. Not yet, Melanie wouldn't give up that easily.

*   *   *

Kelis texted Frederick, to let him know he'd get protection soon, then concentrated on Ferryl/Claris' problem. The sorceress needed a legitimate place to stay before someone noticed her living in the church. Too many people were getting curious about her always being in Brinsford. Twice Laurence dropped her off in Stourton on the way to take Kelis and Abel home. She caught a bus back out to Brinsford, but the bus service wasn't good enough to do that regularly. Ferryl/Claris had to sell the gold fairy to pay for lodgings, which meant finding a reason to spend the whole day in Stourton.

In the end Kelis asked if they could all go to the local swimming baths for a change. Laurence agreed, though he made Kelis promise not to play tricks with the water. Turning the cola in his glass into a waterspout that neatly filled Kelis' glass had made him very wary. On the way into town Abel and Claris asked to be dropped off in the town centre, knowing Laurence wouldn't mind getting Kelis on his own for a while.

As soon as they were alone Ferryl/Claris went into the public toilet and came out with brown hair. She didn't want the Leech Firstseed to see her wandering around town. The first two shops Abel and Ferryl/Claris tried weren't interested in buying a gold fairy. One because the woman behind the counter clearly thought they'd stolen it, the second because of the lack of any hallmark. The next possibility, an old shop, had a magical hex inside the counter so some were still operating. Luckily both Zephyr and Ferryl could see the tell-tale flow of magic.

Abel felt almost relieved, in a way, because it still felt wrong to be selling magical gold. "Maybe we'll have to find another way." He showed Ferryl/Claris the list from the internet. "This one here is the last possibility for something like that. Unless we pawn it, but they'll want proof of ownership at least."

"This is the receipt from when Laurence bought the Sprite." Ferryl/Claris held up the piece of paper and it blurred, showing an address in Manchester and a date three years ago, and now the price and description showed the piece to be gold. "I had forgotten hallmarks. Now I have been reminded, they are easy. I will look at several gold items before trying to sell this, then a little heat and air will put the hallmark onto the base."

"All right, one more time. If it doesn't work, we leave it for today and maybe think again."

"First, there is another problem, the real reason neither wanted to buy from us. You are clearly a schoolboy, while I am not really old enough nor dressed to be selling such an object. We can't change you, so go in first and be ready to cause a diversion if anyone in there causes trouble." Ferryl/Claris tapped Abel between the eyes. "He or she may be like Frederick or Stan, and possibly see something wrong with the receipt." Abel heaved a sigh of resignation, and agreed.

Though he hadn't realised what Ferryl meant to do about her appearance. He stood inspecting a small display of watches and straps when Zephyr alerted him. "Ferryl Shayde comes."

Abel glanced, looked again and gaped. As he realised and turned away the one consolation was that a schoolboy probably would stare at the young woman coming into the shop. It wasn't just the long blonde hair, the tight fitted top or her short skirt and high heels. Somehow Ferryl/Claris exuded a suggestion she might be what Kelis' mum would call morally suspect. Though her manner, hesitant and maybe shy, didn't quite gel.

Ferryl/Claris moved around the shop, then asked to see two gold pendants and a figurine before unwrapping the fairy and asking if he'd buy it. She sounded cautious, unsure and reluctant as if she wasn't really sure. When the proprietor admitted he might, if it really was hers and real gold, her voice sounded a little embarrassed as she gave her cover story. Abel wasn't sure if she'd aimed at sounding like a wronged fiancée or dumped mistress, but either would fit.

The fairy reminded her of the man who bought it so she wanted to sell it. Abel kept on inspecting watches and straps, stifling his impulse to look to see the expression on the proprietor. The receipt didn't raise any questions, nor did the hallmark. Ferryl/Claris' cautious attempt to raise the price sounded as if she needed the cash but didn't want to admit it, and Abel had a completely uncharitable thought. How many times had Ferryl done this in the past, sold magical jewellery to an unsuspecting sucker? The whole act looked polished from his perspective, but maybe just convincing to the victim.

Even the hesitation before asking if she could possibly have it in cash, because there might be a difficulty at the bank, sounded natural. For a moment Abel poised, wind glyph forming, when the proprietor asked for identification. Ferryl/Claris passed him something that he considered sufficient, and he began counting out notes. Abel left the shop. He didn't want to hang about long enough for the man to remember the schoolboy if the fairy turned to silver or dust tomorrow. He headed across the street and waited at the first corner.

Ferryl/Claris ignored Abel, so he gave her a bit of a start and followed until she walked behind a skip and a brown-haired Claris walked out. Ferryl/Claris smiled and hooked an arm through Abel's. "He will make a good profit on that. We should walk past and look in the window in a few days."

230

"How often have you pulled that trick?" It came out without thought, but that had been nagging away at Abel.

"Not often because selling magical gold used to be more difficult. I have used a similar seeming or manner to get out of trouble, or to stop someone who recognised my host from prying. Most men will not press a woman too hard about her circumstances if she suggests she has fallen from grace. Especially if she also intimates she is short of money."

Abel settled for a muttered "probably not." He reluctantly shelved Ferryl's past, because any humans involved were long dead. "How much did you get?"

"Just under three thousand pounds. Enough for lodgings." Ferryl/Claris patted her bag, back to the large one sent by Claris' mother instead of looking like a slim leather clasp.

"Should we be wandering around the shops with all that cash? We wouldn't want to get mugged." Abel realised his mistake as Zephyr suddenly came alert in his tattoo.

Ferryl/Claris turned with a big smile. "That would be entertaining." The shopping after that opened up Ferryl's understanding of the modern world. "Elasticated! Just a word, but a new one and without any real meaning until now. Sorceresses who have not perfected putting diamonds in bone will be using elastic to carry a store of magic. The watch straps might work, but so will an elasticated belt. We can fasten them tight to keep the glyph in place."

"Not too tight or they'll hurt. That or the band will cut off the circulation." Abel still wasn't sure even the watch straps would stay over one spot. "You'll end up with a red mark every night when you take it off. We will, because I'll risk it for an emergency boost." The pair of them were approaching the swimming baths. "Remember, no asking water to move aside or water spouts."

"Just a minute." Ferryl/Claris nipped into the public loo and came out her usual self.

Ferryl/Claris took her time changing into her swimsuit which meant Abel stood waiting for her a few minutes, but Kelis and Laurence didn't notice. They were laughing and splashing each other, just a little, and chasing each other. By the second time round Abel realised Laurence swam just slow enough to let her duck him after about half a length. He caught himself thinking about how Kelis wasn't at all skinny now, and squashed the sudden pang. Abel felt sure it was getting easier.

On the way back Laurence kept teasing Kelis about not learning to swim because she could breathe stood up in the deep end. For once Kelis found jokes about her height funny, probably because they were jokes that applied to Laurence as well. Now Laurence wanted to go to a water park, which went well beyond Abel's comfort zone because he'd never done much swimming. He kept quiet, reassured by remembering that he could politely ask the water to spit him out again.

Revelations

Unfortunately the money didn't solve the accommodation problem because cautious enquiries showed that nobody in Brinsford wanted a lodger. At least Stan, the usual gossip-monger, wouldn't cause trouble. He liked having Ferryl/Claris drop in for a cuppa, though Abel thought it might be to check on her progress. The food had filled her out until her clothes no longer looked baggy, and her colour went from pasty to a healthy light tan.

Ferryl/Claris stayed hidden when Mr. Forester visited Brinsford for business meetings, because he would recognise her from Jenny's Acro practice. Jenny still liked to check up on Ferryl/Claris, and top up with tree magic, so she usually found an excuse to have a walk around the village with the other three. Despite having said she wanted to stay clear, Jenny obviously felt she should keep an eye on Claris. She eventually confessed that seeing Abel wasn't as creepy as expected, probably because most of the time they were in meetings.

This time Mr. Forester had a sheaf of planning application papers. They showed what Frederick needed to do to his house to get varying degrees of acceptance up to a full nursing home. "That house in town really will make a good refuge, a charity where battered wives or something similar could go."

"The old church here in Brinsford would be even better. There'd be no husbands sneaking around a little village like this." Abel's mum darted a glance at him, then at Kelis' mum.

"Yes, secluded like that nobody would even notice a couple of women living there." Rob's mum's mouth twitched as she glanced at Rob.

"After all, nobody has noticed Abel stashing his girlfriend there, have they?" Kelis' mum looked round the table, then at Mr. Forester. "That's what we wanted to know. It looks like Jenny is in on it as well." There wasn't much use protesting, because all four teenagers looked as if they'd been poleaxed. They stayed that way as Mrs. Ventner brought Mr. Forester up to date. Mrs. Turner, a definite busybody, had wondered who the squatter was because Abel, Kelis and Rob obviously knew her. Others had noticed Ferryl/Claris walking around the outside of the village with the three of them to get to the Dead Wood, or up the village street to Stan's or Castle House. The four adults sat back and eyed their children.

"You didn't honestly think we wouldn't notice, did you?" Abel's mum shook her head in disbelief. "She's got bright red hair for starters you idiots. Then you all start asking around for lodgings, and I noticed some sheets whizzing around in the drier that aren't mine." She narrowed her eyes at Abel. "Once we compared notes I knew that girl wasn't going home by bus. I have to use that service if my car's broken down and it doesn't run that often."

"So is she really hiding from bad people or is it an excuse to meet in secret?" Abel cringed because as Rob's mum said that, Mr. Forester shot him a suspicious glance. After all, Jenny had allegedly been a secret girlfriend.

"Bad people, honest." Abel glanced at Mr. Forester. "We don't meet alone."

"Does Laurence know? Have you been meeting him over there when you go out with these two in the evening?" This time Kelis tried to look innocent as she denied it.

Eventually the four parents got the whole story, or the public part. Claris wouldn't go back to town, for any reason, not yet. The solution came as a complete surprise. "Right, in that case she'd better move in here so I can keep an eye on her. Though you three and Laurence will be off every few days so Abel will still get time with her."

"How come Rob doesn't get to go on these trips?" Abel's mum fixed him with a look. He'd no idea what she thought, but the truth couldn't hurt.

"We can't cram Rob in Laurence's car." Abel bit back the bit about Melanie going.

"I could go, but then Claris would be unhappy. She feels safer with Abel." Rob stopped as a big smile lit up Mrs. Ventner's face.

"I can solve that. Why don't the five of you take the BMW?" She looked around the table where everyone looked back baffled. "Apparently it's mine. I've had a new BMW as a gift from my soon-to-be ex-husband every year even if he never mentioned it. He sold the old one in my name, some sort of tax avoidance thing, then claimed expenses for using my car at work. I can't even drive, but it's sat there insured for any driver until next year."

"Bonny's Tavern can use a company car?" Mr. Forester glanced at Jenny. "You know this Claris girl, don't you? Will I recognise her from the Acro dancing?" Jenny nodded. "Then after we've done with the business, I'll go and ask her to come over. She can verify what's been said so we can be sure you've told us everything." He looked back at Abel. "Can she afford lodgings?"

"Mum won't mind."

"Sorry Kelis, but if she can pay it would be handy. We will lose the house, completely, when the bank takes it for the business debts." Mrs. Ventner sighed, then braced herself. "As business partners you should know there'll not be much money from me. We won't be completely broke because in addition to the car I also have a mystery bank account where he paid my mystery wages for the mystery job I did. What's in it is mine, all clear and legal because I'm not responsible for the debts."

With a little smile she turned to Kelis. "You have a little nest egg as well. Your dear father gave you regular gifts for birthdays and Christmas, then sold them and put the money into your own mystery account. Something to do with a regular gift being tax-deductible. I've talked to the bank and daddy dear won't be getting near any of it now."

"How soon will you have to leave here?" Mr. Forester looked a little guilty. "I'm sorry, but we need to know for the business." His wry look at Abel's mum didn't have much humour. "It's a pity we haven't got the church. We could have had our first homeless customers."

"We should be all right at Christmas but it will all be over by Easter at the latest." Mrs. Ventner managed real humour. "Since I'm allowed to take furniture, we could have really fitted the church out. I'll have to either sell it all or find storage, because the bank aren't having my comfy chair or kitchen set. These chairs can go as a gift to Bonny's Tavern, wherever it ends up."

"I'll find you storage if you need it. We've got plenty of places I store building supplies. Considering what we've all just learned, maybe we can leave Frederick's house until another time? Then we can get that young lady over here and clear that up at least." From his look Jenny's dad still wasn't happy about the explanations to date.

"I need the loo before I go and get her. Nerves?" Because Abel felt sure nobody would be allowed over there without parents, so he needed privacy. A few minutes later Zephyr flew off, safely out of sight of his mum, to make sure nobody's suspicions were confirmed. While Jenny and her dad went to get Ferryl/Claris, the other parents continued the inquisition.

At least Ferryl/Claris had exactly the right manner and answers to get everyone partly off the hook. They all got an ear-bashing but no groundings and no police, which looked a definite possibility for a while. Mr. Forester certainly felt that way, as did Kelis' mum. Abel knew he'd get the third degree when Ferryl/Claris sat down next to him, holding hands with their shoulders touching so they could communicate. At least that settled anyone's doubts about Jenny's reaction to the alleged break-up, it didn't bother her at all.

Ferryl/Claris moved into Kelis' house that night, with Rob and Abel bringing all her stuff across the next day. Abel survived the earache from his mum, while Kelis, Jenny and Rob weathered their own storms. The results were definitely unexpected.

Not Claris' mum visiting Brinsford after Claris admitted where she lived. Ferryl/Claris still refused to go home, but finding her daughter living in a big house with Kelis' mum mollified Mrs. Ellsworth a little. Instead, completely out of the blue, her mum started a campaign to get the school to accept Claris back again. That way Claris could repeat last year and take her A-Levels.

*   *   *

Mrs. Ellsworth also visited to help the other parents at the official Tavern meeting, the one for every player where there'd be no mention of magic. Laurence turned up in tight jeans, riding boots and a frilly shirt, carrying what might be a real rapier which he refused to unsheathe. He told Kelis he'd had to promise not to, or his dad wouldn't let him take it. The sombrero with a peacock feather set the lot off, though Laurence swore he'd do better. Many Taverners brought food and soft drinks as promised, which were set up on the front lawn because this time the crowd simply wouldn't fit in Kelis' house. A quick count came up with a hundred and seventeen young people ranging from thirteen to twenty-five, with at least a third making a creditable attempt at a costume. Almost all the rest wore a couple of badges with magical symbols, or something else from the game.

There were two other schools represented now, a local academy as well as Shannon's church school. News about supporting a real charity had gone round like wildfire, with dozens of suggestions about how to fit it into the game. Although many preferred the usual smash and grab quests, a good few were really interested a different type. Those wanted a way for players to improve their levels, or maybe earn health bonuses, if they could prove a certain level of real charity work. That would take some doing, though Abel felt sure Mr. Forester would push the designers to manage it.

Samantha, Rob's big sister, had played Bonny's Tavern with him and Melanie a few times so she declared herself qualified to attend. She swore that her 'costume' of a crop top and shorts with a strip of cloth hanging from the back of her waistband looked like Ferryl Shayde. Melanie came in her full kit as Cackle the Crone with a beat-up toy fox as her bound creature. That still wasn't a playable character but Cackle and a few other subsidiary types such as Champ the Tavern bouncer had real fans. Rob's dance with Lovingly Sculpted turned into three when someone told her who'd come up with the name.

Abel finally had a character, Wind Chaser the sprite catcher. His jeans, boots and an old shirt with the sleeves torn off weren't much, even if the colour glyph meant his wooden sword and knife shone like metal and his shirt looked like leather at first glance. Several magic symbols on wooden discs, hung around his neck on leather laces, and a dozen badges bearing more magical symbols allegedly protected him from prowling sorceresses. Ferryl/Claris, with her red hair and a dress patterned like flames, showed that one of them had got through his defences. Abel's main costume accessory made all the magic users laugh. The wide thin balloon tethered to his arm, with fangs and eyes drawn on with felt tip, really did lunge and swoop realistically. It would, with a totally real Zephyr inside it. She had a wonderful time, even remembering not to hunt properly while wearing her rubber suit.

The number of happy young people crowding onto the last bus to Stourton underlined one thing. Even if they hadn't sold a single copy yet, Bonny's Tavern had a fan club. Mr. Forester, helping the other parents with policing the crowd, wanted to sell them a beta version. None of the designers were that confident yet. At least this meeting wasn't as bad as the birthday party, because nobody did any magic. Afterwards Rob's big sister had plenty of questions, though mainly about phone numbers. According to her Rob should have a list of all the members, and any real brother would let his sister have a quick look.

The party managed something else, it blew away a lot of the worries about bullies, sorcerers, Creepio and leeches. Abel and his friends relaxed into really enjoying this summer holiday. Better yet, with the BMW Abel no longer felt guilty about Rob not coming on the days out.

*   *   *

The first time he took the keys Laurence looked wary about driving an almost new BMW belonging to someone else. Mrs. Ventner wouldn't take no as an answer, confessing she'd been worried about Kelis having an accident in Laurence's small car. As a bonus, having Rob along took some of the attention off Abel and Claris being together.

The big party meant Kelis had finally relaxed around others while with Laurence. Once she started talking about her outings to theme parks and other attractions, several of the Taverners wanted to come along. Shannon and other Taverners with licences promised to borrow a parent's car when they could, while Jenny thought she could persuade her dad to let someone drive one of the pickups from his building business. The summer passed in a blur of days out, glyph practice and game design. Meanwhile Claris put on weight and exercised until she regained her Acro Dancer's figure. As a side effect Abel found it increasingly hard to remember it was all an act when Ferryl/Claris decided she should kiss him.

Two days before Laurence went off to Germany he asked Kelis to a dance at his house, a fancy dress ball so she could wear her Windcatcher sorceress outfit. As a surprise Ferryl/Claris turned the circlet for her head into real gems and gold, though she complained that the plastic took a lot of work. Her mum and Rob's sister Samantha helped Kelis get the makeup and her hair right, and her crowning glory fixed in place. She even went in the BMW rather than risk her hairstyle in Laurence's Corsa. When Prince Charming finally brought Cinderella home, she texted Rob and Abel to say it had been fabulous but wouldn't talk about it the following day.

*   *   *

Kelis finally talked properly at the next Bonny's Tavern meeting, the day Laurence left for Germany. He had completely fooled her about the evening. Laurence wanted her in the long silky robe for a dance but not a fancy dress one. Some of his German relatives were there, expecting Laurence to bring Seraph or no partner as usual, and he'd wanted to really floor them. According to Kelis, Laurence's mother had been in on the plot. She'd loved the robe and whole look but altered the hair and makeup so it wasn't quite so sorceress, then to top it off she'd loaned Kelis a necklace to go with the circlet.

Kelis had danced all night, because Laurence's two cousins made a huge game out of trying to steal his new girl. They were even more determined after finding out she played a sorceress, wanting her to show them magic spells or turn Laurence into a frog. The pair apparently practiced fencing, and at one stage fought a mock duel over Kelis until Laurence defeated them both, allegedly. They'd asked her to come to Germany for Christmas, to a real ball, and generally treated her as a princess. So had Laurence, his family, and the other relatives from Germany. Not a princess maybe, but as if Kelis belonged.

"Are you going to be all right, or will you mope about him for the next two weeks?" Rob had a little smile, but both he and Abel were worried. The summer holidays had been brilliant, the best ever, but by the time Laurence came back they'd be in school again. There'd be no days out for Kelis then, not if Laurence started work as well.

"I might look a bit wistful? It's traditional, otherwise the next sucker might think I'm totally heartless and run a mile." Both of them stared as Kelis laughed. "I'm not all starry-eyed, I promise. This summer has been lovely, but I always knew how it would end. Laurence will go off to work, abroad some of the time, and K'liss Windcatcher will don her disguise as the innocent schoolgirl Kelis." She really did look wistful, for a moment. "Though it really has been nice, just enjoying myself for once without that pig waiting at home. Or Henry lurking to cause trouble, though I've barely thought of him since Easter."

"Are you sure you'll be okay?" Abel wished he'd kept his trap shut when Kelis smiled, a sort of sad-and-dreamy one.

"Yes. After the dancing, before I came home, we went for a walk around the grounds. I told Laurence I really enjoyed summer, but he was a bit old for me. I won't have time for a real boyfriend, not the sort who'd want to take me out at weekends, not while I'm studying for A levels." Her sad face probably meant Kelis wasn't totally sure. "Laurence said okay, but hoped I'd still answer his calls if he needed an emergency princess or sorceress." Kelis took a deep breath and looked at the pair of them with a bright smile. "So that's it."

Her tone meant Kelis didn't want to discuss it anymore. "That just leaves the usual problem, what to do about Abel's girlfriend." Rob turned with a huge smile. "Let's hope the teachers are prepared for her first day greeting."

"Definitely. Though going by past performance, she might not last that long. We'd best warn the rest of the girls at school." Nothing wistful about Kelis now she'd started on her favourite tease, Abel's girlfriends.

Though Abel had his own ammunition now. "It'll be Rob's fan club causing raised eyebrows. After all, Claris might not be there."

"Don't bet on it. Claris' mum reckons she's got a meeting this week. That means the school must be considering Claris retaking the year, and that is one very determined lady." Kelis shook her head. "I wouldn't put pure bribery out of the question."

"Never mind your love lives or my host's mother, who may not need bribery. Look what I've got." Ferryl/Claris placed a long strip of black cloth on the table. "The ends of the belts are elasticated, and that fastening can be tightened as much as you wish." She turned it over, to reveal a row of oblong shapes fastened together by short lengths of wire. "These were steel, and I used heat to fuse the wire to the blocks before altering the whole strip to gold. The whole belt is a single store, waiting to be filled with magic. Then if the glyph on this block," she tapped the engraved one, "is lined up on a glyph in the skin, that extra magic is always available."

"Wow, brilliant." Kelis glanced down at her waist, then at the belt. "Do I have to burn another tattoo?"

"No, a drawing should be good enough, though the best way is to place it under the skin. The same way as the glyphs on the tree roots that feed the barrier in Castle House?" Ferryl/Claris turned to Abel. "Though Abel couldn't manage that last time he tried."

"Not likely. I burned those glyphs on, which would really hurt inside my skin. It'll be marker pen until we learn to heal." Abel glanced at his own waist. "The belt might still slip a bit. How far is too far to connect?"

"We'll experiment, and you are wrong about burning. This version is more like colouring the skin, but under the surface. Learning to recognise how materials are made or skin is constructed will help with being able to do that." Glum faces greeted Ferryl/Claris' smile, because none of them could get even a hint of that yet. Zephyr had tried to help Abel, but he couldn't understand what she thought she saw so it might be wrong.

"At the worst we can hook a thumb behind the belt and picture the glyph on it, pull magic that way?" Rob picked up the belt. "Crikey, it's a good job we all exercise."

"A couple of the Taverners reckon magic training works better than diets. One reckons it's the first time she's ever managed to lose weight. The rest are finding out that exercise really does stop their arms hurting after casting. We could make a video and call it Fitness is Magic to finance the Tavern?" Abel took the belt from Rob. "How about what I first suggested, a bar to carry in my pocket? I still reckon this or the watch strap will slip too far. The strap definitely does because we marked it, and Rob's skin, before he jumped about a bit."

"You mean he rolled about like a ferret in a wasp's nest, which definitely moved the strap too far. Though once again that would be a store even if the sorceress had to put a hand on it." Kelis touched her little silver angel. "I suppose one of those big solid gold necklaces would work the same, except I'd have neck muscles like a bull. Or Henry. Crikey, he'd carry enough magic to flatten a town."

"Henry? I haven't seen him all holiday?" Abel thought hard but no, they'd not seen a sign.

"We might not see him again. After all, he doesn't need more schooling to be a farmer, not with growing up on a farm. He'll probably inherit half his Dad's." Rob drooped sadly. "Oh dear, I'll really miss him."

He grinned, straightening up. "Like toothache."

"He's learned his lesson. Now I want lessons on putting glyphs under tree bark. That sounds safer than under my fair skin." Kelis stuck her nose in the air and sneered at Rob. "It won't matter to Rob of course. Barbarians are supposed to have big ugly scars all over." The meeting degenerated into the usual wrangling, except for making plans to draw things under the bark of the trees in the Dead Wood.

Leaving both Kelis and Ferryl/Claris behind still seemed a bit odd when Rob and Abel left Tavern meetings. So far Kelis' mum seemed happy to have a lodger, and had definitely eased off on the paranoia about Kelis walking round the village without Rob or Abel. On the way back, a shadow called from behind a wheelie-bin. "Sorcerers. The batlins have agreed. If the sorcerer lets us scavenge all the bins in the streets around the house and gives us a safe haven we will split the meld. In return we will guard the garden, keeping out any magical creatures and especially tethered watcher-birds. When will you know if he agrees?"

"He agrees. You'll be leaving as soon as Jenny can persuade her dad to let her borrow the pickup truck again." Abel watched the Goblin creep off back towards the churchyard. "With Laurence gone we won't have a driver so we'll not be going out as often. There again, we'll be back at school in a week." The two Olds and a Batlin had travelled in the boot of the luxury car, so their trip scouting had been easy to organise.

"Wrong, we've got three volunteers to drive a BMW and two of them have a moped or scooter to get out here without needing a bus." Rob glanced at Abel. "We can go out every single day, though we'll have to pay our way."

"We already do, ever since we sold the fairy though Laurence always insisted on paying for Kelis. We'll just be eating burgers rather than going to restaurants for meals." Abel heaved a huge mock-sigh. "Just when I'd learned how to eat peas without a spoon." They'd also be paying for more petrol, because Laurence always insisted on paying at least half. Poor for an Earl came nothing close to what they thought of as skint, though Laurence never made a big thing of it.

* * *

It only took Jenny twenty-four hours to persuade her dad to loan her the pickup truck for the day. Three other Taverners came along to supply a driver and help with the transfer. With Eric to drive the BMW, along with Una, that made ten of them to disguise eight short tubby green munchkins nipping out of the lychgate and into the flat back. In theory nobody would see, but even Kelis wasn't totally sure about her veil. Once in the truck the goblins became eight stone garden ornaments, while ten batlins swooped down to roost in the emptied tool-chest.

The three original Taverners hadn't really thought about the consequences when they cast veils. Una spent the whole trip fraying their ears. She started by complaining she hadn't been taught the veil glyph, but soon moved on to her real complaint. In common with all the advanced Taverners, Una spent all the magic she absorbed each day practicing the glyphs she already knew. She'd never be able to perfect a new glyph even if someone showed her the veil. Unfortunately the best way to have more magic to spare was to be more efficient when casting glyphs, but the practice needed magic.

At least the goblins themselves diverted Frederick, his three resident Taverners, Effy and the four other town Taverners who were here to work on the house. "Those are the first magical creatures to look like the fairy stories, or some stories anyway. Except the flying ones. Those wings are creepy and confusing. A little fat green cartoon shouldn't have Dracula wings." Rachel, who really liked working on the old house, inspected one of the larger Goblins. "They can really be seen by anyone?"

Abel explained, again, because sometimes Rachel skipped details other than something she could cast. The goblins looked nervous, but relaxed when Frederick showed them his wheelie bins and told them the houses along the road had more. Places like the nursing homes had industrial sized versions. Frederick had a more practical concern. "I know they turn to stone, but won't that damage anything they perch on? The weight I mean."

"Ask them about it, and for a demo." Frederick did, cautiously, and the spectators were treated to a variety of stone creatures. A few half-turned, looking part-stone and part-green so they could still talk. Several perched on the garage or shed roof to prove they didn't weigh as much as stone.

"It is just our skin that looks like stone, great lord. We weigh the same no matter how we look." The Goblin glanced towards the Old, stuffing itself with something from the bin.

"Great Lord?" Frederick looked startled, then cautious.

"The stories say only nobles or sorcerers kept goblins as lookouts, and both like to be called that." It glanced at Abel. "That one does not own the church and prefers to be called Abel or apprentice, but we are not sure about that. The Olds think we should call him sorcerer to be safe."

The Old stopped eating for a moment to interrupt. "The magic users near our home are strange, not like the stories but the dryad said they are young and still training. He warned us their teacher is powerful, so we must show respect." It licked its lips slowly. "We know that part. We saw them wield fire to chase away the Ratlins and to hunt and kill the slithery slippery."

"Can any of you wield fire?" The startled younger Goblin edged away from six proud smiles with flames dancing above their hands.

"They are training as well. Ask the dryads. There are many in the orchard, but they will let you pass." Kelis looked from one to the other. "We explained all this. You guard the gardens, hide as garden ornaments in the day, and raid the local rubbish bins for food at night."

The Goblin nodded. "But the Olds said it is safest to ask, to check that the sorceress meant it the first time." It looked towards the bins, managing to stop the lick halfway, so Abel sent it to join the feast. At least all the talk of respect reassured Frederick, more so when a succession of batlins brought living birds and insects to ask if they were allowed in the garden or not. Kelis' declaration that she'd have a firework display all of her own if they killed harmless songbirds or butterflies had been taken to heart.

Though once the goblins and batlins were settled in, Abel, Kelis, Rob and Ferryl/Claris were surrounded by eager faces. At least the veil glyph had no nasty side effects though the trainees wouldn't have the magic to practice much. The enclosed garden soon rang with laughter as young people managed to cast the glyph accurately and started wondering what they could hide.

"We won't hide too much, or too often." Petra's long face matched most of the others. Those like Effy still squandered magic trying to cast wind glyphs because they hadn't learned control. Despite being more economic, the advanced students ran out of magic before they'd finished practicing. They couldn't try every glyph they knew every day, which slowed their progress.

"Except these four, with all that lovely tree magic." Jenny stopped, hand to mouth, while the rest looked puzzled and then suspicious. "Sorry, it just popped out."

"Not to worry, I told Laurence and Claris knows now. Our dryad-free oak tree gives us extra magic." Kelis stuck to the story she'd given Laurence, that they could only use one tree, and Jenny kept her mouth shut this time.

"A mature oak? Crikey, no wonder you three always perfect the glyphs first. That and Ferryl Shayde as a teacher of course." Una shook a fist at Abel. "Cheat." She turned to Jenny. "I suppose girlfriends get a free top-up, and that's why you're catching up so fast?"

"Ex, remember, though the first zap might persuade a girl to stay friends even with Abel." Jenny shrugged, with a smug little smile. "He lets me get the occasional top-up when I visit Brinsford, for old time's sake." Her look at Claris had a lot of mischief in it, because she knew Ferryl lived inside her. "I'll bet Claris has better control than she tells us."

"How much magic is there in an oak tree? It must have more than a rhododendron." As everyone turned towards her Rachel looked decidedly guilty. "I plead extreme youth and wanting to be better at magic than my brother."

"I can relate to wanting to beat any boy, but fourteen isn't young enough for age to fly as an excuse. Not in this company. What did you do?" Though despite her tone, Petra had a tiny smile as she asked.

"The game notes say everything absorbs magic but plants don't leak it. I tried to get some from a rose bush, but couldn't really cut a good glyph and got nothing. The rhododendron is a big old thing with thick branches so I tried that. I did what you told us, drew the glyph on my hand with a finger and put it over the cut, and this trickle came out." She giggled. "That is truly weird. But I must have overdone it, because the bush looks ill. It's sort of wilted. I've had to use up some of my daily allowance the last week to try and revive it."

Petra laughed. "Me too, except I didn't do as much damage and it was the lilac bush. There isn't a lot and it doesn't seem to top up as fast as I do, but I get a little bit every three or four days." From the smiles or shifty looks quite a few were doing similar. Shawn confessed to taking a trip into the countryside now and then to drain a bit from each thick shoot in a random hedgerow. They all had the same complaints. The plants had to have a stout enough shoot to cut a decent glyph but even then didn't give much magic, and took ages to build it back up.

"So how much in an oak tree?" Petra nudged Jenny. "What does it feel like?"

"I felt wobbly and silly the first time, like when I got squiffy once but a lot more. It sort of rushes in and fills you right up, and it's fresh and zingy." Jenny giggled. "It's still a real buzz. Once you've tried it I'll bet you never get tempted by booze. I doubt even drugs feel that good, and there's no downside to tree magic."

"Hey Rob, watch out, there'll be a line of hopefuls wanting to charm you into giving them access to that oak tree." Justin hesitated. "I realised what Rachel did so I've been more careful, but it's slow going. Could the advanced students get a bit of extra now and then from your tree, Abel? That has to be better than being caught cutting branches in the neighbour's shrubbery."

Effy smiled brightly. "Or the newcomers so we can catch up?" Abel exchanged glances with the other three as an argument broke out over who should get any surplus. Jenny came across, looking decidedly guilty.

"Sorry, it just slipped out." She looked back at the rest. "Will telling them you've got an extra supply of magic cause a lot of trouble?"

"Don't worry Jenny, it had to come out eventually. After all, someone would wonder why we always learn faster. That argument is why we didn't tell everyone. They'd all swarm into Brinsford at the weekends and draw attention to Castle House. Then the locals would try to find out why thirty-odd schoolkids went into the wood and wouldn't be able to get in themselves." Abel took hold of Ferryl/Claris' hand.

"We'd have to make dozens of those pebbles, and someone would lose one. That or an apprentice or witch, or maybe a Leech, would get hold of the glyph." Kelis glanced at the others. "Maybe we'll have to push the

246

experiments on a bit. I've got my gold bar with me?"

Abel asked Zephyr to connect to Ferryl. "Ferryl? How much of a problem is it to let each one have a gold bar's worth to top up once a week?"

"Making that many gold bars will take a long time. It will be another chore, filling them all up at the weekend, and if a teacher catches you with twenty gold bars?"

"How about lead? You said that's nearly as good. The three of us would only have a dozen each in our schoolbags. Four of us if you end up back at school." Abel worried a little if she didn't, because then Ferryl/Claris would spend all day hanging about near the school in case he got into trouble. He noticed Jenny looking at the held hands and spooky-phone with a little smile.

"Lead is almost as good, but will poison the user." The mental voice stopped for a moment and Abel felt a little squeeze of his hand. When she continued Ferryl sounded definitely intrigued. "I'm thinking of putting it in the bone of course, the usual sorcerer way, but you won't be doing that. Carrying a bar of it shouldn't hurt anyone. Once again we are doing this the wrong way round, teaching later lessons earlier, but the circumstances are very different. No sorceress would let apprentices have extra magic except to carry out a specific task for her." Her mental snigger came as a surprise. "Certainly not to improve their glyphs and maybe be as strong as their mistress!"

"Pass that on to Kelis and Rob please, Zephyr, to Jenny as well." Abel waited until the others nodded, then raised his voice. "If you lot have done arguing, you could ask a sorceress for an answer. Politely of course, instead of screaming at each other?"

The group split up, looking a bit guilty and shooting rueful glances at each other. "Not screaming, Abel." Una gave a little shrug and a smile. "Though if only one can get a chance at that tree, and I've got my sword?" At least a few smiles reappeared. "Please Ferryl Shayde, how many of us can top up from an oak tree, if you allow us to?"

Abel answered for her, of course. "All of you, every day, and then it dies. Or we can try an experiment." The apprentices looked disappointed and then cautiously hopeful. "If you can agree, without fighting among yourselves, each of you can have a little extra each week. You'll need a lead bar this big." Abel pulled out an experimental gold bar to demonstrate. "It's about the weight of a bag of sweets, about a hundred grams."

"We've each got one, just to try them. Now you can help the experiment. We put the magic in, but can you take it out?" Kelis took hers out and held it up. "Don't run off with it, because this one is gold. Ferryl insisted for the first tries, because that's what sorceresses use."

"Me too, given the choice. Unfortunately, I can only afford lead. How do we take the magic out? Ah, sorry. Who gets to try?" Una tried to look guilty and failed.

Abel looked them over and shrugged. "If this works the ones who came on the Goblin run can come back to Brinsford with us. Just this once they get a top-up from the tree."

"Blimey, you'd think they'd won the lottery. We really have been spoiled, haven't we?" Rob spoke very quietly but the laughing and joking would have drowned him out anyway.

"I've got some idea how they feel, even if I've been spoiled a little. Not having enough magic to practice is a real pain." Jenny eyed up the small bar. "Will anything metal be just as good?"

"Maybe. Sorceresses really do use gold, or diamonds. Ooh, wait until Kelis shows you her diamond." Rob nodded towards Kelis. "Her boyfriend might be rich, but he couldn't afford a rock like the one Abel gave her."

"Well Kelis? Because I definitely don't remember a rock of any size from lover-boy." Jenny gave Ferryl/Claris the once-over, especially her ring hand. "Claris seems to have missed out as well."

"Laurence is an ex-boyfriend but Rob is right." A happy little smile lit Kelis' face. "Abel really did give me a huge rock, long before we knew about storing magic."

"Not quite a real diamond. I found it, and Kelis liked it." "Help, Ferryl, what do I say?"

"How about the truth?" Abel stared at the spooky-phone. It still led to Jenny and all the other three. Jenny narrowed her eyes. "I'd appreciate it?"

"Good idea, but keep away from making metals and stick to the stone being worthless because of the glyph being visible. Jenny is too smart for anything else, and there'll be little fragments of memories still in there. You don't want her hunting for them." At least nobody could hear Ferryl's voice through Abel's skin.

Abel gave up, because he preferred the truth but magic seemed determined to make him tell an increasing number of porkies. He explained the gem, and that Kelis hadn't known it was real. He hadn't known himself that it could store magic. "I daren't give everyone a blooming great diamond. It'll scratch glass and all that, and someone would be tempted to give it to a jeweller eventually to see if it was the real thing. Then the jeweller would find out it is, but someone had managed to inscribe the inside."

"Curses." Jenny thought a moment, then glanced at the rest. "I'll settle for one a bit smaller than Kelis'? Just me, and I swear I really won't let anyone examine it." She smiled happily. "I'll get one of those kits with plastic gold and jewels for making fake costume stuff and surround it with crap, or put it on an obviously cheap chain. You can do the same for Claris in time. It'll be a way of keeping track of your women."

"Done, now shush." Not only had the rest sorted out who would try the experiment, Abel didn't want Rob or Kelis getting into a discussion about his women. He could already feel Kelis' eyes on him, so he held out the gold bar. "Who gets to try?"

"Me, please." Rachel's smile faltered. "I've had to promise to use my top-up on growth glyphs to heal the rhododendron first. Though any that's left I can use for anything I like, such as a veil."

"It's a good job Justin can see through veils or he'd never know where she'd pop up next." Frederick held out a hand. "I've been volunteered as a beginner, and because it's my house and I'm finding learning is hard work. Now how do I do this?"

"Haven't you got a notebook?" Justin held up his.

"I worry someone will see it, and maybe try something and learn about magic when they shouldn't." Frederick's manner sobered everyone, and so did his next words. "Then they'd end up having a breakdown." Even after the magic transfer experiments proved to be a success, everyone kept thinking about that. Several swore they would be buying lockable diaries, while some were going to hide the information on their phones or computers with a really long, complicated password.

The phones came in handy as various people tried to find out where to buy lead. It wasn't easy because scrap yards didn't want to sell to casual visitors and builder's merchants sold lead-free alternatives. The search came to a halt when Frederick took them to the old kitchen and showed them the thick lead waste pipes leading out through the wall. If someone would help him replace those with plastic there'd be enough lead to make a stack of bars. There was also some old lead flashing on the derelict garage to one side of the house, to get everyone started. The best at casting heat glyphs promptly offered to melt the lead if they could get a top-up from a tree to replace the magic.

* * *

Back in Brinsford Abel realised he also had access to some scrap lead, from the overgrown summer house in Castle House gardens. The roof had collapsed, which made collecting the scrap really easy for Abel and Rob. Back at the church, Kelis helped Abel melt the lead into blobs about the right weight, though Rob reckoned he could make a little mould out of some old bricks for the next attempt. For now, Abel and Kelis drew the glyph on the blobs with an old nail before cooling them with wind glyphs.

Once a few were cool enough, Jenny and Rob took them away to the mystery tree to fill them. When the blobs were handed round everyone tried them, taking enough magic to fill right up, and big smiles broke out. As a bonus, just this once, the crude lead shapes were filled back up. Jenny came back very giggly again, pure fresh tree magic still had that effect on her.

Before going home, Jenny insisted on going to say hello to Kelis' mum. Once everyone left, Kelis told Abel he'd better get on with making diamonds. Jenny had really wanted to see Kelis' rock. His second girlfriend would settle for much smaller than a goose egg, so she could actually wear it without looking ridiculous. Just as well when Ferryl explained just how good diamonds were at holding magic, much better than gold.

After beating it around a little, topping up the bits of lead every week wouldn't be a big chore, even when some rough calculation came up with thirty-eight trainees who would be needing them. That didn't include the seven scattered around the country, but a bit more discussion came up with a solution. Those would be advised to spend a few hours a week draining dregs of magic from a hedgerow or immature trees into a lead bar. The concentrated magic would allow them extra glyph casting sessions. Teaching the plant draining glyphs went into the starter procedure for any new trainees.

*   *   *

During the week before the new term started their GCSE results arrived. With huge relief Abel found he'd got A grades in IT and Graphic Art, with B or C in four others including English and what had to be a barely scraped C in maths. Theoretically, no grades were passes or failures, but everyone knew employers wanted a C grade or better. With gritted teeth Abel agreed with Kelis and Rob, they'd all take biology as an additional subject the next two years to help with their healing.

Kelis had managed six A grades, with C grades in French and science. Kelis and Abel seriously wondered if they could fit in extra science lessons, to help with the earth glyph. Rob's surprise turned out to be an A in science; he'd apparently learned more than he thought. That might explain why he seemed to be progressing faster than the other two in turning earth into rock.

Though when Abel suggested that, Rob gave Graphic Art the credit. He treated the individual grains like pixels in a picture, which could be moved or mixed to give any colour or shape he wanted. At least he thought they would when he perfected recognising the pixels, though he could already sort the softer bits out of a handful of dirt. The other two tried that but hadn't Rob's belief or skill. For once even Kelis had to give him best, though she promised to catch up.

Ferryl/Claris went to Stourton with her mum, without Abel, because the school wanted to interview her. Whatever Mrs. Ellsworth had said or done, the school were seriously considering letting Claris resit the whole year. Ferryl/Claris dressed to emphasise that she still hadn't recovered physically and promised not to command anyone. By evening the three in Brinsford started to wonder if Mrs. Ellsworth had tried kidnapping though a text saying "mum persistent. Will be late," reassured them.

Ferryl/Claris finally came back to Brinsford after dark, delivered by a resigned Mrs. Ellsworth. She'd tried persuasion and bribery, but had no answer to her daughter's obvious fear of living in town. Though once her mum finished nattering to Kelis' mum and left, Ferryl/Claris sounded triumphant. Abel hadn't forbidden mazzlement, so with whatever Mrs. Ellsworth had said and done beforehand the panel would be strongly recommending Claris got another chance.

This time, Ferryl/Claris knew Claris really would be a model student and definitely get superb grades. When Ferryl finally found a long-term host acceptable to Abel, Kelis and Rob, Claris Ellsworth would remember all her lessons and could get a decent job.

*   *   *

Abel soon had another problem. The mystery calls to Claris' phone increased, then his own rang with a withheld number. "Do you still want the key? If not, release the youngling."

"I want the key, but the host is still weak. I want her fully fit, so I can buy her back at the meeting." The first Leech had believed Abel could buy back Rob, so it had to be worth trying on the Firstseed.

"Let me speak to the youngling. It will be able to tell if she is strong enough."

"Nope. You don't get to talk to that thing and plot. You talk to me, I talk to the Leech, and we fix up a date. Then I come to your place, and we negotiate." Abel hoped it would accept a bucket full of magic gold for the key.

The woman's voice didn't sound as if it heard no very often. "No? I have what you want, so I set the terms."

"You don't want your leechy-baby back? Because if we don't deal, it's history."

"You will kill the host, a fellow pupil at your school?" Definitely not used to being crossed up, Abel thought.

"A girl who hated me, and I hated her. Now I've got her hidden away, tied up. What do you think?" Abel did his best to channel Pendragon, some sort of arrogant sorcerer.

"Is that why you wish to buy her, to make her suffer even more?" The woman laughed. "You might find that difficult. Very well, I will give you a number. Call me when you tire of playing with the host, and we will arrange for her to bring you here."

"What if the Leech won't tell me where to go?" Abel didn't think the Leech in the toad would be very helpful, so he had to try and get an address.

"If you say you are coming to meet me, it will be very keen. The youngling will be missing the nest. Do you have a pen?" She reeled off a number and Abel repeated it. "Do not take too long or I may seed another schoolgirl. One you care about." She rang off.

When Abel told her, Ferryl promised to spend more time sifting through Claris' patchy memories. To find any clues she had to relive a speeded up version of Claris' life after being taken, ugly and painful memories. Abel didn't push for details, just asked how far Ferryl had got. Ferryl had found memories of Claris in a night club, then feeling strange and passing out. She woke up completely controlled by the adult Leech that she eventually passed to Henry. After that she'd blacked out again. Claris woke up chained to a wall with the seed awake inside her. Ferryl refused to give details of what happened then.

Claris remembered the pain as the seed grew until it took control of her, eventually turning her into a puppet. Her chains were removed and the Leech moved her to a room with a window, on perhaps the third floor. In among the memories of pain and disgust, Ferryl had seen glimpses of a building Abel thought sounded like a cinema, with a big red sign outside. So far none of the memories came through clear enough to tell which building Claris had been held in before coming to Brinsford.

* * *

Another meeting with Mr. Forester two days before school started led to a final revision in the Bonny's Tavern rules. The game would also be available in German, because Laurence's cousins had sent a message. They would translate the whole thing if Kelis sent them the final English version.

When Jenny's dad mentioned her sudden urge to take extra lessons in biology and possibly science, the three mums pointed out it must be something to do with the game. Ferryl/Claris, at the meeting because she lived there now, already took biology and told them that understanding things like how muscles worked helped to make the monsters more realistic. The same applied to science, so a rock or metal shield in the game would react correctly to an intense point of heat. At least the parents found that funny, a game that encouraged the designers to study harder.

Jenny came over the last day of the holidays to collect her Abel-ex trophy, a sixteen millimetre diamond. She immediately took it into the garden and filled it with magic, producing an elasticated bracelet once her giggling settled down. That held the diamond against a glyph drawn on her skin, uncomfortable but then she could use it to top up during practice. Abel didn't tell her about glyphs under the skin because Jenny kept pushing to catch up. His last attempt, with Zephyr helping, had left his skin itching. Kelis and Rob were hoping he'd figure it out with Zephyr's help, so they didn't have to work through the same problems.

The practice to date had used huge amounts of tree magic, impossible without the Dead Wood, so it would be unfair to even tell the other trainees. Jenny didn't push for extra practice when she visited, but usually ended up getting some tuition. This time she had half an hour of concentrated glyph-throwing before filling up again, and managed a passable raincloud. She also dissolved in giggles again while hugging the tree afterwards.

Jenny seemed torn about Ferryl/Claris getting a letter accepting her back at school. They'd be in some of the same classes, which would seem strange. So would being friends with a previously bitter rival, especially as most of the school had no idea about magic or leeches. Though this year there'd be new captains for the Acro dancers, because Ferryl/Claris would retire due to her health.

As Jenny left, the remaining four inspected the door of Castle House and once more wondered what lay behind it. Ferryl still hadn't found a memory giving a view of the exterior of Claris' prison so maybe they would never know. The first day back at school, now only tomorrow, soon dragged their discussion back to what would happen then.

*   *   *

When the bus pulled up outside the school, a small crowd waited. The Tavern had decided on a show of solidarity, though from some looks it still wasn't for Claris. The first reaction when Ferryl/Claris walked into school among a mixed group including both geeks and ex-seraphim wasn't aimed at her. The canteen looked entirely wrong - chaotic. Taverners of different ages and taking different courses were sitting together, some with their non-Taverner friends. The segregation into strict social and age groups had gone, leaving an entirely different mix.

Many of the older athletes and the more affluent still sat as a group near the door, but now there weren't the same sarcastic comments as others came past. One of the sixth form rugby players even had his eleven-year-old sister and her friend, both starting their first day, sat with him. The previous segregation hadn't been hard and fast, but now it had shattered. Not just because of the Tavern, some of the previous elite who didn't play had joined tables with the sort of teenagers Seraph would never have allowed them to talk to. The extent to which Seraph had used the magical imperative in her voice to stamp her own views on the older students really showed now, even if most would never realise it.

Though as the group around Abel and Claris headed for their usual table, the babble faltered. The tight group were conspicuous so people looked, then began to realise who they were. Abel had argued against the hand-holding in school, but half-heartedly because he'd got used to his alleged girlfriend. Kelis, Jenny and Rob were adamant. He would have to hold Ferryl/Claris' hand now and then to get answers that only Ferryl Shayde had, so he may as well start off that way. If Abel only did it to answer difficult questions some bright spark might realise and nobody could even suspect that Ferryl Shayde had possessed the young woman.

"I was joking before. Now I really am buying a tent and moving into the countryside." The lad who'd made the comment about Jenny and Abel must have been lower sixth because he'd come back this year. "What I can't understand is the other two are walking along with him, and there's not one sign of scratch-marks." A ripple of laughter also led to some really curious looks at Jenny and Kelis.

Jenny put a hand out to ruffle Abel's hair. "He's quite sweet really, and a real gentleman. Just what a girl needs to practice holding hands. A few of the other possibilities seemed too keen on helping me practice Acro dancing in my leotard." Kelis kept quiet for once, though she nodded and smiled quietly as Jenny continued. "Rob might have been a candidate but he's already taken. He's got his own fan club." Since seven or eight younger pupils had called or waved to Rob when he came in, and at least half were female, that diverted everyone for a while. His Taverner fans laughed along with the others and waved again.

Despite the curious looks from non-Taverners when Claris sat with Abel and held his hand, most were more interested in why she'd come to school at all. When the questions started again at lunch, Ferryl/Claris stood up and raised her hands. "You've all got questions, and I won't answer all of them. I'm having to take the year again because I messed up, big-time, and missed the exams. That isn't the worst part, by a long way. I'll just say don't accept an invite to get you into a club, even from three other girls, and definitely don't trade sips of drinks. I'm pretty sure none of them drank any of what I swigged. I woke up in a nightmare and totally hooked."

A storm of muttering and exclamations went around the room, with some very loud comments about just saying no. Ferryl/Claris looked down and took Rob's and Abel's hands, holding them up in view. "Luckily I found friends in very unexpected places, really good friends." She nodded towards Jenny and Kelis, then to a few Taverners. "I'm still not right, that sort of thing leaves a lot of scars. I'm very nervous in public but Jenny recommended a sweet guy, a real gentleman, who might help me through that." She held Abel's hand up a little higher. "I didn't fancy the opposition if I'd asked Rob."

The serious faces began to break into smiles as Rob's fan club cheered. A few students, male and female, asked Claris to tell them when she felt better because they wouldn't mind some sweet hand-holding. Most of the students became serious again very quickly though nobody pushed Ferryl/Claris about what had actually happened, or the hand-holding. Abel would bet those were the subject of the little conversations starting up all over the room.

The looks, quiet asides and occasional remarks of "sweet" when someone walked past Abel died away by Friday. The senior students, from year eleven up, were busy trying to get grips with their new curriculum. That included GCSE biology and science, both of which had a surge of new students. Mrs. Svengy, the biology teacher, looked completely baffled by the wide range of pupils who'd never shown any previous interest.

Within a fortnight everyone seemed to be used to Claris, even the teachers. Mr. Sanders made a point of waiting to take the register the first time Abel had a morning Graphic Art lesson, glancing at the door and then Abel with an enquiring look. He let the sniggers from the class build a little before asking for silence and getting on with checking them in. Jenny began practice with the Acro dancers, not only keeping her place but Mr. Beresford asked her to be one of the joint captains. According to Jenny, when she came over at the weekend to get her diamond topped up, magic training had helped keep her fit for Acro dancing. Ferryl/Claris refused to rejoin even when the sports master asked her, claiming she still wasn't properly fit.

Mrs. Svengy began to get really enthusiastic when it became clear the new biology students weren't just keen, they were carrying out voluntary extra studies out of school. She readily guided them to where they could learn more about human biology, claiming that knowing their own body benefitted anyone. Mrs. Svengy had no idea how much most of her new students agreed with that. Everything seemed to settle down, which should have been a great big warning sign!

Creature Rampage!

As the term progressed, more students began to greet Abel, Rob and Kelis as they passed by. Occasional comments led to the trio realising most were new recruits to Bonny's tavern, beta players who didn't know about magic. Even as the game continued to spread without any sort of organisation, the feedback ironed out any small discrepancies in the rules and gameplay. The spread of the game to younger players had an entirely unexpected result.

Since the weather had brightened up, Abel and his friends were hanging about in the doorway waiting for Jenny to join them on the playing field for lunch. "Hello Rob. Could you and your friends come to look at a problem please? Rachel said you should." Despite her attempt at innocence Diane, Jenny's younger sister, couldn't hide her excitement. "Do you know where Jenny is?"

"Jenny went to see Mr. Beresford. Something to do with the Acro dancers but she should be here in a minute or two. Don't worry, we'll bring her." As Diane turned away Abel sent Zephyr to ask Ferryl/Jenny to hurry. Heads turned as the magically aware Taverners saw the spooky-phone and a few began to drift over to see what was going on.

Diane paused before turning the corner leading to the back of the boiler rooms, the yard where the big waste skips were kept. Students didn't usually come here, but Abel could hear voices even over the sound of Jenny running to catch up. The usually cheerful Diane looked serious now. "We might not need you, but Rachel wanted to have backup just in case." She pointed ahead. "Round there David, one of the boys in our year, is being told he's got to hand over half his lunch money." Her face hardened. "Well not today. The Tavern have found a new mission."

"What mission?" Abel started forward, but Diane got in the way so he stopped. "Zephyr, what's happening? Let the other three know." Invisible to Diane, the sprite flew around the corner.

"Three big boys are telling a smaller boy something. He is frightened but saying no, because seven others are behind him, encouraging him. Rachel has a glyph in her hand, ready to cast."

"Bullying!" Diane had to move or Kelis might have just run her down. Abel and the rest followed, then paused.

The obvious leader of the three larger boys had his hand out to the smaller one, sneering. "Your pathetic friends aren't going to actually do anything. Most of them are girls. Now hand it over or you know what comes next." Abel and his friends were more or less behind the three larger boys, so they hadn't been seen yet.

Rachel, just behind the smaller boy, sneered right back. "You might get a shock, Davy. If he tries to hit you, William, punch him in the face."

Abel winced because he remembered how that hurt his hands when he did it, but when he opened his mouth to say so Jenny whispered, "Hush."

"You'll break your fingers if you try, idiot. I'm going to punch you in the guts, because I'm smart enough not to leave marks. Do we get our money?" Davy raised a fist. He glanced at the boys to either side. "If any of those start, do the same. That includes any girls stupid enough to interfere."

William, the smaller boy, clenched his fists and braced himself. "No more money. Never."

Davy moved forward, one arm raised to block any punch and a fist drawn back to complete his threat. Rachel's glyphs, two of them, flew out to nestle round William's fist and it shot forward. Abel knew how that felt, because Ferryl had used his hand to punch with when they first met. The difference this time was obvious. William looked surprised as Davy staggered back and went down, but he wasn't clutching his hand in pain.

The other two boys had moved forward, on each side of Davy but one stumbled and went to his knees. He'd never realise a wind glyph, an amateur, loose one but perfectly timed, had snatched his foot out from under him. Davy would never know he fell because as he staggered back from William's punch a much more precise glyph snatched his feet from under him. With Rachel that made three magic users in the crowd of fourteen-year-olds. Four, Abel realised as two boys in the group faced the last of Davy's allies. One only had one fist clenched, but the slow magic swirl in the other hand would be much more dangerous if a fight started.

Melanie, Rob's little sister, waved to him and put a finger to her lips as

259

Rachel stalked forward to sneer down at Davy. "Just so you know, you'd better quit the bullying or the Tavern will be after you."

"The Tavern? That stupid game?" Abel could understand Davy's confusion because he felt the same way.

"Yes, a stupid game with a lot of players, and we've got a new mission. We're going to stop you and all the other bullies." Rachel cast a contemptuous glance at the other two. "That includes you." She turned and raised a hand in greeting as if just seeing Abel and the rest. "Why don't you ask the game designers? The Tavern protects the downtrodden. It's in the rules."

Abel had wondered if there still might be trouble because Davy looked livid, but the sight of four sixteen and seventeen-year-olds made him suddenly very cautious. Kelis' voice answered Rachel. "That's right. It might even be classed as charitable and earn them health points when they play." The seven youngsters backing William must all be Taverners because they cheered at that.

"So perhaps you three had better leave now." Abel half expected a teacher to turn up, though they never had when Henry had been slapping him about. He also wanted those three out of here before any of the glyph wielders felt vindictive. Davy might be a brawny lad for fourteen, but any of the girls with glyphs whirling in their hands could knock him and his friends out in seconds. He'd never realised just how dangerous magic might be in a non-magical situation at school.

"You should let them slap him around a little, to make sure he learns the lesson." Ferryl/Jenny sounded eager, but she'd also wanted to stick one of Henry's ribs through his heart.

Meanwhile Diane had reached the rest, where she high-fived Melanie. The others clustered around a bemused William, congratulating him on his punch. All except Rachel, who came over with a big smile on her face. Davy and his friends didn't quite run, but they'd disappeared from sight before Rachel came close enough to talk quietly. "I wanted you here in case it went wrong." She glanced back and smirked. "Though with four real Taverners I didn't expect too much trouble."

"Someone like you could deal with all three, but you've got to be careful about using magic. We don't want Creepio giving us grief." Abel frowned, remembering the punch. "How come William's hand doesn't hurt?"

"I used one glyph to cushion his fist, and one to smack Davy. Not too hard, but he'll have a lovely black eye. I remember how you and Ferryl Shayde met, and what she did." Her smile faltered and Rachel looked a bit uncertain, scuffing a toe in the grass. "We decided that we'd had enough. What's the point of magic and being charitable if we let someone like Davy get away with thumping William?" She firmed up a little. "We tried to back him off with numbers first?"

"Don't worry Rachel. I'll loan you my bat if he gives you grief again." Though Rob suddenly frowned, looking towards William. "Though from bitter experience, Davy will catch William on his own next time."

"No he won't. There'll be a Taverner," her hand came up a little and a glyph swirled briefly to show which sort of Taverner, "keeping an eye on William. Though I suppose Davy might take a swing at the Taverner?" He wouldn't if he saw the gleam in Rachel's eye.

Abel relaxed, because this hadn't been spur of the moment. Rachel and the others had thought it through, and he was all for anything that saved another kid from being bullied. "Now I suppose you'll want to claim the health points for a charitable act?" He smiled over at the group. "All of you?" Though Rachel refused. According to her, this came under taking out the trash. Unpleasant, necessary, and nobody expected to get paid for it, but it made the air smell sweeter. Jenny wondered if she could get the quote in the game blurb someplace.

Although the incident seemed to be over, the fourteen-year-olds really had planned ahead. As the pupils trooped back into school after lunch, Davy had positioned himself to the side of the main doors. Abel hung back to see why, in case of trouble, and his friends stayed with him. They weren't needed. When William came in he walked among a small crowd of classmates. As they approached the door they all punched the air and shouted "Tavern," then followed him inside chanting "William, William, William." It didn't last long, only until the first teacher came in sight but it certainly sent a message. Abel thought he probably looked as startled as Davy and his friends. In Abel's case it was at the numbers of Tavern players, over twenty, because he hadn't thought the younger kids were particularly keen. All the young players he knew had been introduced to

Bonny's Tavern by older siblings.

*   *   *

Davy didn't make any more trouble, or if he did Rachel and her friends took care of it very quietly. Neither Diane nor Melanie knew about magic, but both of them told their elder siblings not to worry. The year ten Tavern had it covered. Careful enquiries showed that the more numerous year eleven Tavern had also adopted the idea. Whatever the pupils were doing they'd managed it without causing any ripples, or none yet.

The next excitement came during the third week of school when the teachers called a fire drill. As he filed out onto the school field Abel realised it wasn't a drill because the Headmaster and Deputy Head were in a fierce discussion and looked puzzled. As the last students, the Upper Sixth, came out of the fire exits voices were raised in alarm. Abel turned to where several students pointed across the field, at the trees. Creatures big and small were racing out from among the trees and across the grass, with a cloud of different types of fae above them! The way some of the teachers and pupils were pointing and shouting, some of the horde must be fully visible.

For a moment Abel reeled as confusion swept over him and his ward flashed icy cold, but then his head cleared. All around him students and teachers were crumpling, everyone but the magically warded Taverners he realised. Claris ran to him and caught hold of his hand. "I mazzled them, full strength. Tell everyone. Advanced Taverners take the large creatures, beginners the small. Quick!"

Glyphs were already arrowing across the grass, but in a scattered response and many weren't very strong because the throwers were rattled. Luckily the mazzlement also seemed to confuse the larger creatures like Skurrits, a muddy-green wolf-like creature with a ruff of orange porcupine quills, a yellow snake with tiny pincered legs and covered in short, white, knife-like points and a white glittery lizard with red horns and jaws like a coachman beetle. The smaller ones kept coming, a bewildering array of types. Abel had never seen anything like the gleaming black rat-scorpions or grey ratlins veined with virulent blue and purple, now mixed with familiar types like Hoplins, Globhoblins and Thornies. The few that Abel recognised were hunters, and were heading for the fallen pupils.

"Taverners, form a line. Strongest aim at large creatures, beginners at the fae. Intermediates take smaller creatures. If you can barely use wind, blow fae away from everyone else." Abel sent a tight, very hot glyph into a lizardy thing, searing off half its jaw and one horn. It spun away then started back towards him. "They're tough. Watch every glyph all the way to the target. Don't waste magic."

"We'll run out. There's too many." Abel glanced at the speaker, a new trainee who could barely float a leaf.

"We won't but if you do I want you to go and help anyone who passed out. If they are attacked, your ward will allow you to smack fae away by hand or stomp them." Abel drilled two hot glyphs into a wolf-thing that had a broken front leg but kept coming. "They can't sting you as badly." A glyph came past him, split into eight or nine rapidly growing shards of ice, and tore into a wolf-creature from every direction. It dropped and started bubbling.

Ferryl/Claris threw him a quick glance. "I can't hold back now. If I stick close everyone might think it's you three."

"Four." Jenny stood just beyond Rob, helping to shield the other side of Claris, mostly using pure fire because she wasn't good with combinations. To Abel's other side Kelis duplicated Ferryl/Claris' feat, but only managed three shards. Abel used his wind and fire combination to torch a crippled Leggy-snake and the one crawling over it, before Kelis' wind glyph picked both burning creatures up and threw them into a group of nightmare scorpion rats. A growth glyph from somewhere sent the grass up and over the struggling mass, binding them together into one burning heap until the flames finished the job.

That only underlined how tough the bigger creatures were, which meant some smaller ones got through. A swarm of furred Horn-Toads reached several unconscious students, trying to gore them though the triple spikes were foiled for a moment by clothing. At least a third of the defenders were distracted, concentrating on pick the toads off without hitting innocents. "Everyone, kill the ground creatures first. Beginners hit the small ones. The fae can't get through our wards, or seriously hurt the rest. Anyone running out of magic, kick or slap the fae and smaller creatures off the helpless." Abel concentrated. "Zephyr, forget the creatures. Break up the big clouds of fae. Don't wait to kill them, scatter them."

"Beware the Flying Fist of Doom!" Zephyr zigzagged away from where she'd been trying to smother a Skurrit, scattering fae. "Fae bopping time!" Despite her speed a line of fae dropped in her wake, stunned or already bubbling into oblivion.

"There, to the left." Kelis sent one solid shard this time, driving a two-metre-long spined terrapin with eight legs and a huge tusked head sideways into a wolf-thing. They tore at each other, forgetting the humans.

Abel saw what she'd spotted, a dozen larger creatures heading straight for the Headmaster and the clump of adults and pupils laid near him. "Una, Warren, save the Headmaster. Only take strong users with you." Five students ran that way and powerful glyphs exploded or tore at the creatures.

"It's the wolfish things. They lead. Kill them and the group scatters." Abel looked where Rob pointed in time to see grass snatch the front legs from under a wolf-thing. It barely hit the ground before the earth surged, burying its head. As it scrabbled, slumped, then began to bubble away Rob staggered. "Curses, that hurt." He put a hand in his pocket, no doubt for a bar of spare magic. The group of creatures following the wolf-thing scattered, a few still attacking while the rest turned to flee. A clump of grass snatched the legs from under another attacker while strangling a hand-sized beetle with cat's paws and claws. Water vapour appeared around a bigger beetle-lizard's head before exploding into steam. It collapsed and began to bubble away.

Abel raised his voice. "You heard Rob, target wolf-hedgehogs, or whatevers. Kill them first."

Jenny flipped her hand up and her wind glyph overturned a tortoise-thing that had kept coming. She promptly smacked a fire glyph into the exposed belly and glanced at Abel with a wild grin. "Diamond magic!" Beyond her one of Rob's fan club had his rounders bat, smashing smaller creatures away from fallen pupils.

The glyph from behind Abel looked like one solid something until it unravelled into a net, collecting five scorpion-rats before wrapping around the main target. As the glowing red mesh tightened, the wolf-thing and smaller victims started bubbling before they hit the ground.

Earth surged and along the line four more of the creatures stumbled as the playing field snatched one leg and held it fast. A thistle exploded under one, growing straight up through its body. "Flower power!" That sounded like Rachel. All along the scattered line of Taverners, magic users steadied and retargeted, and in a flurry of mainly wind and fire glyphs the wolf-things went down.

Within a few frantic moments the attack faltered. Many Taverners were now holding their lead bars of reserve magic, while others had run right out and were kicking and swatting at fae or stomping Thornies and smaller creatures. Despite that, enough had the magic to finish the larger creatures or send them scampering or slithering away. Probably twenty sparks of fire swarmed past Abel. He launched five, the best he could control, and they were joined by possibly eight or nine from Kelis, some from Rob and even two from Jenny. A miniature firestorm enveloped the fae in front of them, scattering the survivors. "Fae-hunt! Small and tight, save magic."

In response to either the display in front of Abel, or his shout, a cloud of sparks and wind glyphs swarmed out from the advanced Taverners. They washed over the fae around the fallen students, either burning them or battering them into the ground. "Ratlin-hunt? Give me the fire, Abel." Abel grinned back at Kelis, tossing out a continual line of small, tight fire glyphs as he once had for Ferryl. Kelis caught them with wind glyphs before driving them one after the other towards her targets.

"Zephyr, come back. We don't know what's in there." Most fae were scattering now, flying frantically back towards the trees and escape, but a flying fist of doom hadn't given up.

She stopped reluctantly, hovering. Three quick tight fire glyphs fried the three biggest fae flying past her. "I could get more?"

"We might need you to help if they come back." Abel walked forward, driving a windhammer into a crippled Skurrit and stomping a small something pinned by a tight web of grass but still moving. Both began to bubble away. "These aren't finished yet." All along the line Taverners moved forward, crushing or burning trapped, stunned or crippled creatures. Just in time. Some of the adults and students were stirring, shaking their heads in confusion. A few cried out, because fae or creatures had bitten, stabbed or stung them.

"We'll never explain this." Kelis straightened, taking her hand from inside her blouse. She smiled at Abel's look. "Just because I can't show that stupid great rock doesn't mean I can't carry it sometimes. I put some magic in it to top up lead bars for some of the trainees. Just as well, my belt is empty."

Ferryl/Claris' quiet voice sounded subdued, really worried. "Mine too. Maybe it won't matter if someone saw me. There'll be investigators all over this and then the church. They'll realise what I am and try to force me out of Claris."

"Not a chance." Rob, Kelis and even Jenny echoed Abel, which cheered Ferryl/Claris a bit.

"Church. Good idea. Creepio seems to like a challenge. Let's see if he can keep this secret. After all, I'll bet some of the injured are churchgoers." Kelis looked around with a satisfied smile. "He can't use God's SAS, because we did that bit."

Abel glanced around as more people began to stir, and several were definitely injured though mainly stings as far as he could see. "A teacher will call 999 anyway, so the ambulances will be here before long. I'd better call Creepio sharpish so he can fray my ears, then hopefully try and keep most of this out of the news." Abel didn't think that would happen, but Creepio had to be his best shot. As usual he had to leave a message first. "Huge creature attack in Stourton. Non-magicals hurt at comprehensive school."

Sure enough, as baffled or stung students began to gather in small groups, his phone rang and Creepio started on the ear fraying. "What have you done now?"

"Driven them off, but there's students and teachers stung or bitten." Abel explained, briefly. "Someone must have removed our barrier posts, or only the largest would have got through."

"Check that when you can. Are the emergency services on the way?"

"Yes."

"Then stop worrying." The phone clicked and went dead.

"Well?" Kelis, Rob, Jenny and Ferryl/Claris watched with a mixture of impatience and apprehension.

"Don't worry, that's all he said." Abel looked around. "Now let's see if we can help anyone."

"Me for starters. I'm knackered because I had to use magic, not brute force. I loaned my bat out anyway, to someone who'd run out of magic." Rob suddenly grinned. "Did you like the instant grave? Though it took more magic than I expected."

"Hey, fancy glyphs my man!" Abel staggered, then Rob as a hand connected with their backs. "Who buried that cursed thing's head? I swear I nearly choked when I saw that." They looked round to see the only two of the rugby team to have managed magic so far. The Tavern wasn't a popular game among the players. Neither were past leaf fluttering, but a glance showed their hands and forearms were scratched and bitten so they'd done their part. The wounds meant they'd gone past swatting fae and small creatures to seizing and crushing them.

"Rob did that. Are you feeling okay?" Abel looked pointedly at their wounds.

"It's like a grass burn, when we slide. This feels like about fifty metre's worth. That would be a record in a game. I reckon I drop-kicked a Hoplin nearly that far before it disintegrated." Both of them laughed, possibly a bit high on survival. Quite a few seemed to feel that way.

"Typical macho rugby players." Though for once there wasn't any malice in the comment. "Well done with the leg grab thing whoever it was." Warren scowled. "My magic ran down a bit but having the cursed thing's leg nailed to the field made it a sitting duck."

"I want to learn that net, and the multi-glyph ice shard. Who did that?" A tired-looking Justin looked hopefully from one to the other.

"Rob is the earth wizard, and the Glyphmistress can manage a little thing like multiple shards. Ferryl created the firestorm." All true, even if Kelis only managed three shards. Abel avoided the net. He doubted Ferryl wanted to teach yet another advanced glyph even to him.

"While General Abel marshalled the troops and directed the battle. We were all over the place at the beginning until he started chucking out orders." Jenny managed a sort of salute.

Una patted Abel on the back as she came past. "He got us organised to save the Headmaster. It's a pity I can't bring a sword to school."

"Or General Ferryl, I reckon." Warren had a half-smile, looking at Abel's shoulder. Abel just shrugged.

"While Abel did nothing of course. He didn't even hold anyone's hand." Jenny smirked at Ferryl/Claris because she knew General Ferryl hadn't been telling Abel anything. "You must be slipping."

"Considering what Abel was throwing, he'd have burned my hand right off. Though I certainly felt safe among you four." Ferryl/Claris looked past Abel. "Here comes the first ambulance."

Una came back, helping Rachel. "Rachel is a bit young for this. She more or less drained herself and it's hit her hard."

"Give me your lead bar please, Una." Kelis put one hand in her blouse again, where she'd undone the second button, and held the small lead bar with her other hand. "Here you go, Rachel."

The fourteen-year old took the bar, concentrated, and straightened with a little smile. "Whew, thanks. Here Una, you'll want what's left in there. Did you see the thistle?"

"And heard. Flower power?" Further discussion had to stop as the ambulances pulled up and professionals began to deal with the injuries, freeing the teachers to get the pupils organised. Abel felt Zephyr flow back into his arm, and a definite drain on his depleted reserves of magic. "Well done. Are you all right?"

"I am a bit dizzy. Too much bopping. Did I get enough?"

"Yes, and your fire glyphs were very small and well controlled."

"Oh. You saw. Was that all right? I wasn't sure but I couldn't bop them all." Zephyr sounded worried.

"Every bit helped today. If anyone noticed they'll think you were Ferryl. Can you manage spooky-phone to tell everyone they remember nothing? We all fainted, just like the others." The smoky lines shot out, connecting to a dozen at a time. Many of the recipients looked over to nod agreement.

"Does your tattoo need a boost?" Kelis put her hand in her blouse again.

"She would appreciate it, if you can spare it?"

"Just a bit. There's a few others looking drained, exhausted. I'll work around them." Abel passed his gold bar and soon afterwards drained the magic back out of it. Maybe he should carry an extra belt? He'd ask Ferryl if she could make more. Kelis set off to top up any Taverner who looked particularly tired.

*   *   *

While teachers checked on students and directed them towards prefects or the ambulances, Abel's group headed towards the trees. One glance showed all the hex posts were gone, not just thrown aside. "Dryad." Abel tapped on the tree, letting a little magic tap as well. He was too angry to be completely polite today. "We wish to talk, and will not accept no." A branch creaked. "The next dryad will consider more carefully if you drop a branch. The charred stump of this tree will make it more polite."

"You do not have enough magic left."

"Not right this second, but I can come back later. You saw how many of us there are. Now please tell me who took down those posts."

"Two magic users, strong ones. They threatened to burn us if we interfered." The dryad sounded sullen, but worried. Being caught between warring sorcerers was a dryad's nightmare.

"Then it's a pity you didn't let us have a bit of magic for our barrier. The glyphs would have protected you and combined your magic." Abel's mind spun. Sorcerers? "Would you recognise them?"

"Humans all look the same, but they had hoods as well. They said you were not proper sorcerers, that you were barely trained." Branches rustled on several trees.

"Are we?"

"No. We watched. We did not realize what would come, then we did not expect you to stop them." Branches rustled again, across six or seven trees. "We caused no harm."

"Will you let us use your magic now, to strengthen the barrier?"

"No. We will not stand between sorcerers. All our histories tell us that we will burn if we do." Abel didn't answer, mainly because he didn't trust his temper. Pointing out that not helping could get them burned wasn't fair.

"The teachers are calling, Abel." Rob tugged his arm. "Don't do what I'd like to, because we're being watched." Abel turned away and the group headed back across the field. As he did the St. John's Ambulance Brigade arrived and split up among the students, checking everyone who wasn't by the ambulances. The teachers were directing everyone into year groups, so Claris and Jenny left Rob and Abel as the lads re-joined Kelis. With so many others around them, there wasn't much chance to talk.

"Now young fella, did you get any injuries?" A St. John's man pulled Abel out of the crowd. "Here, you need some on this on that scratch." He produced a swab then dropped his voice. "You slept through it all, Abel. Some students might have hallucinated, but that's to be expected with a gas leak."

Abel frowned, then realised this must be Vicar Creepio's man. "What about the bites and stings, and the state of the grass?"

"The gas drove a nest of hornets crazy. The grass will be dug up which will explain its condition." He nodded towards the school gates where two men with cameras were trying to get in past a very determined man in a yellow hi-vis vest. "Their long-range pictures won't be very clear, nor will any film if a TV crew arrive."

"The medics in the ambulances will get a really good look, and they'll make reports." Abel inspected the nearest ambulance and paramedics and they looked genuine.

"We have a few people in the hospital and on some ambulances. A little creative paperwork, some judicious muddling of memories, and seemings over the wounds to make them look like stings will deal with most of it." The St. John's man kept dabbing. "By tomorrow magical healing will leave irritating bumps instead of the nastier wounds. After that, anyone else will begin to doubt their own memories of what happened."

"What, all the students? They saw creatures before passing out. The big wolves and the spiny snakes at least." Abel really couldn't believe it would be as easy as it sounded.

"Varglin and Beinsnork, bonesnakes? They are strange companions." The man chuckled and patted Abel on the shoulder. "No matter, we will deal with it. We get plenty of practice, though not usually on this scale."

He looked quizzical. "I'm told you can tell everyone else who needs to know?"

"Yes. Though I'm still not convinced you'll get away with it."

"Don't worry, some of us have had a lot of practice. Smoke, mirrors, magic, and a little help from the good Lord can do wonders. It's a bit more subtle than knocking everyone out." He raised a hand to stop Abel's reply. "Which was the best thing at the time." The St. John's man raised his voice. "There you are young man. That shouldn't give you any more trouble." He turned away towards another student.

Abel asked Zephyr to spread the news, smiling as the St. John's man stopped for a moment to stare at the spooky-phone lines. Several Taverners looked decidedly sceptical, but there wasn't anything else any of them could do. Though even as he thought that, Abel saw a small glyph strike Rachel's very conspicuous giant thistle and it wilted. Within minutes other very small glyphs were growing bits of grass on the worst of the burned patches.

The Headmaster and a small group came to a decision, and split to get everyone lined up. The school would be closed today, but open tomorrow unless the parents were notified. Any student feeling ill after leaving here should call the doctor, or ask a parent to take them to A&E. The school buses would be here in half an hour. Anyone unable to get home or juniors who didn't have someone waiting there could stay at school.

* * *

When Abel, Rob, Kelis and Ferryl/Claris got off the bus at the end of the lane they didn't feel much like celebrating the unexpected holiday. Even a diversion into Castle House Gardens to fill up themselves and their belts and gold bars with magic didn't raise their spirits much. Sitting there quietly filling up the twenty-one empty lead bars and one diamond collected at school, none of them could make up their minds. Had Pendragon launched the attack and if so, why? If not, who could it be?

Ferryl wondered if a rival sorcerer had done it to embarrass Pendragon, believing he protected the school. In that case it could be the start of a take-over bid, but seemed too public. According to Ferryl, sorcerer disputes were quiet affairs that never drew public attention. Eventually they went home, where they all professed complete ignorance because they'd passed out. At least Rob had corroboration from a very confused Melanie when Samantha went and brought her from school.

By nine o'clock, Abel knew who'd launched the attack. He'd had two phone calls, the first a very annoyed Pendragon complaining about the embarrassment in 'his' town. He wanted to know if Abel had taken his watcher bird, because the last it saw was students collapsing. Ferryl/Claris thought the mazzlement might have hit it as well and possibly broken the link.

The second call came from an angry Leech boss, the Firstseed. According to her, one of her people had been keeping an eye on Abel and his friends, and seen the youngling's host attending school. The host looked much healthier than when they left her outside the village, strong enough for a meeting. The attack was to demonstrate what might happen if Abel and his friends didn't cooperate. If there were more delays, the next attack would be directly on pupils. Firstseed would seed four, from among those who seemed to be his friends. Abel did his best, explaining the host wasn't able to manage without the youngling yet and he really did want to buy her. As a compromise, he'd agreed to meet by the end of October. He had to call with a date within three days.

"We'll call Vicar Creepio. He'll find her and sort out the whole gross mess." Rob glanced at Ferryl/Claris. "Or do we want four more Claris' to try and fix? We haven't got enough Ferryls. Unless you two can make a bunch of Zephyrs to do the job?"

"No, please. Don't make me do that."

Though Ferryl scotched the idea anyway. "They couldn't even if we made them. Even Zephyr couldn't spread herself through a person properly, not well enough to fix the damage and control a mind. She isn't strong enough yet and hasn't the experience."

Abel ignored Zephyr being theoretically capable of that with more training. "Zephyr won't do it. She is really, really worried we'll ask her." Which Abel wouldn't do, not after that plea.

"So we ask Creepio?" Kelis shook her head. "No, because if he finds her and turns loose God's SAS he'll get the key. Then he'll use it to open Castle House, the church won't be able to resist the temptation. He really wants whatever it is in there under control or dead."

Ferryl/Claris looked worried at that idea. "What is in there hates the church. Key or not it would attack. He has no idea what he'll rouse and will not bring enough backup to survive."

"Then the church will bring up the heavies, and Brinsford is rubble." Abel thumped the desk. "We've got to go to the meeting, but we need to know where. Can we get it out of the Leech? Ferryl?"

"Not unless it is back in a human." Ferryl/Claris sounded resigned. "I will spend all my time looking through Claris' memories. I found a clear view of the sign, but we need the actual building." Ferryl/Claris wrote it down. "Do any of you recognise this?"

"That sounds like a bargain store, carpets or sofas, that sort of thing. It'll be on the internet." Rob looked happier. "Can't you work out the angle from the window to narrow down where Claris was looking from, Ferryl?"

Unfortunately all Claris' memories were muddled with fear, pain and sheer panic. After going around and around Ferryl agreed that if she couldn't get a better fix, she'd go and scout the street. That would be a last resort. If a Leech spotted them the first they'd know would be four schoolchildren going missing. Abel would ring the number tomorrow and arrange to meet on the last day of October, to give them as long as possible. That would be Halloween, which seemed appropriate.

At least there'd be no awkward questions over the attack. None of the Taverners could believe what they'd seen on the local news at six o'clock. Exactly as Abel had been told, the local authorities ascribed the collapse of the students to a burst gas main, and the wounds to hornets. None of the pictures showed fang, claw or horn marks, only big red bumps from stings. St. John's Ambulance Brigade really were a division of God's SAS, or their medics at least.

The school remained closed the next day, with local news showing diggers ripping up part of the school field to fix the alleged main. Confused survivors, including two Taverners, were interviewed but told reporters they hadn't seen a thing. Despite the strange circumstances, the national news never picked up the story at all. All the Taverners exchanged very cautious texts, but daren't really discuss something they allegedly slept through.

That evening Abel had another call, from Creepio. "Thank you for your prompt action, and your silence. Your Taverners are very disciplined for young magic users. Can you give me more details now?"

"Thank you for God's medics." Abel explained the attack including the bit about the two sorcerers or strong apprentices and Creepio promised to investigate. The denial of magic and suppression of sightings and incidents lay at the heart of the old pact. If some sorcerer had been so blatant the Magical Council would be asked to act, and from the tone the asking wouldn't be polite. Creepio didn't sound happy when he pointed out that even unaligned apprentices could keep the rules, so a sorcerer would need a very good excuse.

Abel asked about all the different creatures, and apparently most of them lived in the countryside but never came into towns. Creepio seemed puzzled how anyone had rounded them up and then kept them focussed on the humans rather than each other. He finished by telling Abel to use the trees to strengthen the protection at the school. When Abel said the dryads wouldn't agree, Creepio told him to insist.

The last part annoyed Kelis and Rob when Abel told them. Upsetting all the dryads by threatening some of them wasn't a road any of them wanted to go down. Creepio would probably threaten to burn the lot but he had the usual church indifference to the fate of magical beings and God's SAS to back him. Jenny, who had come to Brinsford to talk freely and collect her recharged diamond, thought singeing one wouldn't be too bad.

*   *   *

The small, slightly guilty looking group of Taverners waiting as Abel got off the school bus didn't wait for any questions. "The dryads want to talk to you." Una turned and led off across a school field that showed no signs of burning or the diggers. Magical landscaping had removed every sign. Abel, Kelis, Rob and Ferryl/Claris glanced at each other, baffled, and followed. On the way Kelis passed out the recharged lead bars.

"Greetings, dryad."

"Greetings, sorcerer. We have reconsidered. The situation has been explained and our trees will provide magic to power your barrier, providing we are not harmed by the link or the effect."

Abel felt Ferryl/Claris' hand in his and connected through Zephyr. "Will we have to give them all a pebble, Ferryl? I'm not keen on giving them stone glyphs as protection in case someone nicks one. They'd use it to get into Dead Wood."

"But a stronger barrier would even stop the larger creatures, and we could use the tree magic to strengthen the boundary all around the school. It is possible if we construct a different glyph for this barrier, or the dryads are warded. Though they may consider that a binding."

"I understand, dryad. We can build a barrier strong enough to stop even the worst creatures, but would need to give you a ward to keep you safe." Abel glanced up, startled as trees all around them creaked threateningly. "That is not a threat."

"Why not? Your apprentices have threatened if not directly. If we will not help, they say the trees may as well be cut down to provide timber for stakes!" Branches waved and leaves rustled as the nearby trees showed their reaction. "We will not be bound!"

"I never said that. I wouldn't harm...." Abel stopped and thought. If another attack came through, and killed a student, how would he feel? "I would never threaten that or burning, but I may act in anger. If a child is killed then I may lash out in anger. I would regret damaging a tree, but maybe too late for tree and dryad. I will not bind anything."

Zephyr popped out of his arm and connected to the tree. "I am not bound. I am free if I wish, but protected." The connection disappeared. "Sorry Abel, I forgot. I shouldn't connect to dryads."

"Don't worry, you already did it once before. But try to remember." Either the dryad had whatever information Ferryl worried about or it hadn't, too late to change it now.

At least Zephyr's intervention had some effect. "Protected but not bound? Would we have a tether?"

"A Tavern mark on each dryad would suffice."

"Just a mark such as this." Abel pulled out a wooden plaque. He always carried a few in case someone needed them to protect a friend or relative.

"If you put that on us, it is a binding." Leaves rustled, but not quite as threatening. The other dryads were still wary.

"Draw it yourself. We'll bring inks from the school and you can test them first. If you all agree, we will weave a barrier to stop anything but a full sorcerer. Since the links to the barrier will also connect your trees, you might even be able to stop them as well."

"But not you."

"I will be able to pass the barrier. Even so you might be able to defeat me if you are linked, but not if I bring the other Taverners. You will have to agree to us maintaining the barrier and you mustn't kill innocent trespassers, the non-magical type." The school bell rang. "We must go now. Look at this and please think about it." Abel tossed the plaque down and the whole group pelted back across the field as the last students went through the doors. There wasn't even time to talk via Zephyr as the group split up to reach their lockers and classes.

*   *   *

Abel left the dryads to think until lunch-time when despite a chill in the wind he, and some others, took their lunch to sit under the trees. They'd barely sat down when the shimmering of a veil around each tree announced the arrival of the dryads. No talking from inside the trunk now, at least a dozen were in plain sight. Abel noticed the veils didn't include his own group, leaving them in view of the other students braving the weather. The plaque landed on the grass next to him. "There is no harm in there. The intent is protection, with some sort of healing that is not activated."

"The additional part gives some relief from pain and encouragement to heal." Kelis glanced at Abel. "As the original creator intended. That only works when drawn on the skin."

"Or bark." Twiggy digits scraped the front of the nearest dryad. "Does it matter where the mark is?"

"No." Kelis seemed content to discuss it so Abel kept quiet. "We put them where we can stroke them. It is comforting."

"That might be a new thing. The wind hints of a dryad rescued, and others who live protected but without marks." Abel reflected that the wind seemed very well informed. Something more than birdsong and mouse chatter had passed that information though the dryads weren't trusting to the wind, not entirely. As the discussion worked through what had been done at Brinsford and Frederick's house, the dryads admitted to knowing of Dead Wood and Sorcerer's Keep.

The talking went on all dinner break, a windy, cold hour. Luckily every student under the trees had practiced fire and wind, though they kept the warm air away from nervous wood-creatures. Eventually the dryads somehow came to an unspoken, silent consensus and the spokes-dryad passed it on. If the humans would come tomorrow and explain exactly what the barrier would do, and the amount of magic involved, they would seriously consider an agreement. After explaining they'd be away until Monday, the quietly jubilant group made their way back to classes.

Not all were jubilant. Abel, Rob and Kelis were pleased but cautious as Ferryl explained how difficult the weaving must be. To include dryads but not all dryads, and those with Tavern marks but not everyone who drew a Tavern mark, took carefully orchestrated intent. In addition, this barrier would dissuade teachers and pupils from coming into the trees, but couldn't harm any who pushed hard.

Designing that kept all four busy during the weekend, instead of worrying about the Firstseed's ultimatum. In four weeks they had to find the Leech lair, the place most of the nest lived, and come up with a plan to keep Firstseed from seeding students. If they couldn't, all four agreed they'd have to send in Vicar Creepio Mysterio and God's SAS.

*　*　*

The weeks crept by, filled with school and glyph homework as well as building what really did become a very complicated barrier glyph. A dozen drawings were scrapped as a tiny test version showed a flaw. Eventually the dryads copied the Tavern glyph onto their bark in permanent ink before Kelis, Rob, Abel and Jenny, orchestrated by Ferryl/Claris, spent hours crawling under trees hidden by a veil. Despite what she'd said about keeping her distance, Jenny had somehow become a permanent part of their group. According to her, watching Abel with Ferryl/Claris had removed most of the weird factor. She now felt sure he'd never broken their guidelines, and instead took to occasionally teasing him about never getting a real kiss.

* * *

Ferryl worked hard on searching Claris' memories, and found clearer views of what the internet showed to be old cinema selling second-hand furniture and carpets. Claris never went outside the lair, possibly because of her emaciated appearance, so she never even saw the front door. The weekend before Halloween, in pure desperation, Abel and Ferryl/Claris went to look for the house.

After the taxi dropped them off near the store, the pair of them walked over to browse. Abel wore a hoody and Ferryl/Claris a seeming of a young schoolgirl with long blonde hair, and both wore gold belts and carried extra lead bars full of magic. Rob, Jenny and Kelis lurked around the corner, also loaded for magical bear. Ferryl/Claris had a casual look round. "It is somewhere close because Claris could see this side of the shop from the front window. We must hope there is some sign." Unfortunately the area all looked a bit run-down, covered with creatures, litter and graffiti. The pair of them walked along the road on the same side of the road as the cinema, casually glancing across at the opposite buildings.

Ferryl stopped and turned to Abel. "Put your arms round me for a few moments, and look over my shoulder. There are no creatures actually going into the tall building with the glass doors covered in posters. There are hexes around the windows, but I need to get closer."

"I see them. Why are there none on the door?" Abel moved his shoulder closer to Ferryl/Claris so Zephyr could ask her by spooky-phone.

"The Leeches would find them uncomfortable. We will have to walk in through that door, because the window hexes will include alarms. Unless I can break them quietly." Ferryl/Claris turned but held onto Abel's hand. "Let's cross the street and innocently wander up that alley at the side. Then I can judge how strong the hexes are. If we walk near the building wall, Zephyr can fly straight upward to inspect the higher windows."

A few minutes later they were walking slowly down the alley hand in hand, aimlessly kicking at trash. Zephyr shot back into Abel's arm as a door further down the alley opened, connected briefly to Ferryl, then snatched the spooky-line back. "Leech coming."

Four men came out, all wearing jeans and hoodies, led by an

impeccably dressed young woman. "Time to go." Ferryl's arm tugged gently and Abel turned to head back to the street."

"What do you two want?" Abel felt a chill and a wash of compulsion telling him to answer the woman. It was gentle but he thought he'd best pretend it worked. Either that or start running.

"Nothing, just looking around for someplace private." Abel kept his head down inside the hood so his face stayed hidden.

"We can find you somewhere private back here?" The compulsion came again, pulling at him, but Abel wasn't going any nearer the door.

Ferryl/Claris butted it. "We want someplace without people." She tugged at Abel's arm. "C'mon. I'm getting itchy. Need my fix." "I'll pretend I'm an addict needing my fix. Leech compulsion has difficulty overcoming Morphine and opium addiction."

"We can fix you up in here?" One man indicated the doorway. "Good stuff, and cheap."

"No." Ferryl put a hand in her handbag, tugging Abel back a few more steps. "I've got the stuff, just need a place. You touch me I'll cut you." One of the men took a step forward and Abel tensed just a little.

"Shall I bop him?" Zephyr sounded wound up and raring to go, which calmed Abel down.

"Not yet Zephyr. Not unless they get close, then smack the Leech."

"Ffod bop ready."

But the Leech-woman put out a hand to stop the others. "Typical junky. Let her go. She's not worth the noise and aggravation." Meanwhile, Abel and Ferryl/Claris made the last three steps to the alley entrance, turned and walked quickly away.

"Now we know. The sides are watched, and that door is guarded. Those are very good hexes for a Leech, they are not usually very adept. I cannot break into the windows to sneak in, so it is smash and grab or walk in the front door. Unless the higher windows are less well protected?" Ferryl raised her voice, whining a little. "Come on, let's get home. There's no-place round here."

"Just hang on until then, all right. No cutting anyone." Abel tried not to smile at that. "Zephyr, what about the other windows?"

"The same glyphs as the bottom ones. Very strong. I could get in the door and bop the guard?"

"Not all four." Abel passed on the rest as the pair walked around the corner to find the other three waiting impatiently. "We found it, but we'll have to go to the meeting with Ferryl/Claris pretending to have a Leech."

"Curses. She'll not let us all in. You could try for taking a bodyguard, just one of us?" Kelis looked past Abel to the corner. "Were you spotted?"

"Sort of but Ferryl got us out." He explained. The discussion in the bus on the way back had to be quiet and guarded, but even when they could talk freely nobody had a better idea. Though if it came to it, they now knew exactly where to direct God's SAS.

*   *   *

Abel called Firstseed as instructed, and she didn't sound happy. "I have received more information on the school attack. You are more powerful than expected so I will not meet you at our lair. Write down this address." Abel wrote it down, mind racing.

"How will I know you?"

"You won't and my appearance is irrelevant. Leeches can detect each other regardless of the host, so the youngling will tell you who I am. That way I can be sure your companion is the youngling, not one of your sorceresses in a seeming." The Firstseed still seemed wary. "You bear the bloodline of the sorcerer? If not, you cannot touch the key."

"Yes." Ferryl swore his relationship to the sorcerer had allowed Abel's blood to break her binding seals.

"Come alone, except for the youngling. Do you still wish to buy the host?"

"Yes. What's the price?" Abel crossed his fingers for something he could afford but it didn't work.

"If you can touch the key, we will bargain. If not, you have nothing I need. Come at six pm, without your apprentices. I will have watchers." She paused for a moment. "Walk across the square. Come by taxi, not in your own vehicle."

"Your people keep away from me. If they close in I start throwing glyphs. If we go into a room and I see more than one other person I blow a wall out." Abel thought hard but that covered it. "I'll be there with the youngling."

The new instructions spoiled any vague plans they'd already made, though Ferryl still felt hopeful. The Firstseed would probably take Abel to her lair anyway because she wouldn't want the key exposed. At least they now knew why nobody had tried to get into Castle House, the key needed a blood relative of the sorcerer. The Leech recognition signal seemed insurmountable until Ferryl/Claris suggested taking Leech-toad with her, in a pickle jar in her handbag. Hopefully the Firstseed would think Claris was still the host. That left the other problem, how to recognise the Leech.

Zephyr's quiet excited voice sounded in Abel's head. "I can do that?"

"How? She will be an adult, and they are almost impossible to detect without getting very close." Ferryl paused. "How did you know a Leech would come out of that door, Zephyr?"

"I can feel them, ever since I fought the Leech in the garden. I went into it, a little." Zephyr shut up, the whole incident still worried her. After a pause, she continued. "I feel the Leech in Castle House garden as soon as we pass the barrier, but didn't realise I would feel any others."

"You almost became part-Leech, spreading through it to possess the creature, which gave you a true understanding of them. You recognise their scent, or a vibration, whatever they use." Ferryl/Claris smiled happily. "She will not expect that!"

"I still don't want Abel swanning off someplace I can't follow." From the set of her jaw, Kelis wasn't budging on that. "I'd rather bring Creepio. He'd catch her right out in the open." Kelis closed her hand, as if crushing something.

Rob glanced at Abel's arm. "Zephyr can't go and look for her anyway. She'd see the tether."

"I can set her free?"

"No! Too soon!" Zephyr sounded close to panic. "Struggling with the leech, and healing Rob, and sometimes hunting or fighting, I lose myself. I must have my way home!"

"Can Abel attach the tether again afterwards?" Jenny shrugged. "Since he tethered her in the first place? Then if Zephyr just followed, without any fights or hunting? If she stayed high but well back, Zephyr could send us a spooky-phone and direct us if I borrow dad's pickup."

All eyes turned to Abel's tattoo, then Abel. He shrugged. "I didn't set the tether. As far as I know, if I tell Zephyr she's free, she is."

"True if you have intent. I can teach you to reset the connection, because it isn't a real tether. It would take both of you. If Zephyr liked freedom, she needn't come back." Ferryl looked at the tattoo. "Even Zephyr can't be sure until she is free."

"I am sure. I do not want to go, but if it helps Abel I will do it. I will be the fearless Ffod, but I will come back without bopping anything."

After a short, very simple lesson for Zephyr and Abel, talk turned to what-if. Anything could happen once the Firstseed found that Ferryl/Claris wasn't the youngling. Even if that worked out, the best scenario they could come up with ended in a pack of Leeches chasing Abel and Ferryl/Claris through Stourton. They'd need backup waiting, preferably the sort that could tackle a Leech head-on.

A score of possible plans were dissected, discarded or adapted but all of them relied on the Taverners, all the stronger magical ones, being willing to take chances. By the time they'd made provisional decisions on who to ask for diversions and who might fight, Jenny had to go home. Another fifteen minutes and her dad would be phoning to remind her about the time, and right now she needed him in a good mood. Kelis went off to make a private phone call of her own. She wanted all the backup possible, even an ex-boyfriend.

Firstseed Firefight

The next few days passed quickly, with many Taverners at school distracted by Halloween. The magical ones were planning on using their new skills to liven the night up, but as a diversion and without actually breaking the compact. Abel worried exactly where that line might be, but with his skin at stake he wasn't going to be too picky.

Some Taverners, the younger ones, couldn't get permission to be out late at Halloween, but most of the older ones promised to be there. The Taverners had all been revolted by what the Leech did to Claris and horrified by the attack on the school, and were keen to dish out some retribution. Eric had the number for Creepio, to ask for God's SAS to rescue Abel or to flatten the Leech lair once Abel and Claris escaped.

Abel, Rob, Kelis and Claris had a late pass for Halloween, allegedly to join their friends in haunting Stourton. All four wore old sheets torn into rags and fake blood. At least when Frederick arrived on the back of Shawn's scooter, the age of their chauffeur reassured the parents. The pickup truck parked under a veil outside the church, filling up with Goblins, might have caused misgivings.

The conversation on the way to town would have caused parental palpitations. In Stourton Jenny waved goodbye as the pickup peeled away to deposit the goblins and collect her troops, while Frederick pulled up by a taxi rank. After some last frantic good wishes Abel and Ferryl/Claris took a taxi to meet the Firstseed. Kelis and Rob took another taxi, but they'd keep back out of sight. With a big smile Kelis dropped a bright yellow colour glyph on the roof before climbing in, so Zephyr could find her.

When Abel and Ferryl/Claris arrived in a small square outside a pub throwing a Halloween bash, Zephyr went on alert. She slipped out of Abel's shoulder and began to swoop around low to the ground, where nobody would notice a ripple in the moving shadows. Within a couple of minutes she arrived back. "Tall, thin woman in black trousers and top and a red cloak. She has long black hair. Over near the pub door."

"Fly free, Zephyr."

"Back soon."

Abel's arm felt empty, just when he'd got used to a resident again. He didn't have time to reflect on that, because as the pair of them walked towards the woman Zephyr described she smiled to welcome them. Abel had to choke back a comment. The Blood Leech had come dressed as a movie vampire in skin-tight leathers with a crimson cloak and plastic fangs. Instead he braced to throw glyphs, because if Leeches communicated more than a feeling of being nearby the youngling would be screaming for mummy to rescue it.

"You feel concerned, youngling. Do not worry. Soon you will be home again." She turned to Abel. "We will wait while friends check the crowd. You are young for a sorcerer. I am told it is not a seeming."

"I'm an apprentice. My teacher wants me to get the key."

She held up a hand to stop Abel saying any more. "You were not followed. Youngling, take him by taxi to the lair. That one over there. I will follow with others, in case of trouble."

"Remember, you and one other." Abel didn't want a car full pouncing on him, even with Ferryl/Claris to help.

Ferryl/Claris had already turned away, heading back towards the taxi the Firstseed had indicated. Her hand slipped into his. "I dare not speak to her. I do not know what voice a Leech would use, or what it would call the Firstseed." "Look, the taxi is empty."

"A proper hackney cab, loitering about so far away from the cab rank in the town centre. How lucky." Which Abel knew it wasn't, the Leech must have called for it or owned the driver. He inspected the taxi driver as they got in, wondering if the man could be carrying a Leech. According to Ferryl's hand he wasn't, so Abel relaxed. At least everyone would know exactly where to go because Zephyr would recognise the building.

The trip didn't take long. When the taxi stopped Ferryl leant forward to whisper "Please stay" and touched the man's hand, held out for the fare. He slumped, asleep. A car pulled up behind, a low, sleek red convertible with the Firstseed driving and two other young women aboard. When Abel held up two fingers, one pouted and stayed in the car. The Firstseed didn't even pause. Even as she opened the glass doors a shadow flickered along the bottom of the building where it met the pavement, then up

Abel's leg and arm.

"The Ffod returns!"

"Are you staying?"

"Of course. Shake hands please." That came closest to describing the sensation of reconnecting. Abel reached out with his magic to clasp an ephemeral something, and the two twined around each other. With a little zing they were one, connected. "Home again." Zephyr sounded even more hyped than usual. "The others follow, but well back. I was to tell them if it is not this house."

Abel wanted to tell Ferryl, but daren't. The other Leech woman waited in the lobby while Abel went up the lift with just the Firstseed and Ferryl/Claris. Apparently there was already one woman in the room with the key. Abel stopped the one attempt the Firstseed made to talk to Ferryl/Claris, claiming he didn't want them exchanging code words. On the third floor the Firstseed took them down a long corridor to the end room, and opened the door. Abel glanced inside to find an otherwise healthy-looking woman, sat in a wheelchair with a blanket over her legs. "Magic flows around the object under the cover on the table. None around the woman. The walls, floor and ceiling, even the windows, are webbed with magic. They will be very tough to break."

"Good, nobody can break in." Abel nodded to the woman and walked in, still holding Ferryl/Claris' hand.

"This is a saferoom, except the door has been left free." Abel squeezed Ferryl/Claris' hand in reply.

"Before I ask you to open the case, I must pay the courier. This woman undertook a very dangerous journey to retrieve that case and smuggle it here, in return for a service." The Firstseed walked across to the wheelchair, leant over the woman, and began to vomit up a Leech!

"Hey, stop that!" Abel reached out an arm but didn't get any further.

Ferryl/Claris whirled and pinned Abel's arms to his sides, pushing him back. "I cannot allow you to interfere with the Firstseed." "The woman agreed, and the Firstseed will be weaker in that body. She believes she has me to help her so it doesn't matter."

"But the woman doesn't know. About the pain."

"It is a bargain. The Firstseed will keep it." "We'll take the woman and Firstseed with us, and give her the toad option. Now stop struggling." Ferryl's smile looked just a little hyper. "Or I'll do what Firstseed probably thinks I've done, get a lip-lock to seed you."

Sheer shock stopped Abel. The Firstseed thought he'd have kissed Claris and turned up freshly seeded, easy to subdue? That explained why she wasn't worried about Abel's magic, and maybe the comment about him playing with his captive. Meanwhile the erstwhile Firstseed slumped to the floor, her Leech gone, while the new Firstseed in the wheelchair straightened with a smile. "That's better. The last host had become difficult to keep alive."

"What about the bargain? Healing and all that." Abel stared at the tall, slim woman now curled up with a tiny ribbon of blood coming from her mouth.

"Why waste the time and effort on this one? She is alive, and if we pour enough blood into her the seed might save her. If not she will feed the seed while it grows a little, then we will put it into a healthier host when she dies. I cannot allow her to be free, not now she knows about the key." The woman turned, rolling the wheelchair to the table and pulling the cloth aside. "The key is inside this." The Firstseed reached out tentatively as if to tap the case, and a fat blue spark snapped at her finger. "This body could touch it while she had no magic, but it has detected the change. Do you still want to touch it?"

Abel didn't hesitate, either this worked or it didn't. He touched the case and nothing happened. "Now what?"

"Put a thumb on that latch, please." Abel did. It stung, then the case clicked and the lid opened slowly. Inside, nestling in what Abel thought must be silk, lay an ornate key. He wasn't sure if the strange twisted engravings were glyphs, but he'd bet the gems held magic.

"Magic, strong magic, curling round and through the key. It looks very, very dangerous." Zephyr sounded really cautious, as did Ferryl when Claris' hand took hold of Abel's. Abel reached towards the key.

"That is enough, young man. Now the case is open, I will take the key. You will be rewarded." The Firstseed reached for the key but squealed in pain as blue-green lightning lashed at her hand. She stared at the burns on her flesh, the key, and then Abel. "Very well, you have a bargain. Open the door to Castle House for me and the host is yours to do with as you wish. The youngling will leave her. I will even place the woman under a strong compulsion to obey you, always, if you wish her compliant."

Ferryl/Claris let go of his hand as Abel put out a cautious finger, more cautious after Zephyr warned him. "The magic is reaching out, around your finger and your hand." Abel took a deep breath and kept going until his finger made contact. "The flows have altered. They have thickened, swirling back and forth." Relief coloured Zephyr's voice in Abel's head. "The flows have quietened and withdrawn, though your finger is still in them."

Abel picked the key up. "I'll make you another bargain. I take the key away with me and we give Claris a choice, stay or come with me. Then we negotiate a price, in gold or something similar because I prefer not to steal."

Ferryl/Claris didn't wait to be asked. "I choose to leave with Abel."

A massive surge of compulsion crashed over Abel, but his ward flashed icy cold and shrugged it away. Though when he looked, it wasn't him the Firstseed had aimed it at. She stared at Ferryl/Claris in shock. "How did you resist? Youngling, kill the host!" Compulsion hammered down again.

"Sorry, that option won't work as expected." Ferryl/Claris put her hand in her big handbag to lift out the large pickle jar with holes punched through the lid. "Yeuk. Nasty." Inside the toad twitched once more before falling still, blood pouring from its mouth. The youngling leech crawled out, but had no-place to go.

"You have failed the nest. Die!" Even as the Firstseed spoke, Claris' finger moved on the jar and Abel saw magic glow. The Firstseed stared at the jar and then Ferryl/Claris, enraged, but the anger changed to caution as she saw the glyph forming in Ferryl/Claris' free hand. Another started to form in Abel's free hand as he tucked the key away in his pocket.

"Bop time?" As Zephyr flew free to hover over Abel's shoulder the Firstseed's caution turned to alarm.

"Very well. You keep the key and woman."

"No seeding children. We know what you look like, and we know where your lair is." Abel's mouth stretched in what wasn't a pleasant smile. "We also have the phone number of an Archbishop."

"Worse still, we could let Braeth Huntian know where to come?" Ferryl's bright smile promised carnage.

The Firstseed began to back her wheelchair towards the door. "Very well. You have made your point. I will not challenge sorcerers and church together." She shuddered, the first sign of real fear, and eyed Zephyr. "No Blood Leech will risk Huntian."

"What about her?" As he glanced at the ex-host Abel could see her chest move so she still breathed, but barely and she hadn't even twitched since dropping.

"Take her if you wish." A vicious grin twisted the Firstseed's face. "That one will not survive if you remove the seed, and it will kill her if you do not supply blood. Seed, wake the host." The woman began to thrash, weakly, and scream. "A present." She whirled the chair around and shot through the door, turning to head down the passage. As she did the door began to swing shut.

"Stop it! The door!" Zephyr got there first but rebounded as magic crackled. Abel grabbed the edge of the door and hissed at the pain that ran up his arms, but he held on. "Here!" Ferryl/Claris threw a chair, which Abel kicked into the gap between door and jamb before gratefully letting go. He shook his arms to get rid of the remaining tingling. Ferryl/Claris bent to the woman and touched her. "Sleep." She stopped screaming. Glyphs swirled in Claris' palms as the sorceress inspected the door, then they shot out to strike the hinges. A slow hissing and sparks came from both pieces of metal before the door swung back open.

Zephyr shot out through the gap, but returned just as fast. "Many people and magic." Abel looked around the edge of the doorway. Almost by instinct he threw a glyph at the Firstseed's wheelchair, over halfway down the long corridor towards a crowd gathering by the lifts. One wheel crumpled and it fell over. The Firstseed cried out in pain but rose, hunched over and obviously having difficulty making the limbs work. "Huntian, they bring Braith Huntian. Kill them!" Abel hit her leg with wind, reluctant to burn a crippled woman, and she fell backwards towards him.

Ferryl/Claris didn't sound happy. "Curses." Abel glanced back to see her inspecting the windows. "Can you hold them while I open this?"

"Break it. Use a chair?" Abel kicked the one near the door towards the window leading to a balcony. "Is there a fire escape?"

"Sort of. I'll need magic, and care. This room would have sealed once the door closed, but now I believe I can unpick the glyphs around the glass. The glass won't break, not unless you brought three or four extra belts?"

"Just two, as you know." Abel looked out of the door again, sending a wind glyph to disrupt the glyph pulling the Firstseed down the corridor towards two robed figures with cowls covering their faces. He threw a fire glyph at them, but it hit an invisible wall and did no more than scorch the walls each side. "They've got sorcerers and a shield." He used a quickly formed ice shield to deflect a wind glyph downwards where it punched through the corridor carpet and floorboards. "They are stronger than me."

"Use fire. Burn the corridor if necessary." Ferryl/Claris tossed a belt full of magic. "I need finesse, not strength." When Abel looked again the Firstseed had begun to crawl, but a Ffod shot along the corridor and knocked a hand out from under her. As Zephyr zigzagged back up the corridor, avoiding or deflecting glyphs, a voice called out telling everyone not to harm the Firstseed.

Abel didn't need a second hint. His wind glyph snagged her foot and dragged her, screaming, two metres towards him. This time, as one of the sorcerers used wind to disrupt his glyph, the other threw tight fire glyphs. Abel dodged back. When he looked again, his blood chilled and he threw himself backwards just in time to avoid a hail of bullets! He stopped worrying about the Firstseed being a woman, putting his hands around the door to send a long blast of fire and wind like a flamethrower towards the gunmen. This time the glance showed the men were actually gunwomen, the two who had been in the sports car. They'd stopped while flames splashed on the shield but raised their guns again when the fire died. Guns couldn't shoot with the shield up!

Though that might not be much of a help. Vapour boiled out of the air to extinguish the flames and now Abel saw a hulking shape behind the sorcerers. "There's a Troll, as tall as the corridor and a lot fatter than the baby one."

"Still a young one, but older so heavier. Smash the floor so it daren't risk coming forward." Ferryl/Claris sounded distracted, her hands spread out near one side of the French window. Sparks and puffs of vapour showed she'd been making progress.

"Easier said than done." But Abel only muttered as he peeped again and loosed fire glyphs at the floor near the shield. The guns, raised to fire, stopped when the faint sheen of the shield reappeared. As Abel fired off more glyphs he noticed the Firstseed crawling away from him again, using the wrecked wheelchair as cover. He flicked it up and over her to hit the shield and dragged her back a few metres. As the chair fell the shield went out, more vapour dowsed his fire and the guns came up. Four pistols now, all held by women.

"Ffod!" Zephyr went down the corridor like a bullet herself, but a crazy ferret-bullet, bouncing off the floor, ceiling and walls while firing off small glyphs. The shield came back up, sharpish, but glyphs arrowed out towards Zephyr and she reversed. The sorcerers were intent this time, the glyphs closing in as she raced towards Abel and he tried throwing counter-glyphs. Zephyr barely made it, zipping through the door and twisting to the side and into her tattoo as Abel diverted another windhammer through the corridor floor. The last two glyphs, unguided now the sorcerers couldn't see her or them, curved through the door and across the room. One burned off the wallpaper in a big circle, while the other smashed the door on a sideboard.

Abel felt magic drain through his link as Zephyr topped up, and gripped the belt Ferryl had thrown. A glance showed she'd got over halfway round the window now. Another glance, out the door, showed the Firstseed had nearly made it to the shield. Then there'd be a firestorm coming this way. Abel had tried smashing the floor but couldn't get the force from this angle, but he looked at the two holes punched in the boards near him and smiled. Those sorcerers might be stronger or more skilful but he could be sneaky. "Zephyr, if I throw a glyph out of sight, can you catch it and aim it?"

"Maybe? I have a link to your magic." Abel explained. "A flying fist of boom!" Zephyr hovered as Abel built a strong, tight windhammer.

He fired off a few un-aimed fire glyphs with the other hand to keep the sorcerers occupied. Once the glyph sat, ready, Abel pulled more magic from the belt and started to build a big fire glyph in the other hand.

"Don't hang about, Zephyr. If this works, it'll be spectacular." Abel dropped the windhammer down through the hole in the corridor floor. "Go!" As Zephyr followed it Abel used that hand to send a scattering of quick wind and fire glyphs down the corridor to keep the sorcerers busy. He felt a stuttering down the link as Zephyr pulled magic so controlling the glyph must be difficult.

He knew when it hit, about four metres of floor-boarding and tattered carpet at the other end of the corridor flew up into the air! Stunned by the amount of damage Abel froze for a second, then yelled, "Zephyr, run!" He leant out into the corridor, perfectly safe because the opposition were definitely distracted, and angled his fire glyph through the hole as Zephyr flew out. This one didn't have to be precise.

Down the corridor the dislodged floorboards were still falling, while the boards partly inside the shield tipped up because they were no longer supported at one end. The Firstseed and a gunwoman were scrabbling for a grip when the Troll slid through the group and down into the hole. One sorcerer threw himself aside but the Troll bulldozed the other robed figure, two gunwomen and the Firstseed over the edge. A ball of fire rose through the shattered timbers as Abel's fire glyph found a target on the floor below, creating an inferno. Abel couldn't help flinching at the thought of Creepio's reaction. His face hardened. The magic belts were nearly empty, but he could spare some for one target.

As the robed sorcerer went over the edge he used wind to support himself across the gap, losing control when flames billowed up around him. Now he clung to a splintered stub sticking out of the wall and his cowl had fallen back, baring his face. Abel's mind spun when he recognised Elrond. Was Pendragon working with a Leech? Even as Abel formed the windhammer glyph Elrond's mouth opened and familiar tendrils and then a glistening shape appeared. Elrond thrashed, still clinging on for dear life, as an adult Leech crawled out of the apprentice's throat. Abel loosed the glyph, splattering Leech blood all over the man's face.

"Look out." Abel glanced back and moved over as the entire French window floated across the room and slid into the corridor, on edge. "Our own shield." Sure enough the other sorcerer and at least one gunwoman had recovered enough to respond, but their glyphs and bullets bounced off the glass. "The glyphs in that glass are good work, better than anything a Leech could manage." Ferryl/Claris looked out, safely protected, and her face set. Abel stuck his head out, staying behind the glass, just in time to see her small glowing net wrap around Elrond's head and pluck him off his refuge. With a long scream he plunged into the flames.

At the other end of the corridor, beyond the blaze, another Troll smashed a hole in the corridor wall and a gunwoman followed it out of sight. Abel stepped back and looked at the walls of the room. "It'll come through the rooms parallel to the corridor, out of sight until it gets here. Can it break this wall down?" The mere thought worried Abel. He'd only been able to hold the rest off because they were at the opposite end of the long corridor, in plain sight. At least the sounds and flashing lights from down in the street below meant the cavalry had arrived.

"It can now, because wrecking the door and window glyphs has weakened the rest. Time to leave before the bonfire gets here as well. Creepio will be upset." As she giggled Abel wondered if his own face reflected the manic grin on Ferryl/Claris'. She pulled his hand. "Call off Zephyr. Our transport is waiting."

The sprite still hovered behind the glass, popping up now and then to fire off small glyphs while shouting "pow, pow" down the link. At least she kept the remaining sorcerer concentrating on her.

"Come on Zephyr." Abel hesitated. "What about her?" The sleeping woman still lay on the floor. "She'll burn."

"Grab an arm. You'll need the other hand when we jump."

"What!"

"No fire escape. Use wind to slow your fall." Ferryl/Claris caught hold of one of the woman's hands and dragged her towards the balcony. "Come on!" Abel shrugged and went for it. Next time Ferryl said "sort of" a fire escape he'd ask questions. He dragged the remaining magic from a belt, feeling Zephyr flow into his arm even as Ferryl/Claris scattered glyphs ahead of them. "Look out below!" The bottoms of the metal legs crumbled into dust and the balcony railing toppled out of sight. Ferryl/Claris never gave Abel a chance to have second thoughts. She plunged straight over the edge, still holding the rescued woman's hand.

Abel summoned a wind glyph as he followed, blasting it downwards with his free hand while tightening his grip on the woman. At least she wasn't heavy, especially with Ferryl/Claris holding the other arm. Abel could feel magic draining away as they fell, slowly but still too fast, and hoped Ferryl had enough left to cushion all of them the last few feet. Zephyr zoomed out of his arm as a shot rang out, closely followed by a shriek above and to the side. A screaming, flailing woman fell past them as Zephyr returned, dropping the pistol before wrapping around Abel's hand and wrist. He wasn't sure if the sprite helped with lift, but the extra grip stopped him dropping his half of the shared burden. Ferryl still had a firm grip at the other side.

A sudden blast of wind slowed Abel, and then the pavement shocked his feet. "You were always useless with wind." Kelis reached for Abel's hand to drag him towards the taxi, then switched to helping lift the woman because she'd crumpled to the ground. "Shannon is driving. We've put the driver in the boot." Ferryl/Claris dropped the arm she held and turned, her wind glyph lifting a man with a baseball bat from his feet and smacking him against a building. She turned, caught hold of the rescued woman's feet and backed into the cab. The four men Abel had met before were unconscious or dead, scattered across the entrance to the alley, while smoke drifting out from behind them hinted at more destruction around the back door. Another five men lay scattered along the pavement in front of the building, all out for the count. A crunching noise brought Abel's head round to see two humps of warped concrete grow out of the step to block the front doors. Rob waved and headed towards him, then stopped.

Another opponent had arrived, a man but definitely Leech-ridden because he ignored the deep slash across his arm and a piece of wood driven into his thigh. Kelis fired off wind and an ice shard, and Rob tried to snatch his foot with the pavement, but this man shrugged them off. Whatever magical protection he had, the glyphs just bounced as he strode straight towards Abel. Ferryl cursed, trying to get past the rescued woman and back out of the cab but the man gave a sudden, startled yelp. He dropped from sight, leaving his head poking out of a neat circular hole full of dust. The dust began to solidify, tightening the hole but not completely filling it in. "I'm out." Rob looked drained, staggering to the taxi. "There was bleddering metal down there as well." He more or less fell in the front door as the rest crammed into the back.

"Hang on!" Shannon, dressed as a zombie nun, accelerated away with a shriek of tyres. "It's a good job you stole a proper hackney cab, it saved us hijacking ours. If I was Mark I'd be in real trouble. His church believes in confession." She swerved around a parked car and accelerated again. "Send up the firework."

"Zoom!" Zephyr flew out of the window and went straight up. Although none of them could see it from inside the cab, one huge, spectacular firework blossomed above Stourton. Zephyr spun in the air, flinging off a thick shower of multi-coloured fire glyphs before diving back down to catch the cab. Abel wasn't sure how many Taverners had turned up, but they'd certainly know when to start the diversion. Eric would be contacting Creepio if he hadn't already done so, which should keep the Leeches occupied.

"Where are the rest?" Abel looked forward, out of the windscreen, but couldn't see any Taverners.

"We came in the pickup with Jenny and all six of the Taverner hit squad turned up. They used everything they'd got to flatten the heavies out the front while we hopped out, then ducked while the pickup got away. Shawn came past the other way on his scooter with Una on the back, strafing anyone still standing." Kelis laughed, sounding almost hysterical. "We didn't get chance to try the front door, because that lot came out of the alley. Shannon and Rob smashed the side door and set fire to it then helped me finish off the men." She stopped laughing, suddenly totally serious. "Who's that?"

Abel twisted his head to look back at whoever Kelis had seen, careful to keep his feet off the woman laid on the floor. A young woman and two men had climbed out of a window and were piling into the sports car. "Bad guys."

"Grab me." Kelis lunged across him to hang out the window so Abel wrapped his arms round her waist. He could see Kelis concentrate, firing glyphs upward. She squinted back towards the sports car, paused, then pulled her hands sharply down. As Kelis struggled back in through the window a loud clang sounded behind. "Bullseye. I wanted to dump it in the driver's seat, but they all looked human."

"Probably not the driver." Abel twisted to look and the Leeches had been catching up fast. Now the once beautiful, sleek vehicle screeched to a halt in a shower of sparks as the engine connected with the road and one wheel rolled off to the side. Abel stared at the cause, a giant block of ice embedded in the bonnet. "An iceberg? As Yoda might say, conspicuous it isn't."

"Ice is always falling out of airliners according to the internet." Kelis elbowed him. "Now unhand me, varlet. You've already got one woman, and you've just kidnapped another." Abel hurried to let go of her waist, conscious that he'd been enjoying the contact. That magical link must still be working.

"You did it, you did it." Rob, sat in the front, pointed and started laughing. "All this going on and you made him blush." The lead bar in his hand explained his sudden recovery.

Though Kelis' and Ferryl/Claris' humour faltered when Shannon started laughing hysterically. After all, that's not a good thing for the driver to do. The rest joined her as eight Goblins, fully visible of course, rampaged down the footpath. A couple of them jumped on car bonnets to leer at the drivers while others scattered litter or stole any food in sight, but just seeing them created all the chaos anyone could wish for. A cloud of batlins pulled at hats and hoods, tousled hair or hovered in front of faces. The green invasion disappeared down an alley towards the next street, leaving bedlam behind them.

"Those are the ones Eric brought in Jenny's pickup truck. They'll be garden ornaments again in five minutes. Laurence brought a Land Rover and took most of the goblins from Frederick's house. He's set up a diversion the other way." Kelis smiled happily. She'd been wary about asking a favour, but Laurence had come good. The traffic slowed down as more odd things happened all around them. A big luminous yellow balloon wobbled across the road, then burst into a half dozen that hurtled off in all directions. An isolated cloud spilled a tiny purple downpour onto one car which screeched to a halt, and horns sounded.

The rest of the Taverners had come to help, as promised. A white, billowy shape drifted out of a grating in the road, slowly wafting through a group coming out of a pub. They tried to beat it off, shouting and screaming, but cold water vapour isn't easy to remove with a glyph directing it. Zooming or drifting eerie lights, invisible hand claps, smoky shapes, dancing sparks, hovering handbags and a plethora of other noisy or strange-looking glyphs spread out ahead of them. The traffic ground to a halt. "Come on." The group abandoned the cab, while Rob opened the boot so the driver would be all right. Shannon pointed. "Your transport is this way but we'll have to walk." She let a glyph go and the group ahead scattered as the lad in the centre began frantically scrubbing frost from his hair.

Ferryl/Claris touched the driver as they left. "Wake." A very small glyph drifted back as she walked away. "Just a bit of mazzlement so he doesn't remember the last trip or two very well." At the other side of the road a cloud of sickly green vapour with two glowing fire glyphs like eyes chased people along the pavement.

"Make way, make way please. She's drunk." Kelis parted the pedestrians for Abel and Rob to bring through the ex-host, still out for the count. At least her vampire costume helped explain the red around her mouth. "Crikey, she's as tall as me." A few minutes' walk, a couple of turns and Shannon headed for her mum's car as Frederick waved them over to the BMW. His face fell when he saw the ex-host, but he waited for explanations until they were on the way back to Brinsford. As soon as the car reached Stourton town limits, Zephyr flew out and up to let off a giant blue firework. The Taverners would know the mission had finished, though some might be having too much fun to stop yet.

*   *   *

Frederick promptly started worrying about the rescued woman. He wasn't the only one. The rest of them knew that a seed would need blood, lots of it and quickly. A text to Jenny, 'big b-bank withdrawal tomorrow, please' followed by the reply 'really? Ok,' dealt with getting enough for tomorrow. None of them were going for long-term feeding this time, though this host might not survive the night anyway. On the way back to Brinsford Zephyr flew parallel to the car but out over the fields. Four times the BMW stopped for Abel and Ferryl/Claris to follow spooky-phone and collect the stunned rabbits. Each time the four humans looked away while Ferryl/Claris drained them down the woman's throat. Asleep or not, she greedily gulped down every drop.

By the time the BMW had pulled up in Brinsford, everyone had their story straight. A group of idiots, throwing fireworks and probably drunk, had stampeded along the street and run their group down. That should cover the bruises, small cuts, burns and grazes. Stripping off the charred bandages and asking Zephyr to become a magical blood-vacuum sorted out the clothes, sort of, leaving a few burns and a couple of tears. Abel, Kelis and Rob gave up on Guy Fawkes this year. They'd be grounded for at least five days.

When he found out where she'd sleep, Frederick almost insisted on taking the rescued woman back to his house in Stourton. Instead he accepted that Ferryl was the best jailor until tomorrow, when the woman's fate would be decided. The BMW sat inside a veil until Shawn arrived on his scooter to take Frederick home, by which time another veil had hidden the ex-host being carried into the church. Kelis and Ferryl/Claris, also veiled, raided Kelis' house for a quilt to wrap up the sleeping woman and bribes for the Goblins. Not because the seed would escape, Ferryl didn't think it would be capable yet, but so they could warn her if the woman woke up.

The BMW drove out of the village, unveiled and drove back in to deposit the four of them. As Frederick left Brinsford on the back of Shawn's scooter, he could probably hear Mrs. Ventner's alarmed voice when she saw her daughter and Claris. Rob and Abel headed for home; going through this once would be bad enough without suffering Mrs. Ventner's version. Half an hour later the "banned from using the car until Christmas" more or less summed up the reactions of all the parents. At least nobody ended up fully grounded, just restricted to the village except for school.

Abel felt sure the other four did the same as him, staggered off to bed as soon as possible. Throwing all those glyphs had shattered him.

* * *

Abel suffered another inspection and more earache when he staggered out of bed in the morning, though the ear-bashing wasn't as bad. The local radio had reported a riot by a crowd of yobs, throwing fireworks and water and possibly releasing hallucinogenic gas. Abel couldn't even be sure if that came from Creepio's people or genuine reactions. The reports had definitely backed up his alibi, and taken the edge off mum being annoyed about the small burn holes in his jeans.

Jenny called to say she'd be over to visit Kelis for a top-up. By the time she arrived, and Abel had joined them with Rob, he had some news. "I don't reckon Pendragon knew Elrond was there. He's just screamed at me down the phone, but only for drawing unwanted attention. We are definitely on the agenda for the next Magical Council meeting. The Firstseed had been paying him for protection. I thought he'd burst something."

Rob scowled. "Didn't you tell him she's a Leech? Or that Elrond is? Was."

"Tell him we killed or at least seriously singed his apprentice? I think not. I told him about the Firstseed but that seems to matter less than whatever she paid him for the hexes. He set into me for causing a Leech war as well. Apparently the Firstseed will seed hundreds of people and attack every magic user in Brinsford." Abel smiled just a little bit. "That might not happen, what with her burning in hell about now. Even if she survived the fire and drop, I'll bet Creepio got her."

Though Kelis' reply wiped the smile away. "Now that's the phone call I'm worried about."

"If he comes here and finds that woman, she's dead. He'll pull out the seed and that'll be it." Ferryl/Claris shook her head. "A bigger Leech would keep her alive, but from Claris' memories a seed is little more than hunger. It will finish her to feed itself."

"Firstseed wanted her dead so she couldn't blab." Abel put his hand in his pocket for the key, and placed it on the table. "About that."

Everyone inspected it for a few minutes. Kelis reached out a cautious finger but both Zephyr and Ferryl warned her to stop. A very nasty looking bulge of roiling magic had started coming to meet her. "So when do we open the door?" Kelis looked from one to the other. "Do we need backup?"

"If it works, no. If it goes in the door and doesn't work I can't see anyone ever getting in, so I'm hopeful." Ferryl/Claris looked thoughtful.

"We might want to deal with the woman and Creepio first. If he turns up and the door's open?"

"He'll want to go in." Rob finished it off. "Then we run and hope." He frowned in sudden thought. "Have you still got the Leech, the first one?"

"Yes, though the toad is dead. That's a point. Why did you save the Leech, Ferryl?"

Abel didn't expect her to look embarrassed. "I don't know. A sort of reaction, because the Firstseed tried to kill it? I should have just laughed and given her the jar."

"You're stuck now." Kelis smirked. "You're responsible for it."

"I am not!"

"Oh yes. If you save a life, it's up to you to make sure the life was worth saving. Or why bother?" Kelis might have sounded totally serious but Rob started giggling and Abel grinned at Ferryl/Claris' expression.

"I am? No I'm not. Am I?" She turned, appealing to Abel.

"It sort of makes sense?" Abel had no idea where Kelis got that from, or how she'd kept her face straight, but she'd definitely caught Ferryl.

"That's the answer." Though from Rob's wicked grin Ferryl might not agree. "We need a bigger Leech to keep the woman alive, and Ferryl must find it a better life. Bingo. Then when Ferryl has wriggled out of Claris' mind and can help the woman, we pop Leech back into a toad. Maybe a bunny for an improved life." His face fell. "We'll never get it out again will we?"

"Not a chance. The other part might work, because it had to have been growing for three or four months before we trimmed it a bit. It knows how to maintain a human." Kelis hesitated, glancing at Ferryl/Claris. "That's if she can't feel anything while she's asleep. Otherwise I vote for Claris getting a sudden wake-up call and having to live with some bad memories or a few months of total amnesia."

"The woman might be having nightmares, but maybe not because she's not twitching. She can feed while asleep, or the Leech can, so that's possible." Jenny looked hopefully at Ferryl/Claris. "Can't you and Zephyr scare it again?"

"Not enough, now it knows the result. Wait until we see if it still lives." Ferryl/Claris nipped out to bring the jar.

None of them liked what she brought back. "That smells, and it'll get worse." Rob waved a hand in front of his nose. Nobody had noticed last night with the scorched cloth and general tiredness but a whiff of blood and something unpleasant came out of the holes in the lid. Inside the Leech lay, barely moving, half submerged in dead toad and blackening blood.

"It needs blood." Ferryl/Claris glanced at Kelis. "We should just kill it."

"No. It liked old blood with magic put into it, so let's try just the magic." Abel reached out a hand and let magic spill from his palm, down through the lid. The Leech definitely strengthened, waving its tendrils. "It looks too small."

"The magical tendrils, invisible even to you, are much longer and have suddenly strengthened." Zephyr sounded cautious. "Perhaps it needs the blood to grow bigger, and the magic for the other part of it?"

"But we still can't control the Leech." Kelis sighed. "Curses. It looks scared, but we don't know how scared."

"Zephyr could contact it, the same way she did Bugsy?" Abel immediately found himself in a mental tussle with a frantic Zephyr. Eventually they agreed that a spooky-phone, while she stayed connected to Abel, wouldn't threaten her sense of self. The result gave them definite food for thought. The Leech seemed utterly terrified, achingly lonely, and felt deserted. It wanted something, some sort of reassurance or belonging, but Zephyr couldn't understand or describe it. The nearest feeling she could think of was her wanting to be in the tattoo to be safe.

"There's only one way to find out. We take the woman and the Leech into Castle House gardens, show the Leech and give it two choices. It saves the woman or dies." Ferryl/Claris picked up the jar. "There may be a way to make it stick to a bargain." She wouldn't elaborate, only pointing out they'd better get it done before Creepio turned up because he definitely would sooner or later.

*　*　*

Carrying the woman up the Main Street, under a veil, seemed surreal.

Once again Kelis commented on her height, while Abel wondered at how light she felt. Jenny tucked an inscribed pebble in the pocket of the tight leather catsuit and pocketed her own before opening the gate.

With the woman laid out, still sleeping, Jenny took the blood she'd brought from her backpack while Ferryl/Claris set out a jug and glass. Kelis placed the jar and Leech inside the protected cage where it could see or sense the woman and presumably the Leech seed. The four of them sat in a half-circle while Ferryl/Claris unscrewed the jar lid. She tipped the dead toad and live Leech out, still in the cage.

"Leech? We have a bargain for you. You must know there is a seed in this woman. We are about to kill it. We want you to go into the woman and save her. There is blood to help you do so." She leant forward, glaring at it. "I am told I owe you this chance, so take it. If you fail, you die. If you succeed, we will find you a more pleasant host when she can live without you, but not a human." An evil smile spread over her face. "You will leave when told, because I will bind you."

"No!"

"Yes!" Kelis caught hold of Abel's arm. "Ferryl didn't say kill. If it's willing and saves the woman, we can't have another mess like we did with Claris. This way Ferryl can order the foul thing out and we can stick it in whatever we like." Her lip curled as she looked at the Leech. "She can even order it not to hurt the woman."

"It can't be in there long. We don't want to be buying and feeding it blood all over again." Jenny looked a little bit ill. "I remember enough of that."

"But we don't need lots of blood, just lots of magic. Remember?" Rob nodded as the rest realised. "Though she'll need food to build her up." He eyed the woman. "And clothes. There's not much room for growth in that."

"My clothes will fit her for now." Kelis' face fell. "But how do we explain another squatter in the church? Mum would send her straight to a hospital."

"First things first." Abel hesitated, then made up his mind. "Zephyr, use spooky-phone to ask the Leech if it agrees to be bound by Braeth Huntian. Bound, not killed and bound. If it does she will guarantee it a better life than in a caged toad." A little smile touched his lips as Ferryl/Claris made a wordless sound of protest. "She owes it that." Ferryl subsided, scowling, while Kelis smiled happily, Jenny giggled and Rob chuckled.

"I will try." Spooky-phone reached out as Abel leant forward and repeated the terms to the Leech. This time it didn't seem to be frightened, waiting for the line to touch it. "The magic tendrils are reaching to greet me." Zephyr sounded nervous. She connected, and moments later broke contact. "The answer is yes, now, immediately. It is desperate to belong, or be part of or be accepted, I'm not sure. The Leech definitely understands binding and life."

That floored Abel. He'd expected a no but now, despite his misgivings, he had to agree to a binding. The Leech really did seem keen, crawling through the mess towards the cage bars and Ferryl/Claris. She looked resigned. "I thought it would be too frightened. Very well." A glyph floated out and settled on the Leech's front, glowing once before sinking it. "It is done. Not a tether or link, a true binding, it will obey any command I give."

"But you'll ask first. It's good manners." Abel laughed at the look that brought, but quickly sobered. "How do we kill the seed?" The Leech moved to the bars, reaching out to the woman. "Well that would be a sort of poetic justice, and worth a try."

Kelis picked up the cage and opened the door. "Right, blood-bag. In you go." She shrugged at the looks from the others and held the cage near the woman's mouth for the Leech to clamber across. After grimacing at the mess left inside, Kelis sat down again with the rest to watch. "How long will it take?"

"I've never heard of this, though there were rumours of bound Leeches now and then. They were supposedly used to help sorceresses control nobles." Ferryl/Claris concentrated on the woman. "Be ready with the blood. She looks very ill."

Perhaps three minutes later the woman stirred and her eyes snapped open. Her head shook a little and her limbs trembled. "Your glyph keeps her asleep but I woke her enough to talk in a dream. I need food to save her, please, Firstseed." Her eyes were fastened on Ferryl/Claris. Abel really wished he'd had his phone ready to capture Ferryl's look of pure shock.

"Here Firstseed." Jenny held out a glass. "Nicely warmed and magicked for you to feed your baby." Ferryl/Jenny hesitated then took it and fed the woman without a word. By then a warm jug of blood containing plenty of magic waited to top the glass up. Ferryl/Claris kept almost speaking then deciding against it, while the rest stifled smiles and let her get on with it. When the last of the blood had gone the woman, still trembling, spoke again. "My thanks, Firstseed. The host will sleep until she is saved, then I will wake her. We will need water then, please." Her eyes closed and the trembling stopped.

"I am not a Firstseed!" That did it, the rest started rolling about laughing.

Abel finally got himself under control. "You are until that woman is well enough for you to explain to the Leech. Come on mummy-leech, let's get your baby tucked up." He dissolved in laughter again. Though actually the woman slept in the garden for a while, until all the magic belts and bars had been filled from the trees. As usual filling her diamond left Jenny giggling, though not so much this time.

With the woman carried back to the church, under cover of a veil again, the rest tried to work it all out. Eventually they gave up. Even if Ferryl didn't spawn the Leech, Firstseed seemed be the Leech word for boss. More importantly, right now Ferryl wanted to talk about Claris. She'd start waking her up tonight, but couldn't wipe out all the memories of the Leech without complete amnesia. Claris would have memories of the memories scattered through every minute since she'd been taken. Complete amnesia would lead to doctors trying to recover something, and fragments might be left. To wipe out every last hint, Ferryl might have to leave Claris unable to walk or talk until she learned all over again.

In the end, if it came down to the choice of bad memories for Claris or screaming agony for the woman, Claris would lose out.

*　*　*

The short conversation when the Leech awoke extended even Ferryl's understanding of their society. It needed to belong to a nest. Abel and Huntian had killed the Firstseed, shattered the nest and destroyed the lair, and the survivors fled. When pressed, the Leech felt the Firstseed die, and every other Leech that had been killed. The seed it killed had already been dying, because it couldn't stand the loss of the nest and being taken away. The Leech had offered to do the killing because if attacked a seed released toxins, but it had trusted a nest member to get near. Now this Leech considered itself part of a new nest. It had been accepted by a powerful Firstseed, Braeth Huntian, stronger than any Firstseed ever known.

It drank water and explained it would need much blood to rebuild the host to where she could live without help. When asked it explained the stomach could only accept liquids, but agreed that human food would have what was needed. The Leech confirmed what the five of them now suspected, it needed the magic more than the blood itself. Without magic it couldn't maintain the woman or encourage her to regrow. With a draining glyph drawn on the back of its neck so it couldn't learn it the Leech searched for magic as instructed. The reaction when Ferryl carefully lined up the glyph on a lead bar full of magic showed it could draw magic directly. After that the Leech seemed quite enthusiastic, or possibly a bit drunk.

Five relieved teenagers left the woman sleeping peacefully. The goblins were watching, not because of bribes but in hopes the Leech made a break for it. "I'll be a lot happier buying packet soups than blood." Jenny had a proper bounce in her step after that had been sorted out. "Zephyr should be able to find enough rabbits for what the Leech itself needs."

"No need to feed any blood. We'll liquidise the raw rabbit joints though I'm volunteering Ferryl for that, and for cleaning the liquidiser afterwards. It's traditional, mummy cleaning up after the baby." Kelis ignored the evil look from Ferryl/Claris. The Leech had agreed to call her Ferryl, but obviously still thought of her as Firstseed.

"Does she change the nappy as well?" The three girls had stripped off the catsuit and dressed the woman in a nightdress, but she would need carrying to the washroom.

"Not a chance. The goblins can carry her to the toilet when necessary, even if nobody is there." Ferryl stomped on ahead, oblivious to the gleeful smiles behind her. "Nor am I feeding her every time and washing her."

"She'll be asleep most of the time." Abel felt happiest about that. The

Leech would keep her asleep so the woman had nightmares, not waking terror, and would experiment with making the dreams more pleasant. She had to wake enough for control, for feeding and the washroom, but not completely. He hoped the present eagerness to please the new Firstseed would continue. If it did Claris would get some choices, in a few days' time when she had woken enough to decide.

*   *   *

The evening news, even the national news, reported the students rampaging through Stourton as a prank that got out of hand. From the sounds of some interviews the tricking had gone on for some time after the mission accomplished signal went up. Some might even have been drunken revellers joining in, because many were in costume anyway. The fire that gutted a small block of flats only made the local news. Miraculously there had been no loss of life, though several people were having treatment for burns, falls and smoke inhalation. A shot of the crushed sports car blamed falling masonry that miraculously missed the driver.

Even while Abel helped his mum wash up after tea, he wondered if God's medics had been at work. His phone soon told him. "We must meet to discuss your latest fiasco. I presume you will insist on Castle House and this time it suits me as well. Two pm tomorrow."

"Three if you want to talk to everyone." Abel wasn't sure when Jenny would be able to get over. She seemed keen to be part of it all and had already met Creepio, and could always look innocent whenever she wanted to. That might help.

"Three. I will bring assistance, but will respect our agreement. You will have a chance to answer my questions."

"Try asking Pendragon why his apprentice fights alongside a Firstseed. I'd like to know." Abel shut his mouth but too late. Creepio had got under his skin and now he'd let the gremlin out.

A long silence followed. "I will need more than that."

"We'll explain what we know." Abel had no idea how he'd prove it. It would be the word of four or five teenagers against the word of an established sorcerer, Pendragon. His word and Ferryl/Claris' actually, because the rest hadn't been in the fight upstairs and there'd be no other witnesses from there. His phone went dead. Abel sighed in resignation and texted the others to confess.

*   *   *

Jenny definitely wanted to be there. The five of them were in the garden early, so after Abel for permission Ferryl gave Jenny proof she was trusted. With Jenny's permission she drew on the teenager's arm with her finger, something totally invisible which would allow her into Dead Wood at any time. Jenny went out the back door of the gardens into the wood and threw Abel her pebble, braced to run towards him to get it back, then relaxed. She straightened slowly, cautiously, then twirled a couple of times. "That pebble doesn't work completely. It still leaves me a little bit uneasy, but now the place feels lovely, welcoming. You could find me here anytime."

"That glyph Ferryl drew means you are welcome, literally. Please don't tell anyone?" Abel looked around the woodland. "Or we'll be putting on bus trips."

"I'm sorry about telling everyone about the tree. I'll be a lot more careful this time." As she came past him and collected her pebble to go into the garden proper, Jenny kissed him on the end of the nose. "That's thank you." Abel almost pointed out that Ferryl drew the glyph, but Jenny already knew that. At least it kept his mind occupied as they chatted, until Zephyr announced two cars driving towards Brinsford. Both were surrounded by church magic.

*   *   *

One car stopped a quarter of a mile back, while the other stopped at the magical boundary and Vicar Creepio Mysterio got out. He left at least two other people in the car. This time there wasn't a hint of humour on the churchman's face when he stopped opposite Abel. "I must have explanations. Firstly, what did you release?" He pointed at Castle House. Abel looked at the other four, baffled. He didn't even have the key on him; he'd buried it in Castle House garden for now.

"Nothing." The total truth.

"Not a Leech hunter, or some sort of magical predator?"

"He has caught a Leech, or one talked before it died. They have spoken

307

of me." Ferryl's voice had some humour at the next bit. "Or Zephyr." She held Abel's and Kelis' hands to communicate. To make it less obvious, Jenny held Abel's other hand and Rob held Kelis' with his free hand on his bat.

"You caught a Leech and it talked of a hunter on the wind." Creepio looked startled, then suspicious so Abel carried on. "The Leeches were screaming about some legendary something, but that's not what they saw. You wanted to see my shy passenger? Please do not try to investigate." "Zephyr, please fly out far enough to show the tether, hover a moment or two, then come back in. He cannot harm you through the barrier."

"The Ffod is not frightened."

Creepio's eyes widened, then narrowed as he watched the shimmer appear and then flow back through Abel's sleeve. "That is not what I expected. It is not as large or strong as the one they spoke of, which would definitely not be tethered to your tattoo." He switched subjects. "What on earth were your Taverners playing at? What part of secrecy did you misunderstand?"

"Student pranks, basically harmless. I'll bet none of the victims suggested real magic. We needed the diversion." Abel shook his head as Creepio opened his mouth. "Listen first, then we'll answer questions." He stifled his smile at the annoyance on Creepio's face, another one who preferred to set the rules. Abel explained, including the Leech in Henry and the badger, Claris arriving, the freeing and the ultimatum by the Firstseed. The only bit he missed was possession or any mention of Ferryl Shayde.

Creepio had questions, but Claris confirmed she'd had a Leech in her and it had been tricked out, and their version of the hunter on the wind had caught it. Abel confirmed the Firstseed had died and as far as he knew, the nest had broken and scattered. Creepio even accepted that he would have probably tried to open Castle House if he had the key, but insisted he would have brought the strength needed to deal with anything inside. Ferryl's hand didn't agree. Kelis' remark about ice from airliners brought a real scowl, as did real goblins loose in the town. As they finished Creepio accepted the basic story made some sort of sense, for suicidal amateurs, but wasn't satisfied that Elrond had been there. He needed better proof before accusing a sorcerer of having a Leech-ridden apprentice.

Though at least one other thing worried him. "Who is the Earth sorcerer? You are all novices yet I found a wounded man up to his neck in dust, in a hole in the road. Totally unharmed by magic, but the hole had closed enough so he couldn't get out. I commend your restraint with others as well. All the humans we found were alive though some were very badly injured."

"Even the women?"

"Those were Leeches, and no longer human. Though you can apparently reverse that situation." He gave Claris a long look. "I really would like to see a medical scan of your torso sometime. I also want to speak to the Earth sorcerer or sorceress. Now." Again Creepio looked braced for a fight.

"Sometime you might get that scan." "When I am no longer in here."

"But you can meet the earthmover now. Rob, take a bow." Rob did, with a silly smile.

Creepio definitely didn't believe him so Rob waggled his fingers. "I hate wind, fire and water, but earth just makes sense." A tiny glyph flew out into the road, well clear of Creepio, and a small piece of tarmac crumbled. "See? It's easier to just undo things, make them into dust, than squish dust into rock. Though that hole really hurt me even if I picked a spot over a drain to reduce the amount of solid. It drained every drop of magic so I didn't quite get it closed properly."

"The part about using a drain convinces me, because only the caster would know. I'm still not sure about this breaking of the nest and Elrond being there. Pendragon is screaming about a Leech war and hundreds being seeded. Convince me." There wasn't an ounce of give in that.

"I will ask my friends what might work. Please ignore the messenger." "Zephyr, ask them all about showing the woman in the church. We don't have to give a location until he agrees not to kill her or the Leech. Then the Leech can answer the awkward questions about the nest thing."

Creepio watched Zephyr closely as she hovered and connected spooky-phone. "I had a report of this sort of thing. It is why I wondered about an ancient fugitive."

One at a time all four answered Abel, all with the proviso the Vicar promised not to kill the informer. Ferryl/Claris insisted he must swear on his cross. When Abel confessed to having rescued a seeded victim, alive, he thought Creepio would burst a blood vessel. Creepio simply didn't believe the part about the host being awake throughout the Leech possession, but Claris finally persuaded him. As Ferryl had already explained, everyone thought the ex-host woke up healed and happy.

According to Creepio he had scores of interview reports to confirm that. After the explanation he accepted that a host that had been used badly for forty years needed help. Eventually Abel asked for the promise. Creepio had to know what was coming. He barely twitched when he found out Abel had a live Leech, though the tame part made him sneer.

*   *   *

It took a little while for the Vicar to agree to sending the cars back to the main road, but without that the five teenagers wouldn't leave Castle House gardens. Once the cars left, Zephyr flew up high to watch them. On the walk through the village Abel felt sure Creepio had to stifle an urge to reach out and touch spooky-phone. Though once the Vicar realised they were heading for the church his blood pressure started to go up again. "That is blasphemy!"

"Saving a life is blasphemy? Or a soul according to you. Maybe two, do Leeches have souls?"

"No magical creatures do." Abel didn't argue because he'd no idea if humans had.

Instead he pointed out the church had been abandoned. The Tavern had even had to drive out Ratlins and a Kalkatrie. Learning what had been in the churchyard didn't help Creepio's mood one bit. He asked a lot of questions about the Kalkatrie before pointing out it was usually called a Cockatrice and should be extinct. Abel stopped him at the lychgate. "Now listen to me please. This Leech will talk to you and supply your proof, but please keep the cross and dog collar covered. You'll terrify it."

"It might need terrifying."

"Already dealt with." "Zephyr, warn the Leech there is a visitor and get the goblins out of sight." Though the last bit didn't really work, not from the glares Creepio gave the gargoyles. "They scrounge from the village bins, keep the rats and nasties down, and pick up litter."

Creepio stopped and looked closely at Abel. "Pick up litter?"

"It's the deal. That or they leave." Creepio didn't answer, he just shook his head and went into the church. He shook his head again at the clean interior, obviously well aware it had to be brownies and pixies. Abel opened the door. "This man wants to know why you are sure the nest was broken. The Firstseed insists you tell him." That earned another shake of the head, but Abel had already explained the Leech always called the boss Firstseed.

The woman's eyes opened, and her limbs trembled a little. "I am trying to make this a dream, so she does not wake. What should I say?"

"The truth, without naming your new boss."

"How do you know the nest is broken? I am told they will retaliate, seed more innocents." Creepio looked poised to go for his cross.

Though Creepio didn't worry the Leech as much as Ferryl had. It looked cautious, but not frightened. "I felt our nest die, one after the other. Thirdseed came here in a boy and died, the Ninthseed died here in a badger but the nest stayed strong. Then this one and his nest killed Firstseed, and second, fifth, sixth and seventh. The Eighthseed still lived as we left, as did the second sorcerer, the Tenthseed. I was Twelveseed. Thirteenseed still lived, the church one, and three Newsfeeds in the cellar. So did the Newseed in this one, but I killed it before it poisoned the host. The nest shattered and the lair burned."

The vicar looked horrified. "Seventeen? Seventeen leeches, two in sorcerers? Who were the sorcerers?"

"I do not know names. Fifthseed and Tenthseed took over the sorcerers, as they cannot be seeded. Fifthseed died in the building as this sorcerer and the hunter fought them and the Trolls." For a moment Abel thought Vicar Creepio would lash out. His fists knotted and veins stood out on his forehead as he glared down. "Sorcerers! Trolls!" It sounded a lot like a curse, but Creepio calmed a little afterwards. "Who is this host? Why is she so ill?"

"She hosted Firstseed for many years so her mind and body are broken. She remembers much of the time with Firstseed, but was meant to die to keep secrets. I have not found a name." The woman's eyes went to Abel.

"Tell him why."

"She knew of the key. Firstseed meant to force this sorcerer to open Castle House. But the hunter took me from my host, so she faced two instead of one. And the hunter."

The harsh sound as Creepio turned to Abel might have been a laugh. "No wonder the Leeches we captured are terrified. You really did it, you and your shy friend. You realise you have the luck of the devil himself?"

"No devil involved, just a lot of friends. Only three of us inside the nest, but there were many more outside."

"Hah, yes. Just so that you know, we found the missing Fourthseed in the alley. She'd crawled in there with both legs smashed, probably jumped from a window when the place went up in flames." Abel remembered Zephyr dealing with the woman shooting at them, and her falling, and kept quiet. "One Leech bled out in the car before we arrived. She didn't have a seat belt so she hit your block of ice much too hard. Another didn't get out of the building before we got there so we killed it." He calculated for a moment. "That would be the eighth and eleventh seeds according to you. The other two car passengers needed intensive care, but are not Leeches. The Leech in the hole must be called Thirteenseed. That man is a priest, and still alive. The church is indebted for that." Abel kept quiet about some Leech hosts still being human as the Vicar's lip lifted in a snarl. "I will insist Pendragon gives up his Tenthseed apprentice, or he'll lose all of them. That particular sorcerer will not be bothering you, or anyone else, for some time."

One part of that stood out, to Abel at least. "You owe us?" Because the remarks from Jenny's dad suddenly popped into Abel's head.

"Not much, considering the shambles we are clearing up. Enough to not report this until you get the woman and Leech clear of the church. I want to see her once the Leech leaves." That sounded like the church throwing orders about again, but Abel thought Creepio probably did that quite often.

"Enough for us to keep her here until she's healed, and rent the church as a sanctuary? For battered wives and other victims?" Abel almost held his breath, trying to keep his face calm as Creepio peered at him.

"You are serious?" Abel nodded, once, standing very still for what seemed like ages as Creepio thought about it. "It will be suggested. Much depends on the result of my talk to Pendragon." The Vicar's shoulders dropped, the tension leaving. "The woman can stay here as long as she is healed. How long must she live in pain?"

"She sleeps most of the time. The Leech will not grow into organs except to keep them working and build them up, and does not drink blood. It will leave once she can survive unaided." Abel hoped the Leech didn't mention nightmares or yesterday's blood-fest. "Leech, let her sleep now." The woman stilled, only her gently rising and falling chest showing she lived.

Creepio sighed. "That is something, possibly a minor miracle. I hope her mind recovers as well, eventually. There is something very wrong here, both the way hosts are treated and Leeches taking a churchman and sorcerers. Please walk back with me and explain all this properly, in very small words. I will need them for my report." That might have been a joke, but it didn't sound like it. Abel, Kelis, Ferryl/Claris, Jenny and Rob walked back through the village with the Vicar while spooky-phone brought everyone up to date. They combined to reduce everything to the smallest words possible.

When they'd all wound down, Kelis just had to ask. "So what do you think? About the church?"

"Churches are sometimes leased, occasionally sold. Never to a sorcerer, or for a Leech sanctuary as far as I know. I am grateful it isn't my decision." Creepio inspected the door to Castle House. "Let me know if you open that, preferably in advance. There are many eyes on you now, so do not give someone the excuse they want." He heaved a big, dramatic sigh. "The angels may watch over fools and innocents, but angels may not be enough next time." Turning on his heel Creepio left, pulling out his phone to call for a car.

"Let him know in advance?" Ferryl/Claris watched as the slim black figure walked away.

"Not a chance." Rob grinned. "We've got backup for the angels, a Ffod."

"Angel bop!" Ffod headed skywards to watch the church cars leave.

Open House

Two days later a letter advised them that if Bonny's Tavern, or any charitable enterprise, wished to lease the church in Brinsford they should apply. The letter gave the address for a Bishop, and a list of criteria. Jenny's dad and the three mums were really pleased, and immediately applied, but the whole affair could take months. With luck it could be a refuge in time for Kelis and her mum to move in as caretakers.

The teenagers were more concerned with feeding up the woman in the church, hiding under veils this time, while Ferryl worked on waking up Claris. Jenny brought some diversion, the progress on preparing Bonny's Tavern for a launch. Kelis really wanted to understand, as did Ferryl/Claris because she soaked up anything new. Rob and Abel tried, but preferred actual designing, though even that didn't work. None of it really detracted them from one gradually growing obsession.

All of them really did mean to carefully consider the dangers in opening the door. They all fully intended examining the key, and the glyphs and magic flows in Castle House door, before bringing one near the other. Unfortunately, none of them could go into Stourton over the half-term, which meant they spent too much time near both door and key.

"School the day after tomorrow." Rob glanced, not at all casually, in the direction of Castle House.

"We'll need to concentrate at school, without something distracting us." Kelis just happened to turn her head towards where Abel had buried the key.

"We should find somewhere warmer to meet in winter." Jenny's innocent look swept around the cave and came to rest on Castle House, showing above the trees.

"I'm a bit worried the damp will mess up that key, buried like that." Abel's growing smile matched the other four.

"It could be dangerous?" Ferryl/Claris started to smile as well.

"But we have Ffod!" A shimmer shot skywards and swooped down to hover hopefully.

"All in favour?" But only Abel raised his hand as the rest stood up.

*   *   *

Five minutes later Abel stood in front of the door, a carefully cleaned key gleaming in his hand. Zephyr tucked herself away in the tattoo, just in case she triggered anything, while Ferryl/Claris stood just behind Abel. Kelis took one flank and Rob the other, three steps back. Jenny stayed behind Ferryl/Claris because despite intensive practice her magic still hadn't caught up. "Come on! Key in slot, turn, click. It's not rocket science."

"You didn't see the key zap Firstseed's hand, Rob." Abel carefully slid the key in and turned it clockwise. Nothing. Anticlockwise and he felt a little give, a tingle in his hand and it turned smoothly. Everyone waited, breathless, but nothing happened.

"Try the handle."

"I will! Just give my heart a chance to slow down, right?" Abel took hold of the big brass doorknob and turned it, but it wouldn't move either way. "Curses."

"Take out the key. The sorcerer wouldn't leave it in the lock." Kelis summoned a small wind glyph. "If it tries anything I'll knock you away."

Abel slid the key out, easily because the whole slot had turned with it, and he put it in his pocket. This time the doorknob turned and with a click the door opened a crack. "So far so good." He let go of the handle and pushed the door. It swung smoothly out of the way, and all five inspected the room, or six because Abel could feel Zephyr's interest.

"Magic flows all over. It is like the room with the Leech in, but not a web. Coils and pools, stores that must power something."

"All I see is double doors with a table next to them, and a little chest on top. Those and the great big stone frog-dragon coiled in one corner and the big pot with a dead vine that's spread all over the opposite wall. Why do I think the frog and vine are watching me?" Rob didn't laugh for once. "They are, aren't they?"

"Perhaps, or probably. Perhaps they will only watch, because Abel used the key." Ferryl/Claris sounded cautious. "After all, the sorcerer wouldn't want to fight his way into his house every time."

"Maybe I'll just tickle the frog and see." Even as Ferryl/Claris turned to protest Kelis let the small glyph go. It reached the door and dissipated. "Or maybe I won't. So no chucking magic at them from out here."

A strained voice sounded from behind them all, Jenny. "Maybe no chucking magic at all? Please? This extremely worried apprentice votes for calm negotiation."

"Or I just walk in." Despite the objections Abel put out his hand towards the doorway, then past the threshold. "Nothing, not even a tingle."

"A wall of magic appeared when the glyph approached. It is not there now."

"Zephyr will warn me if something is annoyed." "Pull in spooky-phone please." Abel pushed his arm right through, almost up the shoulder so his tattoo passed the invisible boundary. "Zephyr?"

"Nothing. It does not mind me at all, but perhaps I should not fly out just now." Considering how exuberant the sprite usually sounded, she must be really worried.

"What does Zephyr say?" Ferryl/Claris came nearer, her finger almost touching where the glyph had hit. "I can't feel anything."

"Perhaps we shouldn't all go in. Though I hope we can, eventually, without a blood transfusion from Abel." Kelis had summoned another glyph, warily watching the frog-dragon and dead tree.

"If you can get the chest, we can look inside. It might have a key, or a badge or something. The sorcerer must have let others in." Rob inched closer, reaching out to poke a finger at nothing. "Or maybe we can just follow you."

"I doubt it. The sorcerer would probably have taken people in there as captives, or possibly tethered apprentices." Ferryl/Claris hesitated, her fingers just short of going through the doorway.

Abel had made up his mind. The doorway wasn't reacting to him, so he took a step through into the room and stopped. "Nothing. There are a few wisps, like a fine net across the room, but they are not reacting to you." Reassured he started towards the table and the chest, keeping an eye on the frog-dragon. Abel began to relax as he came closer without a reaction, but just as he reached for the little chest, the frog-dragon opened its eyes! Blue with sparks in them, just like the stone guardian he'd met.

"Look out!"

"Watch out!"

"Get out!"

Abel agreed with Kelis, he turned to leave but something snagged his foot. When he glanced down a piece of dead vine had wrapped around his foot! Abel loosed a small hot glyph to burn it off, looked towards the door and froze. Ferryl/Claris had followed him and now she had been targeted by a dozen dead branches, all trying to get a hold. Behind her the door began to close.

"Come on!" Through the door Abel saw a Kelis windhammer explode against the doorway and the door hesitated, then continued. Jenny threw wind as well but the door pushed through. Rob's glyph seemed to be absorbed without any effect. Burning off another thin branch, Abel headed for Ferryl/Claris.

"Hold the door open." Ferryl/Claris gasped that out as she fought fiercely using wind, fire, steam, ice and even trying to pin branches to the wall. "Can't affect the stone or walls." That explained Rob's failure. Abel reached past her, feeling something brush his leg as he darted forward. The door slowed a little more when he grabbed it, but kept going. As it reached the last few centimetres Abel pulled his hands back rather than lose fingers, and turned.

The stone frog-dragon had taken longer than the vine to wake up, but it had now uncoiled onto all eight legs. From the way it shrugged off Abel's fire and wind glyphs being late to the fight wouldn't matter, not with its targets trapped in an enclosed space. Ferryl had only one hand throwing glyphs now. The other arm had been swathed in branches though the smoke coming from the cracks meant it wasn't a secure hold.

Abel grabbed the twisted rope of wood connected to Ferryl/Claris' arm and summoned fire. He hissed with pain, but the wrapping on her arm loosened. As he switched to ice to freeze it, a thud shook the whole room. The door swung open, billowing smoke! Abel put his shoulder to Ferryl/Claris and pushed. She twisted her arm. With a crack the frozen wood shattered and she staggered back, towards the door. "Keep going."

As Abel kept pushing Ferryl/Claris fired glyphs back over his shoulder or past him. Another step, a stumble, and they went down in a tangle but outside!

Rob darted in to snatch something off the ground, jumped back and inspected it. The door slammed shut. "Scorched, but the glyph is still clear." He showed Abel the rounders bat with a long scorch mark up one side.

"Are you all right? Both of you?" Jenny had an arm under Abel's, and moments later Kelis helped get him and Ferryl/Claris to her feet. After a quick inspection showed that apart from Abel's blistered hand he seemed all right, everyone looked at the sorceress.

A tremble in his shoulder reminded Abel. "Zephyr? Are you all right."

"I am sorry. I tried, but the air burned." She sounded very subdued.

"Then hiding was the best thing." Abel passed that on while Ferryl/Claris healed long cuts and bruises on her arm, and a few on her legs. She would need a new dress, but luckily had plenty now.

"What now?" Everyone turned to look at the closed door. Abel turned back to Rob. "How did you get the door open?"

"It never quite closed. I got the bat in the way just in time." Rob showed the scorch again. "The door kept trying, then something must have overloaded."

"I'm not a real expert, but how about Ferryl keeping outside the next time? It only started when she went through the door. Even then the room never attacked Abel." Jenny sounded tentative but both Rob and Kelis nodded.

Ferryl/Claris looked embarrassed, and confessed to worrying about Abel being in there alone. After going around it a few times, the five of them inspected the door. It had locked again, the slot turning back to vertical. Abel tried the key, very carefully, and it opened. So did the door, to reveal the room looking as if nothing had ever happened. No scorch marks, no burned wood or splinters, and the frog-dragon had curled up neatly in the corner again.

This time nobody crossed the threshold but Abel, and Zephyr stayed in his arm as he walked slowly up to the table. After a slight hesitation he picked up the box. The frog-dragon's eyes opened, which almost gave him a heart attack, but it didn't move. "Magic flows are stable. Some still curl around you, but only light ones." Abel took a step towards the door, then another, and then walked quickly out of the room. This time he turned and closed the door as he left, then locked it because it didn't happen automatically.

*   *   *

Despite Kelis wanting to look right now, Abel insisted on taking the chest, wooden with thick gold decoration, to their cave. Opening it turned out to be simple. He put his thumb on a glyph just like the one he'd seen on the key case, it stung and the lid swung up. The box held a folded sheet of paper and a gold coin. "Ooh, instructions." Kelis stopped, her hand halfway towards the box. "Come on, take the letter out."

"I'd like to see the coin closer. A sovereign I believe." Though Ferryl/Claris waited as well, until a cautious Abel had taken both out of the chest.

"There are glyphs in this, buried out of sight." Ferryl still didn't touch the coin, probably because of the magic Zephyr saw building up as she came near.

"Never mind that. The letter might tell us what to do." Jenny inched closer. "Maybe it's a treasure map, or there's a secret way in past all the traps." Abel opened out the thick, folded paper and she looked past his arm. "Oh. Well maybe not."

"Huh? 'If ye lay claim, bring the coin and box.' Lay claim to what? The coin?" Rob twisted to look back over the trees. "Or the house. What does the rest say?"

"That's the whole message. A bit cryptic but the rest is an address in Stourton where we'll hopefully get an explanation. We'll have to get Frederick or someone to…." Abel tailed off into silence.

"You can't go, not until Christmas. Still, that's only five weeks. Sort of?" Jenny smiled brightly, but with an effort. They had the next clue, and absolutely no way to use it. In theory Jenny could take the letter and coin, but that idea died when she tried to pick up the coin. It glowed when she got close and Zephyr warned of magic gathering.

"At least that gives us time to get that poor woman sorted out, and Claris back home." Abel put the coin and letter back in the chest. "Jenny can have a look in town see if the place is still there? Then at Christmas we can take a trip. I'll bury this in the garden." Abel laughed. "With the sorceress's glyph, the key, and this chest we'll need that treasure map, Jenny."

Despite a few tries at finding a way round it, everyone agreed they'd have to wait. In the interim there were glyphs to practice, and a frog-dragon to add to Bonny's Tavern game because Jenny liked it. Somewhere along the line the parents would sort out if the church could be leased, which would give Kelis and her mum an emergency home if necessary. The break would also let everyone research property rights. If Abel could claim Castle House, would he have to wait until he was eighteen? Rob also reminded them to check the treasure trove option. There might be something valuable in there.

None of them were keen, but it looked like the exploration would be on hold for another five weeks. Jenny swore she'd keep her mouth shut, and by the time the five of them went back to school they'd sort of got used to the idea.

THE END

The next book in the series
Ferryl Shayde III - A Very Different Game
will be coming soon.

Abel's World

Brinsford - a small village in rural England, eight miles from Stourton

Consists of:

Main Street - with pub and small shop

Brinn Lane - off village green, leads to a small bridge then up valley to local farms

Riverside Close - a dozen council houses

Castle Road - road from village to main road half a mile away

Residents:

Abel Bernard Conroy - 16 - lives with Mum, Dad died - accident at sea

Christine Conroy - Chris - 41 - Abel's widowed Mum, has part-time job

John Tyler - Rob's Dad

Terri Tyler - Rob's Mum

Rob Tyler - 16 - Abel's best friend

Melanie Tyler - 14 - Rob's sister

Samantha Tyler - 19 - Rob's sister

Jessica Ventner - Kelis' Mum

Kelis Ventner - 16 - Abel's best (only) female friend

Stan - local pensioner and reputedly poacher - has a shotgun and an old Jack Russel called Bugsy

Mr. Copples - local farmer

Henry Copples - 16 - local bully

Tyson Copples - 19 - Henry's brother - bully with crossbreed dog Cooch (Cuchelain)

Stourton - Town eight miles from Brinsford

Kielby - village six miles from Brinsford - home of Jenny and Diane

Stourton Comprehensive - local secondary school

School year groups: 11 = GCSE year, 13 = A-Level year

Mr. Sanders - Graphic Art master

Mr. Beresford - Sports master

Mrs. Svengy - Biology teacher

Arabelle - 17 - one of the seraphims - Acro dancer - year 13

Claris Ellsworth - 17 - seraphim - bubbly redhead Acro dancer, likes the rugby players - year 13

Diane Forester - 14 - Jenny's sister - year 9

Jenny Georgina Forester - 17 - seraphim - Acro dancer for school team year 12

Justin - 16 - beta in town - year 11

Laurence Horatio Sperrick - 17 - seraphim - minor nobility but not wealthy, attends local comprehensive - Acro dancer – year 13

Petra - 17 - game beta lives in a nearby village - year 12

Rachel - 14 - Justin's sister - year 9

Sarah Russel - 16 - beta in town - year 11

Seraph Angelique Bellamy-Courts - 17 - wealthy young woman who manipulates the rich, influential, athletic and good-looking to form an elite, the seraphims - year 13

Una - 17 - game beta in town with character costume - year 12

Warren - 16 - game beta in town - year 11

Others

Local:

Eric - 20 - Warren's big brother

Frederick - 53 - adult who sees magical creatures and has befriended a dryad. Lives near Elmwood Park in Stourton

Jake Forester - Jenny's dad, a big builder and businessman.

Mark - 18 - neighbour of Petra's, devout catholic

Shannon - 17 - beta - church school - catholic - year 12

Shawn - 19 - friend of a friend of a beta

Kieran - 16 – First Taverner outside local area - lives in Hope Valley in the Pennines - year 11

Vicar Creepio Mysterio - Kelis' name for a Peripatetic Archbishop interested in Castle House

Pendragon - local sorcerer who has a monopoly on magical contracts in Stourton.

Elrond - a senior apprentice to Pendragon, not a favourite

Ferryl's Magical World

Magic: - A power that permeates the air, but cannot be utilised in its raw form. All living creatures absorb magic but plants are unable to dissipate it. Trees are the greatest natural reservoirs of magic, if old enough. Animals from insects to elephants will dissipate any surplus in an uncontrolled fashion, unless they are sentient and learn to utilise glyphs and store more.

Glyphs: - Patterns drawn or etched on solid objects or in air or water, used to control magic and give it specific purpose. The strength of a scribed glyph depends on the magic put into it, and the medium it is drawn on. Glyphs inscribed in metal are the strongest, scribed in air the weakest. Effect of a thrown glyph depends on amount of magic, skill, and intent behind it. The four basic glyphs are air, fire, water and earth. Combined with each other and created glyphs of increasing complexity, almost anything can be accomplished. Conversely, a slight mistake can be catastrophic or fatal.

Veil: - A concealment glyph that can be anchored to an object or a person. The amount of concealment depends on the intent and magic poured into it.

Spun slowly anti-clockwise a veil obscures living beings from unmagical sight though the magically aware can still see through it and will detect the veil itself as a shimmer in the air. Spun faster it conceals plants and manmade solids such as metal or glass, faster still dead organics such as wood and leather. Spun at very high speed the glyph uses impractically huge amounts of magic but can conceal anything, including even its own shimmer, from magic users. Beings made of almost pure magic can still detect the intense magical activity, but not the veil or what is concealed.

Another identical glyph spun clockwise at the same time extends the size of the globe concealed, faster means larger.

*   *   *

Gods: - Possibly originally sorcerers who have learned how to draw magic from worshippers using a symbol or mark. Their power grows with the number of prayers, but old gods act quickly to crush young ones. Gods fade away as worshippers decrease but are eternal as long as one worshipper still lives. Legend claims that the glyphs were stolen from the first God.

Sorcerer or Sorceress: - Advanced glyph wielder who has learned how to prolong their life either with magic or at the expense of other living creatures. They are usually wealthy, live in a well-guarded home and keep a wide area clear of any large or particularly dangerous entities.

Witch or Warlock: - Minor magic practitioner unable to progress to sorcerous glyphs. Sells charms and hexes, and removes or creates minor curses. They have a normal lifespan, usually training a replacement who will also support them in old age. The profession is dying out in the countryside and smaller towns due to the current disbelief in magic and magical creatures. There are fewer paying customers to provide a living so apprentices prefer to take up other jobs.

Bound Servant: - A being branded with a mark allowing a glyph wielder to control them completely. Will ignore pain or injury, hard to kill because partly protected by brand.

Tethered servant: - Usually a sorcerer's apprentice. The tethering allows free will but can be used to communicate, inflict pain or death, or drain magic.

Creatures Visible to the Non-Magical

Dryad: - Creature that utilises the magic gathered by trees to protect its home tree and prolong both their lives. Gnarled, bad-tempered, rude creatures, they can manipulate magic to create a veil to hide their surroundings or to change their appearance. Will sometimes trade answers to questions in return for honey.

Stout woody torso, no neck, eyes large, round and are different shades depending on tree. Chestnuts are chestnut brown, of course. Torso matches bark of tree. Legs are short, stout, no knees and end in roots that often embed in ground to help dryad stand. They usually live inside their tree. Arms are thin branches with long twigs as fingers, no foliage.

Can work simple glyphs using tree magic, and protect the tree against magic, rot and disease. Dryads control their tree enough to drop branches on attackers, strangle small creatures with roots or hit them with branches. Full control of the roots and branches takes many, many years of practice.

Asexual, though they can produce facsimile human features to lure humans close enough to steal a little magic. Will occasionally ripen young giving them a basic knowledge of the world, the glyphs dryads can work, and how to control a tree. Dryad seedlings blend into a young sapling and grow together. Both are very vulnerable until the young tree matures and accumulates surplus magic.

Dryads communicate somehow, though they claim to hear everything 'on the wind' or through birdsong and mouse chatter rather than give details. They are sometimes overheard referring to The Wild Wood as if it is a sentient being.

Blood Leech: - Old blood magic remnant that survives by possessing a human and feeding on fresh blood and the magic therein. A single

Leech, a Firstseed, infects healthy humans to create a nest of Leeches. They are connected both by sensing each other and an affinity for the lair, the home of the Firstseed. All Leeches obey their Firstseed and will sacrifice themselves to defend it.

Adult Leeches prefer pale skinned hosts to shed excess heat and wear dark glasses because their eyes show red around the pupils. Most find a willing victim, usually demanding a fixed period of possession (forty years) for the curing of an otherwise fatal illness. Once vacated the discarded host should be left young and healthy but with no memory of the intervening years. If the Leech has kept the bargain they will then live out their lives normally.

Not all Leeches keep the bargain, some leaving the host barely alive and often infected with a seed. These also leave the host with full memories of forty years spent hunting humans and draining blood. If a seeded host finds enough fresh blood, another Blood Leech is created. Even if the host finds a priest or sorcerer fast enough, the seed will try to poison them as it dies. Even if the host survives, the memories may drive them insane.

Goblins: - One of the few magical creatures visible to the non-magical because they eat large amounts of mostly non-magical food. Goblins eat almost anything humans or animals do but prefer junk food (or fruit cake) to raw meat. Raid rubbish bins, cat and dog dishes and bird tables but also eat magical creatures and small animals and birds.

Goblins have been hunted almost to extinction for two main reasons. Firstly, because their gastric juices and wind are very flammable, making them a severe fire hazard. Goblins sleeping near open fires could explode and set fire to the house if they passed wind. Sorcerers still believe a Goblin with indigestion started the Great Fire of London. As they were considered vermin, some sorcerers used captive goblins as entertainment at feasts. Guests would shoot burning arrows at tethered Goblins, or heat them slowly until they exploded. This was considered a public service.

The second reason for their extinction came down to numbers. In the past goblins could reach plague proportions as their melds (clan, family) keep expanding. Even the goblins have no way to limit their numbers except suicide. Sorcerers or the church used to mount hunts to scour the countryside, but if only one survived the meld would grow again. Without the fire hazard, this might have been tolerated, as a reasonable number of local goblins helped to keep rats in check. A Goblin infestation sweeping down from the north of England and wiping out the flea carriers might be why the Black Death petered out in the Midlands.

Goblins of all sizes are dark emerald green, potbellied munchkins vaguely humanoid. They have two short skinny legs with fat feet and five fat flat grasping claws - can be used for perching. Two long skinny arms end in small palms with four long knobbly clawed fingers and a very fat, short thumb. Wide mouth, lots of tiny teeth, long thin tongue and huge appetite. Round, dark green eyes, no apparent ears or nose.

Goblins live in melds (like a clan). The meld always regrows even if there is only one left. Old goblins are called Olds. Their skin crumbles after about fifty years and their internal gases and juices erupt in a small explosion, hopefully not near other goblins or anything flammable. Olds may look for the flame (suicide) if there is a food shortage.

Batlins - Smallest Goblin, their bodies are the size of a thrush. Look like all goblins except for large bat-like wings. Live in caves, barns and attics, very much like bats and usually fly at night to avoid notice.

Ratlins - Size of a large rat, not as rotund as other Goblins, live in burrows and often steal flower bulbs or gnaw roots on living bushes and unprotected trees.

Stonelins - About 1 metre tall. These goblins disguise themselves with a seeming, looking like gargoyles or grotesque garden statues and ornaments.

Hobgoblins - Bigger, tougher and scarier and were used by some sorcerers as guards. Lived in wild places and deep caves, but are now allegedly extinct.

Troll: There are several types, all allegedly destroyed by the church.

Cave Trolls still exist, hiding deep in the earth. An adult is the size of a truck with little magic outside of an affinity for strengthening earth and rock around tunnels. Trolls accrete rock and earth as they grow, bonding it into their skins as armour so most glyphs bounce off an adult. New-formed Trolls are about a metre tall, looking like a fat half-worm on end but twisted like a swirl of cream or soft ice-cream (or a dog poop).

Swamp Trolls, Water (Bridge) Trolls and Ice Trolls are probably extinct, as they were more visible and killed on sight.

Varglin - Almost a large wolf but sickly green mossy fur with long fangs and claws and a ruff of orange porcupine quills.

Amanatik - A spined, eight-legged two-metre long turtle with spiral tusks.

*   *   *

The following are invisible, unless the human is awakened to magic.

Free Spirit: - Any gust of wind, ripple of water or flicker of flame might pick up enough magic to persist, briefly. If that magic is the decaying remnant of a dead creature it creates a Free Spirit, the unthinking and usually short-lived amoeba of the magic world. They are completely defenceless, the favoured prey of many magical creatures especially small fae. Very rarely a Free Spirit absorbs more magic as it drifts here and there.

Feral Spirit: - If a Free Spirit survives long enough it might grow to become a Feral Spirit. These feel hunger, seeking out the stray magic leaking from non-magical beings to keep growing. Gradually any who survive long enough, the rarest of Feral Spirits, learn to deliberately take magic from fish eggs or tiny insects. Over many years, possibly centuries, such Feral Spirits can become dangerous enough to kill larger prey for the magic. When threatened the strongest can kill animals up to humans. Even those vanishingly rare examples are still ephemeral in nature, with few defences, so any magic user or predatory creature might snap them up for their magic.

The final form, so rare it doesn't have a name, is when a Feral Spirit becomes truly sentient. If it learns to possess flesh creatures it becomes harder to find and much harder to kill, and may learn enough magic to be truly dangerous. The church in particular will deliberately hunt down any such creature once they learn of it.

Skurrit: - Pack hunter. Long thin low-slung body with a variable number of short legs and clawed feet, all covered with long, matted dirty brown fur. Has a light brown bald tail and a nearly bald head and snout each about 40 cm long. Tiny red eyes in a small skull with a long thin pointed snout, containing several rows of sharp teeth. Not easy to kill. One alone will probably run from a cat, two or more might hunt it.

Globhoblin: - Warty, globular creature up to the size of a football with multiple legs ending in clawed feet. Will eat discarded food but prefers to prey on the helpless like kittens, hamsters, and baby animals as well as small wildlife. Will also prey on drunks or the ill, using a stinger to draw magic directly. Easily killed by weak glyphs or banished by hexes.

Fursomnium: - Dream Stealer or Eater. The creature spreads webs through bedroom walls to feed on the emotional magic given off by dreamers. If a Fursomnium eats well, for instance if someone goes insane nearby, it can sleep for many tens of years.

Gremlin: - Tiny, creature whose skin and carapace look somewhat like a toothless old man in overalls. They live inside any type of machinery, including electrical equipment, and often cause malfunctions. Those are so that angry or frustrated humans touch the object, and the Gremlin can feed from the leaking magic.

Thornie: - Prickly creature the size of a mouse, vaguely humanoid, prefers fruit but will eat most human food. Infest canteens and rubbish dumps.

Hoplin: - Little creatures looking like a miniature armadillo hopping like a kangaroo, with a mildly venomous bite. Hunt in pairs that can kill rats, mice or a kitten. Useful for dealing with infestations of rats and mice.

Faerie: - Very common rough-skinned creatures in shades and patterns of brown, with long, thin horny wings and a variety of limbs. Absorb the magic in grass or leaves, or sometimes fruit. Eat a little to help remain solid, which leaves tiny blemishes. Too many on one plant can kill grass or leaves.

Fae: - Similar looking but leaner, predatory and larger than Faerie which they hunt. Some hunt small insects or even head lice and are harmless to humans. Larger ones have stings or suck magic from animals such as humans which can leave itchy marks. They can be dangerous in numbers. The natural magical food supply for larger versions is sucked like mosquitoes by the large magical creatures that browse on the magic in plants.

Fairies: - Possibly extinct. Prefer wilderness, living on magic leached from plants especially flowers. Many are bright coloured which makes them vulnerable to hunters such as fae.

Pictsies: - Like to live with humans and their pets where they use their extravagant fangs to hunt lice, flies, insects and spiders.

Pixies: - Live with humans. Absorb the magic leaking from the residents of 'their' house or left on clothes, removing dandruff and loose hair to store a surplus.

Piskies: - Live in gardens, in stock pens, or in the wild, preying on the pests infesting animals. Are useful for dealing with ticks. Like jokes, unpleasant ones if trapped in a house.

Brownies: - Good ones are fanatically tidy. Live with humans if possible and tidy up dust, cobwebs and pet hair, but will leave if humans are either too tidy so there is no food, or too scruffy. If not able to find a small private place, some will actually create mess in most of the house while keeping their personal space clean.

Slimies: - These have a variety of names, none complimentary because they look like dull greenish slugs with brown scaly patches. Very slow, so tend to settle on stains or other food sources unlikely to move. Were useful when stains were difficult to remove, less so with the advent of washing powder and bleach.

Beinsnork: - Old Norse for Bonesnake – metre-long yellow snake with tiny legs, covered in short, sharp triangular blades of bone.

Satan-Steed: - A white lizard two metres long with red horns, and jaws like a coachman beetle.

Ganshbaal: - Glittering black nightmare scorpion rats - the survivors of the rats that bore the Indian Elephant-God Ganesh in his final battle before he faded from the world.

Wealth Toad: - Also known as a Luck Toad. A fist-sized furred three-legged toadish thing with three straight, sharp horns. Not usually belligerent. Will sometimes use a simple seeming to live in homes as a small statuette. Name originally comes from an affinity to gold.

Ruttlyte: - Like a ratlin, but grey and veined with virulent blue and purple. Originally a failed attempt at killing and binding Ratlins. Secretive, and like Ratlins they prefer flight to fight.

Catspaw: - Hand-sized non-belligerent beetle with cat's paws and claws and a single sharp spine down its back.

A profusion of other small creatures exist, grazing or hunting the magic in anything from moss and grass through fleas up to rabbits or small dogs. Those targeting spoiled food are actually after the microscopic amounts of magic in either fungi or germs, with any insects a bonus. Creatures also hunt each other. Cats and dogs can see them but not clearly, just enough to avoid them or fight back. Some are beneficial, but if aware humans prefer to stop most from fluttering, crawling, hopping or slithering into their homes.

Allegedly Extinct Species

Kalkatrie: - The Cockatrice legends are probably based on glimpses of Kalkatrie, a creature created as a tracker by the Greek Gods. The short flat pointed beak with teeth, large eyes and ruff of tiny feathers make the head look like a cockerel, emphasised by the two small chicken-like legs with clawed feet. Stubby feathered wings need magical assistance to lift the creature. The scaled body is long and slim, a fat snake with a long tail tipped by a sting that causes sleep. The Kalkatrie usually slithers but can fly or run short distances. Live in tunnels like snakes.

Dragon - Many types, now all hunted and killed.

Ogres – All known ogres are dead, Bound Shades

Aryadne's Hound - Man/spider hybrid created by Goddess Aryadne to serve her. Live in caves, eat carrion, four spider legs at the rear and four spider-like arms on humanoid torso - well over two metres tall. Allegedly died out when Aryadne faded but one was killed recently near Brinsford.

Created Entities

Bound Shade: - A creature with its spirit captured at the moment of dying and used to keep a semblance of life. Usually controlled by burying a glyph deep inside it, or imprisoning the spirit within a tattoo on the Shade's master or mistress. The Shade will then obey direct orders from the glyph-maker or if sent on mission or left as a sentry follow imprinted instructions, guarding an area for instance. While torpid, a Bound Shade needs only a little sustenance, but once roused it must feed on the living to absorb their magic.

Stone Guardian: - Very hard to kill without magic as the creature is animated by a glyph carved in the heart of the stone and charged with magic. Stone Guardians usually protect strategic locations, hard to detect because they look like stone statues until they are roused.

Pungh Hmmshtfun – (Very old type of Hebrew)

spiritus qui furabatur (Latin)

Koška Smerti (Russian)

Braeth Huntian (Olde Englishe)

Ferryl Shayde - name currently used by a faded sorceress

Review

If you enjoyed this book, please share a short review with us on Amazon, Goodreads or the platform of your choice. Help other readers discover new authors.

Vance reads each and every comment you post and loves to hear from his readers.

Want more? Check out all of Vance Huxley's titles - from dystopian to military science fiction, there's something for everyone.

VANCE HUXLEY

Vance Huxley lives out in the countryside in Lincolnshire, England. He has spent a busy life working in many different fields – including the building and rail industries, as a workshop manager, trouble-shooter for an engineering firm, accountancy, cafe proprietor, and graphic artist. He also spent time in other jobs, and is proud of never being dismissed, and only once made redundant.

Eventually he found his Noeline, but unfortunately she died much too young. To help with the aftermath, Vance tried writing though without any real structure. As an editor and beta readers explained the difference between words and books, he tried again.

Now he tries to type as often as possible in spite of the assistance of his cats, since his legs no longer work well enough to allow anything more strenuous. An avid reader of sci-fi, fantasy and adventure novels, his writing tends towards those genres.